Justice for Amy

Justice for Amy

Andy Van Loenen

Iroquois Point Publishing
Grand Rapids, Michigan

Justice for Amy
Copyright © 2011 Andrew E. Van Loenen III

Published by Iroquois Point Publishing
Grand Rapids, Michigan USA

Printed in the United States of America

ISBN: 978-0-9835759-0-0

Library of Congress Control Number: 2011928304

For what does it profit a man to gain the whole world, and forfeit his soul?
—Mark 8:36

Chapter 1

DAYLIGHT HAD GIVEN WAY TO DUSK as Clay Ramsey pulled into a parking space at the Peninsular Hotel. The parking lot lights had just come on and as he left his car he could see his breath in the crisp late September air.

Ahead and to his left a woman and a man appeared to be arguing. The man reached for the woman and she shrank back, recoiling against the back of a blue Ford and almost losing her footing. She steadied herself with her palms against the fender and then lifted them to fend off the man's advances.

She was mid-30s, blonde, pretty. The man's back was toward him, but Clay could see that he was tall and solidly built, with dark hair.

The man grabbed her upper arms and shook her. She winced in pain and tears glistened on her cheeks in the glow from the parking lot lights. "Please, you're hurting me!" She writhed, struggling to get out of his grip.

The man didn't let go.

Thoughts tumbled through Clay's mind as he walked toward them. Was this a domestic matter between a married couple? If he went after the guy, would the woman turn on him—protecting her man? This situation had "No win" written all over it.

"*Let. Me. Go!*" she cried out, still struggling against his grip.

Clay was close now and her eyes locked with his. "Please help me!"

The man's head jerked around and he let her go, turning toward Clay with wide eyes. "On your way, pal. This doesn't concern you."

Clay took a deep breath and stepped closer. The man pushed him back. "On your way! This is private! *You hear me?*"

"I hear you," Clay said in a measured voice, holding up his hands, palms out. "But keep your hands to yourself."

"Well, keep moving then. We're having a little argument—private."

The woman's eyes got wider. "Please! Please, I don't know who you are but I need—"

The man shot her a quick look. "Shut up," he said. Turning back to Clay he said, "Look, she's had a little too much to drink, that's all."

"Well, it doesn't look that way to me. What's going on here? Why are you hurting this woman?"

The man's face grew a deeper shade of red as he gave Clay another, harder push. "I just told you, nosy, she's had a little too much to drink. Now, *go on, get out of here.*"

Clay again stepped toward the couple. "And I just told you to keep your hands to yourself!"

The man came at him again, this time with fists—a big, wide, haymaker of a right.

Clay instinctively blocked the swing with his left forearm and gave the man a sharp, right jab to the face. Almost immediately the man was sitting on the asphalt with blood running from his nose and a surprised look on his face.

Clay was embarrassed and his right hand hurt, but this was no time to back down. So he glared at the man. *"You wanna keep it up?"*

The man looked up at Clay. "No...no, I'll let it go," he said, lightly touching his face where Clay had hit him.

Clay turned toward the woman. "Do you want to have the police haul him in?"

"Oh no...no, that's all right. It's all right."

Clay looked back at the man. "Okay then, *beat it.*"

The man was beginning to stand. "Now listen—"

"Look, you just got a get out of jail free card. If I were you I'd use it. Now, buzz off."

The man faced the woman as he stood. "Just remember, I was only trying to talk some sense into you," he said as he turned and tramped across the parking lot into the deepening darkness.

The woman, visibly shaking, came closer to Clay. "Th-thanks. Thank you very much. That was...very kind of you."

"That's okay," he said softly. "Did he hurt you?"

"Not so much on the outside. It's more...disappointment than anything else. I...I don't know what to do." Tears formed in her eyes.

"Well, he didn't look like your—"

She began to cry.

Clay wasn't sure what to do. She clearly needed to be held and comforted, but how would she interpret such a move on his part? After all, he didn't even know her. He pulled his handkerchief from his back pocket and gave it to her. Then he gently placed his arm around her. "You're upset...I'm sorry."

"This is just the end of everything. I...I don't know how I'm going to break this—"

"Look," Clay interrupted. "Things are rarely as bad as th—"

"I'm sorry. I'm so very sorry to have caused you all this trouble," she wept out.

"That's okay."

"It must look so sordid and tawdry. I mean...I...I don't know what I mean."

Clay took the chance and gathered her in his arms, gently holding her head to his shoulder. "Shhh, it's all right. He's gone now."

At length, she began to regain her composure so he let her go. "Listen, did you really have too much to drink?"

"No. I don't drink. I just had supper and a cup of coffee with him in the hotel restaurant."

"Well, why don't we go inside and maybe you'll let me buy you another cup of coffee."

"That's very kind of you."

"It will probably do you some good to be with someone for a little while right now and besides, it's cold out here."

They started toward the building. She was still trembling as they walked together into the warmth of the restaurant, but he didn't know if it was from the cold or from her ordeal. Her eyes were still red and puffy and she sniffled a little as they took their seats in a booth.

In the light of the restaurant, Clay saw that she was a very attractive woman. But even though she wore no wedding ring, something inside of her, something he couldn't immediately identify, said "Sister" to his heart.

The waitress appeared, took their orders for coffee, and left.

The woman studied Clay for a moment. "Thanks again for rescuing me."

"It was truly my pleasure. Are you sure you don't want anything but coffee?"

"No, just coffee's fine. I really did eat a little while ago and, to be honest with you, I'm not feeling very well. I don't know if it's all the excitement or what, but I'm not even sure I'll be able to handle a cup of coffee."

Her eyes reflected a sadness that made Clay want to reach out to her. "Speaking of eating," he spoke up, "do you suppose it's true?"

"What?"

"That cannibals don't eat clowns because they taste funny."

"Oh, stop," she chuckled. "That's cute."

"Sorry, poor attempt at humor I guess, but it did get you to smile."

"No, it was cute, and thanks, I needed that," she smiled.

"Well, I'm glad you're feeling better, Ms., uh—"

"Are you from here in Traverse City?" she interrupted.

"No, I'm from Grand Rapids. I've been up here since Monday morning on business."

"Oh? What do you do?"

"I own a medical equipment business. My company just installed a monitoring system at Beason Memorial Hospital." He proffered his hand across the table. "My name is Clay Ramsey."

She shook his hand. "Thank you again...Clay Ramsey."

"Hmm?"

"Thank you for not asking me my name, for not asking me about the man in the parking lot and for not asking me to explain what my trouble is. This whole thing is more than a little embarrassing. And thank you for sitting with me and trying to cheer me up."

The waitress arrived and delivered their coffees.

Clay stirred his cup. "You really feel okay?"

"Yeah, I think so. At least I'm feeling better emotionally—thanks to you."

"That's good. I don't know why, but I feel sort of responsible for you, and I'd hate to think you were going to step outside and start crying again."

"No, I won't do that—I promise."

After several minutes Clay had finished his coffee. She had barely touched hers. He noticed too that she seemed more pale than when they'd sat down. She seemed lost in thought, sitting there with her hands on the table, looking into her cup.

He touched her hand. "Are you okay? Would you like me to have the waitress warm up that coffee for you?"

"No. No thank you. I'm really not feeling well. I think I should go home."

"Well, uh...will everything be all right when you get home?"

"What? Oh, yes. He wasn't my husband or even my boyfriend. He won't bother me."

Clay smiled. "That's good. Let me walk you out."

He put a $10 bill on the table as they left the booth. "Do you have a car here?"

"No. I'll get a cab. There's probably one out in front of the hotel."

"I'll help you find one."

They walked out of the restaurant and through the hotel lobby. As they neared the door, Clay pulled out one of his business cards and stopped at a table to write his room number on the back. He gave her the card. "Look, I mean this in the best way. I'm staying here at the hotel so...if you need me, just call. Okay?"

She looked at the card before putting it in the pocket of her suit jacket. "I've caused you so much trouble already."

"It was no trouble at all. Really...it was my pleasure."

"Well...thank you," she said, tapping the pocket with her fingers.

As Clay suspected, there were no cabs in sight when they stepped out under the canopy. She visibly tensed.

"I'd be happy to take you home," he said.

"You've done so much already"

"It will make me feel a lot better to see you lock yourself safely inside."

She studied him for a moment. "I'm not in the habit of letting men I don't know take me home. But, somehow, I feel as though I can trust you. So thanks, I accept your kind offer."

Clay walked her out to the car and used his remote to chirp the doors unlocked. He then opened the passenger door and held it as she entered. After closing her door, he walked to the other side, got in and started the engine.

Turning toward the woman to ask directions, he noticed a pained look on her face. As he was about to speak she gasped and doubled over.

He felt fear rising inside. "What's wrong?"

She gasped again. "I...I don't know. I have the strangest feeling."

He laid his hand on her shoulder. "You're shivering."

"Yes...I...I know." She gasped and then gasped again, still doubled over. "Oh, oh...it hurts!"

"What hurts? What's wrong?"

"It *hurrrts!* I didn't think he'd—"

"What can I do?" Clay interrupted.

"Oh, help me! Please, please, Clay, help me!"

Her face was ashen, covered with beads of perspiration; she was breathing heavily, her eyes filled with fear.

Clay put the car in gear and raced out of the parking lot in the direction of Beason Memorial.

The woman writhed, crying out in pain as she slumped against the door. He reached over and pulled her back toward him. But she was unconscious. Her head fell against his shoulder.

The car tires squealed in protest as Clay made a sharp right turn into the emergency entrance of Beason Memorial. He accelerated hard and then slammed on the brakes in front of the entry doors, restraining the woman with his right arm. He got out and ran to open the passenger door. The woman lay across the seat. He had to sit her up and hold her with his arm as he used both hands to open her seat belt. Then he gathered her in his arms and ran toward the entrance. She seemed weightless to him as he entered the building.

Lorraine Bulson, RN, sat at the triage desk. Clay recognized her from the training class he had conducted

Justice for Amy

just hours before. Seeing him enter, she rushed to get a gurney. "What's wrong?"

"I don't know. She doubled over in pain and passed out. She's hardly breathing and getting cyanotic." He laid her on the gurney.

Lorraine hit the switch that opened the double doors, and, with Clay's help, rushed the gurney in the direction of the trauma rooms.

Vern Hambrick, one of the ER doctors, stood as they passed the nurse's station desk, fell in step with the gurney and helped turn it into a room. Other familiar faces gathered in the area as Vern moved an empty gurney out from under the monitor Clay's team had installed only a day before and helped replace it with the gurney on which the woman lay.

A nurse opened the woman's suit jacket and then her blouse as another nurse prepared the leads of the cardiac monitor. Lorraine took Clay's arm. "You'll have to come with me now."

"No. She needs me. I want to stay."

"I know you want to stay," she said gently. "But there's nothing you can do here except get in their way. Let them do what they do best. I'll let you know the moment you can go in."

"I guess I should go move my car out of the ambulance entrance."

"Good idea. As soon as you're done, come back and see me."

Reluctantly, Clay left the trauma room, stealing a last look over his shoulder as a nurse placed an oxygen mask over the woman's face.

Chapter 2

CLAY MOVED HIS CAR out of the ambulance entrance into a parking space and sat with his head on his arms against the steering wheel. Earlier in the day he had considered driving the two and a half hours back to Grand Rapids directly from the hospital, but had decided to stay the extra night.

Was it providence that caused him to stay? Was there a purpose in all this? Was he supposed to be there to get her to the hospital? Why did he feel such an attachment to this woman he'd only just met?

He forced himself to focus as he prayed for the woman's healing and well-being. Then he got out of the car and went back into the ER. Lorraine sat at the triage desk.

"Any word yet?"

"Nothing yet," she said. "Has she had many of these attacks?"

"I don't know."

"Oh. I thought she was your wife."

"No. I'm a widower. I met her by chance this evening. She needed a ride home, and I was helping her out."

"Well, if you'd like, I can call you and let you know how she is."

"No, I'll wait."

Clay paced in the area near the desk. After several minutes, Lorraine's phone rang. He raced to her side as she picked it up.

"Triage, Lorraine Bulson speaking." The space between her eyebrows wrinkled as she listened. "Okay, I'll send him in."

She looked up at Clay. "Doctor Hambrick will see you now."

"Where is he?"

"He's in the doctor's lounge. It's the first door on the right, past the trauma rooms."

Clay had a sense of foreboding as the double doors slid shut behind him. The 40 feet of corridor to the doctor's lounge seemed like a mile, and he felt as if he were moving in slow motion as he walked down it.

He entered the doctor's lounge, a small room with an anteroom on the left that held a military-style bunk bed. There were three other people in the room: Dr. Vern Hambrick sat at a small, metal desk in the right-hand corner. Another man and a woman sat on a vinyl sofa on the left. They all looked exhausted.

Vern gestured toward a chair next to the desk. "Sit down, Clay."

"Thanks," he said as he sat.

"This is Wayne Harlow and Judy Miller."

Clay nodded in the direction of the two sitting on the sofa. They both nodded in return, but neither spoke.

"When did this all start?"

Clay looked back at Vern. "I don't know, maybe 2 hours ago."

"Did you register her at outpatient admitting?"

"No."

"Oh. I thought she was your wife."

"No. My wife died three years ago."

"You're a friend of hers, then?"

"Well...yes. What is it Vern? What's the matter with her?"

"What's her name?"

"I don't know. I just met her and haven't had the chance to ask yet."

"I see."

Clay gave a loud sigh. "Look, why won't you tell me what's going on? What's wrong with her?"

"Strictly speaking, I'm not supposed to tell you since you're not her next of kin. But I can see how concerned you are, and you did bring her in. Clay, I'm sorry to have to tell you this, but the woman is dead."

"Dead?" Stunned, Clay took a deep breath and sat back in his chair. He blew it out slowly, his hands on the sides of his face. "What was it? What killed her?"

"We don't know. There were no obvious causes or marks on her except for some bruising on her upper arms. My guess is it's something she ingested, but the medical examiner will have to make the determination."

Clay spoke further with them, but afterward could not recall what was said. Later he found himself in his hotel room, weeping over the woman and over the memories that came flooding over him.

The doctors and nurses had assumed the woman to be his wife, an innocent mistake. How could they know that Jenny was dead? But there was something in this woman's eyes. And something in her voice; a virtue, a quality of joy—in spite of her ordeal—that made her very much like Jenny. That little something, whatever it was, had attached him to her. The attachment now severed, he felt a sense of deep, inexplicable loss.

It was 2:30 a.m. when exhaustion compelled Clay into bed. But visions of the woman haunted his sleep; her last words replaying again and again in his mind as she cried out in Jenny's voice, "Oh, help me! Please, please, Clay, help me!"

A STRANGE WARBLING SOUND pulled at Clay's consciousness. He tried to shut it out, but the irritating noise wouldn't go away. As he roused from sleep he realized it was the telephone on the nightstand next to his bed. He picked it up.

"Clayton Ramsey?"

He blinked several times. "Yes. Who's this?"

"Lieutenant Rick Burke, Traverse City Police Department. I'd like to come over there and ask you some questions about the woman you were with last night. I hope you weren't planning to leave town."

Clay sat up straight. "Of course I'm not planning on leaving town!"

"There's no need to get huffy. As far as we can tell, you were the last one to see her alive."

"I'm sorry. I didn't get much sleep last night. Maybe you can tell me who she was. I'd like to talk to her family."

"We haven't identified her yet."

"Oh."

"I'll be there in half an hour or so."

Realizing he didn't have much time, Clay quickly got out of bed, shaved, showered, and got dressed.

He could smell the pleasant aroma of coffee as he approached the hotel lobby. Having had so little sleep, he imagined he would be drinking a lot of it as he poured his first cup of the day. He purchased a local paper from a vending machine, took it and his coffee to an easy chair within sight of the main desk and sat down.

On the first page of the local section was a two-inch story, one column wide, about an unidentified woman who had died at Beason Memorial Medical Center the previous evening. Clay read the story and was getting up to get another cup of coffee when a man approached the desk and asked for him.

Clay walked up beside the man. "I'm Clay Ramsey." He held out his right hand.

The man shook his hand. "Oh. Rick Burke. We talked on the phone a little while ago." He was early fifties and easily 6 feet tall, with salt and pepper hair cut in an old-fashioned flattop. His baritone voice held the remnants of a Southern drawl.

"Shall we go up to my room?" Clay said, not wishing to be grilled by the police in the hotel lobby.

Burke, however, had other ideas. He plopped himself in the chair Clay had just vacated and motioned for him to sit in the chair next to him. "Where you from, Ramsey?"

Clay resigned himself to his fate and sat down, placing his empty coffee cup on the table between the two chairs. "Grand Rapids."

"You got any identification?"

He produced his driver's license and a business card and handed them to Burke, who gave them a cursory look before handing them back. "What is your connection with the woman who died out at Beason last night?"

"I met her outside in the parking lot of this hotel. She was with a man. They were having an argument, and he started getting physical with her."

"What do you mean by physical?"

"I mean he had a grip on her upper arms and was shaking her pretty violently. She was crying and obviously afraid. She pled with him to let her go, but he wouldn't."

"So you stepped in."

"When she asked me to. I, uh...got rid of the man and took her into the restaurant over there and bought her a cup of coffee." He pointed in the direction of the hotel restaurant. "She didn't have a car so I offered to drive her home."

"When was that?"

"I don't know for sure. Maybe eight, eight-thirty."

"Go on."

"Well, shortly after she got in my car she became violently ill, so I took her to the hospital. She died there. That's about it. I don't know, to be honest she may have died in the car. Her face was awfully blue when I carried her into the ER. I don't know for sure if she was still breathing or not."

"How long did you know her?"

"No more than an hour before we got to the hospital."

"She tell you her name?"

"No."

"Where she lived?"

"I was just about to ask when she got sick."

"How come she had your business card with your room number on it in her pocket?"

"Well, she still seemed upset as we were leaving the restaurant, and I thought she might be worried about the man in the parking lot. So I wrote down my room number on one of my cards and gave it to her in case she needed my help. Believe me Lieutenant, there was nothing improper going on. She was not that kind of woman, and I'm not that kind of man."

"You're just a prince of a guy, huh?"

Clay made a face. "Look, I didn't ask for this. What was I supposed to do, let the guy go on hurting her? What would you have done?"

"If you only knew her for such a short time, how'd you know she wasn't *that* kind of woman?"

"I don't know. She just had a sense of innocence and decency about her. It seemed genuine to me. I'll be honest with you. I could almost wish that wasn't the case. Maybe then I wouldn't feel so torn-up about this."

"So you count yourself a good judge of character?"

Justice for Amy

"Who can say for sure? Every man's way is right in his own eyes."

Burke's eyebrows went up. "Of course it also says, 'The way of a fool is right in his own eyes.'"

"Touché."

"Name of this man she was with in the parking lot, who was he?"

"I don't have the slightest idea."

"You said you got rid of him. How?"

"First, I asked him nicely to leave her alone. He got belligerent and took a swing at me. So I decked him—gave him a bloody nose. He left after that."

"How many times did you hit him?"

"Once."

"What kind of trouble was she having with him?"

"She didn't tell me that either, and I didn't ask."

"But you sat over there in the restaurant with her and bought her a drink."

"Coffee."

"Okay, coffee. No name, no address, no nothing. I guess we'd better do the rest of our talking downtown."

"Sure, whatever you say," Clay replied flatly.

Overnight it had rained, and the day was overcast and uncharacteristically cold, a light drizzle still falling. As they walked out to Burke's car, Clay thought the day a perfect match for his mood.

Burke turned out to be a skillful interrogator. They spoke little of the events of the previous evening as they drove. The conversation was of a more personal nature. Looking back, Clay could see that he did most of the talking. Burke offered little in the way of information about himself but managed to extract information from Clay about himself, his company, his business in Traverse City, and even about Jenny.

By the time they arrived at the police station, Burke seemed less official, and Clay had the feeling Burke had accepted his story of the events surrounding the woman's death.

The formal interview turned out to be little more than a rehash of the interview at the hotel, though this time for a tape recorder and in the presence of a witness to make everything official.

At last Burke said, "We need for you to identify the body."

"But, like I told you, I don't even know who she is."

"I know. But we need an official identification to be a part of the statement we just took from you, for the record."

"Where is she?"

"Still at the hospital. The county doesn't have a separate morgue."

"I see."

"You ready to go?"

Clay wasn't sure he was emotionally ready to see her again. The events of the previous evening still weighed heavily on him, her plea for help and the feeling that she had trusted him and he had let her down. Still, going to identify her was, in some small sense, a way he could help her by helping the investigation into what had happened.

He looked up at Burke. "I guess I'm as ready as I'll ever be."

Chapter 3

BURKE WAS RETICENT AS THEY DROVE out to Beason Memorial. Upon reaching the hospital, they entered through the main entrance and he produced his ID for the receptionist, asking for the house supervisor to let them into the morgue for a viewing.

The receptionist consulted her computer and made a phone call. Then, looking back at him, said, "Please have a seat over there, someone will be up shortly." She pointed at a cluster of comfortable-looking chairs.

Burke sat down within sight of the desk and motioned for Clay to sit in the chair next to him. Then he started in again. "Now, she didn't say anything to you about herself before she collapsed, huh?"

"No. All I know is what I've told you."

"You're sure."

"Positive! Look, I've been putting up with your questions all morning. How about letting me ask you one?"

"Go ahead."

"*What* killed her? The ER doctor thought it might have been something she ingested."

"We're still trying to find out. What did you talk about while you were having that cup of coffee with her?"

Clay felt his face getting warm. "She seemed sad, like she needed someone else to do the talking—so I did. I made jokes. I tried to get her to laugh. I was a great, big cut-up!"

Burke shifted in his chair to face Clay. "Look, I know you're frustrated. You think you've been asked that question too many times. But the truth is, we have virtually nothing to go on here, and making you rethink the events again and again may break something loose that you've not remembered so far."

Clay sat back and put his hands on his temples. "She asked me to help her, and I feel like I let her down. I can't talk to her family because I don't know who she is. She virtually died in my arms, and I don't even know what happened to her. You're right. I'm frustrated. But I shouldn't take it out on you. I'm sorry, Lieutenant."

"It's still early, Clay. We'll get answers...eventually."

A middle-aged woman in pastel green scrubs and a lab coat approached the receptionist. She spoke to the woman behind the desk who directed her to the two men. She walked over to where they were seated, recognition lighting her face. "Hello, Lieutenant Burke. I understand you're here for a viewing."

The men stood and Burke nodded. "That's right. Nancy, this is Clay Ramsey. Clay, this is Nancy Walsh. She's the nursing supervisor here."

"Good to meet you, Ms. Walsh."

She shook his proffered hand. "Please call me Nancy. Didn't I see you in the ER yesterday?"

"That's right. My company put in the new monitoring system. I was here conducting training yesterday."

"I thought so."

They took the elevator to the basement of the building and then walked through a maze of corridors until they reached the morgue. Nancy used a security access card to unlock the door.

The place, though moderately large, was smaller than the picture in Clay's mind. Near the middle of the room was a stainless steel autopsy table with a built-in sink at one end. A large, movable light hung over it.

On the back wall were four large drawers in a single row, about the height of a gurney off the floor. These were the refrigerated compartments wherein lay the dead.

Nancy turned toward the men. "I imagine you'd like to see the Jane Doe who was brought in through the ER last night."

"That's right," Burke replied.

Nancy consulted a clipboard hanging on the wall near the drawers. Then she went to the second drawer from the left and operated a latch on it before pulling it open.

Clay made himself look at the woman's face as Nancy pulled back the sheet. Her hair was messed up and he fought the urge to smooth it down. He turned away, unbidden tears rolling down his cheeks, visions of her smile flooding his memory.

Burke looked for the briefest of moments then also turned away. "Is this the woman you were with last night?"

"Yes."

"Is that all, Lieutenant?" Nancy asked as she slid the drawer closed.

"May I use your phone? I want to get the results of a toxicity screening done on this woman."

"Let me call one of the pathologists for you."

"Thanks."

Burke followed her to a wall phone near the door. She checked a laminated card hanging from it on a length of chain before making the call.

Clay leaned back against a counter. He closed his eyes and in his mind saw again the face of the woman who had cried out to him for help. It was a pretty face; smooth white skin, fine golden hair. He remembered her eyes had been big and blue. Now they were closed, and the yellow-gray pallor of death had robbed her complexion of its vitality.

Her words once again echoed in his mind: "Oh, help me! Please, please, Clay, help me!" He wondered if he'd ever stop hearing them.

Burke returned. "Let's get going."

"Did you find out what killed her?"

"We have to go see a Dr. Van Belkum. Nancy is going to take us down there."

The pathologist's office was in the medical lab; still in the basement, but on the other side of the building. When they arrived Nancy knocked lightly on the door, then opened it. She introduced Burke and Clay.

Van Belkum was a rotund, florid-faced man with a halo of gray hair. He welcomed them into his Spartan office. "Arie Van Belkum. Please have a seat." He gestured to two chairs in front of his desk, and both men sat.

"What can I do for you gentlemen?" he said while resuming his seat.

Burke pulled a spiral notebook from his inside jacket pocket. "We'd like to get the results of a toxicity screen done on the Jane Doe who died in the ER last night." He flipped through the pages until he found the one he wanted. "I spoke with a Dr. Hambrick, and he ordered it."

Van Belkum tapped some keys on his computer and read the results off the screen. "Looks like organophosphate poisoning. Results of the gas chromatograph test indicate a specific substance commonly known as methyl parathion."

Burke rubbed his hand over his mouth. "What is it?"

"An insecticide. It's fairly rare these days. Dangerous stuff. People have been known to get sick just handling it."

"How long does it take to work?"

Van Belkum consulted his computer screen again. "Given the amount of the substance in her blood, I would say 1 to 3 hours. Horrible way to die."

"I got her here as soon as I could," Clay choked out in a voice barely above a whisper.

Van Belkum's voice reflected compassion. "There is no antidote, son. Once the poison was ingested, there was nothing anybody could have done to save her."

Burke cleared his throat. "Can you, uh...let me have a print-out of the results?"

"Sure."

Van Belkum clicked his computer mouse and the printer on his credenza came to life. He retrieved the document from the output bin and handed it to Burke. "Is there anything else I can do for you?"

"I think that covers it. Thank you, Doctor."

They stepped into the corridor, and Clay pulled the door shut. He took a deep breath and blew it out, shaking his head.

Burke turned to him. "Sorry to put you through that."

"It's all right. I know it had to be done."

"Well, it did, but not for the reason I said. There was no official requirement for you to identify her. I brought you down here to gauge your reaction."

"So I'm a suspect?"

"If you weren't, I wouldn't be doing my job."

"This was some kind of trick to get me to confess?"

"It was a test to see if you fit the suspect profile."

"Do I?"

Justice for Amy

"No, you're too cranky and uncooperative. Plus, I saw how much it hurt you to see her dead. To tell you the truth, it didn't do much for me either."

"So, I'm not a suspect?"

"I never write anybody off until the case is solved. But let's just say you're way down on the list."

"Thanks...I guess."

"Come on," Burke said, placing his hand on Clay's back. "I'll buy you some lunch."

Chapter 4

THE EVENTS OF THE PAST 16 HOURS had put the thought of eating far to the back of Clay's mind. But as Burke drove to the restaurant, hunger began to overtake him as he remembered he hadn't eaten since lunch the day before.

As on the way to the hospital, Burke appeared introspective. Clay figured he was probably thinking up more questions to ask him. It seemed Burke's mind was always working, always turning things over, always looking for the final answer. He seemed to be a good cop and was turning out to be a pretty decent guy too.

They had pulled into the parking spot before Burke spoke. "When you were in the restaurant with her, did anybody seem to know her?"

"Not that I could tell."

He followed Burke into the restaurant and past the Please Wait to be Seated sign to a booth near the kitchen, where they sat down. He suspected this was where Burke usually sat when he came here.

The waitress brought two coffees and set them down. "Hi, Rick. Who's your friend?"

Clay wondered what she would have done if he'd said he didn't want coffee. Maybe everybody here drank the coffee or maybe she was a good guesser.

"This is Clay Ramsey."

"You new on the force?"

Burke spoke for him. "No, he's just having lunch with me."

"You havin' the usual?" She snapped her chewing gum.

"Yeah."

"What'll you have, Clay? You want a menu?"

"I'll have the same as he's having."

"Okay, back in a few."

She turned to leave and Burke called after her. "Hey Sally, how about bringing us a pot of coffee for the table?"

"Sure, I'll be right back," she said over her shoulder.

Clay looked at Burke. "So what did I just order?"

"A double cheeseburger with mushrooms and fried onions and an order of home fries."

"You eat that for lunch every day?"

"Not every day, but a lot."

"How's your cholesterol?"

"I never worry about things like that."

"I'll bet your wife does."

"My wife passed away five years ago—ovarian cancer."

Clay was suddenly struck with the similarity of their situations and wondered if Burke had so easily accepted his story about the dead woman because they shared a similar pain.

"I'm sorry."

Sally brought back a pot of coffee and set it on the table.

Burke looked at Clay. "It was a long time ago. I don't know, though; I'm not so sure it's something you ever really get over."

"Yeah, I know."

"You're still in love with her aren't you?"

Clay nodded.

"If you can get to the place where you can look at another woman and not feel like an adulterer, I guess you're ready to move on. Trick is finding one that makes you feel again."

Clay made a wry face. "Feel again. What's that?"

"You never think about getting married again?"

"I guess I'm not ready yet. But I'm not against it, if the right woman comes along. How 'bout you?"

"I've thought about it a lot lately, but I'm not holding my breath."

Clay lifted his coffee cup as if in a toast. "Well, here's to us both and happier days ahead."

Burke gave a wry chuckle as he raised his cup. "The woman who died, she remind you of your wife?"

"Very much. Her eyes, her voice. I don't know, something inexplicable I guess; like her spirit could speak to my spirit without words, if that makes any sense. How'd you know?"

"Just guessed—mostly by your reaction.

Sally came back and set their meals before them. "Anything else, fellas?"

"That will do it for now," Burke replied.

Burke got back down to business as he ate, talking between bites. "Here's what we're up against: all the clothes she was wearing are ordinary, off-the-rack stuff. We'll look for dry cleaner marks, and assuming we find some, we'll run them down. But frankly, that doesn't often pan out these days."

"What about dental records?"

"That only works when you have a pretty good idea who the person is."

"Oh, of course."

"From what you said, she was very likely a local woman. But, so far, nobody's reported her missing. I hate to do it but I might have to run her picture in tomorrow's paper."

"That could be pretty lousy for somebody," Clay replied.

"It's a lousy business sometimes. That guy she was arguing with in the parking lot, did he have a car?"

"I don't know. If he did, I didn't get a look at it."

"What about her purse?"

Clay thought for a moment. "I don't recall that she was carrying one."

"Women don't usually go off without their purses."

Clay scrunched his eyes shut. "I can't picture it in my mind...sorry. So, where does that leave us?"

"Well, judging from the amount of time the stuff was in her system before she died, and from the way you say she acted in the restaurant—sad and unwilling to tell you her name and all—I'm thinking it was probably suicide."

"Suicide? What about the guy she was with?"

"Well, it fits. She told you she was disappointed in him didn't she? Sometimes women want to end it all in front of the guy they're having trouble with—sure wouldn't be the first time."

"Oh, come on, Lieutenant. You don't actually believe that, do you?"

"Like I said, it wouldn't be the first time. It seems pretty obvious that something went terribly wrong in her life."

"Yeah, but suicide?"

"You're emotionally involved, Clay. As a cop, I don't have that luxury. For now, suicide is just a working theory. If better evidence comes along, we'll follow it out to its conclusion."

They finished their lunches in silence. Burke paid the check and drove Clay back to the Peninsular Hotel. The sun had come out and a light breeze had nearly dried the rain. It was turning out to be a nice fall day.

As Burke drove off, Clay turned to the entrance, but decided to take a walk instead.

Burke had good insight and he'd hit remarkably close to home, both in the trip down to the police station and in the restaurant. The dead woman did remind him of Jenny. And, Clay realized, he hadn't talked so much about Jenny in a long time—maybe since she'd died. It was uncomfortable.

It wasn't like he was in denial about Jenny's death or that he was emotionally unable to address the reality of it. He had come to terms with it, but he realized that there was only so far he could go. Burke was right: it is not something you ever completely get over.

So what if I'm still in love with her. I committed myself to her for life. To do less would be to deny every promise I made to her.

Oh, they'd talked about it as young married couples, so deeply in love, are wont to do: *"If anything ever happens to me, I want you to remarry. I don't want you to be lonely."* Noble words they'd both spoken in the invincibility of their youth. Words releasing the beloved, words they never thought would have to be heeded. *After all, we're going to grow old together, right?*

Burke, after five years, was ready to move on. Clay wasn't so sure about himself. Still, his response to Burke's question surprised him even as he heard it come out of his own mouth: "If the right woman comes along."

Where did that come from? He'd spoken without any advance thought. Sometimes, though, off-the-cuff statements reflect the true nature of our feelings. Things we may be unwilling to admit, even to ourselves, given the time for careful analysis. One thing was sure: the life he now led was not the full and happy one he'd expected to be leading at this point. Filling his days with work and friends, while satisfying to a degree, could not, he'd discovered, make the nagging emptiness go away.

Maybe he was ready to move on. After all, he had dated a couple of times and had enjoyed the women's company. Maybe it was simply that neither one of them were the, ever elusive, "right woman." Or maybe he was over-thinking things again. He knew he had a tendency to do that. In any case, things were confusing enough right now without adding all that baggage into the mix—Burke's wound opening questions and the feelings coming out of his responses notwithstanding.

Clay looked at his watch, then turned and headed back to the hotel.

Chapter 5

CLAY WAS STILL MULLING OVER his conversation with Burke when he got to his room. He threw his jacket on the bed and plopped into the one easy chair, putting his feet up on the coffee table. He needed to analyze all the events, put them in order, and try to apply some logic to them. One thing he knew: He didn't buy Burke's suicide idea. However, Burke did raise a good point about the woman's purse. *Where is it?* He closed his eyes, concentrating on the time he'd spent with her, trying to get a picture in his mind's eye of her purse. Nothing came.

He heard a noise and roused. The maid was coming in to clean and he realized he had fallen asleep. He looked at his watch—2:05 p.m. He figured he'd slept for about half an hour. He needed it, and although a little groggy, felt better for it.

Clay spoke cordially to the maid before grabbing his jacket and wandering down to the hotel restaurant. The lunch crowd had mostly dissipated and he sat in the same booth he had occupied with the woman the night before. This time he sat where she'd been sitting and looked for her purse, checking under the table and between the seat and back cushions of the bench. He found 31 cents, but no purse.

The waitress headed in his direction with a menu in her hand. Clay tried to remember if she had been the one who'd waited on them the previous evening. Maybe, but he couldn't be sure.

She walked up to the table. "Would you like a menu, sir?"

"No, thanks, I'll just have coffee."

"Cream and sugar?"

"Black is fine."

"I'll be right back with that." She turned to leave.

"Excuse me, but were you working last night?"

She turned back, a look of apprehension in her eyes. "Yes," she said tentatively.

"Were you working this table?"

Her growing apprehension came through in her voice. "Yes."

Clay smiled in an attempt to ease her mind. "Do you, by any chance, remember me?"

"I'm sorry, mister, so many people come and go. It's impossible—"

"I was with a blonde woman," he interrupted. "She wore her hair in a kind of short pony tail with one of those clip things. She had on a blue business suit and we were sitting in this booth."

"What did you have to eat?"

"Nothing, we just had coffee. We were here for maybe half an hour, 45 minutes at the most. I paid with a $10 bill."

"Oh yeah, I remember you."

"Great!"

"Why do you ask?"

"The lady lost her purse and I thought maybe somebody might have turned it in."

"You're talking about the woman who died last night, aren't you?"

"Yes."

"Some police detectives were here a little while ago asking about her."

"I figured they would be."

"You ought to give them a call. They're trying to find out her name."

"So am I."

"Well, nobody turned in a purse last night so I guess you're out of luck. Sorry."

He reached into his wallet, pulled out another $10 bill, and laid it on the table. "Thanks anyway. I think I'll skip the coffee."

Clay left the restaurant and walked to the parking lot, putting his jacket on as he exited the building. He surveyed the lot, trying to remember exactly where the woman and man had been standing while they argued the night before.

He walked to the spot where he was pretty sure he had parked and retraced his steps until he came to what looked like the right place. In that area of the lot, there was about 20 feet of grass between the building and a curb. Cars parked perpendicular to the building, wheels against the curb.

Clay looked about the parking lot. No one was around. He got down on his hands and knees and crawled on the asphalt behind cars, looking for the purse. He could see all the way to the curb. The third car he came to, a dark blue Ford, concealed what appeared to be the prize he sought. It was between the front wheels, just slightly toward the passenger side.

He stood and surveyed the lot again. Still nobody around. The curb prevented him from accessing the underside of the car from the front, so he walked to the passenger side. He managed to lie down beside the Ford while avoiding a green Chevy that had parked a little too close. Reaching as far under the car as he could, he was unable to grasp the purse.

He backed out, and while standing, hit his head on the driver's side mirror of the Chevy, setting off the car's alarm. Turning quickly, he gave the Ford a sharp bump with his knee and set off its alarm. Things were definitely not going well. He pulled out his cell phone, pretending to be talking on it, as he forced himself to walk nonchalantly back to his car.

Clay sat in his Chrysler and waited. The alarms stopped their offensive din after about a minute. It took longer for him to stop perspiring, for his head and knee to stop hurting, and for his heart to slow down to a more reasonable rate.

Cell phone still in hand, he decided to call his office.

"Good afternoon, Ramsey Medical, Gwen Ramsey speaking."

"Hey, kiddo."

"Clay!" his sister cried. "Where are you?"

"I'm still up in TC."

"Problems?"

"Not with the installation." He sighed. "I'm just taking care of some personal business, so I thought I'd take a few days off. How does my appointment calendar look?"

"Hold on." Clay heard her tapping her computer keyboard. "Your next appointment is with Joe Dixon at Muskegon General, next Tuesday at ten."

"Okay. I'll most likely be back before the weekend."

"Clay, are you all right? You don't sound like yourself."

"I'm fine, just a little tired. A few days off will do me good."

"If you say so."

As he pressed the end button on his phone, Clay felt bad for not telling Gwen the whole truth. But he knew she would worry about him if he told her everything, especially that he was planning to find out what had happened to the woman who had died the night before.

Exiting the car, Clay used his remote to open the trunk. He took out the windshield ice scraper he kept there. It was about 3 feet long and had a snow brush on one end and a squeegee/scraper on the other.

Closing the trunk almost to the latching point and taking the scraper with him, Clay resumed his position on the ground between the Ford and Chevy.

Using the scraper end of the stick, he easily reached the purse and pulled it out to where he could pick it up. Then, carefully getting up to avoid setting off the car alarms again, he headed back to his car holding the purse close to his body so a casual observer wouldn't see it. Opening the driver's door he threw the purse onto the passenger seat, returned the scraper to the trunk, got back in the car, and closed the door.

He picked up the black leather purse and zipped it open. A faint odor of the perfume she'd been wearing reached his nostrils. However, there was no wallet or other identification— nothing inside to indicate to whom it belonged. He found a lipstick, a hairbrush, a pair of reading glasses, a small packet of tissues...and a .38 caliber snub-nosed revolver.

Clay's heart beat fast. Not wanting to add his fingerprints to those that may already be on the gun, he removed a tissue from the package and used it to take the gun from the purse, grasping the knurled handgrips. Three of the five cartridges in the cylinder had been fired. He held the barrel to his nose and sniffed. He was no expert but he guessed they'd been fired recently.

He put the purse on the floor in front of the driver's seat, carefully put the pistol in his jacket pocket and got out of the car. The weapon was heavier that he expected and made his jacket droop noticeably. So he took the jacket off and carried it over his arm. He entered the hotel and took the elevator up to the third floor.

In the safety of his locked room, Clay removed the revolver and inspected it carefully, noting its make and serial number on a hotel notepad. He then returned it to his jacket pocket. Did it belong to the woman? He doubted it—she didn't seem the type. Still, if a woman had reason to fear, she might carry a gun in her purse. But why had it been fired? If she'd fired it at a range, it most likely would have been cleaned and the cartridges replaced. It didn't make sense that the gun would be in her purse with three spent shell casings in the cylinder...unless she had shot someone. If she had, that would be a possible motive for suicide. He was sure that was how Burke would see it.

But he couldn't make himself believe it. She had a quality of innocence about her. Of course, if the gun wasn't hers maybe the purse wasn't hers either.

He remembered seeing something on the news a year or two before about Michigan's concealed-carry law and that permits to carry guns were issued by county clerk offices. He removed the telephone book from the drawer in the nightstand, found the number for the local clerk's office, and dialed it.

"County clerk's office. How may I help you?"

"I'd like to get information about a gun, find out who it's licensed to."

"I'm sorry, we only do concealed-carry permits. If you want to find out registration information, you'll have to contact the police."

"The Traverse City police?"

"Any police agency can do it for you."

"Thanks, I'll give them a call."

Clay hung up the phone and reviewed his options: He could take the gun and the purse to Lieutenant Burke. He knew he'd have to do that eventually. However, it wouldn't guarantee that he'd find out the woman's name. Besides, if the gun was going to feed Burke's suicide theory, it would be nice to have some evidence to counteract it.

Clay couldn't make sense of Burke's conclusions. If the woman knew the gun was in her purse and her purse was lost, why wasn't she hot to find it? He was sure she made no mention of a lost purse while they were together. The most likely meaning was either she didn't know it was missing or she knew where it was and was unconcerned. The former couldn't be ruled out, but the latter seemed more likely. Burke was right: women don't usually go off without their purses.

To avoid Burke finding out about the gun, he could call one of the other police agencies. But that was no guarantee he would get the information he wanted either. What if they demanded he bring the gun to the station? How would he explain how he came to be in possession of it? Worse, what if the gun had been reported stolen?

Clay went to his briefcase, removed his PDA, and began searching through his address book. He found the name and number he was looking for, picked up the phone and dialed.

"Mitch Ferguson."

"Mitch, this is Clay."

"Hey, Clay! What are you up to?"

"I need a favor."

"What can I do for you?"

"I need to get the registration information on a gun."

"Whoa, Clay! What's going on?"

"I'm not in any kind of trouble, but I found a gun and I'd like to know who owns it."

"I'm not so sure I should do—"

"Please, Mitch," he interrupted. "I'll explain the whole thing once I'm back in Grand Rapids."

"Where are you now?"

"Traverse City."

"Well, it's public information. Give me the data."

"It's a .38 caliber snub-nosed revolver."

"Make?'

"Smith & Wesson."

"Serial Number?"

He enunciated the letters and numbers carefully.

"This is going to take a few minutes. How can I get hold of you?"

"Call me on my cell phone. You've got the number."

"I'll call you back shortly."

"Thanks, pal," Clay said as he hung up.

Mitch and Liz Ferguson had moved to Grand Rapids from Roanoke, Virginia, 16 years ago when Mitch was hired as a detective sergeant with the Kent County Sheriff's Department. Shortly thereafter, they started attending Calvary Community Church.

Clay was a new believer at the time and had been married to Jenny for just a few months. He met Mitch through a men's Bible study and they became fast friends. Jenny and Liz hit it off as well and the two couples spent much of their free time together. Clay and Jenny, unable to have children, had become sort of second parents to the Ferguson's son Steve, who was just a baby then. He would be graduating from high school at the end of this school year.

Clay hated to take advantage of their friendship to get Mitch to run down information on the gun, and if there had been another safe way to do it he wouldn't have asked. He was weighing the relative merits of continuing in his quest to find out the dead woman's identity when his cell phone rang.

"Clay Ramsey."

"Ramsey, this is the police! We've got the building surrounded. Come out with your hands up!"

"Right, Mitch, just as soon as I take a bath and feed the dog."

His friend chuckled. "Hey buddy, I've got that info you were looking for."

"Great!"

"You got something to write with?"

"Yep."

"The gun was purchased by Century Armored Services of Traverse City in June of 1993 and licensed to be carried openly by James Curtis Wagner of 5089 Floral Court, in Kingsley, Michigan. There are no wants or warrants associated with it."

"Thanks!"

"Listen, Clay, this weapon hasn't been involved in a crime, has it?"

"Not that I know of. I'll tell you all about it when I see you."

"You still planning on letting us feed you Saturday night?"

"Oh yeah."

"Take care of yourself Clay."

"You too, brother."

As he hung up, Clay's mind filled with questions: Who was James Curtis Wagner? Was the dead woman Mrs. Wagner? Was James the man who'd been arguing with her in the parking lot? Was he responsible for her death? A phone call wouldn't do. The surest way to get the answers he wanted was to drive out to Kingsley and get them in person. Then maybe he would turn the gun and purse over to Burke.

Chapter 6

CLAY STOPPED AT THE FRONT DESK on his way out and extended his stay for another night. After getting in the car, he put the gun back in the purse and stowed the purse under the passenger-side front seat. He had to reach over the console and between the seats to push it under from the rear.

He pulled out of the parking lot and headed toward the address Mitch had given him, more questions tumbling through his mind. *Why is there no wallet in the purse?* Surely a wallet would have contained a driver's license and credit cards—some means by which he could identify the dead woman. *Could she have dropped her purse in the parking lot during the argument and forgotten about it in the excitement? Might some thief have stolen her wallet and thrown the purse under a car to conceal it? And what about the gun?*

He arrived in Kingsley, located south and east of Traverse City, at just past 5:30 p.m. and turned into what looked like a residential area. He cruised around until he found Floral Court.

The street was a cul-de-sac and fairly short; three houses on each side and three more around the circle at the end. The dwellings were small, ranch-style houses that looked to have been built during the 1960s. The second house on the left was 5089. It was a well-kept little place with white vinyl siding and a concrete driveway that widened as it approached an unattached two-car garage on the right. A tall red maple tree in the front yard blazed with fall colors.

No cars were in the driveway as Clay pulled in and parked. He got out, took the sidewalk up to the front door, and pressed the doorbell. He waited. Nobody answered. He knocked.

The inside door swung open. A woman, whom Clay guessed to be in her mid-thirties, was walking away and speaking over her shoulder. "Tom, darling, you're early. I'm not near ready." She wore a robe and was drying her hair with a towel.

"Hello," Clay said through the screen door.

The woman stopped and turned to face him. "Oh. I was expecting someone else. I'm sorry." She approached the door but maintained a discrete distance.

"My name is Clay Ramsey."

"If you're selling something, I'm not interested."

"I'm looking for Jim, Jim Wagner."

"I'm Carol Wagner."

"Oh, his wife. Nice to meet—"

"I'm Jim's widow."

Clay made a wry face. *"What?"*

"Jim's dead. He passed away almost two years ago now. Heart attack."

"I'm so sorry," he said, shaking his head.

"It's okay. I'm sure you had no way of knowing. Several of Jim's friends from Desert Storm have stopped by. I'm sorry to have to spring bad news on you." A look of concern came over her face. "Have you come far? Maybe you'd like to step in."

"Thank you," Clay said, stepping in and letting the screen door go closed.

"Would you like a drink of water?"

"Sure, that would be fine."

She disappeared into the interior of the house and returned in a moment with a tumbler of water. "I have to finish drying my hair," she said, handing Clay his drink. "Why don't you make yourself comfortable? I'll be right back."

Clay walked slowly into the room. Should he tell her he was checking out the gun that had once belonged to her husband? Should he mention that he'd found it in the purse of an unidentified woman who was now dead?

He noticed some framed pictures on the fireplace mantle and walked over to take a look. Suddenly things began to fall into place. On the left was a snapshot of two women and a man standing together in what appeared to be a park. The woman who had died was on the left, Carol Wagner was in the middle, and the man who had been accosting the now dead woman was on the right, his arm around Carol Wagner. Clay's heart seemed to skip a beat.

On the right was an 8 by 10 portrait of the man alone. Inscribed near the bottom-right corner with a silver felt-tip marker was, "To Carol, all my love, Tom."

Clay stared at the picture, trying to make sense of the new information that had suddenly come upon him. This Tom's relationship with Carol Wagner was obvious. But what was his relationship to the dead woman?

He was startled when Carol spoke from behind him. "Do you know Tom?"

Clay turned to her. She had dressed and combed her very blonde hair, but it was still damp. "Tom?"

"Yes. Tom Carlson."

"I know I met him once, but I didn't know his name. Was he a friend of Jim's?" *That wasn't a lie...was it?*

She walked to the sofa and sat down, motioning for him to sit in one of two easy chairs that were separated from the sofa by a rectangular coffee table.

"Tom never knew Jim. I met him about a year ago through my sister, Amy. He's been very good to me and very good *for* me."

Clay tilted his head, a curious look on his face. Perhaps the dead woman was her sister, Amy.

"After Jim died, I was just devastated. I fell into a deep depression and tried to end my life. Then I met Tom at a company function where my sister works."

"Your sister, Amy?"

"Yes, that's right. We're going to be married in the spring."

"Congratulations."

"Thank you," she said. "I wasn't sure if I should mention it, you being a friend of Jim's and all."

"I think it's great." Clay said, not sure if he was actually telling the truth.

"I'm glad to hear you say that. I'm not very courageous and this hasn't been easy for me. I don't know if Jim mentioned our lives together, Clay, but we were very close. But now he's gone and I've finally been able to face that and move on to a new life with Tom. He's truly a wonderful person."

He didn't seemed so wonderful last night, Clay thought, *standing in that parking lot, arguing with and accosting the woman who died—the woman in the picture on the mantle. Amy?*

Clay set his empty glass on the coffee table, stood, and walked over to the fireplace. Carol joined him at the mantle as he again looked at the snapshot.

He pointed to the image on the left. "This is Amy, isn't it?"

"Why yes! Do you know her?"

"We met."

He didn't have the heart to tell her that her sister was dead.

"I have another sister too—she took the picture. We're kind of, 'The Three Musketeers.' I'm the youngest."

"What's Amy's last name?" he asked, careful not to use the past tense.

"Phillips. That's our family name. She was married once but she had a religious conversion about eight years ago and her husband divorced her. They didn't have any kids so she took her maiden name back."

"I see."

"Maybe 'The Three Lonely Women' would be a better name for us—we're all alone now. But I'm living proof that things can change for the better," she said, finishing her previous thought.

Clay looked at his watch. "I really should be going. It's been very nice to meet you, Carol."

"You're welcome to come back at any time. I'm sure Tom will be sorry he missed you."

"Thank you."

It was nearly sunset when Clay pulled out of Carol Wagner's driveway. He drove to a sandwich shop he'd seen earlier for supper.

He still didn't know how the gun figured into the equation, but that was something for Burke to figure out. He'd take the purse and gun to him in the morning. Right now, lack of sleep and a long day were catching up with him.

Darkness had fallen when Clay left the restaurant. As he exited the parking lot, he saw a sign indicating a right turn would take him to Traverse City. He turned right, heading north on Brownson Avenue, hoping it was a shortcut.

Traffic was light on the two-lane blacktop—just one car and it was behind him. He was musing on the events of the previous evening when he noticed in his mirror that the car had sped up.

He turned his full attention to driving. The vehicle was very close, tailgating him with its bright lights on. He could see that it was a pickup truck or an SUV, but the lights were blinding him so he couldn't make out more than that.

Clay flipped his rearview mirror to the night position and concentrated on the road ahead. He was coming to a curve, and because of his unfamiliarity with the road, didn't know how sharp it was. As he approached, he let the car slow some. Suddenly he felt a bump. The idiot had run into him. Another bump. Clay increased his speed, his Chrysler barely staying on the road as he fought to round the curve. The truck dropped back as it went through the curve and Clay stepped hard on the gas as the road straightened out. As the truck completed the curve, it too accelerated.

Clay spotted a yellow, diamond-shaped sign indicating a sharp right curve ahead and he slowed. The idiot pulled up beside him. Clay stepped on the gas and pulled slightly ahead. The truck, matching his speed, pulled alongside him again and edged into his lane. Clay glanced over quickly and saw that the driver was wearing a ski mask. He looked ahead. The sign was coming up fast. He looked quickly to the left again. The driver of the truck was looking at him.

Clay slammed on his brakes. The anti-locks kept him from going out of control, but the car still skidded slightly. He had slowed sufficiently to enter the curve safely.

The other guy was less fortunate. He hit his brakes too late and went straight where the road curved, bumped through the ditch, and came to a stop in a yard. Clay noticed in his headlights that it was an older-model blue Bronco with a white top.

He kept going, exceeding the speed limit in straight sections, until he reached his hotel. He parked under a light close to the main entrance, got out, and checked the rear of his car. The damage was remarkably minor, a couple of small dents and some paint scraped off the rear bumper.

His heart was still beating fast as he entered the building. When he got to his room, he fell on his knees beside the bed and thanked the Lord for delivering him safely out the hands of whoever was trying to kill him.

Clay took a shower, then plopped into the easy chair, and tried to watch television. He surfed through the channels a few times, but couldn't get interested in anything. At length, he climbed into bed.

As he shut off the light and settled in under the covers, he felt more convinced than ever that Amy Phillips had not committed suicide. Whoever had killed her was now after him. He must be getting near the truth. *But what truth?*

Chapter 7

NINE HOURS OF SLEEP and the beautiful sunrise he'd seen on his morning run did much to improve Clay's outlook. As he showered, he wondered if the incident on the road the night before had been a random act. *Still,* he thought, *it would be interesting to find out if Tom Carlson drives a blue Bronco with a white top.* As he dried off, he decided to go downstairs and have a decent breakfast, take the purse and gun to Burke, then head for home. Burke would arrive at the truth eventually.

Clay bought a newspaper from a vending machine as he entered the hotel restaurant. He drank his coffee and read while waiting for his omelet to arrive. Burke was a man of his word. On the first page of the local section was a picture of Amy Phillips. They'd obviously applied some make-up and the photographer had done a good job with the lighting. If the story had not stated she was dead, someone may have mistaken her for being asleep.

Clay thought about one of his favorite passages from the Bible that equated the death of believers with sleep. Perhaps she was asleep in the New Testament sense. After all, her sister, Carol had said that Amy had had a religious conversion. Maybe that's what had clicked between the two of them in the short time he had known her. Maybe she was a kindred spirit, a sister in the Lord.

Clay read the rest of the paper as he finished his breakfast. When the waitress dropped off his check, he asked her to bring him a large coffee in a to-go cup. He took a couple of sips of it before leaving payment for his meal and a generous tip. Then he went back upstairs.

Once in his room, Clay called Burke. "Anything new on the case?"

"No, but we ran her picture in the morning paper. I expect we'll have her identified before the day is out. Good thing too. I've got a murder case on my hands now and I'm not going to have a lot of time to spend running down a suicide."

"What's this other case all about?"

Burke sighed. "It'll be on TV tonight, so I guess it won't hurt to tell you. A man named Harry Clemens. Ever hear of him?"

"No."

"He was an auditor with Greene, Lewis, and Satterlee here in town. Cleaning lady found him dead in his apartment Wednesday afternoon. Shot three times with a .38. He was auditing the accounts at Northern Fruit Wholesalers and found a $25 thousand shortage in the books."

"Northern Fruit Wholesalers?"

"They're middlemen for orchardists around here. Clean and package fruit, mostly apples and cherries, then ship the stuff nationwide. The controller for the company didn't show up for work yesterday or today, and nobody knows where she is. We figure she's good for it. I've got people out looking for her right now."

"She?"

"Yeah, the controller is a woman—named Amy Phillips.

Clay sat on the bed. He needed more information. He had to find out who Amy Phillips really was and, assuming the purse was hers, how she came to be in possession of Jim Wagner's gun.

Burke was undoubtedly correct that she would soon be identified. Clay could guess his reaction when he discovered it was Amy in the morgue: *"She killed the auditor when he discovered her embezzlement and then committed suicide to avoid going to prison."*

He decided right then not to give Burke the gun until he'd made his best effort to find out the truth about it and about Amy Phillips. It looked like he wouldn't be going home today after all.

On his way out of the hotel, he stopped at the front desk and extended his stay for yet another night. Then he got in his car and retraced his path down the road to Carol Wagner's house.

He stopped at the curve where the Bronco had gone off the road. All that remained were deep ruts where his attacker had driven into the wet earth of some unfortunate person's yard. It looked like he'd backed out in the same ruts. On the other side of the road was a fairly deep ditch. Clay could only imagine what might have happened to him had he gone off into that.

As he drove the remaining distance to the house, Clay tried to think of what he would say to Carol. She probably already knew about Amy and would be upset. She would also be upset when she found out he had known yesterday and not told her. And he had no idea what she'd have to say about the gun. He'd have to cross those bridges when he came to them.

Clay parked in Carol Wagner's driveway and retrieved the purse from under the passenger seat. He said a short prayer for Carol before going up to the door. This time she opened on the first knock.

"Hello, Clay," she said flatly.

She obviously knew.

"Hello, Carol."

"You'll have to excuse me, but I really can't visit right now. I just learned that my sister, Amy, is dead." She began to close the door.

"May I come in? I'd like to talk with you about Amy."

She moved back from the door to let Clay in. As he stepped inside, her eyes locked on the purse. She scowled up at him. "Who are you and what are you doing with Amy's purse?"

"Can we sit down?"

She shambled out of the foyer into the living room and plopped down on the sofa. Clay sat across from her in the same easy chair he'd occupied the night before. He placed the purse on the coffee table between them. "I am so sorry about Amy and for what you are going through right now."

She dabbed at her eyes with a tissue. "Thank you. Tom came over early this morning. He showed me the newspaper with Amy's picture and read the article to me. Then he left for the Traverse City Police Department to identify her. I couldn't bear to go."

Clay blinked back tears as his mind replayed how Amy had suffered in her last moments.

"I don't know what you're doing with Amy's purse, but something tells me you're a friend."

"I am, Carol. I was Amy's friend."

"She never mentioned a relationship with anybody."

"We weren't in a relationship"

Clay took a deep breath and sat forward in the chair. "I met Amy Wednesday night. I was the one who took her to the hospital."

Carol's drew a shuddering breath. "Why didn't you tell me this last night?"

"I didn't know who she was until I saw her picture on your mantle and you told me she was your sister. But after talking with you about Jim, I couldn't bring myself to hurt you again." He picked up the purse and zipped it open. "I found this purse near where I met Amy, so I was pretty sure it was hers, but there was no identification in it. Pretty much the only thing in it was a gun."

"A gun?"

He removed the gun with the tissue and held it where she could see it. "I traced it through a police friend of mine to your husband. That was the main reason why I came here yesterday...to find out about the gun. Do you recognize it?"

She recoiled. "It looks like the gun Jim carried for his work. I never got very close to it—I'm afraid of guns."

"Did you know Amy had it?"

"What would Amy want with a gun? I mean...she could have picked it up at any time, I guess. But why? Why would Amy have a gun in her purse?"

"I don't know. But sometime on Wednesday afternoon, a man named Clemens was shot and killed up in Traverse City."

"Harry Clemens?"

"Yes. Do you know him?"

"He worked for some auditors up there. Amy mentioned him. They were friends." She gasped. "What are you *saying?*"

"Harry Clemens was going over the books where Amy worked. He discovered a major discrepancy. $25 thousand is missing. The police believe Amy embezzled it."

"No!" she shouted. "Amy would never do that!"

"Please hear me out, Carol, it gets worse. They apparently have enough evidence to believe Amy shot Clemens to keep him quiet."

Carol stood and began to pace. "No!" she cried again, shaking her head. "How can you say those things about Amy? You said you were her friend."

Clay stood and walked to her. "I'm telling you what the police think. They don't have the gun yet. But I can tell you it's been fired three times. Clemens was shot three times. To the police, Amy was a Jane Doe—they didn't know who she was. By now, though, Tom has identified her. They've already established she died by poisoning and they've been working under the theory she committed suicide."

"No!" She swatted at him with the back of her hand.

"I think they're going to say she shot Clemens to cover her crime then killed herself to avoid going to prison."

Carol's hands clenched into fists and she began to beat on his chest. *"No!"* she shrieked. "Go away! Get out of my house."

Clay pulled her into a hug, trapping her forearms between them. "Listen to me Carol. I only knew Amy for maybe an hour, but in that short time a bond formed between us. I don't think she was the kind of person who would kill or even steal. And I don't think she committed suicide. Her last words to me were, 'help me.' Why would she say that if she wanted to die? I wish I could have helped her. I wish I could have saved her life. Now, I'd like to prove she didn't do this. But I need your help."

As Carol regained her composure she freed her arms, put them around him and pressed herself hard into him, her head against the side of his face. He could feel her warm breath against his neck as she breathed deeply, nuzzling her head against him.

It seemed to Clay that she was coming on to him, and he quickly let her go.

What was that all about? He'd put his arms around her to stop her from hitting him, not for any romantic reason. He knew he'd made no romantic overture toward her. *For goodness sake,* he thought. *She's engaged to be married. Obviously, the stress of her trauma has her emotionally confused.*

He walked her back to the sofa and gently sat her down. She didn't seem to be embarrassed. He was embarrassed enough for both of them. But neither spoke about what had occurred. After she was seated, he handed her a glass of water that was sitting on the coffee table. She took a few sips and placed the glass back on the coaster.

He briefly considered sitting next to her to comfort her, but abandoned the idea and returned to the easy chair as she pulled a tissue out of the box on the table. She dabbed politely at her eyes.

"After Jim died, Amy spent almost all her free time with me. We talked, we shopped, we took little trips together. She saved my life. But that's the kind of person she was: decent, kind, thoughtful...good."

Carol balled up the tissue and held it in her hand. "She'd pick me up every Sunday and take me to church. She wanted me to have the same kind of relationship with Jesus she had, and I might have, but when Tom came along it seemed less important to me. She would die before she would hurt anybody. Besides, she is...she was as afraid of guns as I am. I cannot, for the life of me, understand why she had Jim's gun in her purse."

"Tell me about the church she went to," Clay said.

"Northpointe Bible Church, up on US-31 by Acme."

"Do you know the pastor's name?"

"I'm not sure. Myles, or something like that."

Clay put the gun back in the purse and rose to his feet while zipping the purse closed. "I need to be going, but I hate to leave you here alone at a time like this. Is Tom coming back?"

"He had to go in to work. But my other sister is on her way."

"If you'd like, I'll wait with you until she gets here."

"No, I'll be all right."

Clay removed one of his cards from his inside jacket pocket and wrote his cell phone number on the back. He handed it to her. "Please call me on my cell phone if you need anything."

"All right."

Clay walked to the door, stepped out onto the stoop, and faced Carol. "Did Tom ever get here last night?"

"Yes. He got here a little while after you left. Why do you ask?"

"I thought I might have seen him. Does he drive a Bronco?"

"No, a Taurus"

"Must have been someone else." Clay let the screen door close. "Goodbye Carol, I'll be in touch."

As he backed out of the driveway, he had to wait as a red Mazda drove past and into the cul-de-sac. It turned around, stopped in the circle, and waited. The car was far enough away that it was difficult for him to see, but the driver appeared to be a dark-haired woman. He figured it must be Carol's sister.

As he drove off, he looked in his mirror and saw the car pull into Carol's driveway.

Chapter 8

CLAY REASONED AS HE DROVE that three people had access to the gun: Carol, Amy, and Tom Carlson. A possible fourth might be the older sister, but he didn't have enough information to know one way or the other about her.

Carlson had probably been Amy's ride to the Peninsular Hotel on Wednesday evening. She had to have gotten there somehow, and the pieces seemed to fit. He could have put the gun in her purse and thrown the purse in the parking lot. But who was the guy in the Bronco who had tried to kill him the night before?

Maybe Amy had taken the gun in fear for her life—after all, someone had murdered her. But Clay rejected the idea. It would mean she'd been in possession of the gun before she and Carlson went to the Peninsular, and if that was the gun that had killed Clemens, it would make her the killer.

Maybe the gun in Amy's purse was not the one that killed Clemens. The only way to find out was to take it to Burke. Clay knew he had to do that sooner or later. Sooner was better; he was probably already in trouble for hanging on to it this long. But first he needed to visit Amy's pastor.

Clay turned right when he reached US-31 and drove toward Acme. Northpointe Bible Church was set back from the road on what would now be considered prime commercial property. However, the place appeared to have been built in the 1950s—a classic mission church of the era, concrete block with a brick façade, maybe 100 feet long by 50 feet wide. It was a single-story building with a narrow white steeple near the front of a steeply pitched roof.

The front part of the paved parking lot was empty, but driving around to the back, Clay saw two cars parked against a small extension that came off the back of the building. Two steps and a stoop near the left end of the extension led up to the only visible door. So Clay entered there.

A plump woman with gray hair and wire-rimmed glasses smiled at Clay. "May I help you?"

"I hope so. I'd like to see the pastor."

"May I ask what about?"

"Amy Phillips."

Her eyebrows went up and she gave a little gasp as she fumbled to press the button on an intercom. "Pastor Giles, there's a gentleman here to see you about Amy."

Almost immediately he appeared in a doorway to the right of the woman's desk. "Thank you, Ruth."

He walked out to Clay and extended his hand. "I'm Mike Giles."

Clay shook his hand. "Clay Ramsey."

"Won't you come in?"

"Thank you for seeing me without an appointment."

"That's quite all right. Please sit down." He motioned to a chair in front of his desk. "We saw the story about Amy in today's paper. Needless to say, we've been quite taken aback."

He was in his mid-50s and mostly bald. His baritone voice had a velvet quality to it that was very soothing.

Clay sat down. "What can you tell me about her?"

"Before I answer, could you tell me what your connection is to Amy?"

Clay gave him the complete details.

"You should take the gun and purse to the police."

"That's my next stop. But I want to go to them as a character reference and hopefully disabuse them of the idea that she is a murderer or that she committed suicide."

Giles rested his forearms on the desk. "Any number of people from our congregation would certainly be willing to back up your assessment of Amy's character—including me."

"Thank you."

"Amy came to know the Lord through one of our former members, a woman she worked with, who has since retired and moved out west. I didn't know her before her conversion, but apparently it profoundly changed her life—so much so that her husband left her shortly thereafter."

"Do you know if she was seeing anyone?"

"I don't know for sure, but I would say probably not. Given her history, I don't think she would have gone into a relationship with a non-believer. She was usually here for services and prayer meetings and she mostly came alone. For a while her younger sister, Carol, came with her but that stopped several months ago."

"I heard she had another sister."

"Yes, an older sister—Jean, I think. I only met her once or twice."

Clay nodded as the man continued.

"Amy has...had a real heart for children. She taught a third-grade Sunday school class. She loved those little girls, and they loved her. She would have made a good mother. Those kids are going to be heartbroken."

Clay took a breath and exhaled it through pursed lips, at once glad there were no small children to mourn the loss of their mother, and sad that she'd had no children of her own to love. "Is there anything else you can tell me?"

"She sang in the choir. She was a fine, decent woman. She loved the Lord and she loved people. She was always willing to help anybody."

"Thank you, Pastor Giles. It's not my place, but if it comes down to it, would you mind if I suggest to her sisters that they contact you for her funeral?"

"Absolutely. Let me give you one of my cards."

He extracted a card from a desk drawer and handed it to Clay. "This has my home number on it too. I'm usually either here or there, so please feel free to call at any time."

"Thanks," he said as he rose to leave.

"Thank you for being an advocate for her. Please let me know if I can help you in any way."

The men shook hands and Clay stepped out of his office, slipping the card into his inside jacket pocket. He closed the door and approached the church secretary. "Would you mind if I used your phone book?"

"Not at all." She removed the book from her credenza and handed it to him.

Clay flipped through the book and jotted down the address of Northern Fruit Wholesalers on an index card.

"Thank you," he said as he gave her back the book.

She smiled but said nothing as Clay left the church office.

He drove back toward Traverse City. It was 11 a.m. when he arrived at the place where Amy had worked and Tom Carlson still worked. He cruised around the parking lot looking at cars. Four Tauruses, but no Broncos.

He pulled into an empty space near the entrance to the lot and shut off his engine. Using his cell phone, he dialed Burke's number.

"Lieutenant, Clay Ramsey. I have something important I need to talk with you about. Can I buy you lunch?"

"Yeah, I guess."

"How about that same place we ate yesterday?"

"Okay."

"11:30?"

"That will be fine. What's this about anyway?"

"It's about the dead woman, Amy Phillips. But it would be better if we could speak in person."

"I'll meet you there."

Clay drove to the restaurant, arriving about five minutes early.

Burke pulled in at exactly 11:30 a.m. and parked in a space that had just opened up near the door. Clay had to jog, purse in hand, to catch up with him as he entered the building.

After they ordered lunch, Burke looked squarely at Clay. "How did you know the dead woman was Amy Phillips? I found out myself only this morning."

Clay lifted the purse from the seat and laid it on the table. "This is her purse. Be careful, there's a gun in it."

Burke stared at the purse. "Where did you get that?"

"I found it in the parking lot of the Peninsular Hotel yesterday afternoon, after you dropped me off."

"I had a squad of uniforms searching that parking lot yesterday afternoon. Why am I just finding out about this now?"

"I don't know. I must have gotten there before them."

"What kind of an answer is that? I'm asking why you didn't turn it in *yesterday afternoon?*"

"Look, I could have told you I found it an hour ago, wedged under the seat of my car, and you'd have been none the wiser. But as it is, I've come here committed to telling you the truth about the purse and everything I've found out. So please hear me out."

"Go ahead; let's hear what you have to say."

"I got to thinking about her arguing with that man; by the way his name is Tom Carlson, and your question about her purse. So I went out into the parking lot near where they'd been standing and looked. I found it under a blue Ford.

"Yeah?"

"There's no ID in it but I found a gun—a snub-nosed .38 revolver with three shots fired from it."

Burke's eyebrows went up. "You know we haven't found the gun from that auditor murder I told you about this morning."

"I was afraid of that. I figured it was Amy's purse, although at the time I didn't know her name. I was able to trace the serial number of the gun through a friend of a friend. It's registered to James Wagner, an armored truck guard, who lived down in Kingsley."

"Who traced it for you?"

"Nobody up here. I'm not going to tell you that, Lieutenant. It's public information, so I didn't do anything wrong."

"You're pressing your luck!"

"You want to hear the rest of the story or not?"

"No, Ramsey. The question is, 'Do *you* want to go to jail?' Because that's where you're going if I don't like your story. So, get on with it!"

Clay could feel his heart beating. "I drove down to the address, and discovered the man died a couple of years ago. His wife, Carol, invited me in, thinking I'd been a friend of her husband's. While I was there, I saw Amy's picture on the mantle. She also had a picture of the man Amy had been arguing with in the parking lot, Tom Carlson. He's Carol Wagner's boyfriend."

Burke waited to speak while Sally delivered their lunches. "So why didn't you contact me then?"

"Well, it was late, and I figured you'd probably already gone home. But mostly I really don't agree with you about her committing suicide, and I wanted to find out enough information about her to prove it to you before I came in and identified her. Of course, her picture in the paper this morning made that a moot point."

"What did you find out?"

"Carol is fragile. She was so torn up about her husband she tried to commit suicide shortly after he died. Amy rescued her. I mean, she credits Amy with saving her life; describes her as thoughtful, decent, kind, and good. When was the last time you heard someone described as 'good?'"

"Yeah, well, they're sisters."

"I also found out Amy was a committed Christian. Her pastor at Northpointe Bible Church can to attest to her character."

"Are you a committed Christian?"

"Yes."

"Then you have a bias in her favor."

"But it's not just me. I can produce at least tens of people who would agree with me. And what about you? When I inadvertently quoted a verse from Scripture yesterday, you knew it was from Proverbs and quoted me another verse in response."

"What I believe is irrelevant—we're not talking about me. I see people every day, guilty as sin of some crime—hard evidence against them. They come to me with some fancy story about how they've been 'born again,' and that they'd *never* do anything like that."

"I'm sorry, Lieutenant. I didn't know. But remember, Amy is not trying to convince you of anything. She was just living her life before the Lord as best she knew how. Now that she's dead, those people who knew her and were her friends are saying she lived what she believed."

Burke took a deep breath and blew it out, his features softening. "Clay, you go into this with the presupposition that she can't possibly have murdered Clemens or committed suicide, and you look for evidence to prove your point. The police go into an investigation with no presuppositions, because we're not interested in clearing someone but in finding the truth, wherever the trail leads. And right now it leads to murder-suicide. You're emotionally involved. I saw you grieving over her yesterday, and there's nothing wrong with that. But it tells me you are unable to be objective. Now, we'll talk to Carlson and her sister. And we'll talk to her pastor. I appreciate that you were honest about the purse and gun. But you withheld evidence and obstructed justice."

Clay's head drooped. "What are you going to do?"

"Nothing. But I'll need you to follow me down to the station. We're going to have to fingerprint you to eliminate your prints from the purse and gun, and then you can go. But don't try my patience a second time or I'll throw you in jail so fast you'll be there three days before you know what happened."

"Thank you. I'm sure my fingerprints are on the purse, but I never touched the gun. I used a tissue to remove it and I only touched the knurled hand grips."

At the station, Burke sent the gun to be processed for fingerprints and ballistics, then took Clay to booking to have his fingerprints taken. Clay gave him Carol Wagner's address and then waited...and waited.

He was still in Burke's office when the preliminary results came back. The revolver in Amy's purse was the gun that had killed Clemens, but it had been wiped clean of fingerprints. Clay thought it odd. If Amy had been the shooter, why would she wipe the gun clean, but then keep it in her purse? It didn't make sense. Unless the gun had been planted.

Chapter 9

IT WAS 4:25 P.M. when Clay finally arrived back in his hotel room. The episode with Burke, having to be fingerprinted, and the long, tense wait for the results of the ballistics test on the revolver had taken a toll. Even though he'd spent most of the day sitting, he felt as though it had been a day of hard physical labor.

Clearly he had not been able to convince Burke of Amy's innocence. Of course, Burke had not sat with her in the restaurant or heard her cries for help, or carried her, nearly lifeless, into the ER. Perhaps if he had, he would see things differently.

Talk about presuppositions! First he thinks she committed suicide because of a falling out with her 'boyfriend.' When that doesn't pan out, she committed suicide because she murdered the auditor. What was the difference between Burke's working theory of her guilt and Clay's presupposition of her innocence? They were both presumptions; Burke just called his by a different name. That, plus being a cop, apparently made it all right. But, Clay thought, he'd irritated Burke enough already without bringing that up, and he felt fortunate to have gotten out of it with just a slap on the wrists.

Clay knew he needed to do more for Amy, but he didn't know what. He'd like to be able to give Burke the hard, incontrovertible proof he needed to clear Amy's name, but Burke was in no mood to be helped. Whatever Clay did, if anything, had to be very low profile.

It was 5:30 p.m. when Clay began to pack his bags. He had already extended his stay, so he would remain this one final night and go home in the morning. He could come back if he felt it necessary, but going home would give him the opportunity to step away from this long enough to gain some perspective. Maybe, with the benefit of perspective, he could just drop the whole thing. What was the sense in going on, anyway? Apparently nobody else cared, so why should he? Besides, he didn't have enough clean clothing to stay any longer.

He was still basking in self-pity when his cell phone rang.

"Mr. Ramsey. My name is Joanne Coale. I got your card from my sister, Carol Wagner. I'd like to talk to you about Amy."

"Oh...hello," he said uncertainly. "I'm very sorry for your loss."

"Thank you," she said in an unsteady voice. "I was wondering if we could meet."

"I'm going to leave town tomorrow, but I was just thinking about getting something to eat. Have you eaten yet?"

"No."

"I could meet you someplace, and we could discuss whatever you'd like."

"Do you have a place in mind?"

"Actually, I don't. I'm not from around here, so I'm open to whatever you suggest."

"Do you like Italian?"

"Yes."

"How about Panelli's on Fourteenth Street in, say, half an hour?"

"Okay. How will I recognize you?"

"I have dark hair, not quite shoulder length, and I'm wearing a dark jacket over a white blouse."

After hanging up, Clay quickly shaved. He had never been to Panelli's, but he had a rough idea where it was located and he knew there wasn't time for much else. His white shirt still looked pretty good, so he wore that with the charcoal gray pinstripe suit and red silk tie he'd worn on training day at Beason Memorial.

It was Friday and the restaurant was busy. He cruised around the parking lot before finding a space in the back.

The hostess greeted Clay. "I'm sorry, sir, there's about a 30 minute wait."

"I'm looking for someone who may already be inside; a dark haired woman with a white blouse and a dark jacket. I'm guessing she arrived within the past 10 to 15 minutes."

"Yes, sir. Please follow me."

The dining room oozed with atmosphere—very low overhead lighting and candles in tapered glass containers on every table. A recording of Dean Martin singing *Ritorna-Me* was playing softly in the background.

The hostess led Clay to a booth in the rear of the room and left as the woman looked up and extended her hand. She spoke softly. "Hello, Clay."

"Jo," he breathed, his voice filled with incredulity.

He took her proffered hand and felt something like an electric shock pass through him. As he sat down, he realized he was breathing through his mouth.

"You look pale, Clay. Are you all right?"

"I...I'm just surprised to see you," he said, working hard to regain his composure. "Why didn't you say on the phone it was you?"

"Would you have come if I had told you it was me?"

"Yes."

"Then I'm sorry I misled you. I didn't think you'd come and I wanted to know about my sister."

"I guess I should have put 2 and 2 together when I found out Amy's last name. I knew you lived up here somewhere, but with everything that's happened it just didn't occur to me. I never knew your married name."

She nodded and continued to speak softly. "So, how have you been, Clay?"

He took a deep breath. "Okay," he said while exhaling, struggling to control his breathing and wishing his heart would stop beating so hard. "You too?"

"Yeah," she said, flatly.

"Why did you stop writing?" It was the one question he had wanted to ask her for years, but he was surprised when it blurted out of his mouth.

Her head dropped. "The short answer is...because I met someone," She said softly.

"I'm sorry. That just came out. Stupid question."

"No. You have the right to ask. I should have written and told you." She sighed. "I guess I didn't have the strength of character to do it. Just like I couldn't tell you on the phone earlier that it was me when I knew from Carol's description it was you. I even recognized your voice.

"After, what's it been, 20 years?"

"Yes. Something like that."

Clay, at 21-years-old, had recently been promoted to sergeant in the Air Force when he met 19-year-old Joanne Phillips at Shepherd Air Force Base in Texas. She had just come out of basic training for 16 weeks of schooling in Health Services Administration.

During the four months of her stay, they had fallen deeply in love. At least, that's what Clay thought.

After Jo was transferred to her permanent assignment in Germany, they continued their relationship via mail...until she stopped writing. At first Clay thought something had happened to her. He even tried, unsuccessfully, to phone her. But after a couple of months and several unanswered letters, he knew she'd left him.

Jo had altered his life and he shed many tears over her. But he never heard from her again. Until today.

"So what do you want to know?" His voice had a hard edge to it. It surprised him and he saw her countenance fall.

"Please don't hate me, Clay," she struggled to speak. "I can't even begin to tell you how hard it was for me to call you. I know I don't have any right to ask you anything, but all I want is to know what happened to my sister. If there were any other way to find out, I wouldn't have bothered you. Please," she said, dabbing at tears. "If I ever meant anything to you, tell me what happened to Amy."

If I ever meant anything to you? Didn't she know she had once meant everything to him? She seemed different now, though. She'd grown up, that's for sure. But it seemed to be more than just the standard education everyone gets in the school of hard knocks. Why the tears? Was it just that she was upset about her sister, or was she playing on his sympathy?

No. If he was any judge of people, this woman was hurting.

She placed her hands on the table and he laid his hands over hers. "I'm sorry, Jo," he said gently. "That didn't come out the way I intended. I don't hate you. I've never hated you. I've never even disliked you. I didn't mean to speak harshly."

Justice for Amy

She smiled wanly. "Thank you for saying that." Her tears started again and she removed her hands to attend to them with her tissue.

He waited while she blew her nose. Finally, she looked up, took a deep breath, and laid her hands back down on the table.

Clay took it as a signal to begin. He told her about Amy's run-in with Tom Carlson, and that he'd ended up hitting him.

"Oh," Jo gasped softly, and put her hand over her mouth.

"Anyway, Amy was crying and upset, so I took her into the hotel restaurant and bought her a cup of coffee. She eventually calmed down but wasn't feeling well and wanted to go home." He took a deep breath. "I figure she must have ridden there with Carlson because she didn't have a car. I offered to drive her home but she hadn't much more than gotten into my car before she became violently ill. So I rushed her out to Beason, but by the time we got there she had passed out and was barely breathing."

The memory came back very vividly and Clay's voice caught as he blinked back tears. "I...carried her into the hospital." He took another deep breath. "And helped wheel her into the trauma room, but it was too late. She...died there. I'm so sorry, Jo." He felt a tear run down next to his nose.

Tears welled in Jo's eyes at Clay's expression of emotion.

He looked down, not wishing for her to see his face, and tried to discreetly wipe the tear away. "I feel like I let her down. She was in a lot of pain, crying out for me to help her. I did everything I knew—"

Jo sniffled and Clay looked up. She had pulled a couple of fresh tissues out of her purse and was drying her eyes. He waited, chastising himself for being so insensitive; remembering she had only found out this morning that her sister had died. But she was losing the battle with her tears, her body shuddering as she sobbed and tried to catch her breath.

Clay slid in next to her and put his arm around her. "I'm so sorry," he said, choking back his own tears.

The graphic description of Amy's last minutes and his brief loss of control of his emotions had awakened her grief, and her grief was, in turn, triggering a renewed emotional response from him. *I could have done this if she had been a stranger,* he thought. But seeing Jo again had added too much emotion into the mix. He was sorry to have made her cry.

"Let's get out of here," he said. "I'll take you home."

A waiter arrived at their table and cleared his throat.

Clay turned and looked up at him. "The lady is not feeling well. Is there a back way out of here?"

"Just follow me, sir," he said as Clay helped Jo out of the booth.

He led them to an emergency exit three booths away. "The alarm is silent and I'll tell management that someone opened the door by mistake."

"Thanks," Clay said as the man held the door. He reached into his pocket and pulled out what looked like a $5 bill and pressed it in the man's hand as they stepped into the parking lot.

Chapter 10

THE SUN HAD GONE DOWN and the night was chilly as Clay led Jo across the parking lot. She had begun to shiver and was still crying when they reached his car. He dug in his pocket for his keys and chirped the doors open with his remote. Then he helped her into the passenger seat, feeling a sense of déjà vu as he closed her door.

Clay got in on his side and started the engine to warm up the passenger compartment. Jo removed more tissues from her purse to dry her eyes and blow her nose. Then she took several deep breaths. "Thank you for sneaking me out of there. I'm sorry to have made such a scene. My sister, Carol, has been through some difficult times recently so I've spent all day trying to be strong for her. But...seeing you again today affected me more than I...I—"

She was looking right at Clay trying, but unable, to finish her sentence. She stared intently at him with sad eyes until she once again dissolved into tears. "I'm sorrryyy," she said, dropping her head.

He gathered her in his arms. "There's nothing to be sorry for. I'm here for you as long as you need me," he said softly. He didn't know what she was apologizing for or what else to say, so he just held her as she wept.

At length she sat up, got more tissues from her purse and blew her nose. "I'm afraid I've ruined your suit."

"Don't worry about it. Where do you live? I'll take you home."

"My car—"

"I can help you get it tomorrow or I'll pick it up for you myself. You're in no condition to drive right now.

He winced, wondering if she would interpret that as a chauvinistic remark.

She reached for the seatbelt. "4104 Hubbard Street. Do you know where it is?"

"I have a general idea," Clay said as he began to back out. "But it will help if you give me directions as we go."

He turned east on Fourteenth Street and drove nearly to the end before she told him to turn right. Then they drove for almost another mile before he spotted Hubbard. She was still crying, almost inaudibly, as he turned right onto her street.

He slowed as they approached the driveway she indicated, then turned in and stopped. Jo looked at him. "I'm so embarrassed. I don't know what you must think of me."

He touched the side of her face with his open hand, his fingers wrapping slightly around the back of her head. "You don't have to be embarrassed on my account. I think you loved your sister very much."

"Amy was my half sister. My father deserted my mother and me. When she remarried, her new husband adopted me. He's been my father ever since. I'm four years older than Amy and six years older than Carol. Those two were pretty close these past couple of years since Jim died." She paused. "But that doesn't mean I...didn't love her. *Oh Amy.*" Her tears came again, in earnest.

She rummaged in vain in her purse for more tissues, so Clay open the console between the seats so she could take some of his. Then he got out and opened her door. He helped her out and held her arm as they walked to her front door.

She dug around in her purse for her keys. Finding them, she fumbled with the lock before giving them to Clay, weeping quietly and trying to dry her eyes with the spent tissue as he opened the door.

Clay led her into the living room and gently sat her down on the sofa. In the dim illumination of the porch light he was able to see to turn on a lamp. He picked up a box of tissues from the end table and set it in her lap before he went back, closed the front door and turned off the porch light.

Her tears had let up when he returned and he took a seat beside her.

Justice for Amy

They sat together for a long time. She needed someone to be with her and to lend a sympathetic ear as she talked and cried it out. So Clay listened as she spoke of her sisters, their parents and their lives since she was a little girl. Her tears came in earnest as she related her early memories of Amy, and again when she remembered the deaths of her father and then her mother. She spoke with great affection of someone named Chrissie, whom he guessed to be her own daughter.

There was no doubt that her grief was genuine. As much as he wanted to steel himself against it, his heart broke for her. At least, he thought, she was capable of love. Clearly she loved her family.

Perhaps it was just me she was incapable of loving. He banished the thought as he remembered her tears and how she clung to him at their last parting. He'd be the first to admit that he didn't understand what had happened to them. Still, he wondered, if you really love someone, is there a sense in which it can never be destroyed? Do absence and the need to move on in life eventually isolate that love into a place where it cannot be visited on a regular basis? Or does it morph into nothing but a sad warm spot in the heart?

What about those who, for one reason or another, couldn't move on? The ones for whom the loss of a loved one ultimately spelled their own death. Old people who die soon after their life-long mate, some would say of a broken heart. Or people like Carol who, unable to cope with the loss, try and often succeed in ending their own lives.

At first, before Jenny, it hurt to remember Jo. Maybe he'd never really dealt with losing her. *Is such a thing even possible?* He'd just moved on with his injuries. But Jenny's love had been so powerful it had healed him. The Lord had given him a wonderful treasure in Jenny. He didn't know it was possible to love someone as much as he loved her. Still, occasionally something would bring Jo to mind. And it always came with a touch of sadness.

One thing he knew: love is not something you can walk away from scot-free. There is always pain, the worst kind of pain, for anyone who has truly loved. The kind of pain that counterbalances the intrinsic need that everyone has to be loved, with the wariness of not wanting to endure that kind of pain again. Perhaps it is only the strong who can move on; knowing the value of real love to be worth any cost. Or, perhaps their injuries are not unto death. He didn't know.

Jenny still haunted his memory. The emptiness was perhaps in proportion to the depth of their love. He still dreamed of her, although not as much now, and he feared he would forget what she looked like—not a photograph but the picture he held in his heart. His arms ached for her but he could no longer remember how she felt in them. Once again he was moving on with his injuries—coping, wanting to be able to feel again, but not the pain; fighting against the numbness that wouldn't seem to go away.

Is that what Jo was doing—moving on with her injuries? If she had never really loved him, why had she said it was so difficult for her to call him? What did she mean by her cryptic half statement about how seeing him again had affected her?

THERE WAS MORE TO SAY ABOUT AMY. Clay wondered if Jo wanted to know the whole story or if he'd already said enough.

She drifted into a period of silent introspection so he got up to stretch his legs. He went into her kitchen, found teabags and brewed a cup of tea for her. He brought it to her and held it as she blew her nose, which seemed to be hopelessly stuffed up in spite of the formidable pile of tissues on the end table.

She seemed to recover more of her composure as she sipped the tea. He sat next to her and held her hand for more than an hour, but neither of them spoke. Finally she gave in to exhaustion and slipped into sleep.

Clay sat there for a long while before gently disengaging his hand and slowly standing so as not to wake her. He stepped away from the sofa and turned to look at her.

The last time he'd seen her, she had just turned 20 years old. In his mind, she was the most beautiful creature on the face of the earth: chestnut hair that flashed dark golden when the sun hit it just right; bright hazel eyes that always seemed to sparkle; a cute nose with a little bump on the bridge from where she'd been hit by a softball in the seventh grade; and lips that transported him to some wonderful place whenever she kissed him.

She had aged, but not badly. Her skin was not as soft and smooth as it had once been, and her pretty brown hair was longer now with a hint of gray. But it still flashed gold in the right light. Her eyes didn't seem to sparkle now and little lines and wrinkles edged her face. But she was still beautiful. *And who among us is the same person that we were 20 years ago—outside or in? What happened to her?*

He thought about putting her to bed, but realized he'd never be able to pick her up without waking her. She'd obviously had a really bad day and needed all the sleep she could get.

Finding her bedroom, he removed a pillow from her bed. Then he went back into the living room, placed the pillow on the arm of the sofa and gently laid her down on it. After removing her shoes, he covered her with a blanket that had been over the back of a rocking chair on the other side of the room. In her sleep, she cuddled the blanket around her.

Clay gathered up the pile of used tissues and threw them away in the kitchen. He then washed out the mug that had held her tea. Finally, he wrote her a note on a pad of paper he found on the counter:

Dear Jo,

I thought it best to leave—for your own peace of mind and for the sake of your reputation with the neighbors.

Please call me in the morning. You were so upset that I want to be sure you're okay. We also need to pick up your car at Panelli's. And I would like to take you out for breakfast, if you're willing, to finish telling you about Amy—that is, if you still want to know.

I'm an early riser so don't worry that you

might be calling too early. Call my cell
phone; you've got the number.

Clay

He returned to the living room, leaving the kitchen light
on so she wouldn't be in total darkness if she awoke in the
night. He then placed the box of tissues on the coffee table
where she could see it if she needed it. After turning off the
light on the end table he left the house, locking the door
from the inside and quietly pulling it shut until it latched.

CLAY RETURNED TO HIS HOTEL ROOM. It had been yet
another day charged with emotion, first with Burke and
then with Jo. Certainly not what he'd expected, at least the
part with Jo.

He found his own reactions troubling. Was it just the
raw emotion of the past couple of days added to seeing her
again, or had spending time with her begun to wake up
something in him that had lain dormant all these years?
What was that electricity all about when he shook her
hand? What were those cryptic statements of hers about?
Did she still have feelings for him? Worse, did he still have
feelings for her? Why was he even thinking these things?
What about Jenny?

Too exhausted to think clearly, he fell into bed,
breathing a short prayer: "Lord, show me what to do. Help
me to do what's right—what honors you."

Chapter 11

CLAY HAD HOPED TO SEE THE SUNRISE on his morning run, but the sky was overcast and a light drizzle fell in the chilly, late September air. Still, his spirits were high as he finished his shower and dried off. Running always had that effect on him.

He thought about Jo as he finished dressing. He wondered if she was awake, if she'd seen his note, if she'd call. He wondered, too, if it had been a wise idea to invite her to call.

He had nearly finished his packing when his cell phone rang.

"Clay...this is Jo...I got your note," she said tentatively.

"I'm glad you called. How are you feeling?"

"Much better today, thanks." She paused. "I...I was thinking about your invitation to breakfast and wondered if you...you would like to come here for breakfast? I could whip us up something to eat and then we could go to Panelli's and get my car."

Clay wasn't sure of the wisdom of spending more time alone with her, but maybe she was afraid she would lose control of her emotions again and wanted to avoid embarrassing herself in public. "Sure, that would be fine."

"When can you get here?"

"About as long as it takes me to check out and drive over."

"Well, the coffee's already on, so I'll see you when you get here."

Clay looked around the room one last time to be sure he hadn't forgotten anything. Then he walked down to the front desk and checked out.

He parked in her driveway and got out of car. But as he stepped onto the stoop and rang her doorbell, he suddenly felt nervous and unsure of what to say.

She opened the door. "Hello, Clay. Come on in," she said, stepping back and allowing him to enter.

She was wearing blue jeans and a light blue denim shirt with small embroidered flowers on the front. Her hair was shiny and he noticed it smelled like raspberries as he walked past her.

"Thanks," he said, following her into the kitchen. She fit very nicely in her jeans and he made himself avert his eyes. *This isn't going to be easy,* he thought, as he sat down on a high stool at the counter that separated the dining room from the kitchen.

She turned toward him and smiled. "Thanks for coming over. I hope you don't mind not going out. You don't, do you?"

"No, not at all."

"That's good. Let me pour you some coffee. You still like coffee, right? My daughter, Chrissie, lives here with me. She's 17. She's not here right now. She's with Mike, uh, her dad. We're divorced. She's graduating from high school in the spring and she's really...oh...I'm babbling aren't I?"

"That's all right," he said, smiling.

"No. It's not all right. I'm so embarrassed about last night," she said, momentarily putting her head in her hands. "I hadn't cried at all until Panelli's, and once I started it was like the flood gates opened and I couldn't stop and...well...you were so kind."

"I'm glad I could be there for you."

She tilted her head and fixed her gaze on Clay, blushing slightly. "Thank you for saying that. And for all you did last night...and for being a gentleman."

"I was very honored that you thought enough of me to allow me to share in your grief. You trusted me, and there is no way I would violate that, Jo. But as important as that is to me, even more important is my relationship with the Lord. To take advantage of you would, for me, be an offense against you and a deliberate sin against God."

She continued to hold his gaze for a moment and then spoke. "You're like Amy, aren't you?"

"If by that you mean I'm a Christian, yes, I am."

"When did that happen?"

He thought for a moment. "About 17 years ago, now. My wife, well she wasn't my wife then, wouldn't go out with a

Justice for Amy

non-believer. Really, the closest thing I could get to a date was to go to church with her, which I gladly did just to be near her. But something in me changed, and when I understood the gospel, I believed. She led me to Christ."

"Hmm," she said as she dished out portions of an egg casserole that she'd removed from the oven. "Would you like toast? All I have is whole wheat."

"Yeah, I'll have a couple of pieces"

"Okay." She put four slices of bread in the toaster and pressed down both knobs.

He looked at her. "How about you?"

She shook her head. "Amy and I spoke about it several times. I'm sure she really wanted me to believe. I even went to church with her a couple of times, and it's not like I'm against it or anything; it's just been really hard for me."

Clay noticed that her head was down and that she spoke softly. He was struck again with the feeling that something had profoundly changed her.

"So you really didn't know Amy for any length of time?"

"No. I'd never seen her before Wednesday night and I probably wouldn't have met her then if she hadn't asked for my help. I'll tell you, Jo, this whole thing has been difficult for me, but I'm glad I was able to be there for her. It's funny, but as I sat there with her in the restaurant I had the feeling she was a kindred spirit—a sister in the Lord."

The toast popped and she cut all four slices simultaneously and put them on their plates. He picked up his plate and coffee mug and moved to the dining room table. She followed, sitting across the corner from him.

"Would you mind if I prayed before we eat?" Clay asked.

"No, go ahead."

He picked up her hand. "Father, thank you for this food. I ask your blessing on it that it would be to our good. Thank you also for allowing me to meet Jo again after so long a time. I pray that you will be a comfort to her and to Carol during these difficult days. Thank you for Amy's life and for your wonderful grace that she found in Christ Jesus. In his name, amen."

Jo blinked several times. "Thank you for that," she said, picking up her napkin and touching it to her eyes.

Clay was ravenously hungry. He'd had little more than a bite of his lunch with Burke the day before, and had missed his supper, making it roughly 24 hours since he'd eaten a substantial meal. He attacked the egg casserole. "This is *really* good."

She smiled one of those big smiles that sneak up on people, and her eyes sparkled again for just a second as she blushed. In that brief space of time she was the old Jo again and Clay's heart jumped so hard he thought it would leave his chest.

"Thanks," she said, putting her head down again. "It was my mom's recipe."

"She taught you well."

Suddenly he felt like he wanted to cry. That sunny young woman still lived in there somewhere. But apparently she didn't get out much anymore.

When they'd finished their meals, Clay picked up the plates, against Jo's protestations, and took them to the sink. Taking the coffee carafe, he went to the table and refilled their mugs, then returned the carafe to the coffee maker. He sat down to her further protest, "You didn't have to do that!"

"I know. I wanted to. You worked hard making this wonderful breakfast. The least I can do is let you sit down and enjoy it."

"You always were a nice guy, Clay." She dropped her head again.

There she goes, putting her head down again, like some just scolded puppy going off with its tail between its legs.

He picked up her hand again. "What happened to you, Jo?"

"What do you mean?"

"I mean, you hardly lift your head up. And that talk last night about not having strength of character. That's not the Jo I once knew," he said gently.

"People change."

"I know. But I'm concerned about you, Jo."

"It's a long story."

"However long it takes, I've got the time. What did you mean last night when you said I couldn't begin to know how hard it was for you to call me? Why don't you lift up your head?"

When she didn't speak, he lifted her chin with his other hand and turned her head so she was looking into his eyes.

Her voice was barely audible. "Are you sure you want to know?"

"Of course I do. I loved you once and I'll always care about you."

With that, she let go of his hand and made a beeline for the bathroom. She was gone for a long time and he fought the urge to check on her for fear of interrupting a private moment. When she returned, her eyes were red, swollen, and bloodshot.

"I'm sorry," Clay said as he stood. "I didn't mean to upset you."

"You're sorry? I knew you loved me. You never tried to hide your feelings from me. You were strong and handsome and honest, and your love didn't have any strings attached to it. You just loved me because I was me." Tears were running from her eyes and she wiped at them with a tissue.

"You want to know the funny thing?" she said.

"What?"

"I loved you too."

Clay shook his head in small side-to-side movements. "I don't understand. If I loved you, and you loved me, what happened?"

"You weren't on my agenda."

"What?"

"I thought I could choose to love anybody I wanted and make him love me back. I used to think it was just as easy to fall in love with a rich man as a poor one." She shook her head. "I wanted to marry and retire young and I was willing to do whatever it took to make that happen."

"Jo, I—"

"I betrayed you, Clay," she interrupted. "Aside from my daddy, you were the only man who ever loved me, and the only man I ever really loved. And I threw it away over some stupid dream of being rich and living in a big house and all the stuff that I thought should go along with it. I knew I broke your heart. And that's why it was so hard for me to call you. I'm ashamed for what I did to you."

Clay pulled her into an embrace. "That was a long time ago, Jo. It's in the past. Let it go."

She stepped back from him. "You forgive me?"

"Of course. Now, how about one of your pretty smiles?"

"Please don't say that, Clay. I'm not pretty."

"Of course you are."

"Yeah, well, like I said, you always were a nice guy."

Something continued to hold her down, though he didn't know if she was unable to accept that he held nothing against her or if there was more to know.

Clay took her by the hand, led her out to the living room and sat beside her on the sofa, continuing to hold her hand. "Tell me the rest of it, Jo."

"I can't." She hung her head.

He lifted her chin and turned her face toward him. "Yes, you can," he said gently, looking into her eyes.

She took a deep breath, blew it out slowly, and stared at the opposite wall. "I went into the Air Force so I could get into Medical Services Administration. I wanted that because my goal was to marry a doctor. You were a parentheses. I didn't know I would fall in love with you. Anyway, after I was transferred to Germany, I missed you something awful. But this doctor, Mike Coale, started flirting with me. He was seven years older than me and I was really flattered that he liked me." She hung her head. "I went to bed with him on our first date. I felt so guilty afterward because you and I had never...been intimate in that way. But I was on track for my goal. I tried to convince myself that I loved him, even though deep in my heart I knew I didn't. But I married him anyway and we moved to Cleveland."

She looked down and shook her head as she continued. "We weren't getting along. I knew I'd made a mistake, but I was determined to be a good wife to him especially after I got pregnant with Chrissie. Of course once I had her, I didn't turn him on any more." She shook her head again. "Maybe it would have happened anyway. I don't know, maybe it was because the illicitness was gone out of it.

build a relationship on it."

She blew out a breath and made a wry face. "He was having affairs and he wasn't making any secret about it. I wouldn't let him touch me—not that he really wanted to, but I think it was a way he could exercise power over me. When I stood my ground, he started hitting me. That's when I told him I would call the police and get a restraining order against him."

"What did he do?"

"Filed for divorce. And he made it clear that if I made things difficult for him, he'd do everything in his power to keep Chrissie from me. So I gave it to him—uncontested. All I got was child support for Chrissie. And that's all I wanted. She's the only good thing that came out of all those wasted years. If I didn't have to let her see her father, I wouldn't, because I don't want any of his evil rubbing off on her. That's one reason I moved back up here."

Clay squeezed her hand and leaned against her. "I'm sorry, Jo. I can see how much it hurt you, but I'd say you did all you could."

"I'm not asking for your pity, Clay."

"I'm not offering pity. You made a mistake. But who hasn't? You tried to honor your marriage vows by being a good wife and mother. You're trying to protect your daughter by keeping her from a bad influence. I'd say that makes you an honorable woman. I think you're pretty exceptional. And I think you've paid enough, more than enough, for a stupid mistake you made when you were not much more than a kid."

She put both of her arms around Clay's bicep and laid her head against his shoulder, snuggling against him. "I've missed you so much." Suddenly she let go and stood. "I'm sorry," she said breathlessly. "I forgot. You're married."

"No...I'm not."

"Oh no. Not you, too?"

"No. Jenny was a wonderful woman and we loved each other very much. She died in a car accident three years ago."

"I'm so sorry. Do you have any children?"

Clay shook his head. "These days, it's just me and my sister, Gwen."

"Oh, I remember. She was not much more than a baby back then," she said, sitting down again. "But what about you?"

He shrugged his shoulders. "My friends urge me to go out, but I'm not ready. I don't know, maybe I'll never be."

"I'm so sorry, Clay."

"Thank you."

"Did you say you checked out of your hotel this morning?"

"Yeah. I've been up here all week. Plus, I promised some friends that I'd have supper with them tonight. And I want to get home so I can go to church with Gwen tomorrow. But it's not like I'm on a schedule. We have plenty of time to pick up your car, even have lunch if you want to. But if you've got a busy day, we can go right now."

"No. What with Chrissie being gone until tomorrow night, I was just going to hang around the house, maybe do some grocery shopping later. I'll have lunch with you if you want. It's so nice to see you again, Clay."

"Look, uh...don't take this wrong, but why don't you come to Grand Rapids with me?"

"I don't know, Clay. Where would I stay? How would I get home?"

"You could stay with Gwen. She has a spare room and she'd be glad for the company. I'll bring you home tomorrow afternoon in time for you to pick up Chrissie."

"Oh, I gave her money for a cab. It makes her feel grown up. But I don't want to impose on your sister."

"You don't know Gwen. She'd love to have you. How about I give her a call?"

"All right."

Clay called Gwen.

He smiled at Jo as he replaced his cell phone on its belt clip. "She can't wait to meet you."

"I hope I don't regret this."

Chapter 12

HE LOOKED AT THE RED NUMBERS of the digital clock on his nightstand: 8:45. *Who gets up this early on Saturday morning, much less rings people's doorbells? This better be good,* he thought, as he walked to the bedroom window and peered through the curtains. It was drizzling outside and a police cruiser was parked behind his car in the driveway.

He scrounged around for a bathrobe and then went to the front door and opened it. A uniformed officer and a man in street clothes were standing on the stoop. He spoke through the screen. "May I help you?"

"Are you Thomas Carlson?" the man in street clothes asked.

"Yes."

"I'm Lieutenant Rick Burke with the Traverse City Police Department, and this is Deputy Ben Goodman of the Grand Traverse County Sheriff's Department. May we come in? We'd like to talk to you."

"What about? You woke me up and I'm not even dressed yet."

"It's about Amy Phillips and we'll be glad to wait while you get dressed."

"Come in," he said as he held open the screen door for them.

The men entered the house and Carlson shut the door before speaking. "Please have a seat in the living room," he said, gesturing in the direction of the room. "I'd offer you a cup of coffee, but like I said, I just got up and there isn't any made yet."

"That's all right. We'll just wait while you get dressed."

Carlson disappeared into the rear of the house and the men sat on the sofa. In about five minutes he reappeared and took a seat across from them in an easy chair.

"Mr. Carlson," Burke began. "We know you identified Ms. Phillips body the other day, but can you tell us what your relationship was to her?"

"We worked at the same place, Northern Fruit Wholesalers. She was my boss and we were friends. Well, maybe friends is not the right word. I don't think Amy believed in being too sociable with her employees, but we were certainly on friendly terms. She introduced me to her sister at the company Christmas party last year and I've been dating her, Carol, for the past seven or eight months. We're going to be married in the spring and Amy wasn't against it. Does that answer your question?"

"I think so. Were you engaged in an argument with her in the parking lot of the Peninsular Hotel this past Wednesday evening?"

"What are you getting at?"

"I'm giving you a chance to explain yourself, Mr. Carlson. Let me put it this way: you were observed having an argument with Ms. Phillips in the parking lot of the Peninsular Hotel last Wednesday night. We'd like you to tell us about it."

"Am I under suspicion or something?"

"Not at the moment. Whether that continues to be the case depends largely on how well you cooperate with us. See, if you don't want to talk we think you have something to hide. If you keep hemming and hawing, we think you're stalling for time so maybe you can make up a lie. Now, do you need me ask the question again? Or, maybe you'd like to continue this downtown."

"No. I'll tell you. We both worked in the finance department. Amy was the controller and I am a staff accountant. We had a surprise audit. Rumor has it that upper management believed something was wrong with the books. Anyway, nobody knew anything about it until the auditor showed up."

"Go on."

"It turned out that there was a $25 thousand shortage in the books under Amy's sole control."

"What do you mean by sole control?"

"Our computer system allows us to view and print each other's spreadsheets, but we can only make changes to our own. Except Amy, being the boss, could access everything. The losses were in an area that only she had access to."

"So why the argument?"

"Well, at first I couldn't believe it. Amy had always seemed so honest and upright. I mean, she wouldn't take home a paper clip. I didn't think she needed the money, but the system doesn't lie. I guess the audit caught her before she had a chance to cover her tracks. I was trying to convince her to give the money back. I even offered to help her pay it back, for Carol's sake. But she steadfastly denied she had embezzled anything at all."

"You were observed assaulting her and a man had to come to her defense. You want to tell us about that?"

"That guy. I'd like to get my hands on—"

"Are you in the habit of beating people up—women?" Burke interrupted.

"No I am not. I was frustrated with her and I grabbed her by the shoulders and shook her." He held his hands out and mimicked shaking her as he spoke. "She just wouldn't admit it. How could I help her if she denied there was anything wrong?"

"And this other guy?"

"She started crying, and he was near by, and she called out to him. I guess I can see how he might have thought I was hurting her. But man, he smacked me in the face and gave me a bloody nose. It still hurts like heck and I've got a bruise where he hit me. See?" He turned his head so they could look. "I mean, the guy was like a professional boxer or something. I'm an accountant not some street fighter, so I left. Amy didn't want my help and this guy was ready to keep fighting, so I just left."

"You ever hear of methyl parathion?"

"No, what is it?"

"It's a poison. Did you poison Amy Phillips with methyl parathion?"

"*Nooo!* Why would I do that? Carol is the best thing that ever happened to me, and Amy introduced us. I'm grateful to her for that. I really did like her and I wasn't trying to hurt her. I was trying to help her—in spite of how things looked. Why would I risk losing Carol? Besides, I wasn't the one under suspicion for embezzlement. I have nothing to hide. What motive would I have?"

"You're not planning a trip anytime soon are you?"

"No, I'm saving my vacation for my honeymoon in the spring. Why?"

"We'd like you to stick around town for the time being; in case we need to talk to you again."

"Am I under suspicion?"

"Not at the moment," Burke said as he and the officer stood. "Thank you for your time, Mr. Carlson. We'll find our own way out."

Carlson watched from the window as they drove away.

GOODMAN LOOKED AT BURKE as he drove back to the station. "Think he's telling the truth?"

"I think so. If he's right about the access to the accounts, then she looks good for it, as we've thought from the beginning. I'm sure he knows we can and will check, so there's no advantage to lying. He's also short on motive. He's right, he was not the one under suspicion; and I can't see a reason why he'd want to kill her."

"What about the other guy?"

"Ramsey? He's okay—just rescuing a damsel in distress. Carlson probably has a case of assault and battery on him though, if he can come up with a witness. Hard to say how it would go in court, him picking on a woman and all. Still, I give Ramsey credit for loyalty. He did everything in his power to prove she was innocent. He really went the extra mile for her."

Justice for Amy

Chapter 13

CLAY TURNED RIGHT ONTO US-131 for the long leg of the trip south to Grand Rapids. "So, have you been back here very long?"

"A couple of years," Jo replied. "I was worried that it would be hard on Chrissie to leave her friends back in Cleveland. But I had to balance that with putting some distance between us and her dad. She's done all right, though. She's made some pretty good friends up here and I feel much better about it now."

"What about you?"

"It wasn't that hard for me. I didn't have a lot of friends down there. In fact, I can't say that I was really chummy with anybody. Most of Mike's doctor friends were older than me, which meant that their wives were too, at least for the most part; so I didn't have much in common with them. And some of them were into the same kind of repulsive stuff he was into, and I just couldn't get involved with it. I was alone, except for Chrissie, so I decided to come home because I missed my family and I wanted Chrissie to get to know her grandma and her aunts. I'm glad, too, because my mom died last year and she and Chrissie had become very close."

Jo tried to blink back her tears, but ended up getting a tissue out of her purse and dabbing them dry. "I have to say, though, that it hasn't been what I thought. Most of my friends from school have either moved away or are married. It's nice to see them but I always feel out of place because I'm alone. I have acquaintances at the bank, but being the manager and all I really can't say any of them would qualify as personal friends."

"Sounds like it's been a lonely life."

"Yeah, I guess. But I've got Chrissie, and we've become really close over the past couple of years."

"I have the feeling she's very fortunate to have you for her mom."

"What a nice thing to say! You know, it's hard for me to comprehend all that's happened since last night. Don't be offended, but it's almost like I'm waiting for the other shoe to drop. I guess it's hard for me to believe that you can so easily forgive, and treat me as though nothing bad ever happened. Did you really mean it when you thanked God for letting you see me again? I can hardly get my mind around that."

"Yeah, I meant it. It really is good to see you again, Jo. I don't want to minimize what I went through when you left. It hurt—bad. At first it was the not knowing what had happened to you, if you'd been hurt or something. Added to that was not having any sure way to contact you. I think, at some level, I knew fairly soon that you'd left me—I just couldn't accept it. These days I suppose people would say I was in denial, but I don't know if they had a name for it back then. Of course, after a while it became abundantly clear that you'd left me. I guess that's when it really hit me. I was angry about it—angry at you and angry at God for allowing me to be hurt."

"I'm really sorry, Clay."

"It's in the past, Jo. There's no sense beating yourself up about it."

"I guess you've made up with God though."

"Yeah. But not before going down some dark roads. I developed a rather bad attitude about women in general. As far as I was concerned, there wasn't a decent one in the lot. So I basically just used them. And when I got tired of one or she started making noise about commitment, I'd dump her and find another. To say I wasn't a very nice person would be to grossly understate what I was. I thank God for Jenny. She had a heart..." He took a breath and blew it out. "I don't know where I'd be right now if it wasn't for her. It was as if her love healed me."

"You must have loved her very much."

"Yes. But it was more than just her; it was the Lord Jesus too. I'd been carrying around a big load of guilt over all the evil I'd done and thought and said. But with Jenny's gentle leading, I came to him. He has forgiven me of all my sins, past, present, and future. Not only that, but he gave me himself in the person of the Holy Spirit, and the guarantee of heaven too. Truth is Jo, there's enough guilt to go around. I've been forgiven much, and accepted by Christ. I will not withhold forgiveness and acceptance from you."

Clay reached over and took her hand in his. She smiled wanly. "You don't blame me for all that?"

"There was a time when I might have. But no, I'm responsible for my own wrong choices. Nobody held a gun to my head and said I had to do what I did. Please Jo, I am genuinely glad to see you again, and genuinely glad to be riding down the road with you right now. I'm hoping we can be friends."

"I'd like that, Clay. I'd like that very much."

"Good. Then what do you say we make the first order of our friendship that we not bring up past transgressions but look ahead, starting today. Deal?"

"Deal," she said, giving his hand a squeeze before letting it go. "I can't get over how much like Amy you are. She spoke much the same as you about forgiveness and acceptance and heaven."

"I'm not surprised," Clay smiled. "The Bible says that if anyone is in Christ, they are a new creation, a new creature in Christ. 'In Christ' is another way of describing someone who becomes a Christian. It's the common experience of all those who have been truly born again. This is a poor illustration, but it's like walking past a storefront that has a sign in its window that says, 'Under New Management.' It's the same old building on the outside, but when you go inside you see that everything is different than it used to be—new, better. It's an inside job, done by the Holy Spirit, and it's something that is impossible for a person to fake for any length of time."

Jo was silent for a moment, looking down at her feet. At last she spoke. "There's more to understand about this isn't there?"

"Yes. And when you're ready, I'd love to tell you about it."

They rode on in silence for a few minutes until Clay spoke again. "Did you say that you're a bank manager?"

"Yes. I'm a branch manager at Merchants and Growers Bank of Traverse City. All three of us girls were blessed with a good head for figures. I guess we must have gotten it from our mother. Anyway, I worked in a bank down in Ohio and was eventually promoted to management. After the divorce, I was looking to come home and was having my mom watch the jobs section of the paper for me. When a branch manager job opened up at M and G, I applied for it and got it. We're a small, mostly local bank but it suits me just fine. I like getting out at five o'clock. I like being part of Chrissie's life—being her mom. What about you? Didn't you work on medical equipment in the Air Force?"

"That's right. It's what sparked my interest in doing it as a career. I finished my degree in clinical engineering, mostly by extension, through the University of Maryland before I got out. Then I worked in a hospital for a while, and that's where I met Jenny—she was an RN, a critical care nurse. We not only got married, we went into business together.

"Carol's a nurse; an LPN. She doesn't work as a nurse though. She has an associate's degree in business. She's the office manager at Westbay Surgi-Center," said Jo.

"Really?" He thought for a moment. "Is Carol, uh...different? I mean, I've only met her twice, but she's not like you, or Amy either, as far as I can tell."

Jo chuckled. "Carol comes on kind of strong sometimes. She can be kind of imperious—self-absorbed. It was worse when she was a kid. She wanted what she wanted, when she wanted it; and woe-be-unto anyone who stood in her way. And she didn't seem to worry too much about whether she was hurting someone else to get it. Gave our folks fits. She's a lot better now than she used to be. I guess she's more-or-less outgrown it, although she can still be pretty unfeeling sometimes. I don't think she means it or even realizes she's doing it."

Jo shifted in her seat. "I was surprised when she said she was getting married. I mean, I didn't think she had the disposition for it. But next thing we know, she's marrying Jim. Two months later he shipped out to the Gulf. Came back with Gulf War Syndrome, and later came down with diabetes. Seems like she just ignored him most of the time after that. On the other hand, she faithfully gave him his insulin shot every day before she left for work. Carol is a study in contrasts, I guess—an acquired taste."

Apparently a taste Tom Carlson has acquired. But that doesn't explain why she seems to have acquired a taste for me, Clay thought. However, he decided he'd said enough. Jo had sufficient on her plate already without having to be concerned about Carol's relationship with Tom.

They drove on in companionable silence until Jo spoke. "Clay?"

"Yeah?"

"There's more to know about what happened to Amy, isn't there?"

Clay picked up the story from where he'd left off the previous evening and told her everything he'd found out, as well as everything he suspected.

"This is unbelievable!" she exclaimed when he finished.

"I know! It seems like I've been fighting for her since the moment I met her, but I keep running up against a brick wall. I'd stake my life that she didn't murder anybody. I'd like to be able to prove to Burke that she's innocent or at least get him to assume she is and investigate, but he's already ticked off at me for challenging him on his suicide theory. He's been fixated on the idea from the start. Then when he found out about Clemens, the auditor, he dovetailed that into his theory as the reason why she committed suicide. I cannot accept that. Her pastor called her, 'a fine, decent woman,' and everything I've been able to find out about Amy bears that out. She did not commit suicide, Jo. And she didn't murder anybody either. Somebody killed her, and it's probably the same person who killed Harry Clemens."

"But what about that...whatever it was that tried to run you off the road? Surely he can't just ignore that."

"The Bronco? I didn't tell him about it. I don't know, it could have been a coincidence. I mean, nobody knew I was going to Carol's house and I'm sure nobody followed me there. On the other hand, Carlson would have a reason to go to Carol's house and he may have seen me arrive and then waited for me to leave so he could ambush me on the road. If he thinks I'm closing in on him for...what he did, he'd have a reason for wanting me out of the way. But, to be honest with you, I was so glad just to be allowed to leave the police station that I didn't want to bring up something else I couldn't substantiate. I guess I took the coward's way out. Sorry."

"I don't think you took the coward's way out. It wouldn't have done anybody any good for you to go to jail." She hesitated a moment. "Do you really think it's Tom?"

"I don't know. The only thing I have to go by is what I saw out in that parking lot. But I do have an idea."

"What?"

"I was thinking I could check to see if he has an old Bronco stored in his garage. Maybe he uses it for off-roading and Carol doesn't know about it."

"Oooo," she said softly.

"What?"

"Given all that's happened, do you really think you should? I mean, if you're right—"

"Amy asked me to help her," he interrupted. "I couldn't save her life. I'd like to save her memory, if I can."

"Tom has been very good to Carol and I have a hard time believing he would be the type of person to do something like this. And for Carol's sake, I hope it's not true. But you're right; we need to check it out."

"We?"

"You and me," she replied.

"Listen, if Carlson is our guy and he discovers we're checking him out, there's no telling what he might do. I'll do this. You stay out of it."

"Just a minute! She was *my* sister. I'm coming with you and that's that."

"Think about Chrissie."

"Chrissie's a big girl. But more importantly, so am I. Look, Clay, I appreciate that you want to protect me, but two are better than one here."

Clay could see the resolve on her face. "You're not going to be dissuaded are you?"

"Nope. If you're going, I'm going—period!" She turned her face to look out the side window.

"Jo?" he said softly.

"What?" she said petulantly, still looking out the window.

He reached over and gently turned her face back to him. "Now would be the time for another one of your pretty smiles."

Her own smile caught Jo by surprise and she blushed, turned her head, laughed, and turned back to face Clay, still blushing and smiling.

Clay smiled back. "We'll both go. But we'll be *very* careful."

At some length, Clay spoke again. "By the way, my friend Mitch...the cop..."

"Yes?"

"His wife's name is Elizabeth. We call her Liz."

"I'm very gratified that you shared that with me, Clay," Jo chuckled.

"I thought you'd like to know, seeing as we're going to their house for supper tonight."

"Oh, I forgot. You did say something about friends having invited you for supper tonight. I don't know, Clay. I'm sure they're not expecting you to bring some stranger traipsing along with you."

"You're not 'some stranger' Jo, you're my friend. I'll call Liz when we get to Grand Rapids, but I know it won't be a problem. They'll accept you because you're my friend, and later they'll accept you because you're their friend."

"THANKS FOR COMING TONIGHT. I hope it was okay—that you didn't feel out of place," Clay said as they left Mitch and Liz's driveway for Gwen's apartment.

"I had a very good time. They're both really nice. I especially like Liz. I think we'd end up being close friends if we didn't live so far apart. You don't know how nice it is to have an adult woman to talk to."

"Oh, I don't know; I think I'm finding out how nice it is. But you're right; she's a nice lady. They're both very special to me."

Jo socked him playfully on his arm. "Smart-aleck!"

"Hey, I like talking with you."

She smiled and turned her head, aware that she was blushing again.

Andy Van Loenen   83

She turned back toward Clay. "Is hugging normal, or was Liz trying to make me feel welcome for your sake?"

"Both. I'd say she definitely wants you to feel accepted. But we all hug more these days. I don't advocate hugging just anybody. But as far as friends and loved ones are concerned, I think when you care about them you ought to let them know it as often as possible."

"Does this have anything to do with Jenny?"

"Liz is one of those people who hugs a lot. But yeah; I think what happened to Jenny made us all more aware that there's no guarantee that just because you get up in the morning, you're going to live the whole day out and go to sleep in your own bed that night. I suppose that's caused us all to become a little more like Liz has always been."

Clay pulled into a parking space at the apartment complex and shut off the engine. He led Jo to Gwen's door and rang the doorbell.

Gwen opened the door and threw her arms around him. "Oh Clay, I was so worried about you. You sounded so down when you called on Thursday that I just didn't know what to think. Then, when you told me you were bringing a woman back with you, I *really* didn't know what to think."

"Thanks sis, I love you too," he said, kissing her on the cheek.

Clay introduced the women as they sat down in the living room.

At length, he got up to leave. "Pick you up at the usual time tomorrow?"

"I don't know." She turned to Jo. "Jo, will you be going to church with us?"

"Yes, I planned to."

"Okay. Then yes, pick us up at about a quarter to nine."

"Okay," he said as he walked to the door.

Jo followed and embraced him at the door. "I'll see you tomorrow."

Surprised, Clay held her for a long moment. She felt good in his arms—very good; and he found himself resisting the urge to kiss her. He cleared his throat. "See you tomorrow."

He made sure the door was locked and left the apartment, pulling it shut behind him until it latched.

JO RETURNED TO THE LIVING ROOM and resumed her spot on the sofa.

Gwen scooted forward in her chair. "Now that he's gone we can talk. So, what have you done to my brother?"

"I don't understand. I haven't done anything to him."

"You've done something to him. I can't remember the last time I saw his eyes sparkle like that, and his voice is different."

Jo laughed. "I haven't seen Clay in 20 years, so I can't judge what's different about him."

"Did he tell you that he was married and what happened?"

"Yes. He's very plain spoken and honest. That hasn't changed; he's always been like that as far as I know."

"Yeah, you always know where you stand with Clay. But when Jenny, uh...his wife died, it was like a part of him died too. Someone who didn't know him before might never have noticed. But for those of us who did, it was like he never fully recovered. He just worked all the time and seemed so sad. I still cry for him sometimes because he couldn't seem to break out of it, and nobody else could break in. He'd be angry with me for saying this, but I don't think he would allow himself to feel again because he hurt so much. But now all of a sudden he seems like his old self again. You two were more than just friends, weren't you?"

"Yes."

"Were you lovers?"

"Not in the modern sense of the word, but yes, we were very much in love and would probably have married if I hadn't messed things up. But it's a long story—too hard for me to talk about. I never dreamed I'd see him again. And I wouldn't have if he hadn't tried to help my sister, who died on Wednesday. Last night was the first time I've seen him in all that time and everything's kind of in a whirl for me right now."

"So you're saying you still have feelings for him?"

"Well, I've not been pining away for him all these years, but you can't have what we had together and not feel something. You see, I found out too late that he was the other half of my heart. But to answer your question: spending this day with Clay has begun to reawaken my feelings for him, and it's very scary for me because I don't know if he feels the same."

"Well, I wouldn't presume to speak for Clay, but I will say that I think something good is going on in him and I think you're the cause."

Jo smiled. "Let's keep this between you and me, huh? Clay and I have been thrust into a bad situation together and I don't want that to influence him. Maybe when our lives get back to normal he'll discover if he has any real feelings for me."

"I'm so sorry about your sister. Is it something you can tell me about?"

Jo explained what had happened to Amy and how Clay came to be involved.

"My emotions are in turmoil. One minute I'm filled with sorrow about Amy, the next, I'm filled with joy about meeting Clay again and the possibility that there might be something for us."

Gwen had sat, quietly taking everything in. But when Jo finished speaking, she went over to the sofa and sat down beside her. "I'm going to be praying for you, and for Clay too," she said, taking Jo's hand in hers. "And if there's any way I can share this burden with you, I want to. I mean that, so please stay in touch with me. Maybe the only thing I can do is pray for you, but I want to help. I will also not tell Clay how you feel—that's for you to say. But thank you for telling me. I think Clay is a very lucky man...but somehow, I think he knows that."

Jo put on her pajamas and climbed into bed. She lay there, and for the first time since she was a young girl, she prayed: "God, thank you for sending these people into my life. Thank you that they seem to genuinely care about me and are so willing to be there for me and even to pray for me. Thank you for Clay, whom I feel like I've known all my life. Thank you for his kindness to me and whatever it is that's happening between us. I hope it's real. I don't know if my heart can stand to be broken again. Thank you for Amy's life. I truly believe she is with you now. Amen."

Her thoughts then turned to Amy and how she had tried to express her joy about her relationship with Jesus and eternal life. Jo realized that even now, she didn't fully understand.

She wondered if her tears would ever stop as her emotions caught up with her and she once again found herself crying softly. Something was different this time though: the sadness for her loss was not as deep and there was peace and a spark of joy mixed in with it.

When at length she drifted off to asleep, it was with the belief that things were truly okay with Amy—that she was happy. And, much to her surprise, she was overwhelmed with the sense of how her own life was about to radically change. But somehow she had a feeling of peace about that as well.

Chapter 14

WHEN HE ENTERED HIS HOUSE, Clay picked up his mail off the floor under the slot in his front door. He was exhausted, but he took the time to shred the credit card offers, recycle the other junk mail, and file the bills so they could be paid at the start of the month.

It felt good to lie in his own bed, and he was desperately tired, but he took the time to pray: "Lord, please give me wisdom that I might do your will as it relates to Amy Phillips. Thank you for your saving grace in her life. Please help me to know what to do about Jo. Seeing her again, after all these years, has begun to awaken feelings in me that I didn't know still existed. I'm certain she is not a believer and I am constrained, for righteousness' sake, not to yoke myself together with her. But I have the idea she cares for me as well. She's been through a lot with her husband's adulteries, and the divorce, and now with Amy. I don't want to hurt her any more, and I don't want to be hurt either. Please show me what to do. And whether this comes to anything or not, I pray for her salvation. Also, I pray for strength that I might worship you acceptably tomorrow. Please help me to set aside all other thoughts and concerns that I may place my whole focus on you, that my worship might be pleasing to you. In Jesus' name, amen."

He lay there waiting for sleep. In spite of his weariness, in spite of how good it felt to lie in his own bed, his mind wouldn't slow down enough to allow him the rest he so desperately wanted.

He thought about Jo—her embrace at Gwen's door, and tried to examine his feelings toward her. They weren't what he'd anticipated on Friday night. Neither was it mere friendship, as they'd talked about earlier in the day. That

Justice for Amy

embrace made it more. Or did it? They'd spoken about Liz's penchant for hugging and letting the people you care about know that you care. Maybe that was it—she was just expressing friendship.

Why had she felt so good in his arms—like she belonged there? He could almost still smell her hair and feel her nuzzle her head next to his. Why had he had the overwhelming desire to kiss her?

Was she expressing more than mere friendship? Why did it suddenly matter so much to him? This was all very confusing and certainly not the path he'd planned to go down. Still, a part of him wanted to walk that path: otherwise, why the feelings?

He couldn't deny that he was beginning to see Jo in a different light; the way he'd seen her 20 years ago. Where would *that* lead? She'd been on her own for at least a couple of years, and was apparently content to stay that way. That being the case, these feelings could only lead to more heartache. But how do you make feelings go away?

He could cut his losses and just take her home tomorrow, drop her off, and call it quits. Pull the plug before it gets a chance to get going. Maybe that would be the best thing all around. If he could do it.

It was well after midnight when Clay finally fell asleep.

SUNDAY TURNED OUT TO BE BRIGHT AND SUNNY.

It was exactly 8:45 a.m. on Clay's watch when he rang Gwen's doorbell. She looked through the peephole before she opened the door. "Hi, Clay, we're almost ready."

Clay kissed her on the cheek. "Hi, kiddo. You're looking particularly pretty today."

"Thanks," she said, socking him on the arm. "And don't call me that."

She padded back to her room to put on her shoes. Clay walked into the kitchen, poured himself half a cup of coffee and leaned back against the counter to drink it.

In a moment she came out again with her shoes on. "Jo will be ready in just a sec. Are we going to Granny's Kitchen for lunch today?"

Clay didn't answer. He was staring past her; she turned to see what had caught his attention: Jo had entered the room. She was wearing a navy blue suit. The open jacket covered a conservatively cut, light pink scoop-neck top that looked like silk, and was worn outside of her skirt. Her hair shined in the light, reflecting its dark golden highlights, and she was wearing just a hint of the same light pink lipstick she'd worn on Friday night. Clay was transfixed.

"Clay?"

He didn't answer.

"Clay." she said, nudging him with her elbow.

"What?"

"Get you're eyes back in your head. You're making the lady blush."

"I'm sorry," he said. He then turned to Gwen. "What did you say?"

"Are we going to Granny's for lunch today?"

"Seeing as Jo is our guest, I think we should go where she would like to go."

"I don't want to impose on your grandmother," Jo said.

Clay opened his mouth, but Gwen spoke first. "No, it's a restaurant, Granny's Kitchen. We go there almost every Sunday after church and Clay springs for lunch."

"If you go there every Sunday, it must be good, so it's fine with me," she said, smiling. She walked up next to Clay and looped her arm around his. "Especially if Clay is paying."

It was Clay's turn to blush. "Come on you two, let's get to church," he said, picking up Jo's travel bag on the way out.

When they walked in, they spotted Mitch and Liz talking in the narthex and walked up to join them. However, Liz and Gwen, as if by conspiracy, took Jo off somewhere. So Clay and Mitch went into the auditorium and sat down.

They sat in silence for a moment until Mitch spoke. "Jo seems like a nice lady."

"Yeah," Clay said flatly.

"What? Did you two have a falling out or something?"

"No, it's not that. It hit me last night and again this morning that I have begun to think of her as a whole lot more than a nice lady or just a friend. Truth is, she's doing something to my heart."

"Okay. So help me out here, Clay. A good-looking woman, whom you've known for over 20 years, is friendly and nice. Even better, she likes you well enough to take a trip with you. You're single, she's single. And you're worried because you think you have a romantic interest in her? Duhhh? This is a good thing, Clay. Be happy. Or is it your goal to turn into a wizened old curmudgeon?"

"It's not that, Mitch. I think I'm getting some signals from her that she would like to be more than just friends too, and—"

"Have you seen the way she looks at you?" Mitch interrupted.

"No."

"Well, I'd say she's definitely interested in being more than just friends. Liz noticed it too and remarked about it last night after you guys left."

"But you see, that's just the point. I have not felt anything for a woman, any woman, in three years. Suddenly Jo reappears in my life and, without even trying, resuscitates something in me that I thought was long dead. But here's the rub: she's not a believer. So, while my heart wants to pursue her for all I'm worth, I have to content myself with just being her friend until she comes to faith. *If* she comes to faith. And that's the frustrating thing—if."

"Ah, I didn't know that. I see your problem. Have you spoken to her about the Lord?"

"Yeah, a little."

"So, did she get angry with you or turn you off?"

"No. Actually, she seemed interested."

"Well, there you go. I'd say your job is to be faithful and to wait on the Lord's timing."

"Yeah, you're right, of course. But pray for me, will you? Jo too."

"I'll pray for you. And so will Liz. In fact, buddy, we already are praying for you and we'll keep on. The Lord has allowed you two to get together for a reason. He will work it out, I'm sure."

"What are you sure of?"

Their heads turned right simultaneously. It was Liz speaking. The three women had arrived to take their seats.

"Oh, we were just talking about something the Lord is doing," Mitch replied as the men stood up.

Liz was either satisfied with the answer or knew enough not to question further. She didn't press the issue.

WHEN LUNCH WAS OVER, Clay dropped Gwen back at her apartment. Upon exiting the car, she leaned in the passenger side window and gave Jo a one-armed hug. "It was so nice to meet you, Jo. Let's stay in touch."

"I'd like that. Goodbye, Gwen."

Clay waited until Gwen entered her apartment and waved from the window before leaving. He then set off to his own house to change his clothes for the trip.

"You two are pretty close, aren't you?" Jo observed.

"Yeah. Since our folks died, we're all each other have in the way of family. I guess that's brought us closer than we might otherwise have been."

"Who's this Bill she keeps talking about?"

Clay chuckled. "That's her beau, Bill Douglas. He's an associate pastor of our church, and the major item on Gwen's mind at any given time. Last Sunday he asked my permission to ask her to marry him. Talk about something that will make you feel old. I don't think he's asked her yet, though. I'm pretty sure I would have heard her scream all the way up to Traverse City."

They both laughed.

Clay turned into his driveway and parked. "You want to come in and change into something more comfortable for the trip?"

"Sure."

He retrieved her bag from the back seat and led her into the house and to a spare bedroom where she could change. He continued on to his own room and changed out of his suit into a pair of khaki pants and a green and tan checked shirt. He also packed a couple of changes of clothes, toiletries, and underwear in a bag.

He met Jo in the hallway as she was leaving the spare room. She was wearing blue jeans and a white mock turtleneck under a light blue, waist-length, fall jacket that she wore open with the sash untied. Clay looked at her with approbation. Twenty years ago she had been like a powerful magnet, drawing him inexorably to herself. There was no doubt in his mind that he was feeling the pull of her

Justice for Amy

again—not that she was trying. It was something in him involuntarily responding to something in her; the same something that had drawn him to her all those years ago.

She broke his reverie. "I hope you don't mind me wearing jeans again. Truth is, I practically live in them when I'm not working."

"No, I don't mind at all. You look good in jeans. But then I always said you could make even a burlap bag look good."

"*Claaay.*"

"I'm sorry."

"Are you? I'm flattered."

"Okay, I'm not sorry."

"You have a beautiful house."

"Thank you. It's kind of big for just me to rattle around in. I've given some thought to selling it."

"Was this Jenny's house?"

"No. We sold our little house in Westgate and had just purchased this one when she died. Of course she was in it, but she never really lived here. If the deals hadn't already gone through, I probably wouldn't have moved. Although, maybe it's just as well I did; too many memories in the old place."

Clay grabbed his jacket, picked up a couple of containers of bottled water and they left for Traverse City.

After they were under way, Clay asked, "How'd things go for you last night at Gwen's? Did you sleep well?"

"Great. We had a nice talk, and when I finally got to sleep I slept like a baby."

"Finally got to sleep?"

"I did something I haven't done for a long, long time. I prayed last night. And I have the most remarkable sense that everything is okay with Amy, and that she's happy."

Clay reached over and picked up her hand. "I'm so glad to hear you say that. The Bible says of Christians that to be absent from the body is to be present with the Lord. I have no doubt that she is with God today in heaven and blissfully happy. And I'm glad you know that now, in your heart, so you'll not be overcome with grief over all of this."

"You know, Clay, belief seems to come so easily to you, just like it did to Amy. You seem so settled in it, just like she was. And me, I want to believe. But it's hard for me. I think of my father abandoning my mom and me. I think of how hard I tried to make my marriage work, and what Mike did to Chrissie and me, and it's hard for me to think of God as being loving. And look at Amy; first her husband breaks her heart because she took a stand for God, and now it appears someone has killed her. Where was God when she needed him? And it's not just us; there's a lot of evil in this world and a lot of people are hurt by it. I want to believe, but it's just so hard for me."

Clay sent up a quick prayer. Her question was fair, the honest response of a heart that was genuinely seeking but unable to overcome the barrier her intellect was throwing in the way. He asked for wisdom to be able to give her an answer that would help her see the truth and get over the obstacle.

"I don't know if I can give you specific answers. I mean, I don't have any way of knowing what goes on in Mike's heart—why he would leave you and Chrissie. I see you and I think that if a man were fortunate enough to have your love, he'd have to be an idiot to throw it away. But he made a choice, and that is part of the answer to the larger question I think you're asking. You've stated it in a personal way, but I think it really has broader implications. Tell me if you think this is a fair way to state it: 'If God is totally good and loving and he created all things and pronounced them very good, why is there evil in the world?'"

"Yeah," she said pensively. "Seeing as good and evil are polar opposites, it seems very inconsistent to me that a good and loving God could create evil. Yet, nobody can deny that there is evil in the world. So yes, I guess that's the question."

"I've struggled with this too, especially after Jenny was killed. I think that to understand it, you need to ask the next logical question: 'What is evil?' And even language tends to mislead us a little here because, in the context of the question, evil is a noun, a thing. But is evil really a thing? If it is, and God created everything, then he is not a good and loving God."

"Well, I hadn't thought about it in just those terms, but yeah, that's just what I'm struggling with."

Justice for Amy

"What if evil were not a thing in itself but a corruption of the good God has made?"

"What are you saying?"

"Well, suppose you had a good wool skirt hanging in your closet and moths ate holes in it. Evil is like the holes in your skirt, but it is not the skirt itself. Because it has no existence in itself, evil can only exist *in* something good. And because it requires good in order to exist, nothing can be totally evil. For example, a totally moth-eaten skirt is no skirt at all."

She thought for a moment. "Okay, you're saying that evil is not a thing, so God didn't create evil and is, therefore, not responsible for evil."

"Yes, that's exactly what I'm saying."

"Okay, I can accept that. But if God is good and loving, he would destroy evil, and if he is all powerful, he could destroy it."

"Right. But if you think about it in terms of evil only being able to exist in something good, the question then becomes: 'What good thing does God have to destroy in order to destroy evil?'"

"Oh, I think I see where you're going."

"The good is freedom—freedom of choice. That's why I said that Mike made a choice. The drunk driver who killed Jenny also made a choice. That both of them were bad choices with evil outcomes goes without saying. And while I'm not trying to make you feel bad, you also made a choice, which you knew was wrong when you made it. I have too. We all have. And sometimes even simple choices can have profound and lasting consequences beyond anything we might have imagined when we made the choice to begin with."

"Go on."

"Well, the thing is, even God can't do something which is actually impossible, like make something be both true and false at the same time and in the same way. Similarly, it's just not possible to force people to choose good and maintain free choice. Forced freedom is no freedom at all. So the only way to destroy evil is to destroy free choice. But when there is no free choice, in the moral sense, neither is there the possibility of moral good. Unless it is possible to hate, love is not possible. If a person cannot choose to curse God, neither can he choose to love and worship God. So the only way for God to destroy all evil would be for him to destroy all good too."

"Okay, that makes sense. But are you saying, then, that they just get away with it?"

"Not at all. While evil cannot be destroyed without destroying free choice, God will eventually defeat evil by separating good persons from evil persons based upon what they freely choose. Those who end up in heaven as well as those who end up in hell will, in each case, be where they are as a result of their free choice. In this way, God actually uses the power of free choice to defeat evil. But of course, in the ultimate sense, that time is not now while we live this life on the earth. Now we are often affected by the bad choices people make, and that we ourselves make. But we also often benefit from the good choices of others and ourselves."

She sat, obviously in thought, for several minutes. At last she said, "It makes sense to me, but, frankly, it is far more intellectually satisfying than it is emotionally satisfying."

"I know. But think of this: Your father abandoned your mom and you, and that hurt you both. But I'm betting the man you've called your daddy really loved you a lot; and your mom too. And I'm guessing the feeling was mutual.

"You chose to come home again, your mom chose to help you find a job, and someone at the bank chose to hire you. All of these things have benefited you and Chrissie— not to mention your mom and even me, because I get to see you again. Sometimes the benefits of the subsequent good choices we make greatly outweigh the pain of the bad choices we've made. Who can say? Someday you might just end up forgetting about all the hurt you've gone through with Mike too. And as long as we live, we are free to choose heaven."

"We need to talk more, but I need time to work on this. Honestly though, what you said about my daddy helps. I've benefited from his and my mom's good choices. They loved each other and me and my sisters very much."

"It would be a whole lot easier if we didn't have to factor our own good and bad choices into the equation wouldn't it?"

"Yeah, for sure."

"Listen, Jo, I hope I didn't make you feel bad by what I said. I know you tried to do the right thing. I know you genuinely tried to love Mike. You just weren't able to counteract his ongoing wrong choices."

"No, you didn't make me feel bad at all. In fact, you're the one person who has always made me feel good about myself. Really, at some level, I knew all along I was reaping the results of my own wrong choice about even getting involved with Mike in the first place. I mean, I've often thought how dumb I was to do that. Honestly, I'm grateful we talked about this because I've been so close to it that I haven't been able to get it in perspective. It finally seems like now I can step back and get a good look at it. And that helps...a lot."

"That's good," Clay said, obviously relieved. "But I wouldn't call you dumb. We all make dumb mistakes sometimes. It's part of what makes us human."

They drove a while before Clay spoke again. "Are you planning on going to work tomorrow?"

"I guess so. I can have three days of bereavement leave, but I don't know if I should take it because I don't know what the police are going to do about Amy. I have some vacation coming though, so I could take some days off if you want me to. What are you thinking about?"

"Tell me what you think about this: I can go to Lieutenant Burke tomorrow and try to get him to release Amy. That way maybe I can save you and Carol from having to deal with them about that. I'm thinking that if you feel up to going to work tomorrow, maybe you'd have a way to check on how much money Amy had in the bank— assuming she banked with you. If she had a fair amount of money in the bank and no recent big deposits, it would be evidence that she had no motive to embezzle from her employer. Maybe then I could get Burke to be reasonable about investigating."

"Oh, that's a great idea! And, yes, she did bank at M and G. Not only that, but I can tell you we each had a trust fund from when our parents died. It came to about $100 thousand for each of us. I've been saving mine for Chrissie's education and it's worth close to $110 thousand now. If Amy didn't use hers, it should be worth about the same; plus whatever she had accumulated in the bank apart from that."

"Great. Is it possible to get a history of her deposits and withdrawals too?"

"Should be."

"You're not going to get in trouble for this are you?"

"I don't think so. I'm an officer of the bank and she was not only a customer, but also my sister. I don't think there'll be any problem."

"Great. Now one more question: Where did you go with Gwen and Liz this morning?"

"Oh," she laughed. "We were just trading phone numbers and e-mail addresses so we can stay in touch. And by the way, if I don't get the chance to say it later, thanks for this weekend. I almost feel like you took me to another planet— a planet where people really care. It meant a lot to me," she said, bending toward him and giving him a peck on the cheek.

Clay could feel his face getting warm. "I hardly know what to say. The pleasure was really mine. I was just happy to get a chance to catch up with you after all these years. I hope I also get a chance to meet Chrissie when we get back."

"Hmm, I never told her about you, so I'm sure she'll be shocked. But I don't think she'll be home quite yet."

"Well, we've still got to go to Tom Carlson's and check his garage for a Bronco. That is, if you're still determined to go. Honestly though, I'd feel a whole lot better if you weren't."

"I meant every word I said yesterday, Clay. If you're going, I'm going."

Clay removed his cell phone from its belt clip and gave it to Jo. "We'll be there before long. Maybe you'd like to give Carol a call and see if you can surreptitiously find out if Carlson is at her house."

"Good idea. I've been wanting to check on how she's doing anyway."

She punched in the number and pressed the send button. The phone was ringing when she put it to her ear.

"Carol? This is Jo."

"Oh, Jo. I've tried to call you a couple of times. Where have you been?"

"I've been down in Grand Rapids for a while. How are you doing?"

"I'm okay. Tom's been with me most of yesterday and again today. It's been good to have him here. I wouldn't have wanted to go through this alone. You sound like you're in a car."

"I am in a car. I'm on my way back right now. It's a long story; I'll tell you about it later. Is Tom there with you now?"

"Yes. I'm going to shower and wash my hair. Then we're going to drive up north for a color tour, and then stop on the way back for supper. Why don't you come with us? We'll wait for you."

"No. Chrissie will be back from Mike's any time now, and I'm tired anyway, so you go and have a good time. I'll talk to you tomorrow."

After she hung up, Jo gave Clay back his cell phone. "Tom's there with her now. They're going on a color tour, and then out for supper. Looks like we're clear to check out his garage."

"Great," Clay said, as he turned west onto M-113. "I assume you know where he lives."

"I don't know the number, but I know I can find the house. You'll see what I mean. It's not too far from Carol's. I'll show you where to turn."

Chapter 15

"DID JO SAY WHERE SHE'S BEEN ALL WEEKEND?"

"Apparently she's been in Grand Rapids. She said it was a long story and she'd tell me later. She's on her way back now. She called from the car."

"I didn't know she had a cell phone."

"I didn't either. Chrissie's wanted one, but the last I knew Jo was against it."

"Maybe she caved under the pressure," Tom laughed.

"Maybe. Chrissie can be persuasive when she wants to be. Hey, I'm going to take a shower and then we can get going."

"Okay. While you're doing that, I'm going to run home and get my jacket. It's going to be cool tonight," he said, heading for the door."

"Umm. Give me a kiss."

He kissed her. "I'll be back before you get your hair dry."

CARLSON'S HOUSE WAS LOCATED AT 1931 WALNUT STREET. It was a small ranch with a gable roof and dark shingles. Like so many houses built in the 1950s, this one had wide lap siding. However, it stood out because it was painted pastel pink.

The narrow concrete driveway, to the right of the house, led to a detached one-stall garage. It sat back from the house about 6 feet its left side roughly even with the right side of the house.

The back yard was enclosed with a 6-foot privacy fence made of wide, dog-eared fence boards. Judging from the fence, the property lines were about 10 feet on either side of the structures. But the back yard was comparatively deep, maybe 60 feet.

Clay pulled up in front of the garage and stopped. They sat there for a moment after he shut off the engine. Jo was looking straight ahead and appeared to be deep in thought. In the quiet, he could tell that her rate of breathing had increased. She jumped slightly as he touched her arm. "Scared?"

"A little nervous, I guess. I know it's silly; nobody's around, but I feel like I'm doing something wrong."

Clay resisted the urge to gather her in his arms. "I can't do this Jo. I can't make you violate your conscience. I'll take you home right now and come back here alone."

"No! I meant what I said. I'll be okay. Aren't you nervous?"

"A little. But I know I'm doing this for a good cause."

"I agree. So we'll be nervous together. Let's get this over with," she said, opening her door.

The gate, which ran between the back right corner of the house and the front left corner of the garage, was a little less than 5 feet high and made out of the same dog-eared boards. It was hinged on the garage side and held closed by an old-fashioned screen door hook on the inside.

Clay reached over the top of the gate, lifted the hook out of its eye, and pulled it open. He held it so Jo could enter. He followed her in and a return spring closed the gate.

A sidewalk went to a stoop that was nearly centered on the house. The garage roof extended out about 8 feet into the yard to cover a concrete patio, 4 by 4 posts supporting the roof at its edge. The garage itself had no side window, but it did have a windowed entry door near the front. Next to the door was a plastic garbage can, and next to that a gas grill. At the far end of the patio was a hot tub, and in the yard a picnic table.

Tom Carlson drove up in time to see the gate swing closed. Parking in front of the house, he exited his car and quietly shut the door. Then, jogging around to the left side of the house, he quietly entered the back yard through another gate.

Clay put his hand on Jo's forearm. "Why don't you go around the back of the garage to the other side to see if there's a window there."

"Okay," she said, and began walking toward the back of the garage.

Clay walked to the side door of the garage. A curtain obscured his view of the interior, so he tried the door. It was locked. The two curtain panels, though together at the bottom, had a small gap between them near the top, so Clay stood on his tiptoes and peered into the garage through the gap. Empty.

Carlson walked softly to the corner of the house and peered around it in time to see Clay try the door. Seeing that Clay's back was turned, he advanced toward him, staying near the house and picking up a large rock from a stone border around some shrubbery planted near the back stoop.

As Clay left the door and began to walk toward the back of the garage, Carlson rushed at him, the rock held high in both hands.

At that instant Jo came around of the corner and spotted Carlson. Clay saw the look of terror on her face as she screamed. He instantly knew she was looking past him and turned to look.

Jo's scream startled Carlson and he hesitated, missing Clay's head and hitting a glancing blow off the back of his right shoulder. The rock flew from his hands and embedded slightly in the soft earth.

Clay fell forward, knocking Jo to the ground as he went down next to her.

"Claaay!" she screamed, terror in her voice. Carlson, dumbfounded, stared at her and stepped back.

Clay was stunned. "I'm...all right...I think. Are you all right?"

She sat up. "Oh, Clay, you're *not* all right, you're *bleeding!"* Jo quickly got to her feet and helped him up. "I've got to go find something to stop the blood."

"I have a handkerchief in my back pocket," he said, moving his arm and shoulder joints around, determining that nothing was broken.

Jo was crying and her hands were shaking as she found the handkerchief and began to dab at Clay's shoulder with it.

Carlson stammered, "Joanne. What are you doing here? That's not your car."

She gave him a withering glare. "Tom! You jackass!" she shouted. "What do you think you're doing? You could have killed him with that rock!"

"I'm sorry. I didn't know it was you. I thought he was a burglar. But now that I see who he is, I'm going in and call the sheriff."

"Tom, please wait a minute," Jo said, seeking to diffuse the situation. "We haven't broken into your house, or garage, or done any damage to anything."

"So I take it you're a *friend* of his?"

She put her arms around Clay and pulled him close, as if her embrace could somehow shield him. "Yes, Tom. And we need to talk to you. Can we go in?"

"Wait till Carol hears about this."

"Is she with you?"

"No, she's home taking a shower. I just came back to pick up a jacket. And it looks like it was a good thing I did."

Jo repeated her question. "Tom, can we please go in and discuss this?"

"Okay, come on in, but I'm only doing this because you're Carol's sister," he said with resignation.

Carlson entered first, followed by Jo, and then Clay. They walked to the living room and Jo sat close to Clay on the sofa. His shoulder was still bleeding a little and she was paying close attention to it, dabbing at it with the handkerchief. Carlson sat across from them in an easy chair. "Now, why are you here? And, I'm warning you, it better be good or I will call the police."

Clay spoke up. "We came here because I wanted to see if you have an old Ford Bronco in your garage."

"A Bronco? I don't own a Bronco. And what difference would it make if I did?"

"Thursday night somebody in an old Bronco tried to run me off the road. Given the guy was wearing a ski mask, I think he was trying to kill me. And given what took place between us on Wednesday night, and what happened to Amy, I wondered if the guy was you."

"*Me?* Look, I admit I don't like you, but up until just a few minutes ago I didn't know you were even still around here. Sure, I didn't like getting punched, but that's no reason to kill you. I mean, why?"

"Well, I witnessed the altercation you were having with Amy out in the parking lot. And let's face it; if you were the one who killed her, you'd have a reason for wanting me out of the way."

"I *did not* kill Amy. I don't know how many times I have to say it. The police were over here yesterday asking me the same thing. I suppose you were responsible for that too."

"I'm afraid so. Look, Jo doesn't think you're the type of person who could do something like that, and I trust her judgment. But I had to see for myself that you don't have a Bronco. I'm sorry I hurt you out in that parking lot, but you have to admit, you were manhandling Amy and had her in tears. What was I supposed to think?"

"I was very frustrated with her. But it was no cause to do what I did. I can't begin to tell you how sorry I am for that—especially in light of what happened to her. But the police are saying it was suicide."

Clay stood and extended his hand to him. "Can we put this behind us?"

Carlson remained seated, but shook Clay's hand. "Sure," he said flatly.

Clay sat back down. "Would you mind if we ask you some questions? We're trying to understand what happened with Amy."

"Sure, I guess." His voice was still flat.

"Do you know what happened to Jim Wagner's gun?"

"Yes. I have it. I took it from Carol's house because she's deathly afraid of guns."

"Can you explain how that gun happened to be found in Amy's purse?"

"What?" he said, rising to his feet and walking toward the rear of the house.

Clay and Jo looked at each other, but there was no time to speak because Carlson returned in less than 30 seconds carrying a wooden box with a hinged lid. The lid was open, revealing a velvet-covered cutaway in the shape of a snub-nosed revolver. By the look on his face, Carlson was perplexed. "I don't know what to say. It was here the last time I looked."

"When was that?"

"I don't know, maybe two or three months ago."

"Any idea who might have taken it?"

"It just sits on my dresser. I suppose anybody who's been here since the last time I looked could have taken it."

Clay changed the subject. "What can you tell us about Wednesday night?"

"Well, an auditor showed up on Monday afternoon to do a surprise audit. By Wednesday afternoon we all knew there was a shortage and which accounts were affected. So after work, we went over to the Peninsular to discuss the matter. We go there sometimes for lunch because it's close to the office. Amy's car was in the garage so she rode with Jake. Anyway, we discussed what was going on and what to do about it over supper, but really didn't get anything resolved. Jake had to go, so I said I would take Amy home. We talked for a little while longer and I pleaded with her to return the money. I even offered to help her pay it back. But she steadfastly refused to even acknowledge she'd taken it. Of course, you know the rest."

"Why are you so certain that she took the money?"

"Because all our spreadsheets and ledgers are computerized and password protected. The doctored accounts were in an area that only Amy had access to."

"Could she have shared her password with someone or could someone have gotten her password somehow?"

"Anything's possible, but it's unlikely. She was the department manager and she was a stickler for security. If someone was caught sharing passwords, they'd almost certainly be fired."

"Who is this Jake guy? He a friend of yours?"

"Jake Morgan. We're not best buddies, but yeah, we're friends. I've been over to his place a few times, he's been here a few times; you know how it is."

"When was he last here?"

"I don't know. A couple of weeks ago—something like that. We watched the Detroit Lions' season opener." He gestured toward a large screen TV. "You're not thinking he took the gun are you? I mean, he's fairly new at NFW. He barely knew Amy."

Clay shrugged. "Speaking of Amy, was she ever here?"

"Yeah, she was here a couple of times with Carol. It's been a while though, two or three months. Look, I've got to get going. Carol's probably wondering what happened to me."

"Listen, Tom," Jo said. "We came over here like we did out of concern for Carol. We're sorry for the intrusion and I hope we can put this behind us." Clay was nodding in agreement.

"It's all right. I'm not angry anymore, now that I understand what's going on. I'm concerned about Carol too. They were so close and this has hit her hard. I wish there was some way to protect her from the fallout that's sure to come up over what Amy has done."

Jo opened her mouth to speak, but Clay, sensing what she was going to say, nudged her leg and she didn't. Instead he spoke. "We'll let you get going." They both stood to leave. "Once again, I'm sorry about Wednesday."

"Yeah, me too."

When they were in the car Jo said, "How's your shoulder?"

"It hurts like heck. But, I don't think he did any serious damage; at least it doesn't feel like anything's broken."

"I'll take a look at it when we get home; get it cleaned up and get some ointment and a bandage on it."

Home? Why not say, my house or the house? Did she misspeak, or did she think of him as somehow belonging to her, and home as being the place they belonged? It had been a long time since he'd felt he belonged to someone. He suddenly realized that it had taken only a couple of days for him to get back to where the idea of belonging to Jo, and her belonging to him was not an unpleasant thought.

He was almost glad Carlson had struck him with the rock. Not for the pain but for Jo's response: The way she'd cried over him and cared for him, and the way she had tried to protect and defend him spoke volumes about how she felt about him.

Clay was nearly overcome with emotion. It felt so good to have someone care about him again. He was suddenly struck with a realization of the depth of his loneliness. He was able to hold back tears, but his voice was ragged as he responded to her. "Thanks, Jo."

"Hey, are you okay?"

Justice for Amy

"I really am. Thanks too, for reading my mind in there when I nudged your leg. I hope you didn't think I was being cheeky with you."

"That's all right. But what's the deal anyway, do you want him to go on thinking Amy is guilty?"

"No, I don't. But I think it serves our present purpose to let him think that. I want to check out this Jake Morgan guy, and I don't want Tom inadvertently warning him that we're suspicious."

"I was thinking the same thing! Maybe we can read each other's minds."

"Scary, isn't it?" Clay smiled.

"I don't know. I kind of like it."

"Me too. I like it a lot. And speaking of scary, thanks for being there, and for standing with me and identifying yourself with me the way you did. I might be dead or on my way to jail right now if you hadn't been there."

"So you *are* glad I came."

"I'm very glad you came."

Clay started the car and set off for Jo's house. "Are you getting hungry?"

"Yeah."

"Would you like to go someplace?"

"No."

"Oh."

She let him hang for a moment. "I want you to let Chrissie and me make us all some supper," she said, smiling, delighting in her little joke.

"Oh! That's even better," Clay smiled back.

When they arrived at the house, Clay carried Jo's bag in for her and set it outside of her bedroom door as she directed him into the bathroom.

He removed his shirt. Dried blood had stuck the fabric to the wound. He winced at the pain and it started bleeding again as he pulled the shirt away.

Jo hoped Clay couldn't tell her hands were shaking as she dabbed peroxide on his cut. But being so close to him—his flat stomach, his muscled upper body, his spicy cologne, the heat radiating from him—something about his presence, was having a profound, if involuntary, effect on her.

She threw the used cotton ball in the wastebasket. "There," she said, her voice a little husky. "A little antibiotic ointment and a bandage and you'll be as good as new."

She applied the ointment to a large bandage and gently placed it over Clay's cut, pressing the edges well so it wouldn't come loose. "There you go."

Clay turned to face her. Her breathing had increased and she was blushing. He realized that his breathing had increased too as he bent his head down and kissed her lips. She didn't resist.

Jo's arms came around Clay's back as his arms went around her and they pulled each other close, her soft lips conforming to his. It seemed to him as if he could taste her. She tasted good, and she felt so good pressed against him. All he knew was that he wanted this moment to go on.

When at last they released each other, Clay was trembling inside and felt weak at the knees, as if he should sit down to keep from falling down. Both of them were breathless and Jo leaned back against the counter top.

She was still blushing and tears were streaming down her face.

Clay took hold of her hands and spoke softly. "Hey, are you all right?"

She didn't respond, but continued to cry softly. She let go of Clay's hands and pulled a tissue out of the box on the counter to dry her eyes.

Clay was filled with remorse. "I'm so sorry, Jo. I shouldn't have kissed you. I was way out of line. Please forgive me."

Still not speaking, she flung herself into his arms and pressed her lips against his. He could feel her warm tears on his face as they held each other in another long kiss.

When at last they separated, she was able to speak. "My nose leaked on you. I'm sorry," she said as she wiped the area above his upper lip with her balled-up tissue.

"That's all right," he said softly, as she pulled another tissue from the box and dried her tears from his face before drying the tears from her own face and then blowing her nose.

He gently pulled her back into an embrace and she nuzzled the side of her head against his shoulder. "Don't be sorry," she said. "I wanted you to kiss me. I've been wanting you to since yesterday morning."

"Then why the tears?"

"I don't know. I guess it's just been too much for me to process. Up until Friday night I had convinced myself that you hated me and that I'd never see you again. Then, suddenly, you appear, and now all this."

Tears were coming from her eyes again and Clay felt as if his heart would jump out of his chest as he raised her head and gently kissed her again.

When their kiss broke, Jo returned her head to Clay's shoulder and they held each other for a long time, until by unspoken consent, they released.

Clay held both of her hands in his, and as they faced each other she said, "I should go find Chrissie."

"Let me get a shirt on first, lest she get the wrong impression about what's going on here."

"Oh...yeah. While you do that, I'll take care of my luggage."

Clay put his torn shirt back on and went out to the car to get another one from his bag while Jo picked up her bag and carried it into her bedroom. Her knees still felt weak.

When they were ready, Clay went into the kitchen and Jo went to get Chrissie. She was gone several minutes before she reappeared with the young woman, who appeared to have been sleeping.

"Clay, I'd like you to meet my daughter, Christine." The girl stepped forward demurely with her hand extended. "Chrissie, this is Mr. Ramsey."

She took Clay's extended hand. "I'm very pleased to meet you, Mr. Ramsey."

"The pleasure is mine," he said, smiling and shaking the girl's hand. "And if it's all right with you, and with your mother, please call me Clay."

She glanced briefly at Jo. "All right...Clay."

She was well mannered and just a little shy, but she had her mother's beauty and bearing. Jo had obviously raised her to be a lady.

After an exchange of pleasantries, Jo walked behind Clay and placed her hands on the back of his rib cage, lightly pushing him in the direction of the living room.

"You go and watch TV while Chrissie and I make us something to eat."

Clay obeyed.

After supper, Clay insisted on helping with the dishes. When they were finished, Chrissie returned to her room to do her homework while Clay and Jo returned to their places at the dining room table.

Clay's countenance had fallen somewhat and Jo noticed. "Something wrong?"

"I have to go back tomorrow, no later than early afternoon, to prepare for a meeting I have in Muskegon on Tuesday morning. I'd cancel, but it could mean losing a very lucrative sale if I do."

"That's all right, Clay. Remember, I'm going to work tomorrow too. I've got to check on Amy's accounts."

"Oh, that's right. Maybe you can see if you can find anything on Jake Morgan while you're at it."

"Good idea. I'll see what I can do."

"Listen, Jo. I want to see you at least one more time before I go. Could we maybe have lunch tomorrow?"

"Yes, I'd like that very much," she said, picking up Clay's hand in both of hers. "There's a sandwich shop on Park, just south of Front. Why don't we meet there at about 11:30?"

"That sounds good. Jo...I've not wanted to bring this up, but I can't avoid it any longer: Where would you like to have Amy taken?"

She sat for a moment without speaking. At last she took a deep breath and sighed. "Ryerson's, I guess. That's where my mom was."

"Would you consider letting Amy's pastor do the service?"

"I hadn't thought about it, but yeah, I'm sure that's what she would have wanted."

"His name is Mike Giles, and it's Northpointe Bible Church out in Acme."

"Yeah, I've been there a couple of times with Amy. But I didn't remember his name—thanks."

"I'll talk to Lieutenant Burke tomorrow morning. Hopefully I'll have some information for you at lunch. Can I get your phone numbers—work, home, cell phone? Your e-mail address too."

"So far I've managed to survive without a cell phone," she said, standing up and going for her purse. She removed one of her business cards and returned to the table, flipping the card over and writing the information on the back. She passed the card to Clay, along with his own card that she had been given by Carol. "How about writing your home number on the back of this?"

Clay did as she asked. "I hope you don't mind if I call."

"You'd better call." Her smile was wan.

"You know I will, Jo," he said, standing and pushing his chair back into its place under the table."

Jo stood. "Time to go, huh?"

"Yeah," he said, walking toward the door.

"See you tomorrow at lunch?"

Clay pulled her into an embrace. "It's a date."

She spoke softly. "Goodbye, Clay. Drive carefully."

"I will," he said. They kissed, this time less intensely. "Goodbye, Jo."

They released each other and Clay left the house. Jo stood in the doorway and watched until he drove out of sight and then closed and locked the door.

"MA-OMMM!"

Startled, Jo turned around to face Chrissie. "Have you been standing there long?"

"Long enough! Mom, we need to talk."

Jo walked over to the sofa, sat down, and patted the cushion next to her. "Well, come on and sit down. I have nothing to hide, so fire away."

Chrissie sat next to her mother on the sofa. "Mom, last I knew you wouldn't even have a male goldfish in the house. Now all of a sudden, you've spent the night with a man in Grand Rapids, and I come out here and find you wrapped in each others arms and kissing."

"Whoa! Chrissie, please, it's not what you think. I'm sorry there wasn't time to fully explain to you what's going on. But I assure you, it's nothing improper."

"Well, what *is* going on then?"

Except for the parts that were inappropriate for Chrissie to hear, Jo explained, in detail, all that had taken place since she'd first met Clay over 20 years ago. She concluded by saying, "I didn't sleep with him and he didn't expect me to. Before we left, he made arrangements for me to stay with his sister—that's where I stayed. And I went to church with the both of them this morning."

"From what I could see, you two seemed pret-ty close."

Jo blew out a breath. "I think we're falling in love with each other again. I know it seems sudden, and it doesn't make any sense, and I can't explain it, except to say I just have a feeling this was meant to be. He respects me as a woman and as a person. His interest is in my heart, not in what I can do for him or what he can get from me. He cares for me, and I can't pass that up. I don't want to pass it up. Please be happy for me, Chrissie."

Tears were standing in Chrissie's eyes as she pulled her mother into a hug. "Oh Mom, I am happy for you." Releasing her, she continued. "Maybe you think I was too young to understand, but I know it broke your heart when Dad left. It broke my heart too. And I know you were being strong for me, but I heard you crying yourself to sleep for weeks and weeks. I know how lonely you've been, and how hard it's been for you to trust someone again. I guess I'm just trying to protect you from being hurt."

"Thank you, sweetheart," Jo said, briefly hugging Chrissie again. "I didn't realize how perceptive a young woman you are. But I want you to trust me on this. I know it's possible my heart could be broken again, but it's also possible that Clay and I could have something beautiful together that will last a lifetime."

"I know. I hope you're right, Mom."

"I know it sounds crazy, but I have this sense that he'd rather walk through fire than hurt me."

"Well he's definitely a hottie...for someone your age."

Jo smiled. "He certainly is easy on the eyes...for someone my age."

They both laughed.

Chapter 16

CLAY DROVE TO THE PENINSULAR HOTEL. He backed into a parking space and caught a glimpse of himself in the rearview mirror as he turned to face the front. He was grinning. He was still grinning when he got to his room and saw his reflection in the mirrored closet door. He wondered if the desk clerk, who checked him in, thought he was a couple of bricks short of a full load. But he didn't care. His heart and mind were full of Jo, and his grin was not one of self-satisfaction; it was there as a lasting effect of her.

It probably was foolish of me to kiss her, he thought. *Taking our relationship to this level will undoubtedly complicate things. But who am I trying to kid? It's already complicated.* She had occupied almost his every waking thought since he'd met her again on Friday evening. Kissing her had been the right thing to do—at least he hoped so. It was good to feel alive again, and it is not good that man should be alone.

Where did *that* come from? He realized that in his mind, he had misquoted Genesis 2:18. Still, it was true, "...It is not good for the man to be alone." But on the heels of that thought came the words from Second Corinthians, "Do not be bound together with unbelievers..."

Clay didn't know whether to thank God for giving him a rich and wonderful treasure or to ask his forgiveness for being so presumptuous as to do what he had done—let his heart rule his mind. He thought of Mitch's words from earlier in the day. "The Lord has allowed you two to get together for a reason, and he will work this out..." He hoped Mitch was right, for he feared Jo was already indelibly etched on his heart.

He got on his knees beside the bed to pray, and spent considerable time there before the Lord, but prayer was difficult. Did he really want the Lord's will; or was he engaged in the fruitless exercise of trying to conform the divine will unto his own human will? He prayed fervently for Jo and for himself before finally retiring to a night of fitful sleep.

It was 4:13 a.m. on the bedside clock when Clay awoke. It was too early to get up, so he laid there and thought. First of Jo—he could call her. No, she would be asleep and he didn't want to wake her. She was facing a difficult week and would need all the sleep she could get. He wished there were some way he could shield her from the pain and sorrow that would inevitably come once the police released Amy's body for burial. But he knew he couldn't. At the very least, he would be here for her at the funeral, and, if possible, before that too.

His thoughts turned to the events of the previous day. Was Carlson telling the truth? Did he really think Clay was a burglar or did he recognize him from the parking lot on Wednesday night? If he did suspect a burglar, why not call the police? After all, an armed burglar posed a very real threat. On the other hand, if Carlson had recognized Clay, he would most likely assume he was unarmed. And if he had connected the rock with his head, it surely would have crushed his skull, almost certainly killing him. Do burglars wear khaki pants and expensive sports shirts?

Clay shuddered. He was thankful Jo had been there and had screamed. Surely the Lord had used her to deliver him from danger. "Thank you, Lord," he breathed. Nevertheless, something about Carlson nagged at him, but he couldn't quite put his finger on it.

And who was Jake Morgan? Clay realized he knew nothing about him, save that he, like Carlson, was a staff accountant at Northern Fruit Wholesalers, and had once worked for Amy. Good that Jo would be checking his accounts today along with Amy's. But what if he didn't bank at M and G? Could she still find out anything? He didn't know.

Credit check! Maybe she could run a credit check on Morgan. Surely that would give some indication of where he was financially. And why stop with Morgan? Why not find out everything they could about Carlson too? He wondered if Jo would be able to do that, or if she'd even consent to it. The only way to find out was to ask her.

Did either of them have criminal records? Mitch could probably find out. Of course, he still had to explain to Mitch about why he'd asked him to run the serial number on Jim Wagner's gun. He made a mental note to talk to him when he got back to Grand Rapids. He would come clean with him and ask for his help. Mitch was a cop with a cop's mind—he knew how to investigate.

IT WAS 4:20 A.M. WHEN JO AWOKE. What a weekend it had been; especially last night—like a wonderful dream. More than that though, somehow the love that was blossoming between her and Clay was giving her her confidence back. His kisses, his arms holding her...ummm.

The beauty of it was that, like before, he didn't seem to want anything from her, except to be with her and care for her and protect her. Somehow she felt compelled, as if by some invisible force, to go to him. She actually wanted to go to him, to be with him, to share his life. This was so good. She couldn't remember the last time she'd felt this alive.

But it was so lonely here now. She thought about calling Clay, but it was too early. He had a big day ahead of him and he could use the sleep. Even so, she wished he was here with her where he belonged, so she could cuddle up next to him and feel loved and secure in his arms.

Maybe it was because he wasn't in her bed right now. Maybe it was because he respected her. Maybe it was because he really listened to her and cared about what she thought. Maybe it was because he was more interested in giving and sharing than he was in just merely getting. Maybe it was all these things...and more.

Maybe he didn't want her! No, he wanted her all right. If those kisses were any indicator, he wanted her as badly as she wanted him.

Poor Clay. She wondered if his shoulder still hurt from where Tom had hit him with that rock. Tears welled in her eyes as her mind replayed the event. But good had come from it, in that it had brought them closer together. His words had been so sweet and his kisses had shaken her to her core.

That stupid Tom! What could he possibly have been thinking—going after Clay with that rock? Burglar indeed! Clay didn't look like a burglar! But then, she thought, were burglars a category of people you could identify on sight?

Maybe it would be prudent to find out as much as she could about Tom as well as Jake Morgan. Good idea, she thought, as she drifted back to sleep.

IT WAS 5:30 A.M. WHEN CLAY FINALLY GOT UP and went for his morning run. When he returned, he showered, and dressed, and placed a call to Jo.

"Oh, Clay, I'm so glad you called."

"Something wrong?"

"No, I just wanted to hear your voice. I woke up early, about twenty after four, and almost called you."

"You should have, I was awake."

"What were you doing awake at that hour?"

"Mostly thinking of you."

"Ummmm. Funny, 'cause I was mostly thinking of you."

"I tell you, Jo, we can read each other's minds."

"So what am I thinking now?"

"Well, I'm thinking I'd rather be there, speaking face-to-face with you, than talking with you over the phone."

"Okay, I'm convinced. I was also thinking it might not be a bad idea for me to see what I can find out about Tom today as well as Jake Morgan. I just can't get past what he tried to do to you."

"Whew! Seriously? I was thinking the same thing. I was also wondering if it would be possible to run credit checks on each of them."

"That could be difficult. I would need to have their Social Security numbers to do that, and there are charges involved, but I'll see what I can do."

"I'll pay whatever charges there might be, but don't get yourself in trouble with the bank over this. I don't want your reputation to be damaged."

"I want to do this if I can. Somebody spoiled Amy's reputation, and I want to restore it if possible. After you left last night I finally got around to reading the Sunday paper, and there was a front page article about Amy in there. Without coming right out and saying it, they made her out to be a thief and a murderer. It really burns me up."

"I was afraid of that. I'm so sorry. We'll fix that if we can."

"I'm just worried about her funeral. I don't know what's going to happen. Although I did talk to Carol last night, and she agrees we should have Amy's pastor do the service. I guess I'll call him later."

"Maybe it would be better if you didn't publish an obituary, but just notified her close friends and let her pastor notify her friends from church. That might keep away the gawkers and those with ill will toward her. You could place a memorial notice the following day. But do what you think is best."

"I'm just afraid nobody will come. She deserves better than that."

"I know. I wish I could fix it today. But all I can promise is that I'll be there for you, Jo. We'll get through this together."

"I wish you were here right now," she said, her voice faltering.

"I'll hang up and come right over."

"No. I've got to get ready and go to work."

"See you for lunch then, at 11:30?"

"See you," she said softly.

Clay read the morning paper as he ate his breakfast in the hotel restaurant. Mercifully, there were no articles about Amy. He wondered as he finished his coffee if Burke would be in the office yet. He decided he'd drive over, taking the chance that he'd be there, and work out the details of getting Amy's body released for burial.

Burke was there, and the body could be released, but not on Clay's signature. He needed a witnessed signature of a next of kin. Still, he was nice enough to allow Clay to hand carry the release form over to Jo for her signature; and Clay was allowed to witness it. However, he wanted a photocopy of Jo's driver license as official verification of her signature. Clay didn't know if the man didn't trust him or if he was a stickler for procedure, but he complied without question or complaint. He wanted to be in Burke's good graces when he was finally able to bring him the evidence of Amy's innocence.

When Clay returned to the police station with the signed form, Burke called Ryerson's Funeral Home to pick Amy's body up at the hospital. Clay was able to speak with Stanley Ryerson on the telephone, and made an appointment for as soon as he could drive over there to discuss the arrangements.

Ryerson asked, but Clay wasn't sure how the manner of Amy's death would be listed on her death certificate. To assuage the man, he guaranteed payment of all expenses and fees in case her insurance wouldn't pay. Apparently the fellow had read yesterday's newspaper. Before he left he gave the man Jo's and Carol's contact information, and got a business card from him to give to Jo.

He checked his watch as he left the funeral home. 10:45 a.m. He went back to his hotel room to collect his belongings and call Amy's pastor. However, when he got through to the church secretary she said that the pastor wasn't in the office on Mondays. Clay thanked the woman and hung up. Then, consulting the card he'd been given, dialed his home number. A man answered.

"This is Clay Ramsey. We spoke last week about Amy Phillips."

"Yes. I remember you. What can I do for you, Clay?"

"It's about Amy. I spoke to her sister, Joanne Coale, about what we discussed—you doing the funeral service for Amy. And she and her sister, Carol would both like that."

"Well, as I said, I would be honored to do it."

"I'm meeting with Joanne for lunch today, and I wanted to give her your number, if that's all right."

"Of course it's all right for you to give her my number."

"Thanks. Listen, uh...could I ask you a big favor?"

"What's that, Clay?"

"I've been talking with Jo, Joanne, about some of the issues in her life that have made faith difficult for her. She has valid questions, and I've tried to answer some of them as best I can, but I was hoping you might extend an invitation to her and her daughter to come back and worship with you all. Kind of take her under your wing, as it were."

"By what you're saying, and by your tone, I'd say that you care about her."

"I do. More that I can say."

"What was it that brought you to the Lord?"

"Now, of course, I realize it was the Holy Spirit working in my heart. But looking back I can see he used many things in my life. Ultimately though, it was love that got me. I came to realize I was lost and destitute in my sin, without God, without hope. Then he showed me Jesus and opened my understanding so I could know his love for me, and how he gave himself for me for the forgiveness of my sins. Once I understood, I suppose you could say I ran to Christ."

"So you know this is something God does, not man."

"Yes, I know that. But I also know that the Bible says, '…how shall they believe in him whom they have not heard? And how shall they hear without a preacher?' and that's why I asked."

"Don't worry, Clay, we're singing off the same page. I just wanted to be sure you understood that my job is to be faithful to the Word of God and that he is the one who does the saving. Still, I will do everything in my power to make her feel welcome here. And I think I can safely say that she will be warmly received by the congregation as well."

"Thanks. That's all I'm asking. Well, I've got to get going if I'm going to make my lunch date with her. Thank you so much, Pastor Giles."

"You're welcome, Clay."

Clay rang off and hurried to check out so he could get to the sandwich shop for his lunch with Jo. When he arrived, he found all of the on-street parking spaces full, so he parked in a ramp across Park Street from the shop.

Jo was already seated at a small table when he walked in. She smiled and waved when their eyes met and Clay's heart jumped at the sight of her. He walked to where she was sitting and picked up her hand as he bent to give her a peck on the mouth. "It's good to see you," he said, sitting down and giving her hand a squeeze before letting it go.

"It's good to see you too—for more than just a few minutes when I signed that paper. How is your day going so far?"

She was stunningly beautiful in a black dress and bright red jacket with jewel-like black buttons rimmed in gold. But that was just the visible part of the package that was Jo. That which was unseen about her was, in Clay's mind, just as beautiful. Why some man had not snatched her up

Andy Van Loenen 119

before now was a mystery to him. But he was glad, and he thought himself very fortunate indeed.

"It's going a lot better...now." He handed her Stanley Ryerson's business card. "Lieutenant Burke released Amy, and I paid a visit to Ryerson's to get things started. You'll want to give them a call sometime this afternoon. I also contacted Amy's pastor, Mike Giles, and he is also waiting for your call. I wrote his number on the back of Ryerson's card. That's his home number. He's not in the office on Mondays, but he said it's okay for you to call."

"Thanks, Clay, you've made this easier for me."

"I wish I could go through this for you."

She reached out and took his hand. "You've done so much already. This whole thing would have been vastly worse for me if you hadn't been here. I can't tell you how grateful I am for that and for—"

Clay hung his head. "I feel like I'm betraying you by leaving just when things are starting to get difficult."

Jo placed her fingertips under his chin and raised his head to face her. "Clay, I will hold you in my heart until you're able to come back to me."

Clay smiled wanly. "And I will hold you in mine."

At that moment a dark haired man in a white shirt placed two sandwiches on their table. "Two turkey clubs," he said, as he turned and walked away.

Jo looked back at Clay. "I hope you don't mind that I ordered for us. I couldn't remember, so I took the chance you'd like turkey. The closer to noon the busier it gets around here, and I have a meeting at one o'clock."

"I don't mind at all. Thank you very much. At least let me pick up the bill."

"No, you pay at the counter when you order. My treat."

"Well, thank you."

Without looking back, Jo lifted her right hand and gestured backward with her thumb. "Do you see who else is here?"

Clay scanned the area where she had pointed until his eyes fell on a table near the back of the room. Tom Carlson was engaged in an animated discussion with another man whose back was turned to them. Apparently it was a joke, because suddenly both of them broke out laughing. Then, just as suddenly, they pushed their chairs out, stood up and began to walk in their direction.

"They're headed this way," Clay said, sotto voce, his lips barely moving as he looked straight at Jo.

There was no time for her to respond as Carlson spotted them and stopped. "Joanne...and Clay." He spoke as if they hadn't seen each other in a long time. "Jake, you know my fiancé, Carol; this is her sister Joanne, and her friend Clay...I'm sorry, your last name escaped me—"

"Ramsey," Clay added, standing and extending his hand.

Jake was about five foot ten or eleven and maybe 160 pounds. Clay guessed he was in his early thirties.

"This is Jake Morgan," Carlson continued as Clay shook the man's hand.

"Nice to meet you both," Jake said. His voice was slightly higher than baritone.

"Nice to meet you," Clay and Jo said simultaneously.

Carlson looked at his watch as Clay sat back down. "We've got to get back, but I wanted to stop and say hi. See you both later."

"Bye," Clay and Jo said as they left.

Jo spoke first. "Well, at least we know what he looks like."

"Yeah. Have you been able to find out anything so far?"

"Yes. First about Amy: she has not touched her trust fund, so the value of it is a little under $110 thousand. But more than that, she was having $1 thousand a pay period going into the bank via direct deposit for at least 7 years—that's as far back as I could go. The value of that account is now over $168 thousand. Plus, I remembered that she bought a new car, I think 2 years ago, and paid cash for it. I also remembered she has a 401-K through work, but I don't have any way to know the value of it."

"So you're saying she had about a third of a million in liquid cash, plus her retirement account."

"Plus her house, which she could easily have converted to cash if she needed to."

"I'm going to make sure Burke hears this. Clearly, very clearly, she had no motive to embezzle anything. But how about Carlson and Morgan?"

"I haven't been able to find out anything at all on Morgan, but I've got a couple of more streets to go down before I call it quits. Tom does bank with us though, and has about $3 thousand in savings, and another $2 hundred in a checking account. I ran a credit check on him and his scores are in the high 500s. That's not particularly good, but it's not particularly unusual either—a lot of people have bad credit. The range is 400 to 900. But the strange thing is, he apparently doesn't owe any money right now.

"Why is that strange?"

"Well, his 24 month history shows a lot of 3s and 4s, meaning payments 60 to 90 days late. Some of it was on a car loan he had through us. But it looks like between April and July of this year he paid off his credit cards, and paid off a lump sum of not quite $10 thousand due on his car."

"So it looks like he came into some money."

"It seems so. Of course, it doesn't mean anything by itself, but it is unusual. Another unusual thing is that he was a joint contractor on several department store credit cards that were all paid off and closed at consumer request in 1995."

"Why is that unusual?"

"Joint contractor almost always means there's a spouse. Plus, men don't usually carry department store credit cards. I'm guessing he was married, and maybe divorced in 1995. Thing is though, without a name and Social Security number, I can't run a check on the wife—assuming there was one. Another thing too: I'm guessing he's not from around here as his report shows he worked for a Beacon Lakeside Corporation at some time in the past. I checked and there's no local company by that name. It might be in Muskegon though, because he had a loan through a Muskegon bank."

"Good work, Jo! I wonder if Carol knows about the wife?"

"I was wondering that too. But I can't think of a way to sound her out about it without her thinking I'm prying, and without raising a bunch of questions about why I'm suspicious. However, if I get an opening, I'll see what I can do.

"Even so, it's very interesting information. Like you said, it doesn't mean anything by itself. He could have come into the money legitimately, or cleaned up his act and just saved it. But it is instructive, and it would be interesting to compare to Morgan's report if you're able to get anything on him.

"I'll keep working on it."

"You know, we've become quite the detectives. Maybe we could become the new Nick and Nora Charles."

"Who?"

"You know, The Thin Man. Of course I'm too big for William Powell and you're much too pretty for Myrna Loy. Plus, we'd have to buy an Airedale."

She smiled. "You watch too many old movies."

"Well, you are prettier than Myrna Loy—much prettier."

"If you say so."

"I do say so. And I never lie. You ready to get going?"

"Yeah," she sighed. "I guess that means you have to go now too, huh?"

"Yeah, it does—as much as I want to stay," he said as they left the shop hand in hand."

When they were out on the sidewalk, Jo spoke. "I walked over here. It's only about four blocks."

"Would it be okay if I drove you back?"

"I'd like that," she said as they set out across the street.

When they got to the car, Clay unlocked the doors with his remote and opened the passenger side door for her. She did not enter. Instead, by unspoken consent, they embraced, eagerly finding each other's lips and pulling each other hard together, as if by so doing they could meld their two persons into a single being.

When at last they released their kiss, they held each other; savoring the seconds of their remaining minutes together, until a car rounded the corner of the ramp into the area in which they stood.

They released each other, and Clay gently cupped her face in his hands, giving her a brief, soft kiss on the lips before helping her into the car. More than ever, he did not want to go.

They drove in silence down Front Street until they reached the bank. Stopping, they exchanged another brief kiss. "Be safe, my Clay," Jo said, opening the door.

"You too, sweetheart. I'll call you tonight."

"I'll be waiting," she said, as she closed the door.

Clay ignored the driver behind him, who was blowing his horn, as he watched Jo disappear inside the bank. Then, continuing west on Front Street, he drove out to M-37 and turned south.

He drove home in silence, wishing for no music or talk or noise to break the enchantment she held over him.

Chapter 17

"GOOD AFTERNOON, NORTHERN FRUIT WHOLESALERS. How may I direct your call?"

"I'd like the payroll department please."

"That would be Finance. Would you like to speak with someone in particular?"

"No. Just whoever is responsible for payroll."

"That would be Barbara Lockhart. One moment, I'll transfer you."

She waited: one, two, three rings, and was expecting to go to voice mail when the phone was answered.

"Finance, Barb Lockhart speaking."

"Barb, this is Jo Coale from Merchants and Growers Bank."

"Yes. How may I help you?"

"I'm trying to verify that you have a Jacob Morgan on your payroll. I understand he works there, but I'm having difficulty confirming it."

"We do. And the reason you're having difficulty is probably because his name is Morgenstern. He has informally shortened it to Morgan, and that's what everybody knows him as, but legally it's Morgenstern, with an 'e'."

"Oh, that explains it! Thank you very much Barb. You saved me a lot of time. Just to be sure though, can you verify his SSN?"

"I really shouldn't, for security reasons, but let me call you back."

"Okay, let me give you my number."

"No. Don't give me your number. I'll look you up in the book and call right back. Sorry, can't be too careful, you know."

"I understand completely. I'm at the main branch—downtown. I'll be waiting for your call. Thanks for your help, Barb."

Armed with Morgan's real last name, Jo once again checked to see if he had any accounts with M and G Bank. He didn't. However, she was able to run a credit check on him after Barbara Lockhart called back with his Social Security number.

She felt bad about misrepresenting her purpose to the woman, but if she'd given her real reason for wanting the information she doubted Barb would have been at all cooperative. Besides, she had no intention of exploiting Morgan. Her only goal was to clear Amy's name. But to do that, she needed to know who might have had a motive to embezzle $25 thousand and make it look like Amy had done it. And Morgan's credit report did not look good. But there was no time to worry about that now. She would discuss it with Clay tonight when he called.

Jo got up from her desk and closed her office door. Returning, she called Carol at work to verify that she would be able to go with her to Ryerson's to make funeral arrangements. She then called the funeral home to make an appointment for early evening. After calling Carol back with the time, she called Mike Giles at home.

"This is Joanne Coale. You spoke with Clay Ramsey this morning about my sister, Amy Phillips."

"Yes, I did. He said that you and your sister would like me to officiate at her funeral. I would be honored to do that—Amy was very dear to us. Did you have a time in mind?"

"Right now we're thinking about Th-Thursday, if-if that would be all right," she said, her voice beginning to falter. Hearing her own voice speak the words arranging for Amy's burial suddenly brought the awful finality of it all crashing in on her and tears began to well in her eyes. She fought to get control of her emotions as she sniffed and pulled a tissue out of the box in her desk drawer. Drying her eyes, she continued. "I was hoping for sometime in the afternoon, but I haven't spoken with the funeral director yet."

"Well, afternoon is fine. Why don't you call me when you get it worked out with them. And if you'd like to have it at the church, we'd be honored to do that as well."

"Yes. I think Amy would have wanted that. Also, because of the publicity, I am not planning to publish a notice in the paper. I was wondering if you could notify Amy's friends from church about the viewing and the service once I figure out when they can be."

"We'd be happy to do that. I can have the deacons call their care groups and notify the whole church."

"Thank you very much. I'll call you back as soon as I know something."

"You can reach me at this number day or night. Is there anything I can do to help with this?"

"Thank you, but Clay made all the preliminary arrangements before going back to Grand Rapids. I pretty much just have to follow up."

"Oh. He's not with you?"

"No. He wanted to be, but he had to go back. He's coming back up here as soon as he can though."

"I hope I'm not talking out of turn, but from talking with him this morning I can tell that he cares very deeply for you."

"No, you're not talking out of turn. I know that. And the feeling is mutual."

"Do you have anyone to be with you right now? My wife and I, or just my wife, if you'd prefer, would be happy to come and be with you."

"That's very kind, but I'm at work right now, and I'll be seeing my sister, Carol, soon after."

"All right then, but you call whenever you need to and we'll be here for you."

"Thank you, Reverend Giles."

"HEY," SHE SAID, STOPPING IN HIS CUBICLE. She hiked one leg up and half sat on his desk, managing to get just enough thigh showing to be provocative.

"What can I do for you, Barb?" he replied flatly.

"I'd like a million dollars. But I'll settle for drinks tonight after work, seeing as you're asking, and seeing as I did you a favor today."

"You know, Barb...I don't drink. And what are you talking about, doing me a favor?"

"I verified that you're employed here for M and G Bank. You apply for a loan or something?"

"I don't have the vaguest idea what you're talking about."

"Somebody named Jo called from there to see if you really worked here—didn't know your legal name is Morgenstern."

"But I'll bet you set them straight, right?"

"Sure. I verified your name and Social Security number for them. Wouldn't want to hold up...whatever it is you're doing."

"Yeah, well, thanks, Barb. I don't know what I'd do without you."

"Hey, don't mention it. Uh...look, if you really don't drink, I'm a good cook."

"I think my girlfriend would object to that."

"Okay, Jake. Can't fault a girl for trying—maybe some other time."

"Maybe," he said as she walked away.

Tom Carlson's voice came from the next cubicle. "What was that all about?"

"Aw, who knows? That woman's had the hots for me practically since the day I started working here." He stood up and walked into Carlson's cube. "She must have 15 years on me. She's almost old enough to be my mother. Apparently some guy named Joe from M and G Bank was checking on my employment. She probably just made it up to get me into her evil clutches."

"You know that woman we met at lunch, Carol's sister, Joanne? Her friends call her Jo and she's the manager at the main branch of M and G, downtown."

"No kidding? You think it could be her?"

"How many Jo's could they have?"

"Is that Joanne with an 'e'?"

"Yeah. And her last name is Coale, like the mineral, but she spells it funny, with an 'e' on the end; C-o-a-l-e."

"Humph. Barb didn't say if it was a man or a woman. Maybe I ought to go ask her."

"Hey, I would. I mean, if you're not doing business with them, why would they want to verify your employment?"

"Good point. I guess I'll go ask Barb. But do me a favor, will you?"

"What's that?"

"If I'm not back here in about 3 minutes, come and get me. Say I have a phone call or something. If she ever gets me in her office with the door closed, who knows what might happen to me."

"Okay," Tom laughed.

JO ARRANGED FOR BEREAVEMENT LEAVE and a day of vacation, so she could have the rest of the week off. Then she went home. Waking up early, Clay's leaving, and the arrangements she had yet to make regarding Amy had done a triple whammy on her emotions. She didn't trust herself to deal with customers or her employees any more that day. She'd just barely been able to beat back the tears on the phone with Reverend Giles. Right now, all she wanted was to go home and cry...and sleep. But there was no time for that either, she thought as she drove. Chrissie would be home from school and she'd have to whip together something for them to eat. Then Carol would be coming over to go to Ryerson's. Then, hopefully, Clay would be calling.

Reverend Giles seemed really nice on the phone—like he genuinely cared about her. Amy had certainly loved that church. Maybe, once all this business was over, she would take Chrissie and start going there. Amy had certainly wanted her to do just that. But she realized now that her anger at Mike, his infidelities, his leaving her, had also translated into anger at God.

Somehow though, after her discussion with Clay about free choice, her anger against Mike had turned into something more benign. Not that she had any use for Mike, but that she didn't actively hate him any more. And was even able to see how her own early choices had placed her in a marriage that had little hope of surviving. Free choice is good. Clay used his to care for her. God is good. People are the ones who abuse free choice.

It had been a profitable talk because her anger at God, she now realized, had also been assuaged. Still, it was a lesson that both she and Clay had, under different circumstances, learned the hard way.

Dear Clay. She thought again of Reverend Giles words, "...He cares very deeply for you." What had he said to the man to make him say that? That he loved her? She longed to hear those words from him.

Somehow, for her, Clay had become the one bright spot in all this darkness. In his heart he was like Amy and Reverend Giles. There was kindness and a love for God. But there was also a fire burning, and she knew it burned for her. Any doubts she'd had this morning about whether he really wanted her were dispelled this afternoon as they kissed and held each other in that parking ramp. It was a heady feeling to be wanted, to be thought beautiful and desirable; heady enough to change her whole outlook on life.

They seemed to belong together. It was like they were always on the same wavelength—thinking each other's thoughts. How could this be? They'd only been together again for a few days. But they were so comfortable with each other it was almost as if they'd been together rather that apart these past 20 years. Maybe God had somehow sent him to her. Who could say? All she knew was that she wanted this to go on forever.

Of course, she remonstrated herself, this extreme headiness couldn't last forever. But the love and kindness would, if she cultivated it—and she intended to use her free choice to cultivate it for as long as she was able. And they'd have their heady moments too.

"Ha," she laughed out loud, amazed that she was suddenly filled with so much confidence. "Restrain yourself, girl," she spoke again into the air. "You could be headed for a major heartbreak." *No,* she thought, *Clay belongs to me...and I belong to him—forever.* It was just that simple, just that settled, just that irrevocable.

JO AND CHRISSIE ATE AN EARLY SUPPER and had not much more than finished the dishes when Carol arrived.

Chrissie settled down to do her homework as Jo and Carol left for Ryerson's Funeral Home.

The funeral was scheduled, with Reverend Giles' agreement, for 2 p.m. on Thursday afternoon at Northpointe Bible Church in Acme. That left Tuesday to notify Amy's friends.

On the way back, Jo suggested a memorial notice be placed in the paper on Friday, and Carol agreed. When

Justice for Amy

they arrived back at Jo's house, they spent some time working on the text of the notice before Carol left for home.

JO PICKED UP THE CORDLESS PHONE and took it with her as she walked to the recliner in the living room to await Clay's call. What a day it had been. She was dead tired, but she knew it was mostly from the emotional roller coaster she'd been on all day. Still, she'd had a settled feeling since Saturday night that things were well with Amy, and because of that none of this was affecting her the way she'd thought it would. It hurt. But it was okay, too. And she was just too tired to try to figure out what it all meant. She sensed that somehow God was involved in this, and not as a passive bystander. Amy's God. The God Amy loved, and whom she claimed loved her. She realized that she had thought more about this God in the past four days than she had in probably the past four years. Reverend Giles' God. Clay's God. Her God? Yes. She had a strange awareness, as she drifted off to sleep, that this same God loved her too.

"MOM."

Chrissie put her hand lightly on her mother's shoulder. "Mom."

"Hmm," Jo said, rousing out of sleep. "What is it, Chrissie?"

"It's CoCo. I can't find her anywhere."

"Where did you look?" Jo rubbed her eyes while yawning.

"In my room, and your room, and all around."

"Did you look in the basement?"

"Nobody's been down there."

"When did you last see her?"

"I don't know. Sometime after you and aunt Carol left."

"Well, maybe she's in the garage using her litter box."

"I'll go look," Chrissie said.

"Okay. I'll check the basement, just in case she got down there somehow."

Jo checked the basement while Chrissie checked the garage. Finding the cat in neither place, they instituted a thorough search of the main floor. CoCo was not to be found anywhere.

"Could she have slipped out when you and Aunt Carol came in? You know how sneaky she can be," Chrissie said when they returned to the kitchen.

"I don't know, honey. She might have, I just wasn't paying attention."

Chrissie went outside and called and looked around for her cat. She was crying when she came back in 15 minutes later. "I can't find her...anywhere," she said through her tears.

Jo pulled her into a hug. "Don't worry, honey. She'll most likely be sitting on the back steps in the morning, proudly displaying a chipmunk she caught or something."

"You think so?" she sniffed, clearing her nose.

"Sure. And I'll check outside for her one more time, before I go to bed. Now why don't you get your PJs on, and I'll come in to tell you goodnight in a little while."

"Aw, Mom!"

"Come on, it's a school night."

"Okaaay."

Jo resumed her place in the recliner as Chrissie went off to her room. She picked up a book she'd been reading and operated the lever on the side of the chair to lift the footrest. Then, reaching overhead, she turned on the floor lamp behind the chair and adjusted the arm to move the light to the best place for reading

She had just opened her book when the phone began to ring. It sounded muffled and she realized it had gotten caught between the cushion and the side of the chair. Digging it out, she answered on the third ring:

"Hi, sweetheart."

Her heart jumped. "Hi, sweetheart," she said, suddenly breathless. "How are you?"

"Would you laugh if I told you I already miss you?"

"No, because I miss you too."

"In that case, I have some bad news. I won't be able to come up tomorrow—unless I come up late. It looks like I'm going to be in Muskegon until after lunch and I won't be able to touch base with Mitch until evening."

"Oh."

"After that, Gwen pretty much has my schedule clear, although I may have to go to Madison, Wisconsin on Friday. I'm not sure yet."

"You're not trying to avoid me, are you?"

"Of course not. Why would you even think such a thing?"

"I'm sorry, Clay. I've had a tough day. Then, to top everything off, Chrissie's cat seems to have gone missing and she's upset. But I shouldn't have taken it out on you."

"I'm sorry too—sorry you've had a hard day. I know you've had a hard way to go these past years. And I would guess it's probably hard for you to trust a man again. But you can trust this: I have no plans to avoid you unless you tell me you don't want me around any more. And In the mean time, I'll go on counting myself fortunate that you've allowed me to get close to you again."

"Oh, Clay."

"Oh, Jo."

They both laughed.

Clay was the first to speak again. "So were you able to get any information on Jake Morgan today?"

"Yes! First of all, I found out his real name is Morgenstern, Jacob Morgenstern. He just goes by Morgan. He doesn't have any accounts with M and G so I can't check that, but I finessed the payroll person where he works to confirm his name and give me his Social Security number. So I was able to run a credit check on him."

"Clever lady. Find out anything interesting?"

"Yeah, hold on a second."

She got up, got the credit report out of her purse, and continued speaking as she went back and sat down. "His scores are in the low to mid-500s. Looks like he had a car go back to Petoskey National on repossession a little over four years ago, and a bankruptcy shortly after that. He worked at one of those big chain pharmacies, Barrigans in Petoskey, so I'm guessing he's from there. Here's the interesting thing though; he got another car loan through A-1 Auto Finance two years ago. That's one of those high interest places that loan money to people with bad credit. Anyway, he paid it off in May of this year."

"Yeah, that is interesting."

"Another question is, what was he driving for two years? I mean, maybe he borrowed somebody's car or maybe he took public transportation. On the other hand, maybe he was in jail. But I'm guessing at that because he shows no activity between the bankruptcy and the auto loan. His recent history is all 1s though, meaning paid on time."

"Do you know the value of the loan he paid off?"

"No. All I can see is that the original value was $9,980.00. It was a four year note, so I'm guessing there was maybe $75 hundred due on it when he paid it off."

"Anything else?"

"No, not much. Judging from his address, he lives in Carriage Hill Apartments. I can show you where they are when you come up. I hear they were nice when they were built in the late '60s, but they've fallen on hard times and become one of the lower-rent places in recent years."

"Jo, you are an absolute wiz. Of course the problem is, on the face of it, both Carlson and Morgan look questionable."

"Yeah, I know. Guess I wasn't much help after all."

"Don't denigrate yourself; you did just fine. We had nothing but names before—now we have information. All we need to do is narrow it down. I found out something too."

"What's that?"

"I remembered reading something about being able to identify Social Security numbers because the first three digits indicate what state the card was issued in. Anyway, Carlson's first three digits, 5-0-7, didn't look like they came from Michigan, so I looked it up on the Social Security web site and found out his was issued in Nebraska. Apparently he's from there, or at least lived there when he got his Social Security card. It may be nothing, but I'll give it to Mitch along with everything else and see what he can dig up."

"Oh. Mitch has agreed to help?"

"Well, he doesn't know it yet," Clay laughed. "That's what I want to talk to him about tomorrow. I also went to the library and checked, or I should say tried to check on that Beacon Lakeside Corporation in the Michigan Manufacturers Directory, but came up with nothing. Then I remembered you guessed that he'd left Muskegon in '95, and wondered if they might have gone out of business. So I requested the 1994 book, but it is at the state library in Lansing and it will take a few days to get it up here."

"Do you think that's something important?"

"I don't know, could be. I guess I'm trying to get as complete a picture as possible."

"I'm leaning toward Jake right now, but I don't know if it's because I don't want it to be Tom for Carol's sake."

"I know, sweetheart. I love the way your heart works, and I hope you're right. You never know, it may not be either one of them."

"Yeah, but I also know the odds favor it being one or the other of them. I just wish there was a way to find out for sure."

"Well, I talked to my computer network guy today and asked him how someone could get someone else's passwords, and basically there are four common ways:

"One, they just guess until they get it right. That doesn't seem likely to me, though, because Tom said Amy was a stickler for security and she probably wouldn't have chosen something easy to guess for a password.

"Two, it's possible to install software, generically called spyware, on a computer that would capture keystrokes. Most commonly, though, these kinds of things are surreptitiously done by malicious web sites and you'd have to be something of an expert to pull it off, or already have the password to load it locally. This doesn't seem likely to me either—unless one of their IT guys did it; but that's even more farfetched.

"Three, he, whoever he is, could have surreptitiously watched while she typed in her password. This is called shoulder surfing, and if you don't get caught, it's the fastest, easiest, and cheapest way to get someone's password. This is certainly a possibility, but I don't know what the environment is like where Amy worked—whether it would have been possible or not.

"Four, you can buy a little memory device that plugs on the end of the keyboard cable before it plugs into the computer. This thing also captures keystrokes, but can be easily removed and downloaded as plain text at any time. You could see everything the person typed, including passwords. And because it's installed at the back of the computer, it's not likely to be seen. This seems the most likely to me because it can be installed quickly and easily by just about anybody at a time when the unsuspecting user wasn't around. I tell you Jo, I'd like to get in where those guys work to see what I can find out."

"But...how would you do it?"

"I was thinking I could go over there late on Wednesday afternoon and stay out of sight until they close and everybody goes home. Then I would be free to roam around and check things out. Thing is though, I may end up trapped in there until they open in the morning."

"Clay, don't. It might be dangerous."

"Well, let's give it some thought and we can talk more about it on Wednesday when I see you."

"I wish you were here now."

"I do, too. I miss you."

"I miss you, too."

"Get some sleep now. You'll feel better in the morning."

Chapter 18

JO AWOKE THE NEXT MORNING TO SCREAMING. Who? What? *Chrissie!* All of her motherly instincts kicking in, she was immediately awake and alert as she jumped out of bed. Not bothering with robe or slippers, she ran to Chrissie's room. Not there! Another scream. Dining room! She ran into the dining room to find the girl, now in hysterics, holding the open sliding glass door and staring through the screen.

Goosebumps formed on her skin, even under her pajamas, from the brisk morning air and she shivered as she came beside Chrissie and saw CoCo lying on the deck, convulsing in her own vomit.

She pulled the girl out of the doorway and closed the door. Then, turning Chrissie toward her, she shook her by her shoulders to divert her attention from CoCo.

Her hysterics turned to wracking sobs and Jo pulled her into a hug. "Honey, get dressed—now. Hurry. We'll take her to the vet."

Chrissie hurried to her room still sobbing as Jo hurried to hers to throw on jeans and a sweatshirt. She grabbed her purse, pulled a hairbrush out of it, and coming into the hallway, was running it quickly through her hair as Chrissie exited her room, tears still in her eyes, but no longer sobbing.

Chrissie took the brush for her own hair as Jo got a bath towel out of the linen closet to wrap CoCo in. Then, exiting the house, she scooped the cat into the towel and gave her to Chrissie to wrap while she went back in to operate the button that opened the garage door.

As Jo drove toward the vet's office she couldn't remember if she'd locked the house or put down the garage door. But she couldn't worry about that now. She had to get the cat to the vet, she thought, as Chrissie cuddled her pet and cooed to it while weeping, almost silently.

The day was cold and damp, and Jo uttered an epithet under her breath that the car's engine hadn't warmed sufficiently for the defroster to keep the inside of the windshield from fogging with their exhalations. To make matters worse, it was morning rush hour. She wanted to move—fast, but frustratingly slow was the best they could do.

She banged the steering wheel with the side of her fisted hand and hollered, "Come on," as the person in front of her seemed to be asleep at the stoplight, which had just turned green. Then she had to brake hard as the idiot turned right without using his turn signal. She was about to holler again when she noticed the road ahead was clear. The windshield was now also clear as she pressed down the accelerator of her red Mazda.

Dr. Cobb was a kindly old man who reminded Jo of Grandpa Walton. Having had a country practice for decades, he had moved into town and opened a small animal practice when he was no longer able to physically handle large animals and the night-and-day calls to the farms he'd once served.

He was just getting out of his car as Jo and Chrissie drove up.

Jo ran over to him with Chrissie, carrying CoCo, at her heels. "Oh, Dr. Cobb, thank goodness you're here!"

"What is it, Jo?"

Jo opened her mouth, but Chrissie spoke, thrusting the animal in the old vet's direction. "It's CoCo, she's so sick, I think she's dying!" She began to weep again as Jo took the cat from her.

Cobb hurried to the door and unlocked it. "Come on in— hurry, let's get her on the exam table," he said, pushing open first the door to the waiting room and then the door to the exam room.

Jo placed Chrissie's cat on the table and Dr. Cobb listened to various places with his stethoscope and prodded various places with his fingers and sniffed at the cat's mouth. He then stood straight with a sad look on his face, and seemed to be searching for words.

"What is it?" Jo asked.

Well, I haven't seen this for a long time, but it looks like organophosphate poisoning."

"What?"

"I'm sorry, pesticide. A particularly nasty kind that you don't see much any more, especially in the city. I'm so sorry, but she's dying. There's no antidote."

Chrissie backed up, holding both hands over her mouth. Bumping into the wall, she slid down it until she was sitting on the floor.

Jo rushed to comfort her as she spoke over her shoulder. "Is there anything you can do?"

"The kindest thing would be for me to put her to sleep, to put her out of her misery right now."

"Do it," Jo said as Chrissie screamed, *"Nooooo!"*

Jo helped Chrissie up and held her in an embrace, turning her so she couldn't see what was taking place. She cried on her mother's shoulder as Dr. Cobb drew Nembutal into a syringe and mouthed at Jo, "It would be better if you took her out."

Jo took Chrissie out into the hallway and leaned against the wall as she held her and they both wept. She had never been a pet person, and she'd been furious at Mike for giving the kitten to Chrissie when he knew full well she didn't approve. She'd even made Chrissie keep the litter box in the garage, not wanting any smells in the house. In the larger sense though, she refused to be what she referred to as a "cat woman," like some other divorced and single women she knew. But she cried because her heart broke for her precious daughter. Chrissie loved that cat, and had mothered it since it was a kitten. To her tender, young heart it was tantamount to losing a child.

At length, Dr. Cobb joined them in the hallway. "She went peacefully. In the end, there was no pain," he said, placing his hand on Chrissie's shoulder.

Crestfallen, the girl could not speak, but slowly turned and walked out to the waiting room and sat down, her elbows on her knees and her head in her hands.

"What do I owe you," Jo said softly, still in the hallway.

"There's no charge. I'm only sorry there was nothing I could do. If you'd like, I can take her out to my place and bury her."

"I guess so," Jo said.

"Call me when you get a minute and Chrissie is not around, okay?"

"Okay," she said, as she walked out into the waiting room to get Chrissie and go home. "Thank you, Dr. Cobb."

He smiled a sad smile, but did not speak as he stood in the doorway and watched them leave.

JO ALLOWED CHRISSIE TO STAY HOME FROM SCHOOL, and called in to report her absence before making them breakfast. However, Chrissie just picked at her food. When it got cold Jo offered to rewarm it in the microwave, but Chrissie opted to go to her room instead. She was no longer crying, but had become sullen and unwilling to carry on a conversation. She was grieving, and Jo's heart broke for her. She wanted to go to her, but there would be time for that later. Right now, Chrissie needed to be alone.

Taking advantage of the time, Jo called Dr. Cobb. His request for her to call when Chrissie was not around had seemed cryptic to her, but she dared not ask him at the time because Chrissie was so upset.

"This is Jo Coale. I would have called sooner, but I waited for Chrissie to go to her room. You seemed a little mysterious and I wondered what's going on."

"I'm sorry, I wasn't trying to be mysterious, but I have a concern about what happened to CoCo and didn't want to discuss it in front of Chrissie. She was already so heartbroken I didn't want to add to her pain."

"What is it, Doctor?"

"Well, as I said, I think CoCo was poisoned by an organophosphate pesticide. I thought that was strange because you can hardly get the stuff anymore. It was fairly common in the '50s and '60s, but it was so dangerous that it's hardly used now. In fact, the general public can't even buy it. You have to be licensed, and then you have to sign for it. A lot of farm animals, and even some people, died from it—some from just handling it. One gram can kill a human being."

"What are you saying?"

"Just this. It's only because I'm old enough to have been in practice back when this stuff was used regularly that I was able to make a diagnosis. I've seen it before. A younger vet would probably never have picked up on it."

Jo's breath caught as the light went on in her head. "Are you saying she was deliberately poisoned?"

"That's what I think. You living in town, and the stuff being unavailable to the general public makes accidental poisoning very unlikely."

"Who would do such a thing?" Jo said out loud to herself, forgetting she was on the phone.

"I'd hate to think," he replied, startling her. "Obviously somebody who didn't like your cat. But more than that, somebody who has a basic understanding of how the stuff works. If she'd gotten a big dose she would have died within 20 minutes to half an hour, but as it was, she got just enough to kill her slowly, to make her suffer."

"Oh, Dr. Cobb!" Jo agonized. "What did you call that stuff, organo—?"

"Organophosphate. But that's the generic name for it. As I recall, there were two major pesticides in use back then: malathion and parathion. They would both act the same in a living organism, but parathion was probably the more dangerous of the two."

"Thank you, Dr. Cobb. Thanks for letting me know this, and thank you for not saying this to Chrissie."

"I'm so sorry, Jo. I'd give her a few weeks before mentioning another cat. She'll need time to mend."

Jo hung up, then went to her room and made her bed. Catching sight of herself in the mirrored closet door, she remembered she had not showered, or put on a bra, or even socks. In her rush to get to the vet's office, she'd thrown on jeans and a sweatshirt.

Stripping off her clothing, she went into the bathroom, picking up a towel from the linen closet on the way, and turned on the shower. She let it run for a moment before sticking her hand in the water stream to test the temperature. She then stepped in and closed the frosted glass door.

The hot water pouring over her felt good as she washed herself and began to think. Who among her neighbors disliked CoCo enough to kill her? No names came to mind. Of course you never know what people are really thinking, but all of her neighbors seemed friendly. None of them seemed like the type to do something so horrible. Why? The poor cat was hardly ever out of the house. And even when she was, Chrissie kept a pretty close eye on her. Although she did have a habit of sneaking out when someone opened the door. But she rarely left the yard even then.

If the cat wasn't bothersome, why would someone want to poison her?

Was Morgan responsible for this? Did he poison CoCo as a warning for her to back off? According to what Carol had said the night before, he'd somehow found out she was checking on him. Even though the shower was warm, she shivered at the thought. Would she be next? Worse, would Chrissie?

Clay said that Amy had been poisoned. Did he say what with? She couldn't remember. She would ask him tonight when he called. But he didn't say last night that he would call tonight. Should she call him? She wished he was here and that there was no need for telephoning.

The thing about poison, she thought, is that it's not overt like a knife or a gun. It's a secret way to kill someone. By the time they figure out what happened, if they figure it out, it's too late. And of course the killer is long gone. It's the perfect way to kill someone. A patient killer could just plant the poison in some food item and wait for the day it was eaten.

Fear gripped her. Is that what happened to Amy? Did somebody plant poison in her lunch and wait for her to die? Did she even know what was happening to her as she became so violently ill and Clay carried her into the hospital?

Had someone already secreted some deadly agent into her and Chrissie's food supply? Is that what happened to CoCo?

Trembling, she turned off the water and dried herself. Then, wrapping the towel around her, she went into her bedroom and sat on the bed. Her fear began to give way to panic. *Clay, where are you? No, I mustn't panic,* she thought, working hard to control her breathing. In...out...in...out. *I must remain in control. If I panic, he's already won.*

Justice for Amy

She was shivering, but because she was cold. Her power to reason had slowly returned and she began to get dressed. CoCo's food came in a can so it would have been impossible for someone to poison her food. Therefore, she must have been caught outside and given the poison. Canned food would be safe to eat.

She *had* forgotten to lock the door in the rush to get to the vet's office. Someone could have gotten in and poisoned their food. Panic began to rise again. *Maybe they're still here!* No, she reasoned, if someone was here they already would have had multiple opportunities to hurt her and Chrissie in the couple of hours since they'd been home.

Jo finished dressing and stuck her head in Chrissie's room while on her way to the kitchen. She was laying on her bed with her back turned, still, very still. Jo walked in and bent down over her daughter. She heard her slow, rhythmic breathing. Sleeping.

Entering the kitchen, Jo picked out her largest butcher knife and then made a thorough search of the house, basement, and garage. Nobody.

Breathing a sigh of relief, she returned to the kitchen and began to pile all of their fresh food into a garbage bag. Fortunately she'd not been around to do the shopping on Saturday so there wasn't much to throw away.

When Clay called, they'd figure out their next steps. But at least for the foreseeable future, she and Chrissie would be eating out.

Chapter 19

"HI GWEN," CLAY SAID AS HE ENTERED the front door of Ramsey Medical.

"Clay! Hi. I guess I missed you this morning."

"No, I stopped by last night after you left and picked up my stuff. I went to Muskegon from home this morning."

"How did it go with Joe Dixon?"

"Looks like Muskegon General is our newest customer!"

"Oh, that's great!" she said, stepping toward him from behind her desk.

"It sure is," he replied, giving her a hug and kissing her cheek. "I missed you, sis."

"Ditto, big brother. How's things with Jo?"

He struggled for words.

"She's okay, isn't she? Clay?"

"Oh, she's fine. I thought you were asking how our relationship was going."

"Well, I am. It's okay isn't it?"

"Couldn't be better. I was just searching for the right words, I guess."

"To say what, that you're in love with her?"

"Well, she's definitely doing something very nice to my heart. How'd you know?"

"Clay, I've known you all my life. Besides, it's written all over your face.

"Okay, Miss smarty pants."

"Hey, I'm glad. Glad for you, and glad for her. I hope you marry her. And the sooner the better. What do you think about that?"

"I think it's a little soon for that. Besides, I'm not sure if she'll even have me."

"You might be pleasantly surprised."

"I hope you're right. Anything new?"

"Don Cunningham called from Metro in Madison. They definitely want to see you in Wisconsin on Friday morning. I told them you could be there at 9 a.m. I know that's early, but he's booked the rest of the day. I thought you could just fly over. It'll give you a chance to get some flying time."

"Yeah, that's fine."

"And Beason Memorial called. They've not received their stock of BP transducers yet, and were wondering if we had any to tide them over for a day or two."

"Do we have any?"

"Sixteen. But they need them ASAP. Are you heading back to Traverse City today?"

"I hadn't planned on it. I'm having supper with Mitch and Liz, and it's important I talk to Mitch. It may take a while. Besides, I'm just whacked. Anybody else going in that direction?"

"Woody's going to Cadillac. He's out back now. I think he's about ready to leave."

"Okay, thanks, sis. I'll go talk to him."

Clay left the office area and stopped in the storeroom, picked up 12 transducers and put them in a large plastic bag. Then he arranged to have Woodrow 'Woody' Davis, one of the biomedical equipment technicians, take them to Beason Memorial after completing his business in Cadillac. He also arranged to have him deliver his pickup truck to the Cherry Capital Airport in Traverse City and leave it there. In order to accomplish this, Woody's wife would drive Clay's truck, and Clay would pay for them to stay and eat at the Peninsular Hotel. He gave Woody the next day off with pay so the newlywed couple could enjoy Traverse City, then have a leisurely drive back, albeit in a company van.

He then went into his office and caught up on his e-mail and voice mail messages before leaving for the day.

CLAY WAS HUNGRY, but not wanting to spoil his supper he ate only a bowl of chicken noodle soup when he stopped for a late lunch.

He had expected to spend a great deal more time at Muskegon General. But things had gone so well, and so quickly, that he'd ended up with an unanticipated empty space in his day. It was in these periods of down time, when he had no plans and no particular place to go, that his thoughts almost always turned to Jenny. However, as much as he'd loved her, these were not thoughts that he welcomed. Almost three years after the fact, he'd already traveled down every possible road they could take him and found that they all lead to frustration and sadness. But today was different. He was different. Today's thoughts were reminders of something he needed to do.

Clay paid for his meal and left the restaurant. As he drove, he thought of the remarkable job Gwen had done of clearing his calendar. With the exception of a trip to Wisconsin on Friday, he had the whole rest of the week free. But that was Gwen, always looking out for him. He was suddenly moved with the depth of his love for her, and how much he'd miss her when Bill Douglas took her away.

He turned in at the open gates of Oakbridge Cemetery. Driving to the spot he knew so well, he pulled off to the side of the narrow road and parked mostly on the grass. When he'd first started coming here he had to count the stones: 9 up and 3 to the right. That had long since ceased to be necessary; he knew the place he wanted and, exiting the car, walked directly to it.

The gray stone was granite—wide enough for two graves, but only the right side was etched:

Jennifer Lynne Ramsey
Beloved Wife and Daughter
January 23, 1963 – October 16, 2000

Clay took a deep breath and blew it out slowly as he hunkered down before the stone and lovingly touched her name. He had gotten to the place where on most visits, he no longer cried. Today's visit was not one of those.

When he regained his composure, he sat quietly on the ground for some time. He usually didn't speak when he came here. That which was truly Jenny was not, after all, in this little piece of earth that bore her name. On the other hand, it was one of the few tangible things he had left of her. That's why he came here.

That's why today he spoke, and told her about Jo.

He wasn't sure how long he'd sat at her grave, but the sun was low in the sky, and a cool fall breeze had come up making him shiver, telling him it was time to go, telling him it was time to move on. So he left that place knowing things were different now, knowing his trips here would be less frequent, but knowing that things were all right between him and Jenny.

IT WAS LATE WHEN CLAY FINALLY ARRIVED at Mitch and Liz's house. Liz, unflappable as ever, greeted him with her characteristic hug—in spite of the fact that he was 20 minutes past his promised time.

"So, I hear things are going well for you, Clay."

"Yes! We just sold a monitoring system to Muskegon General for their new ICU."

"That's good too, but I meant with Jo."

"*You've* been talking to Gwen." It was a statement not a question.

"She called right after you walked out the door. Tells me you two are becoming an item."

"Well, I won't deny it."

"Mitch told me what you said to him on Sunday, and if I could give you some advice from a woman's perspective... Don't make her guess how you feel. I saw the way she looks at you and she deserves to know, Clay—one way or the other."

Clay chuckled. "Thanks Liz. Between you and Gwen I'm the best looked after guy in Michigan. Truth is, Jo and I were a whole lot more than just friends 20 years ago. This was way back, before I ever knew Jenny. Now I think it's possible that we may be falling in love with each other again. But I don't want to rush into anything—especially with someone who is not a believer."

"Gwen told me you two had a history. I didn't know about her not being a believer though. I guess behind every silver lining is a cloud, huh?"

"Well, it's not that bad. I mean, who knows how the Lord will work this out? Still, it wouldn't hurt to pray for her—for us."

"I'm already doing that Clay, and you know I'll keep on. Jenny was my best friend—" She stopped speaking and quickly turned away.

When she didn't immediately turn back, Clay held his arms out to her. "Come here," he said softly.

She stepped into his hug. "I miss her," she choked out, wiping her eyes with the backs of her hands.

"I know...I do too."

"I know how much she loved you, Clay. She would want you to be happy. And so does Gwen, and so do I. Now go on, get out of here. I'll be okay."

He continued to hold her. "Thanks for caring about me Liz. You couldn't be any more of a sister to me if we had the same folks."

She gave a wan smile. "Remember Clay, you should always do what your sisters tell you—we know best in these matters. Now go on, Mitch is in his office. Supper will be in about ten minutes."

Clay smiled as he let her go. He went to find Mitch as directed, and, given the short time until supper, made small talk until Liz called them to the table. He also avoided discussing matters related to Amy's death and the investigation he and Jo had undertaken into it while they ate. This was something that needed to wait until he could get Mitch alone in his office.

Yet, Clay couldn't shake the sense of foreboding he'd had since early this morning. Everything had gone well at Muskegon General, and getting Woody to take his truck up to Traverse City had been a fortuitous bit of good fortune. Still, something nagged at him. He'd had the urge to call Jo all day, but was putting it off until he'd have the time to spend talking to her without interruptions. Now he was impatient to get in and talk with Mitch, and he was glad when supper and the small talk ended so they could finally get on with it.

He told Mitch the whole story about Amy Phillips, his involvement with her, Burke's murder-suicide theory and his refusal to investigate further; Jim Wagner's gun, and everything he and Jo had found out about Tom Carlson and Jake Morgan. He'd spent some of the previous evening at his computer, committing his thoughts and hand-written notes to a document that he'd printed and given to Mitch.

Apart from occasional raised eyebrows, Clay was unable to read anything from Mitch's face as he told him the story.

When he finished, Mitch didn't immediately speak, but spent some time going over the written information Clay had given him.

At last he looked at Clay. "Quite honestly, this Lieutenant Burke has a pretty good case for murder-suicide."

"Aw, Mitch, not you too!"

"Look, Clay, obviously her sisters are not going to believe she's guilty. And you're in a relationship with her big sister. Isn't it just possible that your feelings for Jo are clouding your judgment?"

"Sure it's possible, anything's possible, but I thought the whole thing smelled fishy before I even met Jo. And look at the facts, man: She made $61 thousand a year, she owned her car outright, she has a third of a million in liquid assets plus her house, and a 401-K. Where is her motive to embezzle a comparatively measly $25 thousand? I mean, why risk her job and her reputation over such a small amount when she's already got a much larger amount at her disposal?"

"Who knows why people do what they do? You'd be amazed at the things I see. The thought of getting caught usually doesn't enter their minds."

"Yeah, but she was a sister, Mitch. Taught a third-grade Sunday school class, sang in the choir. Virtually her whole church is willing to attest that she was a fine, decent woman."

"Thing is, Clay, you don't get to be a police lieutenant by being stupid. I can't help thinking this Burke has thought of those angles. But I will admit you make a good point. On balance she doesn't seem to have a motive, and she doesn't seem to be the type. So what is it that you want from me?"

Clay gave a sigh of relief. "To my way of thinking, either Carlson or Morgan, Morgenstern, is good for it. It almost has to be one or the other of them as they are the only others besides Amy with general access to the accounts. What I would like you to do is see what you can find out about them. Do they have criminal records? If so, what for? That kind of thing. The kind of things I have no way of finding out, but you do. Maybe you could run them through NCIS."

"That's NCIC, the National Crime Information Center. And yeah, I could do that and I could do some other things too. But what are you going to do with the information if I get it for you? You know, if you're right, you'd most likely be placing yourself, and maybe even Jo, in some very real danger. This is police business."

"I know this is police business. And I would never knowingly do anything to hurt Jo or place her in danger. My only goal is to get Lieutenant Burke to investigate Amy's death. My hope is to drop such an overwhelming load of evidence on him that he will have to drop his suicide theory and reopen the case as a murder investigation. I will keep your name out of this."

"I'm telling you, Clay, this is way against my better judgment."

"I'm sure it is, Mitch. And I feel bad about taking advantage of our friendship this way, but I don't have anywhere else to turn."

"You're not going to give up on this, are you?"

"No. I can't. She asked me to help her. It's keeping a promise, a matter of honor. I have to do this."

"All right, I'll see what I can do. But you *will* give the information to Lieutenant Burke. If I find that you're acting on your own, I'll throw you in jail myself for obstruction. I'd rather visit you alive there than dead over in Oakbridge."

"Thanks, pal. I guess I don't need to say time is of the essence."

"No. I know that."

"Mitch, I'm not looking to risk my life—especially now."

"Yeah, well, see to it that you don't.

"Thanks for all your help with this, Mitch."

"You're welcome. Now go home so I can spend some time alone with Lizzy."

CLAY SAT IN HIS RECLINER and reached up to turn on the lamp behind it. Then he plucked the cordless phone out of his lap and programmed Jo's home number as a speed dial. He placed a call to her number. Busy.

He picked up the book he had been reading and opened to his bookmark at the beginning of chapter ten. However, it had been so long since he'd had a chance to read, he went back and reread chapter nine to get back up to speed. He lifted the footrest to get more comfortable.

Finishing chapter ten, he tried Jo again. Still busy. He checked the number on the display to be sure he'd programmed it correctly. He did. He wondered whom she was talking to.

Chapter eleven. Still busy. *Maybe she's on the Internet.*

Chapter twelve. Still busy. He was starting to worry about her.

Chapter thirteen. Still busy. *Maybe she has the phone off the hook. Why?*

Chapter fourteen. *What time is it? 10:37 p.m. No wonder I'm so tired.* Still busy. *You're not avoiding me are you, Jo?*

Chapter fifteen. *I'll just close my eyes for a minute...*

Chapter 20

"TRAVERSE CITY TOWER, Cessna one-niner-four-seven-bravo."

"One-niner-four-seven-bravo, Traverse City tower. Go ahead."

"I am inbound with tango—landing."

"Four-seven-bravo, continue inbound. Plan a straight-in for two-eight and report when you have the field in sight."

"Roger. Will plan straight-in for two-eight and report field in sight."

IT WAS 4:15 A.M. WHEN THE BOOK that had been on Clay's lap thumped onto the floor, awakening him. At first he didn't know where he was, but then he remembered he'd fallen asleep in the recliner while reading a book and trying to call Jo. Had she taken her phone off the hook? He knew that if a telephone were simply unplugged the line would still ring. In order to return a busy signal, it must be off hook—or the line had to be shorted out.

He had gotten up, showered and made a cup of instant coffee before trying to call her again at about 5 a.m. Her line was still busy. He worried about her as he drank his coffee, trying at the same time to think of something he may have done to offend her so she wouldn't want to talk to him. He couldn't think of anything, but he knew that didn't necessarily absolve him. There had been times in his life when he had somehow offended a woman without realizing he'd done so. But Jo didn't seem like the type. He realized that that was one of the things drawing him back to her. Whatever she had been before, she had become a woman without guile. What you saw was what you got; no lies, no hidden agendas, as far as he could tell. She told

Justice for Amy

things straight-out—even when it made her look bad. So he worried all the more that something must be wrong.

He had been the first customer at the restaurant this morning and had eaten his breakfast hurriedly so he could be at the airport as dawn broke.

As he'd done the preflight on his twin-engine Cessna 310-B, he was glad he always kept the fuel topped off to prevent condensation from forming in the tanks. It had allowed him to get in the air quickly today. And now, at last, he was nearing the Traverse City airport.

"Traverse City tower, four-seven-bravo."

"Go ahead, four-seven-bravo."

"I have the field in sight."

"Four-seven-bravo, you are cleared to land, runway two-eight. Welcome to Traverse City."

"Roger, cleared to land runway two-eight. Thank you, tower. Four-seven-bravo."

Clay landed and taxied to a parking spot. He paid for parking, tie down, and refueling for his plane. Then he spent about 15 minutes looking for where Woody had parked his green Toyota Tacoma pickup. Finally spotting it, he used his cell phone to call to Jo's number again as he walked to it. Still busy.

The day was unseasonably cold. It was Wednesday, October 1st and the early morning temperature hovered in the mid-thirties: a harbinger of the winter that would soon be upon them.

A thick mist rose from Grand Traverse Bay and a light fog covered the inland area, making driving conditions less than ideal. Clay's mind conjured up unpleasant images as he drove to Jo's house. He repressed them, telling himself he had no direct knowledge that anything was wrong and that he was allowing his imagination to get away from him. Nevertheless, he wasted no time getting to her house, even exceeding the speed limit when he could see clearly.

He pulled into her driveway, stopped, and turned off the engine. He then went to the front door and rang the doorbell. No answer. The windows in the door were too high up for him to see into the house. And the drapes over the picture window were closed, obscuring any possible view of the living room.

He went around to the back of the house and up onto the deck. The sliding glass doors were locked and the vertical blinds afforded him only a minimal view of the dining room. He saw no movement or any signs of life.

Leaving the deck, he entered the breezeway from the back and knocked on the door to the kitchen. No answer, and it too was locked.

Finally, he walked across to the other side of the breezeway and opened the side door leading into the one-and-a-half stall garage. No car.

Clay exited the breezeway from the front. He stepped down onto the sidewalk and sat on the top step. What had happened to Jo and Chrissie? Had they received some threat by telephone and hurried out of the house, not bothering to hang up? But neither Carlson nor Morgan knew they were being checked out. Did they? He looked at his watch. 8:50 a.m. Chrissie should be in school by now. If he knew which school she went to, he could go there and see if she were there today, and possibly ask her what happened to her mother. No. Jo wouldn't go anywhere without Chrissie. Besides, he didn't know where she went to school. And no school would look kindly on a strange man asking about a student.

He sat there for another 10 minutes and then got up and walked to his truck. As he was about to open the door, he saw Jo's red Mazda coming down the street. She slowed, as if to turn in, and then drove by and stopped. Then she backed up, drove into the driveway and parked behind Clay.

As he began to walk toward her car, she got out and rushed into his arms, not bothering to close her car door. "Oh, Clay! I've been terrified out of my mind. Why didn't you call?"

"Whoa, sweetheart," he said softly while pulling her into his embrace. "I've been *trying* to call you steadily since about 9:30 last night, but your line's been busy. I've been worried sick about you and got here as soon as I could today. Then, when you weren't home, I couldn't imagine what must have happened to you. I'm so glad to see you and that you're okay. Where have you been?"

"I took Chrissie to school. I'm sorry I drove by, but I didn't recognize your truck and I didn't know it was you until I saw you standing there. Where is your car?"

"It's at the little airport I use in Sparta. I had one of my guys drive the truck up here yesterday and I flew in this morning. Now I have a vehicle in both places and I can get here a lot faster by flying."

"Oh, I forgot you're a pilot. You've got your own plane?"

"Yeah. It allows me to get where I need to go faster. At least that's what I tell people. Truth is I also enjoy flying."

She cuddled against him. "I'm glad you're here now."

Jo turned her head and laid it on the front of Clay's shoulder as they held each other in a prolonged embrace, neither of them speaking further. When at last they released, Clay closed her car door and they went into the house.

Jo started a fresh pot of coffee brewing. "I can't think of why my line's been busy all this time."

"I thought you might have been online with your computer last night, but when I still couldn't get you this morning, I worried it might be something else."

"Oh, Chrissie was on the Internet last night researching something for a school project. Once before, something got locked or something and made our phone line go out of order. I had to call the phone company from work and they charged me a service call to turn something off and turn it back on again." She picked up her cordless phone, pressed the Talk button, and held it to her ear. "Dead, just like the last time."

"Where's your computer?"

"In the spare bedroom—I'll show you," she said, leading the way with the cordless phone still in her hand. "We keep it in here so either one of us can use it and not bother the other. Although Chrissie uses it much more that I do."

The room was slightly rectangular, about 11 by 12 feet. Immediately ahead, in the right back corner of the room, was a long folding table that held a sewing machine and a serger. To the left of the door was a twin bed, positioned perpendicular to the door, and about two feet away from the double slide-by doors of a closet. In the left back corner of the room, was the computer, sitting on a desk.

The system had an external modem and Jo watched carefully as Clay turned it off and unplugged the telephone line from it. After a few seconds, he plugged the line in again and turned it back on. "Give the phone a try now."

Jo pressed the Talk button again and held the phone to her ear. "It works!" she said, pressing the button again to turn the phone off. "Thank you, sir!" She turned her face up to Clay and puckered her lips, inviting him to bend his head down and kiss her.

What started out to be a simple peck turned into a full-fledged kiss. And then another, and another, and another. Jo lifted her head and enveloped Clay in her arms as he kissed down the side of her neck, giving as good as she got while they pulled each other tightly together.

Maybe it was because he had missed her so much. Maybe it was because he was so glad she was okay and not angry with him. Maybe it was just Jo kissing him back and holding him close. Whatever it was, it suddenly became apparent to him that they had to get out of this bedroom—now.

Clay cleared his throat and pulled away from her. "Let's go have some of that coffee," he said in a hoarse whisper.

"Okay," she said, blushing a deep shade of crimson.

They held hands as they walked to the kitchen and Jo poured them each a mug of coffee. Then they went into the living room and sat on the sofa. "I'm sorry I don't have any cookies or anything to offer you. I threw everything out yesterday." She sat her coffee down on a coaster on the coffee table.

"Threw everything out?" He looked puzzled. "How come?"

Jo explained in detail how Chrissie's cat had been poisoned and the conclusions she had drawn from her subsequent conversation with Dr. Cobb. She told Clay of her fear for their safety, and how she had been struggling to keep panic at bay since she didn't hear from him last night and she thought she was facing everything alone.

Clay sat his coffee down on the end table and put his arm around her, pulling her close as she concluded. "I'm afraid for Chrissie and I've decided to take her to school and pick her up until this is over."

"I'm sorry, Jo, I had no idea. I can only imagine how terrified you must have been. I'll pick up a couple of prepaid cell phones for you two today so you can stay in close touch. But we should probably drop this whole investigation right now. I don't want anything to happen to either of you."

"No. Too much has already happened and we're getting too close. And now that you're here, I'm not so frightened anymore. We need to see this through to the end. If Morgan is on to us, we'll never be safe. He won't stop until he shuts us up for good. But you're staying here tonight, not in some hotel. You can sleep in the spare room. Right now I'm more concerned about safety than reputation."

Clay nodded. "I'll stay, but tell me something. Why do you think it's Morgan?"

"It's mainly something Carol said. When we were together on Monday night, she mentioned that she had spoken to Tom and that he and Morgan both knew that I had been checking Morgan's financial status. I guess that Barb woman at their company must have told them I called. Anyway, Tom told Carol that Morgan was angry about it."

"Wonderful," he said, sardonically. "How would you feel about staying at my place in Grand Rapids? I'll stay here and see this through to the end."

"I can't do that, Clay. Chrissie has school, and I can't just interrupt her life by pulling her out. Besides, I have to go back to work next week."

"You're right, of course. I guess I just spoke off the top of my head. But with what you've already told me, I'm starting to be afraid for you—both of you."

She kissed his cheek. "Thank you for caring about me Clay; and for Chrissie too. But it looks like we're in this together to the end."

"I talked to Mitch last night, and I'm hoping he'll have some information for me today or tomorrow. Then I can go to Burke with that, plus what we've found out on our own. Maybe then he'll investigate and make an arrest. Hopefully, after that, our lives can get back to normal."

"I suppose normal means you'll be going back to Grand Rapids to stay."

Clay shook his head. "No. What it means is that we won't have to be watching our backs all the time, waiting for something bad to happen to one or the other of us, or all three of us. I do live in Grand Rapids, and my business is there. I have to go back, but not to stay. I want you in my life, Jo. And I'm willing to do whatever it takes to make that a reality, so long as you feel the same. That's why I had my truck brought up here yesterday."

She turned so she was kind of sideways to him and leaned in so she could put her arms around him. They held each other for a long moment before she spoke softly near his ear. "I do feel the same, Clay. I want to be in your life, and I want you to be in mine, and I'm determined to make it work for us this time."

Clay's could feel his heart beating in his chest, and he seemed suddenly breathless. If he'd had any doubt about where Jo wanted their relationship to go, she'd just answered the question in a simple sentence that spoke volumes.

He pulled her close and they held each other in another long embrace until at last he spoke. "Why don't you show me where Morgan lives? Then we'll go over to Wal-Mart and pick up some cell phones for you and Chrissie."

"And then you can take me to Chili's for lunch," she added, removing her arms from around his neck and standing up. "There's one near there and I just love their fajitas."

Clay stood and gently cupped her face in his hands, rubbing his nose against hers a couple of times before giving her a gentle kiss on the lips. "Sounds like a plan."

WHEN THEY RETURNED from an early lunch, Jo showered and prepared to go to the funeral home while Clay activated the new cell phones over the Internet. When she returned to the living room, he gave her one of the phones and showed her how to use it.

She put the phone in her purse. "What are your plans now?"

"I'm a little torn. Somebody has to pick up Chrissie after school. I thought I could do that for you. But it means I'll miss going with you this afternoon. And I'm still planning on going to Northern Fruit Wholesalers before they close at 5 p.m. Then, I want to pay a visit to Jake Morgan. But that means I'll miss going with you tonight too. You tell me though, and I'll do what you say. My main goal is to support you any way I can."

"I'm afraid for you, Clay. Afraid you'll get caught over there, or worse, that you'll get into a confrontation with Morgan and he'll hurt you."

"I know. And all I can tell you is that I'll be very careful."

"Chrissie does have to be picked up, and neither Carol nor I can do it. So you doing it makes sense." She took a deep breath and exhaled it. "I just want this to be over. Go. But be very careful, Clay. Come back safe to me."

"I will."

Jo gave Clay directions to Chrissie's school. He kissed her as she walked out of the door to leave for the funeral home, and watched as she drove out of sight.

Chapter 21

CLAY MISJUDGED THE AMOUNT OF TIME it would take him to get to the school and arrived early, getting a really good parking spot with a view of the door.

He tried to call Mitch's office while he waited, but got his voice mail. As the greeting played, he pressed zero, hoping to have Mitch paged. However, all the operator would say is that he wasn't in and wouldn't be in for the rest of the day. He pressed the End button on his cell phone and keyed in Mitch's home number.

"Liz, this is Clay. Mitch around?"

"No. He's in New York, picking up an extradition. He got a call before he left for work this morning and managed to get an early flight. Won't be back until tomorrow. Is there something I can do for you?"

"No. He was working on getting some information for me. I'll check back with him later."

"Sorry. He mentioned putting something together for you. Said that, if you called, to tell you he'd talk to you on Friday."

"You guys doing okay while he's gone?"

"Yeah, we're fine."

"Thanks Liz. I guess I'll talk to him on Friday."

Clay rang off and called Gwen at work. As she was filling him in on what was going on at the office, he heard the bell ring. In less than a minute the doors to the school burst open and teenagers began pouring out. He quickly ended his call and kept an eye out for Chrissie, not spotting her until she was almost to his truck.

He half stepped out and waved his arm in the air. "Chrissie!"

She walked up. "Clay. What are you doing here?"

He explained the arrangement he'd made with her mother as she got in.

Once they were under way, Chrissie twisted in her seat. "I'm glad you came to pick me up, Clay. I've been wanting a chance to talk to you alone."

"Am I in trouble?"

She laughed. "No. But I do want to know what's going on between you and my mom. What your intentions are toward her."

Clay laughed.

"Don't laugh at me, Clay. I'm serious. She's all I have and I'm all she has, and we look out for each other. Now you've come into the picture, and I want to know what your intentions are toward her."

"I'm sorry, Chrissie. I really wasn't laughing at you. You have to understand that the question you just asked is the one question, usually coming from a girl's father, that strikes terror into the heart of every teenage boy. Just goes to show you're never too old, I guess. How much has your mom told you about us?"

"Only that you two were in love with each other a long time ago, before she met my dad and before you met your wife." She hesitated for a Moment. "She also said your wife died. I'm sorry."

Clay smiled. "Thank you." He took a deep breath. "It's true. We were in love with each other. And up until last Friday, we had neither seen nor heard from each other in over 20 years. Honestly, once in a while something or other would cause me to think about her. But for the most part I hadn't even done that in a long, long time. I never expected to see her again—the subject wasn't even in my mind. So when I ran into her last Friday, it was a complete shock to me."

"That's pretty much the same story she told me, and I can appreciate that. But I want to know how you feel about her now."

"Okay. Since Friday we've begun to get to know each other again. And while it's hard to put precise words on it, I can tell you that your mom has occupied virtually my every waking thought since then."

"Look Clay, I'm going to be up front with you, okay? My mom told me that she broke up with you, and I want to know if you're using her—trying to make her fall in love with you so you can dump her to get back at her."

"Chrissie, I would nev—"

"Let me finish!" she interrupted. "My dad treated her like dirt; like she was his slave. He didn't love her, but she tried her best to be a good wife to him. Finally, he dumped her for some young, blonde hard body with big boobs—*Kimmieee!* I hate him! And when I turn 18 next spring, he'll never see me again!"

"Chrissie—"

"You're the only man she's even so much as looked at since then! You don't know how she hurt, how she cried and cried! You don't know how much courage it took for her to open her heart to you! And I won't see her hurt again! So I want you to be up front with me and tell me the truth! What are your intentions toward my mother?"

Clay couldn't help but admire this young woman who so desperately wanted to protect her mother. She was demanding an answer from him and she deserved to know. So he told her. "I care very deeply for your mother. I think she's falling in love with me. At least I hope she is, because I'm falling in love with her. I'm not planning to dump her. In fact, I would never knowingly do anything to hurt her—or you either, for that matter. My intention is to care for her, and protect her, and make all her days happy ones. But I have to be honest with you, Chrissie, that does not mean things will be perfect or even that they'll work out. But it does mean that *I* want them to. And that's the plain, unvarnished truth."

"Then you and I are going to get along just fine."

"Well that's good," he said with a smile on his face and in his voice. "Because if things do work out with us, I'm hoping that you'll be a big part of it too. Now, what do you say we stop somewhere and pick up some groceries? Your mom is not going to feel like cooking when she gets home and we need to be there for her."

"I like you, Clay."

He smiled big. "I like you, too. You've got spunk. You're a lot like your mom, and I mean that as a compliment. You even look a lot alike."

"Other people have said we look a lot alike, and I guess we are alike in other ways too. But we don't agree on everything."

"No, I suppose not."

"I'd like to get a tattoo, but she won't let me."

"Umm, can't say as I blame her. Never do anything at 17 that you'll regret at 37. Think of yourself as an executive, or a CEO, or a mom with little kids, and ask yourself if a tattoo fits the image."

"Boy, you even *sound* like her!"

"Sorry Chrissie, I only call them as I see them. Still like me?"

"Of course."

"Good."

Clay pulled into the store parking lot and parked before he gave her the cell phone he'd purchased for her. She already knew how to use it—something he reckoned all teenage girls knew by instinct. Then, thinking better of it, he chastised himself for thinking in stereotypes as he showed her where he'd programmed her mom's and his numbers in her speed call list.

When they arrived at home, they put the groceries away and made supper.

Clay had just finished changing into a pair of blue jeans, a light blue denim shirt, and a baseball cap when Jo arrived. Her eyes were red as she entered the kitchen and he could tell that she had been crying. He gently pulled her into an embrace. "How'd it go?"

"It's so hard to see her there, to think about all that happened to her."

"I'm so sorry, Jo. I wish there were some way I could insulate you from all this."

"I'll be all right," she sighed. "I really have a sense of peace about Amy. But now that the day has come, it's just hard to see her lying there. My mind is so full of memories about when we were kids. We shared a lot together, even as we got older, and I didn't realize how much I loved her, or how much she loved me, until I lost her. It-it's like there-there's a big hole in my h-heart." She began to cry.

At the sight of her mother's tears, Chrissie, who had been leaning against the kitchen counter, began to cry as well. Clay opened his left arm and pulled her into a three-way embrace.

They stood there, the three of them, for several minutes, sharing their grief and giving and receiving what solace they could, Clay fighting his own tears as he tried to comfort them.

When they regained their composure, Clay spoke. "I have to be going if I'm going to get over to Northern Fruit Wholesalers before they close."

"I know," Jo said, coming once again into his arms. "Be careful, my darling," she whispered in his ear.

He kissed her lips. "I will. You too."

Releasing her, he walked toward the door.

Chrissie intercepted him with a hug. "Be careful, Clay."

"WHAT DID YOU DO, MAKE SUPPER?"

"Clay and I did," Chrissie replied.

"Where'd you find the food?"

"We went grocery shopping after school."

"Seems like you two have become quite good friends," Jo observed.

"I have to admit, I like him, Mom. I think he's in love with you."

"I think so too. But I wouldn't mind hearing him say it. But you're okay with it, huh?"

"Yup. And I wouldn't worry if I were you. He's probably just waiting for the right time to tell you."

Jo gave her a hug. "So when did you get so smart?"

"Just comes naturally, I guess. I've got a smart mother," Chrissie replied, hugging Jo back. "I love you, Mom."

"I love you, sweetie. I couldn't have asked for a better daughter than you," Jo said, releasing her.

Jo walked to the stove and lifted the lid off the pot containing their supper. "What is this stuff? It smells good."

"Ziti and meatballs in tomato sauce. It was Clay's idea— I hope you like it. He got frozen meatballs and Italian sauce from a jar. We cooked up the ziti and mixed everything together. There's some shredded parmesan cheese in the fridge."

"I'm sure it will be just fine. You two are amazing. I was wondering what I was going to make, and rushed home in time to cook. And here you two have done everything for me."

"Well, to be honest, that was Clay's idea too, although I agreed with him and I did help. He didn't want you to have to worry about stuff like cooking."

"Thanks, honey. Listen, I really need to get some gas in the car, but I didn't want to miss Clay. I thought I was going to have to cook, so I just came right home. Would you mind taking the car over to the gas station and filling it up? I know how much you hate to drive."

"Yeah, right," Chrissie laughed. "I just *hate* to drive. Give me some money and I'll go right now. I should be back in time to eat."

Jo gave her $30 dollars and followed her to the door. "Drive carefully, honey," she called out as Chrissie backed out of the driveway.

Chapter 22

IT WAS 4:45 P.M. ON THE DASHBOARD CLOCK of Clay's truck as he drove past the entrance of Northern Fruit Wholesalers. He'd decided on the way over not to park in their lot so his truck wouldn't stand out after all the employees left for the day. So he pulled into the lot of the business next door and found an empty spot near the lot entrance. He backed in and shutting off the engine, thought of his dad. He had always called backing in "turning the horses toward home." "You never know when you might need to make a quick getaway," he used to joke. All joking aside, it seemed apropos now.

There was a stand of American arborvitae running the length of the property line between the two businesses. The trees must have been 30 feet tall. There was no way his truck could be spotted from the neighboring lot or building. On the other hand, he'd be hard pressed to run through the thick hedge of trees if he needed to make a quick getaway. But he hoped it wouldn't come to that.

Before exiting the truck, Clay opened his briefcase and removed a small tool pouch containing screwdrivers, a pair of needle nose-pliers, wire cutters, and a small flashlight. He also removed a picture ID that he had made the night before on his computer, identifying him as Jim Clayton of Northern Telecommunications Services. The ID was on a lanyard and he placed it around his neck. He clipped the tool pouch to his belt as he exited the truck, certain he had watched far too many episodes of *The Rockford Files* as a teenager.

Clay walked around the hedge and into the front parking lot of Northern Fruit Wholesalers. From his vantage point he could see that the building was fairly large, maybe 100 feet wide by 200 deep. The facade was red brick and concrete, and it had two stories. However, the second story, while running the full width of the building, only covered something over a quarter of the first. On the right, a roadway led from the back of the building to a separate entrance on the street, where a sign with an arrow indicating the loading dock stood. Obviously the back part of the building was a warehouse.

The double glass entry doors were centered on the building and flanked by evergreen plantings on a well-manicured grass strip. It was 4:51 p.m. on his watch when Clay entered through them.

The lobby was the size of a large living room and a corridor ran both left and right behind a receptionist station centered near the back. Dead center, behind the receptionist, was a stairwell leading up. On either side of the stairwell were signs indicating the restrooms.

The pretty, young receptionist was talking on the phone as Clay started to walk by her on the left. She held up her hand, motioning for him to stop as she spoke in low tones into the handset. "Hold on a second."

She looked up at Clay. "May I help you, sir? We're about to close." She held her left hand over the mouthpiece.

Time to think quickly. He had not planned on being stopped by anyone. "Men's room?"

She turned a little to her right and pointed behind her. "It's right there."

"Thanks."

He could hear her resume her conversation, still speaking in low tones, as he walked past. "I'm back. So what did he say when you told him?...No kidding?" Her conversation faded as Clay entered the men's room. He noted, just before he walked in, that there was an exit sign at each end of the corridor. That probably meant there was a stairwell at each end too.

The door to the restroom entered from the stairwell alcove rather than the main hallway, and Clay had to turn right as soon as he walked into the restroom to avoid running into a wall. The wall ran for about 8 feet before it broke to the left, forming a short corridor, about 5 feet wide, that opened into a room about 9 feet wide. On the right were double sinks. Across from the sinks, just in the wide part of the room, was a paper towel dispenser. To the right of the dispenser was a full-length mirror.

Clay bent down and looked through the opening beneath the 2 stalls that occupied the right back corner of the room. He was alone.

On the end of the wall where the corridor broke left was a 2-foot square metal scuttle door that was centered at about 2 feet off the floor. The door had a continuous hinge on the right and a screwdriver-operated latch on the left.

Clay removed the appropriate screwdriver from his tool pouch and operated the latch on the scuttle. He had to hold the screwdriver once he'd turned it because the latch had an internal spring that returned it to the locked position. Keeping pressure on the latch and using the screwdriver as a makeshift handle he opened the door and looked in.

The 4 by 8-foot room was a utility chase where wires, pipes, and air ducts went between floors.

A man in a suit came in to use the facilities. Clay removed his flashlight, pointed it into the opening and stared up, as if looking for something specific. The man washed his hands and left without speaking to him. Half the battle was in looking like you belonged there.

Clay entered the chase through the scuttle. The metal door was spring loaded to close itself automatically and there was no latch mechanism on the inside of the door. However, a small, flat piece of metal in a track could be pushed over the strike plate to cover the hole where the latch would normally go to keep someone from being locked inside. Clay pushed the small metal plate into place and held it while he let the door slam closed. He could tell from the way the door looked in the frame that it was completely shut.

The place was dusty and Clay worked to clear a spot before sitting on the floor and leaning against the wall. He figured he would be there for at least an hour waiting for people to leave, so he shut off his light and sat there—thinking.

CHRISSIE PULLED A BAG OF FROZEN BROCCOLI she and Clay had just purchased out of the freezer and carefully dumped the contents into a pan of boiling water as Jo set the table. "I hope you don't mind frozen. I didn't have the heart to tell Clay we usually buy fresh."

"It's okay," Jo responded. "Certainly not bad for a man. I think he eats out a lot though, because he really enjoys home cooking. But at least he's skillful enough in the kitchen that he doesn't have to eat cold beans out of a can over the sink."

Chrissie laughed. "The thing that gets me, though, is that he doesn't seem to mind helping with cooking or dishes or anything. I don't know if he's really like that or if he's just trying to impress us...you."

"I think that's the real Clay—just the kind of person he is. What do you think, should we keep him?" Jo smiled.

"Definitely!"

Chrissie drained the broccoli as Jo dished up Clay's ziti and meatball concoction. Then she added some of the flowerets to their plates before they took them to the dining room and sat down to eat.

"Are you planning on coming to the funeral home with me tonight?"

Chrissie finished chewing a piece of meatball and swallowed it. "Do you want me to come?"

"Yes, if you don't mind. She was your aunt."

"I know. And I loved her, and I know she loved me. Honestly, I've not been looking forward to this, but I do want to go. I just hope I can keep myself from blubbering the whole time."

"You'll do all right, sweetie. And I'll be glad to have you by my side. Aunt Carol seems sort of disconnected from everything. I guess it's her way of coping."

The two finished eating, cleared the table and did the dishes before changing into appropriate clothing and leaving the house at 6:30 p.m.

CLAY TURNED ON HIS FLASHLIGHT and looked at his watch. 6:35 p.m. The building had become remarkably quiet after five o'clock and he had become accustomed enough to it that he was able to hear sounds he probably wouldn't have paid attention to at other times.

Several people had come and gone from the men's room. Some of them had been cleaning staff. He'd heard their mop buckets roll in and roll out; first above and then in the room just outside his hiding place. He'd also heard vacuum cleaners running in the upstairs and downstairs areas. However, he'd heard no noise he could attribute to a human for the past 15 minutes.

He waited an additional 15 minutes before pushing open the small door that concealed him in the chase. Dark.

Clay climbed out of the chase and held the door while it closed so it wouldn't make noise. He then walked over and turned on the light switch. He noticed that he'd left dusty footprints on the floor, so he went over and got a few paper towels, which he got wet. First he cleaned off the bottom of his shoes and then wiped up his tracks from the floor.

He turned off the lights and waited a few moments for his eyes to become accustomed to the dark before he peeked out of the restroom door. The place was dark except for minimal artificial lighting and the small amount of natural light that came in through the front doors. It was nearly dark outside and would be fully dark in less than 30 minutes.

Clay exited the restroom and went up the stairs. Jo had told him that Amy's office had been on the second floor. The door at the top of the steps was locked and required an access card to enter.

He went back down to the lobby and then tried the stairwells at either end of the building. Both of those doors to the second floor were similarly locked. Terrific.

Struck with an idea, Clay went back to the men's room and climbed back into the chase. Once again he held the metal plate while the door slammed so that he could get back out.

He put his small flashlight in his mouth and climbed on the pipes and ducts up toward the second floor. The chase narrowed significantly as he went up. It was probably only 2 feet wide on the second floor and he really had to squeeze to get past an air duct. He hoped there'd be a scuttle on the second floor because he wasn't sure if he could get back down the same way he had come up.

Once he cleared the air duct he saw the scuttle door. He put his ear against it while sitting on the duct and listened for several minutes. Quiet.

Clay found the small metal plate designed to keep the door from locking and tried to press it in with his thumb to open the latch. It didn't move. He removed a screwdriver from his tool pouch and held the blade against the back of the plate while he sharply hit the end of the handle. The plate slid in, moving the latch out of the hole.

He was sweating as he climbed out into the second floor men's room, but he didn't know if it was from the exertion or from nerves.

He turned on the lights and then washed his hands and face with cold water. After drying off, he used the damp paper towel to clean up his shoes and dusty footprints from the floor before throwing it away. He pulled a pair of latex gloves out of his pocket and put them on. Then he turned off the lights and waited for his eyes to adjust while he listened carefully for any sounds outside the door.

Exiting the restroom, he found himself in the second floor office area. Rather than being completely dark, about every third fluorescent ceiling light was on, giving a moderate level of illumination to the entire area.

To his left was a wall that went the entire width of the floor. The door leading into the walled off area was locked and Clay looked through the window. Judging by what he could see, he surmised the area to be the executive offices. That must mean he was in the Finance department.

The area was set up, for the most part, as an open office. Light green colored cubicles filled the interior space. On the window wall, in the front of the building, were modular offices covered in the same light green fabric.

Clay walked over to the walled section. Each office had a door with a full-height window to its right. Each of the windows had miniblinds on the inside and the name of the occupant, in press-on letters, on the outside.

The third office he came to was Amy's. Her name had been scraped off the window but a faint outline of the letters remained.

Across from Amy's office were the cubicles of Jake Morgan and Tom Carlson. He went into Morgan's cube first.

The desk drawers were without locks and Clay instituted a thorough but careful search so as not to leave any indication the contents had been disturbed. He found nothing incriminating.

Next, he pulled Morgan's computer out far enough so he could check all the connections. He reasoned that if Morgan had used a keystroke capture device, he would have to put it on his own computer in order to download it. He found nothing.

He carefully slid the computer back into its place and went into Carlson's cube.

Again, he carefully searched all of the drawers but found nothing incriminating.

He pulled the computer out too far and knocked the keyboard to the floor. It hit on one corner (the other corner held up by the cord connecting it to the computer) and turned slow pirouettes until Clay picked it up. Fearing he had broken it, he checked it over carefully. There was no discernable damage.

He was about to set it back on the desk when he noticed some writing on the bottom. It was very small and written in pencil:

philla   071amy467

"Bingo," he said under his breath. If he were a betting man, he'd bet a lot of money he'd just found Amy's login ID and password written on the bottom of Tom Carlson's keyboard.

He wrote the characters on an index card he carried in his shirt pocket and carefully restored the computer, keyboard, and mouse to their original locations on the desk before leaving Carlson's cube.

The door to what had been Amy's office was locked and there was a brass-colored metal plate, held on by two screws, covering the latch mechanism so nothing could be pressed into it to open the door.

Clay used a screwdriver to loosen the top screw; he removed the bottom screw completely so he could rotate the plate up, giving him access to the mechanism. Then he used a credit card to defeat the latch. The door opened and Clay reinstalled the plate to its original position.

The room was dark, but he didn't want to turn on any lights because of the windows. It would be a dead giveaway that someone was in the office. He cranked open the miniblinds and shut the door. Then he closed his eyes for a few moments to allow them to function better in the low light.

It looked as though nothing had been removed from the office. At least all of the essential items were there. Her computer, telephone, potted plants, even a half-full bottle of drinking water; all as he imagined they were the last time Amy sat in the chair which he now occupied.

A wave of sadness came over him. Beautiful Amy, with a sparkle in her eyes that couldn't be repressed, even in the face of betrayal by someone she had trusted. A sister in the Lord, a good and decent woman, whose life had been taken from her in the foulest way by a coward seeking to cover the crimes of his own greed.

"Oh, help me! Please, please, Clay, help me!"

Suddenly he was in the car with her again, hearing her cry out to him for help, feeling her slump up against him. The memory was vivid, and it came with tears.

"I'm so sorry, Amy," he heard his own voice whisper. "He's not going to get away with this. I'll see to it that you get justice."

He pulled out a couple of her tissues to dry his eyes and blow his nose. He then stuffed them in his pocket so as not leave evidence of his presence.

Recovering his composure, he turned on Amy's computer and waited while it went through the boot-up process.

At the login screen he typed in "philla" for the user ID and "071amy467" for the password, then clicked OK. The login screen disappeared and the computer finished booting.

Clay double-clicked the icon to open her spreadsheet program. He then clicked on the File menu and scrolled down. At the bottom of the menu, the three most recently used files were listed: majaccts, rcvables, and payables. He clicked on majaccts.

A password box appeared on the screen. The file could be opened without a password for read only access, but for read-write access the password was needed. Clay typed in

071amy467 and clicked OK. A workbook of spreadsheets opened on the screen, displaying all of the company's major accounts. He closed the workbook and tried the other two files. They worked the same way. Then he closed the spreadsheet program and shut down the computer.

He looked at his watch. 8:15 p.m. Time to go. He picked up her water bottle and watered her plants with what was left of her drinking water, not knowing why he did it. He then got up and looked out the blinds to be sure he was still alone before cranking them closed and leaving Amy's office. He was now sure that Carlson had embezzled the money and killed both the auditor and Amy. The only question that remained was whether Morgan was involved.

He walked back over to Morgan's cube and inspected the underside of his keyboard. No writing. He carefully looked around for anything upon which Morgan may have written Amy's passwords, but again he found nothing. Of course, all that proved was that Morgan had not been stupid enough to write something down where somebody else could find it. Maybe the guy had a good memory.

Really, though, Morgan no longer seemed a likely candidate. On the other hand, Clay didn't want to rule him out without talking to him. He also did not want to dismiss Jo's intuition, even though she had admitted she favored Morgan as guilty because she didn't want it to be Carlson for Carol's sake. He would pay a visit to Jake Morgan and get the issue settled if at all possible.

He decided it would probably be faster to leave by the side door closest to where he'd parked. He didn't know if going out from either the second floor door or the door from the stairwell to the outside would set off an alarm. Neither did he know if there were people working in the warehouse at the back of the building. So he ran, first out the second floor door, then down the steps and through the outside door to his truck.

If there was an alarm, he didn't hear it. Nor did he see anyone as he left the neighboring parking lot and drove away. He breathed a sigh of relief. He wasn't certain if he'd broken any laws, but it sure felt good to get out of there.

The temperature had plummeted back down into the mid-30s after the sun went down and Clay shivered as he waited for the engine to heat up, wishing he'd remembered to bring a jacket. It didn't help that he was damp with perspiration. It hadn't been that warm in the building, so it must have been nerves. And what he had to do next wasn't helping either.

He drove to Jake Morgan's building, parked in an open space near the door, and went inside. Morgan's apartment, according to the address on his credit report, was 1-D. It turned out to be the fourth one down on the right.

He knocked on the door. No answer. He waited and knocked again. Still no answer. Apparently the man wasn't home.

He left the building and walked along the grassy strip in front. Each apartment had two windows; one for the bedroom, and one for the main living area. He walked to the seventh window and looked in. The drapes were open but the reflection from the lights in the parking lot made it difficult to see inside. Still, he was able to see into Morgan's bedroom—the guy made his bed. Looking in the next window he was able to see a sofa, a small television, and a kitchen/dining area further in. The place was completely dark. Either Morgan wasn't home or he was giving a real good impression of it.

Clay returned to his truck, started the engine and made sure the heat was on. He sat there, waiting and thinking. How would they break the news about Tom to Carol?

JO AND CHRISSIE LEFT THE FUNERAL HOME right at 9 p.m. A lot of people had come, mostly from Amy's church, and it was gratifying to know that those who knew Amy best would not accept the idea that she was guilty of any wrongdoing. However, by 8:45 p.m. only Carol, Jo, and Chrissie remained. Even Tom had gone before 8:30, needing to get gas and pick up a few things from the store.

Carol left the parking lot as Jo and Chrissie stood in the doorway thanking the funeral director. Then they too set off for home.

After they had gone about a mile, the engine began to sputter and buck. A sense of foreboding came over Jo as she pulled into the right lane and tried to keep the car running.

Chrissie's voice was tinged with alarm. "What's wrong, Mom?"

"I don't know. The motor wants to die. I can hardly keep it going."

At that point the engine quit completely. Jo pulled over as far as she could on the right shoulder, fighting the power steering, which was no longer working now that the engine was dead. She turned on the four-way flashers.

They sat there for a moment, apprehension building, neither woman quite sure what to do. Jo tried to restart the engine. Multiple tries proved fruitless.

Jo looked at the dashboard. The fuel gauge read empty.

"We're out of gas!" she exclaimed. "Chrissie, didn't I send you to get gas before supper?"

"I did, Mom. I swear. I filled the tank up. Don't you remember? I brought you the change."

"Well, how do you explain that we're out of gas *now?*"

Chrissie countenance fell. "I can't explain it. But I promise you, Mom, I *did* get gas in the car."

Jo looked at Chrissie's face, saw the hurt, and she realized that she was taking her anxiety out on her. Chrissie had never given her cause to doubt her word. Stricken with remorse, she replied. "I'm sorry, honey. I believe you. If you say you put gas in the car, it's good enough for me. We were parked in kind of a dark spot. Maybe some kids siphoned our gas for a joy ride or something." She reached over and gave her daughter a hug. "Please forgive me."

"It's okay Mom, I'm scared too."

Jo was rummaging in her purse for her cell phone when a blue Bronco with a white top pulled off the road in front of them, stopped and backed up a little before stopping again directly in front of their car.

Jo's face brightened. "Looks like some kind soul has stopped to help us." She slipped her phone back into her purse.

As the occupant opened the door and began to exit the Bronco, a police car pulled up behind Jo's Mazda and turned on its red and blue light bar. At that, the Bronco driver pulled his leg back in, shut the door and drove off.

Neither woman wanted to stay alone, so the young officer took them both to a gas station and delivered them back to their car. He also poured the fuel from the 1-gallon container into their tank for them and waited while Jo got the engine started. Then he followed them to the gas station and waited while Jo filled the tank and set off for home before driving off.

"Nice guy," Chrissie said.

"I noticed he had his eyes on you."

"Oh *Mom.*"

CLAY LOOKED AT HIS WATCH. Just past 9:15 p.m. He'd been there almost 45 minutes and had grown weary of waiting for Morgan to return. Who knew? He may not come back at all tonight. Maybe he had a girlfriend he stayed with.

He set out for Jo's house, arriving about 9:30, and found the place dark. He was batting a thousand tonight he thought as he waited in the truck. At least he'd finally gotten warm. He should have asked Jo for a key; then he could have waited inside. No, that would be improper. The way their relationship was progressing was good reason to exercise caution—lest they wind up in a situation where they couldn't resist each other. He'd been fighting that since this morning's episode in the spare room. Still, if he were going to be staying there he'd need to have access. Fortunately, Chrissie would be home tonight.

Jo and Chrissie pulled in behind Clay at about 9:45 p.m. and he got out to meet them. Chrissie raced by him without speaking, hurried into the breezeway, and let herself in the house.

"What's with her?" he asked, taking Jo's hand.

"Bathroom," she whispered.

"Oh," he chuckled, bending his head to give her a kiss as they walked.

They followed Chrissie in. Clay held the door while Jo entered, and then made sure it was locked and dead bolted before joining her in the kitchen. He leaned back against a counter and Jo came into his arms, laying her head against the front of his shoulder. He held her for a few moments and kissed the top of her head. "How'd it go tonight?"

"Okay," she replied. "Better than I expected." She took Clay by the hands and led him to the dining room. They sat down and Jo continued, taking Clay's hand again. "A lot of people came—more than I would have guessed. And a lot of them had stories to tell about Amy. Some were the parents of little girls who had been in her Sunday school class. They told of how Amy led their daughters to the Lord. Some of them even spoke, with tears, of how she'd led *them* to the Lord and how grateful they were for her. People loved her, Clay. Everybody I spoke to is just heartbroken about what's happened." She began to cry.

Clay got up and went into the living room to get the box of tissues. He brought it back and gave it to Jo before sitting down next to her again. She dried her eyes and blew her nose before picking up his hand again. Then she laid her head against his arm for a few moments while she regained her composure.

He was debating whether this was really the best time to tell her what he'd found out about Carlson when she began to speak again.

"I saw Jake Morgan there tonight. He came with his girlfriend—Kathy somebody, I don't remember her last name. Nice woman though."

"Really. That explains why he wasn't home tonight. I got tired of waiting for him about quarter after nine and came back here."

"He didn't kill Amy, Clay. I just know it."

"I don't think so either. But what made you change your mind?"

"Well, I had to go to the ladies room. And when I was coming back, Jake was coming in the front door with Kathy. We met in the vestibule, and recognized each other from the restaurant the other day. He asked me if we could speak privately, and I didn't know how to tell him no, what with everybody around and everything. So we went, all three of us, into one of those little mourning rooms that had two stuffed chairs and a table in it."

"I'll bet you were scared."

"I was—at first. That Barb woman told him I'd been checking on him, and he figured out the rest for himself. He is from Petoskey, just like we thought. And he was a pharmacy technician at Barrigans while he was going to college at night, taking accounting classes. Anyway, he was in an accident in 1999 and had a serious back injury requiring surgery. Afterward, the doctor put him on Oxy...Oxy..."

"OxyContin?" Clay interjected.

"That's it. Anyway, he became addicted and began to steal it from the pharmacy. But they caught him, and he spent two years in prison up in Marquette. He told me that he lost everything. That explains the bankruptcy we saw on his credit report."

"His girlfriend was there in the room with you?"

"Yeah, but she wasn't his girlfriend then. They met down here, and she knows everything about him. And that's part of it—see, she was Amy's friend."

"Okay, I'm confused."

"Jake 'found the Lord,' to use his words, through a prison ministry. When he got out, he moved down here to try to start over, and he began going to Amy's church. Problem was, nobody would hire him for any kind of responsible job. That is, until he answered an ad for an accountant at Northern Fruit Wholesalers and Amy took a chance on him."

"Okay, I see."

"Later, when she got to know him more, she introduced him to Kathy. They're going to be married next year."

"Wow."

"Yeah. He loved Amy, just like everybody else who knew her. Maybe more because of all she'd done for him. He credits every good thing that's happened to him, after prison, to Amy. He sat there on the table and wept for her. He didn't kill her, Clay. He told me that not only did he not drive her, but he didn't even know about the meeting she had with Tom on the night she died. And I believe him. I know it makes Tom look like the guilty party, but I believe him."

Clay took a deep breath and exhaled it. "I agree with your assessment."

"You found out something didn't you?"

"I'm afraid so."

Clay spent the next several minutes explaining what he had discovered at Northern Fruit Wholesalers. He concluded by saying, "I wasn't sure when I left there tonight if Jake was involved with Tom in this or not—them being friends and all. But now it seems crystal clear that Tom is in this alone. What's bugging me though is, how are we going to break this to Carol?"

"Yeah. It's bugging me too. But I think we should hold off until after the funeral tomorrow. She's asked him to be a pallbearer and it's kind of late to change that now. As long as we don't say anything to anybody, I can't see where waiting an extra day is going to make a difference. It irritates me, though. It should be Jake helping to carry her out, not Tom. Jake loved her, but they won't let him off for the funeral because it would leave them without any accounting staff."

Chrissie appeared in the entrance to the dining room wearing pajamas, robe, and fuzzy pink slippers. "I'm going to go to bed now, Mom." She walked over and gave her mother a hug. "Goodnight."

"Goodnight, honey. Sleep tight."

"I will. Goodnight, Clay."

"Goodnight, Chrissie," he said as she walked off.

"I think she's kind of taken to you," Jo said after she heard the girl's bedroom door shut.

"I know. And I can't tell you how happy that makes me. She's a wonderful girl, certainly not your stereotypical teenager. You've done a good job with her."

"Well, it hasn't been all roses, but I agree, I'm very fortunate to have her. I don't know how I would have gotten through these last years without her. With all that's happened to the two of us, I think she's grown up a little faster than she might otherwise have done. She's quite mature for a girl her age. And," Jo stood up, "speaking of flowers, thanks for all the flowers you sent to the funeral home. They're very pretty."

"I haven't seen them yet, but you're welcome. I wanted to be sure Amy had a fitting memorial—especially after that nasty story the paper ran," he said, also standing up.

"I'm really bushed, and getting some sleep sounds pretty good to me right now."

"Yeah, me too. I was up before five this morning."

Jo laid her hand on the side of Clay's face. "Goodnight, my darling."

Clay gently pulled her into his arms and held her for a moment before kissing her. "Goodnight, sweetheart."

He checked the front door to be sure it was locked, then turned off the lights as they went to their separate rooms.

Chapter 23

"HELLO?"

"Hi, it's me. Where are you?"

"On the road."

"You get the princess?"

"No."

"Why not?"

"Because the cops showed up about two seconds after I did, *that's why not*. You want me to try and grab her in front of the cops?"

"No...obviously!"

"Look, don't worry, we'll get her; maybe sometime this weekend. I just left there and it looks like somebody's staying over 'cause there's a pickup in the driveway, and I saw all the lights go out in the house. It's probably lover-boy and I'm not going to chance anything if he's there."

"We're going to have to get him too, you know."

"I know."

"Boy, you're in a good mood tonight!"

"I know what the stakes are and I know what has to be done. *Okay?* It *never* was my plan to grab Ramsey at the same time. It's just too risky. Besides, I want to take my time with him—make it hurt."

"Let's not discuss this on the phone, huh?"

"Yeah, okay."

"You coming over?"

"No. I'm going home. I'll see you tomorrow."

CLAY FOLDED BACK THE BED LINENS and knelt down beside the bed in the spare room. The sheets smelled fresh. Jo must have changed them at some point during the day; perhaps after he'd gone to what had been Amy's workplace.

His heart suddenly felt warm as he thought of Jo's care for him.

He spent a considerable time in prayer: praying for Jo and Chrissie, but also praying for himself. It would have been far easier for him to have stayed in a hotel than to stay overnight in the same house with Jo—such was his desire for her. And he would have done just that had she not virtually told him he was staying. Still, her fears were not unfounded, and he wished he'd never gotten her into a situation where she needed to fear for herself and Chrissie.

On the other hand, had he not been so offended at what had happened to Amy and had he not been so determined to see justice come to her murderer, he would have just gone home and never have met Jo again. He shuddered at the thought, for he realized that what he felt for her was much more than just desire. He had come to love her again.

But how to tell her? Did she feel the same? Could she? After all, it had only been a week. Surely she would think him crazy if he told her how he felt. But to him it wasn't crazy; that big empty place inside of him was now full and overflowing.

As he prayed, peace began to flow over him; the certain knowledge that the Lord was in this with them. It was almost as if he could hear the Lord speaking as the words of Scripture echoed in his mind: "Do not fear, for I am with you; do not anxiously look about you, for I am your God. I will strengthen you, surely I will help you, Surely I will uphold you with My righteous right hand." So he continued praying, asking the Lord for continued guidance and asking, if it would be his will, that he would give Jo to him and to give him to her.

At length he climbed into bed, expecting to struggle for sleep. But the peace remained and he quickly gave way to unconsciousness.

JO CLOSED THE BEDROOM DOOR and padded in sock feet and flannel pajamas to her bed. The sheets were cold and she shivered slightly as she pulled the covers over her, wishing she'd thought to turn on the electric blanket beforehand. Nevertheless, she felt secure knowing that Clay was just down the hall. She'd feel more secure, she thought, if he were beside her right now with his arms around her—warmer too. But she knew he wouldn't come to her bed. His relationship with God wouldn't permit such a premeditated breach of trust—in spite of how she ached for his arms. They certainly had come close this morning though. Her heart beat faster at the memory, but she banished the thought.

In her heart she knew that their day would come, and it wouldn't be a cause for guilt. It would be good and pure and honest, and filled with shared love as husband and wife. She'd had that as a settled feeling since last Saturday night when she'd prayed at Gwen's apartment, but had told no one—had barely dared admit it to herself. Nevertheless, she'd had the clear impression that Clay would be her husband. But how could she say such a thing to him? If there was a way to tell him without making him run for the hills she wished she knew it.

As much as she had tried to love Mike, it had never been like this—her heart so thoroughly captivated, so intricately linked to the heart of another. It hadn't even been this way with Clay before, although she knew without a doubt that she had loved him. It was scary—very scary. If the level of hurt one felt was proportionate to the degree in which she gave her heart to another, she knew she risked being hurt like she'd never been hurt before. Reason was demanding with a loud voice that she hold herself aloof, but her heart would have none of it. It was rushing headlong to Clay's heart—willing to take the risk, looking at the prize of life-long love. Maybe love really is more wonderful the second time around.

She turned out the light and rolled onto her stomach, scrunching the pillow under her as she propped herself up on her elbows. Then she spent the next few minutes praying for Chrissie and for Clay; for their safety and hers in the dangerous situation in which they found themselves. She prayed that justice would come swiftly to Tom Carlson and that God would help her to be strong for Carol. Finally, she asked God's blessing and assistance in her deepening relationship with Clay.

She marveled as she dropped off to sleep how, after a lifetime of not being concerned about such things, she'd been doing so much praying lately.

CLAY'S INTERNAL ALARM CLOCK awakened him at 5 a.m. This was his usual wake up time, but he doubted if Jo or Chrissie were even close to being awake.

He got up and switched on the bedroom light, squinting his eyes against the brightness until they became accustomed to it. He walked over to his travel bag, dug out his running clothes and shoes and put them on. Then, picking up the house key Jo had finally convinced him to take, he quietly made his way outdoors and spent the next 45 minutes running through the neighborhood.

Clay dried off from his shower and wrapped the towel around his waist. Then, using a hand towel, he wiped the fog off the mirror before shaving. In his rush to get to the airport yesterday morning, he had forgotten his shaving cream and had to lather his face with hand soap out of a pump container next to the sink.

He dried his face, hung up the hand towel and had just turned to leave when Jo pushed the door open. "Oh, sorry. It was quiet for a few minutes and I didn't know you were still in here," she said just entering the room, trying to make her eyes stay open in the harsh light.

"I was just leaving. Did I wake you up?"

She was still squinting against the brightness, one eye closed, and her voice still had sleep in it. "No...I don't know...maybe. It's my regular get up time anyway."

Clay tilted his head to the side and looked at her.

"Mmmm, don't look at me, Claaay," she groaned. "I just got up and I look awful."

He lifted her chin up and gave her a soft kiss on the lips. "No you don't. You're absolutely beautiful—bed head and all."

She ruffled her hair with her hands. "Liar."

"I'm not lying, Jo. You are beautiful; make up on, make-up off, hair dirty or clean, pressed down flat or soft and silky—*you* are beautiful." He kissed her again and turned sideways so she could pass. "Now why don't you get your shower, and I'll see about getting us some breakfast."

He heard the shower running as he dressed and later as he walked past the bathroom door. Entering the kitchen, he made a pot of coffee.

Clay removed four eggs from the refrigerator, and put four slices of nine-grain bread in the toaster. He waited until he heard the blow dryer stop running before he started cooking, and was just dishing scrambled eggs onto their plates when Jo walked into the kitchen. She put the toast on their plates and took them to the table. Clay followed with mugs of coffee and they sat next to each other, holding hands as he prayed for the meal.

"Yum, this is good," she exclaimed. "What did you do to the eggs?"

"A little cream cheese."

"Umm, I'll have to remember that."

"You know, Clay," she continued, "you are good for a girl's self-esteem."

"You make it very easy."

She turned to him. "Seriously Clay, in the short time you've been here you've changed my life. I don't know if it's possible for you to understand this, but for years now I have felt...ugly and...unlovable." She took a breath and sighed. "I...well...you make me feel beautiful and desirable."

Clay's heart melted within him as he took both of her hands in his. "I think you've been made to feel that way; and for so long that you've accepted it as fact. But it's not true. You are beautiful and desirable. And you're kind and gentle and warm and caring and smart and wonderful too. You are eminently lovable Jo...and I should know because I love you."

Jo closed her eyes and took a deep breath as her arms went around Clay. She pulled in close and he stood with her so they could hold each other closer. She made a small contented sound as she exhaled. "You don't know how I've longed to hear you say those words, because I love you. I love you with all my heart."

They sought out each other's lips and kissed a long and tender kiss. When their kiss broke, they continued to hold each other for a long time.

IN SPITE OF A FEW NOBLE EFFORTS on the part of the sun, the day turned out to be damp and overcast with periods of rain.

Jo's mood grew more introspective as the morning moved toward the time they'd have to leave for the funeral. Clay wanted to hold her and tell her that everything would be all right, but he knew she needed to be left alone with her thoughts. At noon he was about to suggest lunch when she disappeared into her room without comment. She reappeared at about 12:30, dressed in a conservative navy-blue pantsuit with a lacy, but solid matching top, and a jacket without buttons. She was ready to leave for the church.

Clay and Chrissie rushed to get dressed as well. They arrived at the church at about 1:20 p.m. He thought they'd be the first ones there, but the hearse and a couple of other cars were already in the parking lot when they pulled in.

Upon entering, they were greeted by a dark-haired woman, just slightly taller than Jo, but outweighing her by 20 to 30 pounds. She gave Jo a hug and said something to her that Clay couldn't hear.

Jo turned toward Clay and Chrissie. "Clay, this is Kathy...Jake Morgan's lady friend." She looked at the woman. "I'm sorry, I forgot your last name. Kathy, this is Clay Ramsey; and of course you already know my daughter, Chrissie."

Clay shook the woman's outstretched hand. "Kathy Weldon. I'm so sorry we have to meet under these circumstances. Amy was a dear friend of mine. We taught a Sunday school class together, and she introduced me to Jake. He wanted me to tell you both how very sorry he is that he can't be here today. With Tom Carlson taking the day off to be here, they just wouldn't let him go."

Jo slipped away and walked up to the front while Clay and Chrissie continued to speak briefly with Kathy Weldon, who herself had to leave as she was organizing the preparation of food for later.

As the woman walked off, Clay looked up in time to see Jo lovingly brush back some errant strands of Amy's hair with her fingers. She wiped away tears, and then smoothed the front of Amy's blouse. Then, with her hand still on Amy's shoulder, she broke down and wept, hanging her head and covering her eyes with her left hand.

Chrissie started to go to her mother, but Clay caught her by the hand. "I know this is hard, but let's let her have these last few minutes alone with her sister. She needs to say goodbye."

Chrissie stayed but, affected by her mother's tears and her own sadness, began to cry. Clay held her for a few moments and gave her some tissues out of his jacket pocket. At length, they joined her Mother at the front.

They stood there for a few moments in a three-way hug before taking their seats in the front pew. Clay wished there was something he could do or say that could take Jo's pain away. But he knew there wasn't. There was no choice; she had to go through this. He would go through it with her. He would give her every comfort he could. But she had to go through this.

Clay checked his watch. 1:55 p.m. People had been arriving at a fair rate, but now just a few stragglers were entering the church. He scanned over the mostly seated crowd and judged that there were about a hundred people in attendance. However, he did not see Tom Carlson or Carol among them. Finally, about two minutes before it was time to begin, they entered the building and rushed up to the front. Carol sat next to Jo and Carlson sat next to her, on the aisle. Jo, Chrissie, and Clay moved down to let them in.

Clay sat next to Chrissie and looked over at Tom Carlson. He hadn't given any thought to what his reaction would be upon seeing him and was surprised at the vehemence with which he wanted to do him bodily harm; to requite what he had done to Amy, and the pain and sadness of Jo's tears. But the Holy Spirit helped him with Romans 12:19: "Never take your own revenge, beloved, but leave room for the wrath of God, for it is written, 'Vengeance is Mine, I will repay,' says the Lord."

He would contact Lieutenant Burke as soon as he could after the service. It was the right, and probably safest, thing to do. Burke was God's minister with the "sword," the avenger to bring wrath upon the one who practices evil.

Chapter 24

THE FUNERAL ITSELF WAS A CELEBRATION of Amy's life. Many came and gave beautiful testimonies of how she had impacted them for good. Some told of how she had introduced them to Christ. Others recounted episodes from her life; one young woman telling a particularly humorous story of how Amy had accidentally burned her own tent down while chaperoning a group of teen girls on a camp-out several years ago.

Pastor Giles spoke from First Thessalonians, chapter four. He emphasized that Amy's hope, her confidence, was in Christ; and that all the blessings of Scripture, the promises of God, are to those who are in Christ, as Amy was and still is. And because of that, "we do not sorrow as those who have no hope, but look forward with anticipation to the day when Christ himself will return for us; raising some from the dead, and translating others alive to be with him forever." The day when we will see Amy again; but more importantly, the day when we will see our Savior and Lord face-to-face and be welcomed by him.

It was time for the pallbearers to go forward and Clay's heart hurt. It was especially painful to be standing in front of Tom Carlson as they picked up the casket. At least, he thought, he didn't have to look at the miserable excuse for a man. The other men were strangers to him, friends and acquaintances of Amy's from church.

At the cemetery, they sat the casket in the nickel-plated device that held it over the grave. Astroturf covered the dirt that had been dug out, and there was a green, canvas-topped shelter on aluminum poles that was sufficient to keep the rain that had begun to fall again off the smaller group of people who had come to the committal service.

Pastor Giles took his place near the head of the casket and faced the group. He was clearly moved with emotion, and it was with some difficulty that he spoke. "Once, in a conversation with a woman, the Lord Jesus said these words: 'I am the resurrection, and the life: he that believeth in me, though he were dead, yet shall he live: and whosoever liveth and believeth in me shall never die.' Then he asked the woman a question, 'Do you believe this?' And that, beloved, is the question: 'Do you believe this?' When the Lord Jesus Christ spoke the question to Amy's heart, her answer was, 'Yes.' What do you answer when he speaks to your heart?"

He paused for several seconds to allow those present to consider the question before continuing. "If God be for us, who can be against us? He that spared not his own Son, but delivered him up for us all, how shall he not with him also freely give us all things? Who shall lay any thing to the charge of God's elect? It is God that justifieth. Who is he that condemneth? It is Christ that died, yea rather, that is risen again, who is even at the right hand of God, who also maketh intercession for us. Who shall separate us from the love of Christ? Shall tribulation, or distress, or persecution, or famine, or nakedness, or peril, or sword?...Nay, in all these things we are more than conquerors through him that loved us. For I am persuaded, that neither death, nor life, nor angels, nor principalities, nor powers, nor things present, nor things to come, nor height, nor depth, nor any other creature, shall be able to separate us from the love of God, which is in Christ Jesus our Lord."

He bowed his head. "Eternal Father, we humble ourselves before you and ask that you will etch upon our hearts the brevity and uncertainty of human life. Teach us to number our days that we might apply our hearts unto wisdom, and the righteousness which is found in Christ alone; so that when we appear before you it may be to the same glad welcome that our sister Amy found. Thank you for her life, and for the testimony of Christ Jesus she was to all who knew her. In his dear name we pray. Amen."

Looking up, he continued. "Unto Almighty God we commend the spirit of our beloved sister, Amy. And we commit her body to the earth; in sure and certain hope of the resurrection unto eternal life, through Jesus Christ our Lord. Amen."

Clay was standing between Chrissie and Jo as the pastor spoke. Chrissie had been stoic up to this point, having steeled herself against her emotions. But at the finality of these last words she shuddered and began to cry. Clay gathered her into an embrace, almost simultaneously giving her into her mother's arms. He could hear Pastor Giles finishing the benediction as if somewhere in the distance.

"...lift up the light of his countenance upon thee and give thee peace. Amen."

He then invited the mourners back to the church for a time of fellowship.

Clay and Jo remained behind, consoling Chrissie, as the others walked off. At length they too walked from the grave, Chrissie's head against Jo's shoulder and Clay's arm around them both.

Jo sat in the back seat, holding her daughter as Clay drove back to the church. By the time they arrived at the parking lot Chrissie had recovered. Clay pulled into a parking space, shut off the engine, and turned in the seat to look back at Jo and Chrissie.

"I'm sorry I embarrassed you both back there," Chrissie said.

Clay looked at Jo. "I wasn't embarrassed. Were you?"

"Not at all. Don't feel bad, honey. You loved your Aunt Amy. There is no shame in that."

"Absolutely none." Clay reached between the seats and squeezed Chrissie's hand.

The girl gave a wan smile, and they went back into the church.

Once they were inside, Clay looked around but did not spot Tom Carlson or Carol anywhere. He felt bad for Carol. Carlson had, no doubt, convinced her not to come. How would she react to the news that he had murdered Amy? Clay intended to call Lieutenant Burke as soon as they got back to Jo's house, so he guessed they'd find out later in the day.

Kathy Weldon commandeered Jo and Chrissie. "There are some people I'd like you to meet," she said, taking Jo by the arm. Jo turned and looked at Clay, with an "I'm sorry" look in her eyes, as she followed the woman.

Clay smiled and mouthed "I love you" to her before she turned back to Kathy. It did his heart good to see how they both were being accepted by Amy's friends. It seemed like every time he looked up from his conversation with Pastor Giles, someone new was hugging one or the other of them.

When at last it was time to go, Jo had rejoined Clay and they thanked Pastor Giles and his wife for all they had done. They in turn promised to thank, on Jo's behalf, everyone who had worked behind the scenes to prepare the food and set up the fellowship hall. Finally, they invited them all to worship with them on Sunday.

Clay was happily surprised when Jo said that they would. He had planned to go home on Sunday but decided he'd wait until after church to leave.

Both Jo and Chrissie were quiet on the way home, but upon entering the house Chrissie spoke. "I've got some homework I need to get done for tomorrow."

"You don't have to go to school tomorrow, I'll call in for you," Jo replied.

"No. I do. We have a calculus test and it's for credit. I don't want to miss it 'cause I'll have to make it up."

"Well, it's up to you honey. See how you feel in the morning and I'll call you in if you want."

Clay was dialing Lieutenant Burke's number as Jo followed Chrissie to her room. When she returned, he was resting on the sofa, leaning back against the arm with his legs stretched out over the length of the cushions.

"Let me sit with you," she said, moving his left leg over to clear a spot for herself.

Jo sat down and leaned back against Clay's chest. "What did Lieutenant Burke have to say?"

"He wasn't there. They said he won't be back until after lunch tomorrow."

"I guess it won't hurt to wait an extra day."

"No, I suppose not. It will also give me a chance to talk with Mitch and see what he's dug up. Maybe it's better all the way around."

"Maybe. Right now I'm too tired to care whether it's today or tomorrow."

"Yeah, me too. I can only imagine how beat you must be after the day you've had. I'm so sorry, Jo. I only wish there were some way I could go through this for you."

"It's enough that you've been here for me...and for Chrissie too."

"He kissed the top of her head, and cuddled his face next to hers.

"Ummmmm," she said, laying her head back against his shoulder.

In a few moments she was asleep. In a few more moments, he was also asleep.

Clay woke up. He didn't know what time it was, nor did he know how long they'd been laying there. What he did know was that his right leg was asleep and his back hurt, making him very uncomfortable. However, he didn't want to move his arm to look at his watch for fear it would awaken Jo. She felt so good, asleep in his arms, that he wanted to prolong the moment as long as he could.

When at last he could stand it no longer he kissed the top of her head and cuddled his face next to hers again until she began to stir. "Hey," he said softly. "Wake up, sleepy head."

"Umm, what time is it?"

Clay looked at his watch. "About 5:30."

"I should make us some supper."

"I noticed you didn't eat anything at the church."

"No, I just couldn't. But I'm starting to get hungry now."

"You don't need to be cooking today. How about you get Chrissie and I take us out for supper?"

Jo got up from the sofa. "Oooo, my back hurts."

"Yeah, mine too—and my leg went to sleep," he said as she walked toward Chrissie's room.

Clay got up and walked around the room, trying to get the blood circulating in his leg again while Jo disappeared inside Chrissie's room.

In a few minutes she returned. "She doesn't want to go. She's right in the middle of studying and said she'd grab something out of the fridge if she gets hungry. So I guess it's you and me. Let me brush my hair."

They both had light meals and neither said much as they ate. Jo seemed to be in a pensive mood and Clay didn't want to intrude on her thoughts. She continued to brood as they rode home in his truck.

When he shut off the engine in her driveway, he unbuckled his seatbelt and turned toward her. "What is it? What are you thinking?"

She unbuckled her seatbelt and scooched around in her seat until she was facing Clay. "It's something Reverend Giles said at the funeral," she said, bringing her feet up on the seat and hugging her knees. "It's bugging me and I'm trying to understand it."

"Maybe I can help."

"Well...I do believe in God. I'll admit that it might be in a generic way, but I do believe. Amy always talked about Jesus. And today Reverend Giles seemed to be making a point of talking about Jesus; not that he didn't mention God. I know that Jesus is God's son, but when he talked about all of God's promises being for those who are *in Christ,* it seemed like he was making him out to be more than just God's son. Then when he quoted Jesus' words: 'I am the resurrection...'." She paused.

Clay spoke up. "'I am the resurrection and the life; he who believes in Me shall live even if he dies, and everyone who lives and believes in Me shall never die.'"

"Yeah, that's it. And he said that Jesus spoke the question to Amy's heart and she answered, 'yes.' What was he saying? What was it that Amy believed?"

"The woman's name was Martha."

"Hmm?"

"That was the name of the woman Jesus was speaking to. She had a brother named Lazarus and a sister named Mary, and they were friends of Jesus'. Anyway, Lazarus died. Jesus actually knew that, but he didn't arrive in Bethany, where they lived, until four days later."

Clay reached between the seats, got his Bible out of his briefcase and opened it to John, before he continued.

"Basically Martha was saying to him, 'If you'd gotten here in time, my brother wouldn't have died.' Here, let me read it for you," he said, switching on the dome light.

Martha therefore said to Jesus, 'Lord, if You had been here, my brother would not have

194   *Justice for Amy*

died. Even now I know that whatever You ask
of God, God will give You.'

Jesus said to her, 'Your brother shall rise
again.'

Martha said to Him, 'I know that he will rise
again in the resurrection on the last day.'

Jesus said to her, 'I am the resurrection and
the life; he who believes in Me shall live even if
he dies, and everyone who lives and believes in
Me shall never die. Do you believe this?'

She said to Him, 'Yes, Lord; I have believed
that You are the Christ, the Son of God, even
He who comes into the world.'

"See, a big part of Jesus' ministry was healing. He
restored sight to the blind, made the lame to walk, the deaf
to hear, cleansed lepers, and healed all manner of
diseases."

"Yeah, that much I knew. I guess it's common knowledge."

"That's what Martha was dealing with—a man who
could heal. That's why she said, in effect, 'If you'd gotten
here in time, my brother wouldn't have died.' Don't get me
wrong, she saw Jesus as more than just a man. But I think
she saw him as something less than God. Maybe that's
what you two have in common. You believe the things you
know—and that's good, as far as it goes. But Jesus was
about to bring out her faith in a big way, and that's why he
told her that he is the resurrection and the life."

He thought for a moment. "See, we say that seeing is
believing. Faith says believing is seeing. I think that's why
he said, 'Do you believe this?' And her response, while
encapsulated in a single sentence, was huge."

"What do you mean?"

"Well, first she says, 'Yes Lord.' She calls him Lord, and
she says that she believes that he is the resurrection and
the life, and everything else that he just said. And she
makes it clear that, not only does she believe now, but she
has for some time believed that he is God's son, the Christ,
the Messiah. That's the meaning of, 'He who comes into

the world'—it was a common Jewish expression for the Messiah."

"Okay, so what's the significance?"

"Here's the question: which is harder, raising Lazarus after he's been dead 4 days, or raising him at the end of the age? The answer, of course, is neither. 4 days, 4,000 years; when you're dead, you're dead, and raising the dead is impossible—unless you happen to be God. Only God can make such a statement and have it make any sense."

"So you're saying that Jesus *is* God?"

"Exactly. Beyond being the son of God, he is God the Son—the second person of the Trinity; Father, *Son*, and Holy Spirit. One God in three persons. And a short time later, he proved it beyond a shadow of a doubt—"

"By raising Lazarus from the dead," she interrupted.

"Right. Understand that Lazarus was well and truly dead, and had been for 4 days. That which was Lazarus was far away from the cave in which his body was buried. But wherever he was, he could hear the voice of God, and was instantly freed from death. The Resurrection and the Life commanded him to come forth, and his life was instantly restored to his body, and he who had been dead walked out of the tomb alive. One day, all who are in the graves will hear his voice and come forth."

"Okay, it makes sense. He couldn't do that if he wasn't God."

"That's my point. Because he is life itself—eternal life, he is the giver of eternal life to those who believe in him. That's what Amy believed. It's also what I believe. There's more to it than just that, but that's part of it."

Jo thought for a moment. "I want to know more. Like, I want to know what he meant by God's promises being for those who are *in Christ*. But it's going to have to wait because I'm just too tired to go on much more tonight."

Clay shut off the dome light. "That's okay. We can talk more later," he said, handing her his Bible. "Here, you can have this."

"I can't take your Bible."

"Sure you can. Look, I have to fly to Wisconsin tomorrow anyway, so it's not like I'm going to need it right away. Read the whole book of John if you get a chance. It's not all that long and I think you'll find it very helpful in your quest to understand."

"Thank you, Clay. But when you want it back, just say so."

"We'll take it to church with us on Sunday and use it together."

Chapter 25

CLAY WAS SURPRISED TO SEE THE LIGHTS ON as he returned to Jo's house from his morning run. He was about to insert his key in the door when she opened it.

"Hi!" she smiled.

"Hi! I hope I didn't wake you," he said, coming in and closing the door.

"No. I set my alarm. I wanted to make you a good breakfast before you went off this morning. It should be ready by the time you've showered and dressed."

He gave her a peck on the lips. "How nice. Thank you. I guess I'd better get to it then," he said, heading toward the back of the house.

Jo was dishing up helpings of egg casserole when he returned to the dining room. "You seemed to enjoy this so much last Saturday that I thought I'd make it again for you today."

"I love it." Clay smiled as he poured coffee into two mugs and took them to the table. Once again they held hands while he prayed for the meal.

"Thank you for getting up and making this," he said.

Jo smiled. "It's no chore, Clay. It makes me happy to do this for you."

"You make me wish I didn't have to go away today. I'd far rather stay and spend the time with you."

"I'd far rather have you stay. But I'll be here waiting for you when you get back."

"And I'll be back as soon as I can."

When they finished eating, Clay pushed away from the table, collected the dirty dishes, and took them to the kitchen sink. Jo followed with the coffee mugs. "Let's just leave these dishes; I'll take care of them after Chrissie eats. You want some more coffee?"

"No, I'd better not. My plane doesn't have a bathroom," he said with a smile.

Jo put one of the mugs in the sink, refilled the other and set it on the counter to cool. Then she came into Clay's arms and he held her and kissed the top of her head.

"What are you going to do today?" he said softly, in her ear.

"I'm going to go see Carol. Talk to her about Tom and try to prepare her for what's coming. I'm worried about her—how she's going to take the news. I want to be there for her—especially if she tries to do something stupid again."

Clay winced. "Umm, I wish you wouldn't do that."

Jo stepped back from him. "Why not?"

"Well, first, because I'm afraid that if she hears it first from you, she may blame you. I think it would be better to let Burke do his duty and then you can be her big sister. It may go down easier for her if she doesn't associate you as the source of her pain. Second, and more important, I'm just plain afraid for you. What if Tom were to show up while you're there? There's no telling what he might do. I'm more sure than ever now that he tried to kill me this past Sunday. I think underneath his façade, he's truly a violent man."

"But he'll be at work today, and I could call first to be sure."

"I don't know, sweetheart. I just have a real bad feeling about this."

"I'm a big girl, Clay."

"I know you are. And I wouldn't dream of telling you that you must or must not do anything. I'll be more than happy to go with you when I get back."

"The longer we wait, the greater the likelihood of him showing up. But we'll see." She looked at the clock. "You'd better get going if you plan to make your appointment on time."

Clay looked at the clock. "Yeah," he said dejectedly as he turned to leave.

"Hey. Don't I get a kiss?"

Clay took her in his arms and gave her many passionate kisses on her lips and face and neck. "There," he said. "There's something to remember me by."

"Whew!" she said, stepping back and catching her breath. "How could I forget after that?"

They both laughed and Jo spoke again. "Be careful my darling. Come back safe to me."

Clay kissed her one last time. "I will, sweetheart," he said as he turned to leave.

Jo picked up her coffee mug and sipped from it as she watched from the living room window until Clay's tail lights disappeared from view.

CHRISSIE WAS DETERMINED TO GO TO SCHOOL and awakened with her alarm shortly after Clay left. Jo dished her up some of the casserole and made her toast. She then did the dishes as her daughter dressed and prepared for the day.

Jo looked at the kitchen clock when she arrived home from taking Chrissie to school. 9:10 a.m. She got her telephone book from the drawer and looked up the number for Northern Fruit Wholesalers. Then she picked up the cordless phone and dialed:

"Northern Fruit Wholesalers. How may I direct your call?"

"Tom Carlson, please. He's in accounting."

"One moment please."

There was a moment of silence before Jo heard the phone on the other end begin to ring.

"Accounting, Tom Carlson speaking."

She hung up.

She stood there for a moment weighing her possible next steps, then pressed the Talk button again and dialed Carol's number.

"Hi, Jo. Sorry I missed you yesterday afternoon. I wasn't feeling well, and I asked Tom to take me home."

"Are you okay?"

"I'm fine now."

"That's good. Listen, can I come over? I need to talk to you."

"That sounds ominous. Should I be worried?"

"I'd rather talk to you in person, if that's okay."

"Sure. Come on over. I'm not planning to go anywhere."

Jo went into her bedroom and made her bed. Then she checked in Chrissie's room, but her bed was already made. She walked to the spare bedroom and stuck her head in the door. Clay had made his bed, too.

She stood there for a moment and then entered and sat on the foot end of Clay's bed. A wave on melancholy came over her as she realized that she already missed him. She put her hand down on the spot where he'd slept and closed her eyes, her heart warming as she thought of the love they shared. Smiling, she arose and smoothed out the spread before heading into the bathroom.

Jo washed her hands and checked herself in the mirror as she ran a brush through her hair. Then, putting on a light jacket and grabbing her purse, she got into her car and set out for Carol's house.

IT WASN'T UNTIL CLAY WAS ABOUT TO TOUCH DOWN in Madison that it occurred to him that Wisconsin is on Central Standard Time.

He dawdled while getting parked and refueled. Finally, he rented a car and drove to the hospital, arriving at about 8:15 a.m.

Finding his way to the cafeteria, he bought a cup of coffee, found an empty booth in a corner and sat down. He spent the next 20 minutes going over his presentation and contemplating the possible reasons why hospital coffee seems to be universally bad. Then, finding a men's room, he brushed his teeth without toothpaste and popped a breath mint into his mouth.

It was 8:50 a.m. when he appeared at the receptionist's desk and handed the gray-haired woman seated there his card. "I'm here to see Don Cunningham from the purchasing department. I have a nine o'clock appointment."

"I'll see if I can locate him for you, sir. If you'd like to take a seat over there I'll send him over to you when he arrives." She pointed at an upholstered chair within sight of the desk.

Clay sat down and watched the receptionist as he waited. She dialed a number and waited. Then she hung up and dialed another number. After a short wait, he saw her speaking into the handset but couldn't hear what she was saying. When she hung up the phone, she looked up at Clay and smiled before going about her business.

In just over 5 minutes a heavy-set man, about five foot-ten, and with blond hair that was seriously thinning, appeared at the desk and spoke to the receptionist. The woman pointed in Clay's direction, and the man turned and walked toward him, extending his hand. "Don Cunningham, Director of Purchasing."

"Clay Ramsey. Nice to meet you," he said, shaking the man's hand.

"I'm real sorry, but I had to cancel our meeting. I left you a voice mail late yesterday, but obviously you didn't get it. Man, I'm sorry you had to fly all the way over here for nothing."

"Perhaps we can reschedule for a better time."

"No, it's not that. The decision has already been made. Frankly, it was a political thing. One of our doctors, a cardiologist, is on the board. He has an affinity for Philips and was able to push through a decision, bypassing our purchasing committee and process. I'm really sorry. None of us likes it when this kind of thing happens. But it does happen once in a while."

"Well, Philips is good equipment. You won't be sorry you bought it...but you're going to pay a lot more for it than you would have for Mediscope."

"Yeah, don't I know it."

"Here's my card. Give me a call if I can be of service, or the next time you're in the market for monitoring equipment." Clay extended his hand and the two men shook again.

"I will. No guarantees, but our ER is looking to replace its system next year. Small consolation I know, but I'll definitely keep you in mind."

Clay looked at his watch. It was almost 10 a.m. Eastern Time when he resumed the seat of his rental car. As he drove back to the airport he decided that he would fly to Grand Rapids as opposed to Traverse City. He would check in with Gwen, and visit with Mitch in person rather than by telephone, if he was available.

Chapter 26

GWEN WAS GENUINELY GLAD TO SEE CLAY as he walked in the door of Ramsey Medical. She ran to his arms and gave him a long, strong hug. "It's good to see you, big brother. I missed you."

"I missed you, too," he said, hugging her back and kissing her on the cheek.

Clay put his arm around her and walked her to his office. He hung his jacket on the back of the door and they both sat, facing each other, on his green leather sofa.

Gwen spoke first. "Aren't you supposed to be in Madison today?"

"I've already been there. The deal went to Philips yesterday. We never had a chance. Some political thing, I guess. The guy called and left a voice mail, but with the funeral and all, I forgot to check it last night."

"Oh, I'm sorry."

"Me, too. On the other hand, I was going to fly back to Traverse City, but I decided to use the extra time to come and see you. And I'm glad I did. I missed you." He picked up her hand and gave it a squeeze before letting her have it back. "Something's going on with you, isn't it?"

"How'd you know?"

"I don't know. I just have the feeling that you've got some stuff stored up and you want to talk about it."

"Am I that transparent?"

"Only to the people who love you."

"It's Bill. A church in Duluth, Minnesota has offered him a call to be their pastor. They've been a mission church up until now. He'll be their first regular pastor."

"And he's accepted their call?"

"Yes."

"Where does that leave you?"

"He's asked me to marry him."

"That's *wonderful*. What did you tell him?"

"I told him no. I'm not going to leave you in the lurch, Clay."

"Gwen...This is your dream."

"It doesn't matter. I'm not going to leave you."

"Yes it does matter, and yes you are. Your happiness is a matter of utmost importance to me. Now, you sit at my desk and call him right now, and tell him that you love him and that you'll marry him."

"Claaay."

"I mean it, Gwen! He's a good man and he loves you, and nothing would make me happier than to give you away to him at your wedding." Clay got up and got a tissue out of the box on his credenza and dabbed at his eyes.

"Can I have some of those?" she said.

Clay gave her the box and sat facing her again, one leg folded underneath him and the other foot on the floor. He waited while she dried her eyes and blew her nose before putting his hands on her shoulders and bumping his forehead against hers. "I love you, little sister," he choked out. "I couldn't live with myself if I thought for even a minute that I was standing in the way of your happiness."

Clay sat back and took a couple more tissues out of the box. He dried his eyes and blew his nose before he stood and threw them in the waste basket. He walked to the door, took hold of the knob, and began to close it as he backed out. "You call him!" he said as he closed the door.

Clay went out to the front desk and used Gwen's phone to check his voice mail. The only message was the one from Don Cunningham. He listened to it and deleted it, glad for the opportunity to come home and see Gwen. He smiled, his heart filled with joy for her as he contemplated her good news.

At length, Gwen came out of his office. She was beaming and Clay knew the wedding was on. But he put on a game face and acted stern. "Did you call him?"

"Yes." she said, wagging her head and sticking her tongue out at him. She could see right through him and he knew it.

"And?"

"And I'm practically an old married lady."

Clay scooped her up in his arms and spun around with her. She screamed with surprise and he pulled her close. "I'm so happy for you!"

She put her arms around his neck. "If you don't stop this, you'll have me crying again. Now, put me down."

Clay put her down and she went to her desk. "You're really happy about this, aren't you?"

"I'm deliriously happy about this. You deserve to know the kind of deep love that can only come from being one heart with someone who absolutely adores you. I know Bill is that man. And I can hardly wait to be an uncle to your kids."

Gwen blushed. "Well, I'm sure it will be a while before we have kids. What are you going to do for help around here? They want us to start at the first of the year."

"I'll find somebody. It won't be the same, but I'll smile every day knowing that you're happy."

She pulled out a couple of tissues for herself and Clay changed the subject. "Help me think up some nice gift I can take back to Jo."

"Why don't you get her some fresh flowers? You could pick those up on your way to her house. Of course, you could always buy her a ring."

Clay gave a theatrical sigh. "Are you and Liz in cahoots or something?"

"We certainly are. Jo loves you, you know. And you love her—it's written all over your face."

"I think we've had this discussion, Gwen. I know she loves me, and she knows that I love her. How's that for a news flash? Look sis, I can see it happening, but the time is not right yet."

"Well, I guess you know best, but don't wait too long. I'd like to pick *you* up and twirl *you* around before I go to Duluth."

They both laughed.

CLAY CALLED MITCH and agreed to meet him for lunch at Torrey's English Grille. By the time he arrived, Mitch was already seated. Clay saw him waving and joined him in his booth.

"Hi buddy," Mitch said. "I hope you don't mind, but I ordered you a chicken Caesar salad. I know you like them, and I'm on a tight schedule today."

"No, that's great. I'm grateful you were able to get away on such short notice."

"Well, the information I've dug up is somewhat disturbing, and I wanted to get it into your hands as soon as possible, so you can get it to your Lieutenant Burke."

"That sounds serious—"

Just then the waitress arrived with their lunches. Clay grabbed the check and stuck it in his shirt pocket and the two men prayed for the meal.

"I don't mind telling you I'm concerned," Mitch said when they started eating. He pulled a spiral-bound notebook from his jacket pocket and opened it.

"First, your man Morgenstern does have a record. He spent a couple of years in Marquette for grand theft and unlawful possession of a controlled substance. He's on parole now, and as far as I can tell he's been clean since he got out."

"Yeah, we found that out, or I should say Jo did, a couple of days ago. She ran into him at the funeral home and he confessed everything to her. I don't think he's our man. Turns out he's a brother and was pretty close to Amy."

"That was my gut reaction too. He had no priors and nothing after. Looks like he made a mistake and paid for it. Carlson, on the other hand, is another story. He's either an extremely unfortunate guy or a smart killer."

"What do you mean?"

"Well, he is from Nebraska, like you guessed. A little town called Hoskins, not too far from Lincoln. He was married to a woman named Sarah. Seems she was fairly well off—some kind of shirt-tail relation to some folks that made farm implements back in the 1940s and 50s. Anyway, she died in a car crash. Somebody tampered with her brakes."

"Carlson?"

"That's what the police thought. I spoke with the investigating officer," he checked his book, "a Mark Taylor. It's what he still thinks. But they can't prove it because there were no fingerprints in the area where the brake line was cut, and he was in Las Vegas when it happened, supposedly on business."

"Supposedly?"

"He admitted under questioning that that's what he told his wife. But in reality, he went there to gamble and he didn't want her to know about it. Anyway, his alibi checked out, and they couldn't tie him to the tampering, so they had to let him go. Thing is though, they lived on top of a fairly big hill and she rarely went out alone. But on the very night he took off for Vegas, she was going to a baby shower for a friend of hers."

"He inherited...?"

"$400 thousand and change, plus $100 thousand in insurance."

"Wow. I wonder where it all went? His credit report shows him behind in his payments until recently."

"Good question," Mitch replied. "My guess is it went to Las Vegas casinos. In fact, I'd guess the guy has a problem with gambling."

"Why do you say that?"

Mitch looked at his spiral book again. "He moved to Muskegon in 1991, and went to work for Beacon Lakeside Corporation. They were a chemical manufacturer—specifically pesticides. He got married in '92 to a Kristen Little, who was a secretary in the accounting department there at Beacon."

"He's an accountant, you know."

"I know. Anyway, the federal government cracked down on the really dangerous pesticides, and it hurt Beacon. They laid him off in 1995, and went out of business in 1997. But, in '95 his second wife accidentally dies of poisoning."

"Pesticide, right?"

"Right," he checked his book again. "Methyl parathion. Same thing that killed your friend, Amy."

"Oh, man." Clay put his head in his hands. "And I'll bet he was out of town."

"Yeah. He was supposedly up in Mount Pleasant looking for a job. I spoke to the investigating officer, and Carlson did show up for a job interview. However, he's sure they can also place him at a casino there as well. That's why I think he has a problem with gambling. My guess is that he's addicted and needs the money to keep feeding his habit.

"How much did he get?"

"Another $250 thousand. All insurance this time. Apparently this girl wasn't so well off."

"No, but she's just as dead," Clay declared. "No evidence, I suppose."

"No. They searched the place with a fine-tooth comb but didn't find anything. Trouble is, she went out with some girlfriends on the evening of the night she died, and she could have gotten the stuff anywhere. You know Muskegon; it's chemical town, USA. At least it used to be. And of course, Carlson discovered her body. So he had ample time to get rid of what ever it was that held the poison—assuming he did it."

"Do the police know about his first wife in Nebraska?"

"Yeah, they know. That's one reason why they're pretty certain he did it. Too many coincidences. Problem is, they can't prove it."

"You know, I think that's what's been nagging at me about him. Seems like I remember reading something about that in the paper."

"Could be. It did make the papers."

Clay told him what he'd found at Amy's workplace, and Mitch nodded his head while he listened. "He's at it again. I don't think you'll have too much trouble getting Burke to investigate," Mitch said.

"No," Clay said. "There's a definite pattern here. Seems like he gets enough to last him for a while, then he kills again when he needs money to support his habit. I'm worried about Jo's sister, Carol. They're supposed to get married next spring. She's probably next on his list."

"Maybe, maybe not," Mitch replied, flipping a page in his spiral book. "I almost forgot, but I checked to see if Morgenstern or Carlson owned a Bronco, and neither of them do. However, Carol Wagner owns a 1969 Bronco. It was in her husband's name but she had survivor's rights on it and transferred it into her own name in," he looked at his book again, "October of 2000."

"What are you saying?"

"I'm saying she still owns it."

"It makes sense," Clay mused. "That certainly would explain the incident on the road. I thought it was Carlson, but it was her. It was her all along. Carlson wasn't waiting to ambush me, she just followed me from her house! It explains everything—"

Suddenly, the full impact of it hit him. "Oh, no."

"What?"

"She's involved in this."

"Well, I'm saying she could be."

"Oh, no!"

"What is it?"

"It's Jo! She was going over to Carol's house to prepare her for what we found out about Carlson before we went to the police this afternoon."

"Well, we don't know for sure—"

Clay got out his cell phone and dialed Jo's home number, but it rang until the answering machine picked up. He rang off and dialed her cell phone number, but got a message that the phone was off or out of the calling area.

"I've got to go, Mitch, I've got to go." He took the check out of his shirt pocket and threw it on the table. Then he took $25 dollars out of his wallet and threw the bills on the table as he stood up and put on his jacket. "Take care of this for me, buddy. I've got to go."

"Clay?"

"No time to talk. I've got to go. E-mail that stuff to me, will you? Thanks buddy, I owe you big time, but I've got to go. Jo might be in trouble, and I've got to go to her. Pray, man. Pray that she's all right!"

Chapter 27

AS SHE DROVE TO CAROL'S HOUSE, Jo agonized about how she would break the news to her about Tom. Mentally reviewing the past week, it seemed clear to her that Carol's behavior had been strange: remote, detached, almost unemotional. She couldn't recall that she'd actually seen her crying over Amy. On the other hand, she hadn't actually seen Carol all that much. Still, it worried her. If Carol was retreating within herself, shutting out those who love her, she was likely to already be in danger.

They'd never been really close as sisters. Unlike Amy, she'd never found a way to break through Carol's shell. Maybe it was because of the six-year difference in their ages. Whatever it was, Carol obviously didn't feel comfortable enough around her to let her true feelings out. *That's going to have to change*, she thought as she pulled into Carol's driveway. Whether she knew it or not, Carol needed her now more than ever. And she was going to do whatever it took to let her know that she was loved and that she could get past this.

Jo shut off the engine, walked up to Carol's door, took a deep breath and blew it out through pursed lips as she rang the bell.

"Jo. Come in," Carol said as she opened the door. She stepped aside allowing Jo to enter. "Let me take your jacket."

"Thanks," she said, scruffing out of her jacket and giving it to Carol to hang in the vestibule closet. "I hope you don't mind me coming over like this. I didn't mean to be mysterious on the phone."

"Not at all. I saw you drive up and I turned the flame on under the teakettle. It'll be hot in a few minutes and we can have some tea. Come in and sit down."

"Thanks," Jo said, walking in and sitting on the sofa.

Carol sat across from her in an easy chair. "I'll admit that you've piqued my interest. Is this about you and Clay?"

"No—"

"Well, tell me about him," she interrupted. "How are things going with you two?"

"Oh, Carol, I. Love. That. Man. When I haven't seen him for a while and then I see him, I get breathless and my heart practically jumps out of my chest. When he holds me, I just want to melt right into him. And when he kisses me, I get goosebumps all over, and I can feel it down to the bottom of my feet."

"Oooo, you've got it bad, girl."

"Ummm," she purred. "Don't I know it."

"Is he any good in bed?"

Jo shook her head. "That's not who we are, Carol."

"Well, how do you know he can? He doesn't have any kids does he?"

"You know, I'm not worried about it. When the right time comes, everything will be fine. But I'll be honest with you; I'd marry him no matter what, if he asked me. I love him that much. Let's change the subject, huh?"

"Sure. What did you want to talk to me about?"

"It's about Tom. Carol, I'm afraid this isn't going to be pleasant for you. And I wish that I didn't—"

"Just a minute," Carol interrupted. "I hear the tea kettle. I'll be back in a few minutes with some tea for us. I have that Earl Grey you like," she said, getting up and walking past her into the kitchen.

Jo leaned forward, put her elbows on her knees, and rested her head in her hands; regretting that she'd told Carol about her relationship with Clay. Maybe this wasn't such a good idea after all. Carol's relationship with Tom was obviously at a level she had not anticipated. Somehow she'd thought that because they weren't living together, they weren't sleeping together. Apparently they were. There was no way Carol would hear an accusation against him. The only thing this was going to accomplish was to make Carol furious with her—to drive a wedge between them at a time when Carol really needed her.

I never should have come here. I never should have called. This was a bad idea from the beginning. But I've already opened my big mouth. How am I going to get out of this?

Suddenly, she couldn't breathe. Something was stinging her on the neck and it hurt. *Oooooo, it hurts!* She tried to raise her arms to fend it off, but they wouldn't move. She commanded her arms to move, willing them to move with all that was in her, but they wouldn't move. Her legs wouldn't move! Nothing worked! *I'm paralyzed! I can't breathe! What's happening to me?*

Her eyes wouldn't shut. Everything was swimming before them and she knew she was going to be sick. She saw the coffee table moving toward her head and it hit her—she knew it hit her, but she didn't feel it. *I'm lying on the floor. I can't move! I can't breathe! I'm dying! Chrissieeee!* Blackness.

CLAY LOOKED AT HIS WATCH. 1:30 p.m. He was still a good 12 miles from the little town of Sparta where he kept his plane at the small public airport. He drove as fast as he dared. Fortunately, the lunch rush was nearly over, so freeway traffic had lightened considerably.

It was 1:50 p.m. when he pressed the throttles forward on the two-four end of the runway and began his take-off roll.

The Cessna 310-B is supposed to cruise at 213 miles per hour, with a top speed of 232. Clay's airspeed indicator read 240, and the cylinder head temperature was hot—very hot. Still, he kept the throttles as far forward as they would go. This was going to be a costly flight.

As he flew, Clay brought self-recrimination to a whole new level in his reproach of himself for not demanding that Jo stay away from Carol's. He'd had a bad feeling about this. Why didn't he press the issue with her? How could he have been so utterly stupid? Why had he not realized from the beginning that it had been Carol in the Bronco? Who else could it have been? Who else even knew he was there that night? Stupid, stupid, stupid! A male driver never would have allowed himself to be fooled into running off the road. Would he? Well, maybe. Oh, who knew?

He tried to pray for Jo, but all he could manage was, "Father, please, please keep her safe. Please, please protect her." He looked at the small screen on his cell phone, but it indicated that there was no signal. He wished the darn plane would go faster but the indicator still read 240 MPH. At least the cylinder head temperature seemed to have leveled off. He may ultimately ruin his engines, but he probably wouldn't have an in-flight failure. He prayed the same prayer again.

It was just before 2:30 p.m. when Clay touched down at Cherry Capital Airport in Traverse City. He figured his flying time had been in the neighborhood of 37 minutes, over 10 minutes faster that he'd ever made it before.

It was 2:50 p.m. when he finally climbed into his truck and set out for Jo's house. He removed his cell phone from his belt and was about to try Jo's numbers again when it rang, startling him. He pressed the send button.

"Clay, is that you? It's Chrissie."

"Yes. Chrissie, it's me. Is your—"

"Is my mom with you?" she interrupted.

Clay's heart sank again. "No. I was about to ask you the same thing. Where are you?"

"I'm at school. She never came to pick me up."

"I'm on my way to you. Stay put. I'll be there in a few minutes."

"Brad...uh, my former boyfriend is here. He's offered to take me home."

"Do you want to go with him?"

"Not really."

"Then don't. I'll be there for you soon."

"Thanks, Clay."

Clay rang off and rushed to Chrissie's school, forcing himself to calm down as he drove. He wasn't doing himself or Jo any good by letting panic take over. And Chrissie would surely pick up on it too, and be affected by it. At this point, what he needed above all else was to calm down and think clearly. If he could just get that awful feeling out of the pit of his stomach. He put the window down, took several deep breaths and exhaled them.

He pulled into the circle drive in front of Chrissie's school and saw her waiting on the sidewalk near a light post. She was talking to a good-looking young man with blond hair. Clay stopped next to her and she hurried, books held tightly in front of her, to get into his truck. She didn't say goodbye to the young man.

"Is that Brad?"

"Yeah, that's him."

"Nice looking guy."

"He has a problem controlling where his hands go."

"Ah. I see. Well, good for you, Chrissie. You don't have to put up with that kind of stuff." Clay pulled out of the circle drive and headed for Jo's house.

"That's easy to say, but most boys seem to expect it. It's hard, you know—being a girl. Sometimes you feel like you have to prostitute yourself just to get dates."

"You're a beautiful young woman, Chrissie. The right guy will come along and you'll know it because he'll respect you—enough to keep his hands off you. Save yourself for him. The best relationships have mutual respect as a core component."

They had turned onto Jo's street before Chrissie spoke again. "Do you think something could have happened to her? I mean, maybe she got in an accident or something."

"I hadn't thought about that. The last I knew, she said she was thinking about going to your Aunt Carol's house."

Clay pulled into the driveway and shut off the engine. They exited the truck and Chrissie unlocked the side door as Clay checked in the garage for Jo's car. It was gone. He went back to the truck to get his briefcase, and when he entered the house he found Chrissie engaged in a telephone conversation.

"...thanks, Aunt Carol. I'll have her call you when she shows up. Okay, bye." She pressed the talk button, hanging up the phone.

"Not there?"

"No. She hasn't seen or heard from her all day."

I'll bet, Clay thought as he opened his briefcase. He found the number for Beason Memorial and placed the call. Jo was not a patient in the hospital.

He hung up the phone and turned to Chrissie. "Looks like you have homework."

"Yeah, some. But it's Friday, so it's not like I have to work on it tonight."

Clay hadn't thought about that. He thought for a second and finally just came out with it. "I'm going to go look for your mom. I need you to stay here while I'm gone."

"I want to go with you."

Clay thought again for a moment, knowing he couldn't expose her to danger. Suddenly it came to him: "Honey, I need you to man the phone in case your mom calls. Then you can call me on my cell phone."

"I don't want to be alone, Clay."

"Do you have a girlfriend who can come over and maybe spend the night with you?"

"Yeah, Shelly. We stay at each other's houses all the time."

"Call her. Order some pizza or anything you want—on me. Just stay here by the phone."

"Okay."

Clay took $20 dollars out of his wallet, placed it on the counter, and went to the bathroom as Chrissie placed the call to her friend. When he returned, she was hanging up the phone. "She coming?"

"Yeah, she'll be here in a few minutes. I'm scared, Clay. All the strange stuff that's been happening, and now—"

Clay put his arms around her and held her. "I'm a little scared too. But I'll find your mom. I'll get the police involved if I have to, but I'll find her. You guys keep the doors locked while I'm gone, and don't let anybody in—even if you know them—except your mom or me."

"Or the pizza guy," she replied.

"Don't even let him in. Just pay him on the front stoop, let him go, and lock the door again."

"Okay."

"You going to be okay?"

Chrissie nodded her head.

As Clay let her go, he put his hand on the side of her face and scrunched his nose at her. She smiled. "Don't worry, Chrissie. She'll be home before you know it." He wished he felt as confident as he sounded.

He was walking to his truck when a green Saturn pulled in the driveway and a teenage girl got out, bag in hand. Clay spoke as she walked by him. "Hi, Shelly."

She gave him a strange look. "Hi," she said before she disappeared inside the house.

He waited for the girl's mother to drive off and then backed out of the driveway.

Chapter 28

NUMBERS, RED NUMBERS. One-one-two-seven. A clock. It's 11:27. It's dark. Kind of dark. It must be night. No, it's day—the shades are down. Where am I? In bed. Not my bed. My head hurts. My whole body hurts. I can't move.

Jo blinked her eyes several times but still couldn't see clearly, although she could see the clock. She realized then that her contacts were gone. She moved her head up and down and side to side as far as she could. Her neck felt like it was on fire. She moved her shoulders, and pulled her knees up and put them back down. She discovered she could move. Everything hurt, but she could move. It was just her hands and feet that seemed to be stuck. She wondered what had happened. She wondered where she was. Panic began to edge in. She was in bed. Was she dressed? She looked down as far as she could. Yes, she was dressed. She breathed a sigh of relief.

It was starting to come back to her. She was at Carol's house. Carol was making tea. Something stung her. She hit her head and passed out. But where was she now? Carol's bedroom. The shades were down, but she knew it was Carol's bedroom because she'd seen it before. Why couldn't she move her hands and feet? She strained to move them and realized she was tied up. Why would Carol tie her up? It didn't make sense. Panic seized her. Tom did this! Somehow he knew it was her on the phone and sensed she'd be coming to Carol's house. He came after her and did this to her!

Suddenly the door burst open and the overhead light came on. Jo closed her eyes, recoiling against the sudden brightness. Slowly she made her eyes open, allowing them to become accustomed to the light. When she was able to focus, she saw Carol was standing over her.

"Carol! Thank God it's you! Untie me! Get me out of here!"

Carol stood, looking at her, but did not respond to her pleas.

"Carol!"

"No, Jo. I'm not going to untie you. I'm the one who tied you up. You *will* be getting out of here though. Soon. And don't thank your God—he can't help you now."

"Carol?" Jo's voice reflected her confusion and incredulity.

"You always were daddy's little princess, weren't you?"

Jo thought the question was rhetorical, but then Carol slapped her face—hard. *"Weren't you?"*

"I don't know. If you say so."

"You were. Just like Amy was his little angel."

"Carol, what are you saying?"

"You weren't even his daughter! You're the bastard daughter of some other man! You're not even a member of our family, yet *you* get to be the *princess!*"

"Carol, please. Mom was married to my dad. He deserted us."

"The princess and the angel. You both grew up to be holier-than-thou. *'That's not who we are, Carol.'* Well, I seem to remember that you were a pretty hot number for Mike, just like Amy was for Steve."

"Carol, we were married to those men."

Carol slapped her again. *"Shut-up!"* she screamed, spittle flying from her lips.

Jo recoiled at the blow. Her face stung, and it brought tears to her eyes. Carol looked wild, strange, animal-like. Something in her eyes—something Jo had never seen and couldn't identify. Something that said she had left reality behind.

She blinked at her tears and spoke in a small voice. "Carol, I'm your sister. I love you."

"Shut up! You're not my sister!"

Jo recoiled, bracing herself, but the blow didn't come. She began to cry. "I love you, Carol. I came over her because I love you. Please let me go."

Carol's face softened a little. "It's too late for that, Jo. You should have left well enough alone, but *nooo,* you had to stick your nose in where it didn't belong—you and Ramsey. I tried to warn you. Chased Ramsey down the road. Killed your stupid cat. But you just couldn't let it go. Now you have to die. You and Ramsey. You both have to die."

"Carol, please! Think of Chrissie. She needs me. Please Carol, don't do this. *Please!*"

"It's too late, Jo. If Chrissie's smart, she'll go live with Mike. If she's stupid, we'll get her too."

At the thought of harm coming to Chrissie, Jo suddenly was charged with strength, and fought mightily against her bonds, desperately trying to get free.

Carol reached into the pocket of her jeans and produced a stun gun. She fired it in front of Jo's face, causing her to recoil and stop fighting. "You want some more of this?"

Jo instinctively recognized the source of her grief. "No," she said in a soft, small voice.

"Then be a good girl, and lie still, and keep your mouth shut. Tom will be here in a few minutes, and then you get to go for a ride."

Carol reached behind Jo and tested the tightness of the pantyhose with which she'd bound her hands. Then she walked out of the room, turning out the light and closing the door.

Jo kept her mouth shut as she fought against her bonds, every muscle in her body crying out with searing pain. However, her struggles proved fruitless, and at last she gave in to exhaustion.

She began to cry again and prayed through her tears. "Father, please protect my Chrissie and my Clay. Jesus, guard them and keep them safe. I know that you are God, and nothing is too hard for you. Please, please protect them. Amen."

She wiped her eyes as best she could on the bedspread and sniffed several times trying to clear her nose. Then she moved her head out of the wet spot and waited.

It was 11:51 a.m. on the bedside clock when Tom entered the room, Carol following behind him. "Well, well, well. How nice of you to come to us, Joanne. Saved me the trouble of having to come and get you."

Jo remained silent as Tom removed the pantyhose from her hands and replaced it with a large nylon cable tie. Then he unbound her feet and wrenched her up to a sitting position on the bed. Everything began to spin before her eyes. She closed them to keep from being sick. Tom pulled her to her feet, but her legs wouldn't support her and she fell. He stepped back and let her hit the floor. Still, she remained silent.

He wrenched her to her feet again, but she kept her eyes closed as he held her up, half walking, half dragging her to the side door of the house. He held her there, pinned face first against the wall, while Carol went through her pockets for her keys. Then Carol went out and backed Jo's car up to the door.

Jo found that if she opened her eyes to small slits, she could see and things didn't spin too badly. At least she didn't feel as if she'd throw-up. She was silently crying out to Jesus, repeating her earlier prayer when Carol returned and held the storm door open.

Tom spoke. "Now, we're going to get into your car and you are going make it look like everything is just peachy. Otherwise Carol here is going to give you another jolt from her little toy." Carol triggered the stun gun and let it snap in Jo's face a few times, causing her to recoil against Tom.

Carol opened the passenger side back door of Jo's Mazda, and Tom led her to it and into the back seat. Then he bound her feet again, this time with another large nylon cable tie, and closed the door.

Carol locked the house, then got into the driver's seat of Jo's car. Then they left, Tom leading the way in his car, and Carol following as they drove north on Garfield and turned right at US-31, toward Acme.

As Jo sat silently in the back, she could feel herself beginning to recover. She was able to keep her eyes open when she finally spoke. "My earliest memory of you was when Mom and Dad brought you home from the hospital."

"He wasn't *your* dad."

"...when *they* brought you home from the hospital. I was six, but Mom let me hold you. I sat in that big old easy chair we had, the one that had the flower print upholstery, and Mom put you in my arms. I kissed your forehead, and you seemed to look right into my eyes. That's when I started loving you."

"It's too late, Jo."

"I used to baby-sit you. I helped you with your homework. I've never done anything to hurt you."

"You know, Jo, your problem is that you're weak. You're ruled by your emotions. Amy was the same way, so was Jim."

"You killed Amy, didn't you? Chrissie's cat was poisoned with the same stuff that killed Amy."

"No. Tom did. I liked Amy. I was sorry it had to come to that. But she found about us, and about Tom embezzling money from the company. It had to be done. Don't get me wrong, I didn't enjoy it. But it had to be done. It was her or me, her or us. Look, if it's any consolation, I'm not going to enjoy what has to happen to you either. You just got too close—you and Ramsey."

"What do you mean, 'her or you'? Amy would *never* have tried to hurt you."

"She found out about Tom and me. Found some rather hot e-mails he'd printed off and left lying around. Men can be so stupid sometimes. I knew then it was only a matter of time before she figured out about Jim. See, she thought she introduced us, but I met Tom at Amy's office almost a year before that. I stopped by one day because she wanted to take me out for lunch, but she was in a meeting. Tom took me in her office to sit and wait for her, and we, uh... well, let's say we struck up a conversation. The rest, as they say, is history."

"You were having an affair with Tom while Jim was still alive?"

"Uh-huh. See, Jim changed after the Gulf War. He never was the same. It was like he was sick. He got fat, he couldn't get a decent job, he became diabetic, he wasn't very good in bed. I just got sick of it."

"So you had Tom kill *him,* too?"

"No."

"You did it?"

"It had to be done. He was getting suspicious; actually I think he knew about us. But he was weak. One morning I substituted succinocholine for his insulin, then went to work. He was gone before I left the house, so it's not like he suffered for a long time. I felt bad about it. But what was I supposed to do?"

Jo had no idea what succinocholine is, not that it mattered now. "You felt bad about it? You could have divorced him. Certainly it's better than *killing* him."

"And what would I get? He made minimum wage. Now I've got the house free and clear, two cars, and money in the bank."

"Carol, listen to yourself. You feel bad about Jim, you feel bad about Amy, you feel bad about me. Do you think that makes everything all right?"

"Does it really matter? If there is a God, how many times can he throw me in hell? Grow up, Princess. You've got to *take* what you want in this life. There are no handsome princes."

Jo was at a loss for words. There was no response that was adequate. Carol lived or had moved into a psychopathic world—a world in which Jo couldn't speak the language. Had she been that way all along? Was that why people couldn't get close to her?

They drove on in silence, turning right on a street somewhere north of Elk Rapids. Jo didn't see the street sign and she didn't know where they were anyway, but she sensed that they were nearing the end of their journey. They either had to turn again or run into Torch Lake. She prayed silently again for Chrissie and Clay. She also prayed for herself—that her life would be spared, or that God would be merciful and let her die quickly.

Carol followed Tom in a left turn onto a two-track that led to cabin by a small lake. The place looked like it should be a garage, but instead of having a large door for cars to enter, it had a small door in the middle with a window on either side.

Carol pulled up behind Tom and stopped, leaving the engine running. Tom exited his car and walked to the cabin, inserted a key in the locks and opened the door. He walked back to them and opened the car door next to where Jo sat. He got Jo's legs out of the car first. Then he pulled her out and up until she was standing. He spoke to Carol. "Why don't you drive this thing around back where it's not visible from the drive? Then get in my car; I'll be out as soon as I get her situated."

He scooped Jo up in his arms and kicked the back door shut with his foot before carrying her into the house. "Whew, you're a little bigger than your sister, got more meat on your bones. Built better too. Nice headlights. You and me gonna have some fun."

Jo glared at him as he carried her into a small bedroom and laid her on a metal bunk. "What's Carol going to say?"

He took another large cable tie, looped it through the one already around her feet, and secured it to the metal footboard. "Not *now,* sweetheart. I've got to get back to work. But I'll be back later, by myself, and we'll have lots of fun."

Jo shuddered involuntarily, her skin crawling at the thought. He made "sweetheart" sound like a dirty word. "Why don't you just kill me now and get it over with."

"Now, what kind of talk is that? You still have work to do. There's plenty of time for that later, when your lover-boy comes to rescue you. Then you can die together from a drug overdose. Too bad, but you should have known better than to get involved with drugs in the first place. Now, you just rest. You're gonna want to be fresh for me when I get back."

With that, he turned and left. Jo heard the door close and then heard them drive away in Tom's car.

The only light in the cabin came in through the windows. Fortunately, it was a sunny day, not so much for the light but because it warmed the inside of the cabin. Still, it couldn't have been more than 50 degrees in there, and Jo shivered, wishing she had her coat.

She didn't know what time it was, but figured it must be somewhere around half past 12. She had maybe 5 to 6 hours before Tom would be back. She shuddered at the thought, repulsed almost to the point of sickness, his vile words playing over and over in her mind.

Chapter 29

IT WAS 4:04 P.M. when Clay pulled into Carol's driveway, parked behind her car, and shut off his engine. He had no way of knowing if Carol had seen him arrive, but he closed his door as quietly as he could, walked to the side door of the garage, looked in, and saw the Bronco. He then walked to her front door.

Carol opened on his first knock. "Well, Clay. Hello. Come on in." She stood aside allowing him to enter. "May I take your jacket?"

"No. I won't be here very long."

"Well, come on in and sit down." She led him to the sofa and he sat in the spot that Jo had occupied earlier in the day.

"Can I get you something? A soda, maybe?"

"No, Carol. This isn't a social call. Where's Jo?"

"Jo? I haven't seen her all day. Just a minute, Clay, I've got a pot boiling on the stove that I need to go turn off. I'll be right back."

She walked past him into the kitchen and Clay looked around.

He saw a glint on the coffee table and bent over to examine it. A contact lens. He was about to sit up when his eyes fell on a leather strap protruding out a little way from under the sofa. He pulled it and found it to be attached to a woman's purse. He opened the wallet he found inside—Jo's purse.

He sensed Carol was returning, stood, and turned toward her. He heard a snapping sound and simultaneously saw the stun gun in her hand. He instantly knew that if he had stayed seated it would be on his neck right now instead of snapping in the air. He jumped back, tripping over the coffee table and falling to the floor.

She was on him in a flash, going for his throat with the stun gun.

Clay barely had time to react. His left arm was pinned between his body and hers, and he grabbed her right wrist with his right hand. But the angle was too great for him to apply enough force to keep the gun from hitting him. However, he was able to keep it off his bare neck.

He felt it snapping against the stand-up collar of his jacket as he extricated his left arm from between them. Even through the thick fabric he could feel pain.

Finally freeing his left hand, he grabbed her right wrist with it and, using both hands, was able to fend her off.

Still, she didn't let go of the trigger. The spark was jumping between the electrodes just an inch from his face. He could smell the ozone it produced.

Her eyes were wild and her strength was formidable for a woman her size, but he managed to roll her over and get on top of her while continuing to hold off the weapon. He pinned her right arm to the floor with both of his hands.

She writhed under him with amazing power, almost causing him to fall away from her. But he held on tight as she tried to bite his right forearm.

Clay steeled his grip with his left hand and let go with his right. Then, pulling back his right arm, he punched her solidly in the face.

Dazed, she released her grip on the gun and it quit sparking.

He removed the gun from her hand and stood. Her nose was bleeding and she was trying to get up as he reached down and grabbed the shirt under her chin and jerked her up with his left hand. *"Now, where's Jo?"* he shouted.

"Go to hell!" she screamed, trying to knee him in the groin.

Clay sidestepped and fired the stun gun through her shirt into her upper arm. Blood from her nose was dripping on his left forearm.

Her knees buckled and he pulled her back up. He looked around for something he could restrain her with, but found nothing. He dragged her into the hallway and kicked open a door. The bathroom. He looked inside. Nothing.

He dragged her to the next door and kicked it open. A bedroom, with the shades drawn. He reached across her for the light switch and she tried to bite his arm, but he moved it in time and gave her another, slightly longer, jolt with the stun gun.

Her knees buckled again, and this time she was harder to hold up. He managed to turn on the light. There were two pairs of pantyhose lying on the bed.

Clay dragged her to the bed and pushed her onto it, face down. He used one pair of the pantyhose to tie her hands behind her, and the other to tie her feet together. Then he turned her on her side, facing him.

"Are you going to tell me where Jo is, or do want some more of this gun?"

She spit in his face. *"Go to hell!"*

He wiped his face with his sleeve and gave her a shot in the other arm. *"Where is she?"* He snapped the gun in front of her face and she recoiled.

"Someplace where you'll never find her."

Clay opened her shirt and laid the electrodes of the stun gun directly over her heart. He pressed hard so she could feel the sharp points dig into her chest wall. He could see the terror in her eyes and on her face.

"I'm getting really tired of playing this game with you. Now, I'm giving you this one last chance to tell me where Jo is. You can tell me now, or I pull the trigger and go after your boyfriend." He pressed the gun harder into her chest.

"She's at Tom's cabin," Carol blurted, recoiling in panic.

Clay removed the gun from her chest and she relaxed. "Where is Tom's cabin?"

"I don't know."

He pressed the gun back against her chest and her panic returned. "I don't know, I swear I don't know! I've never been there. All I know is that he picked Jo up here and took her there. I don't know where it is! I swear I don't know. If I knew I'd tell you. I swear. Please, I don't want to die!"

Clay removed the gun from her chest, buttoned her shirt, and turned to leave.

"You could have had me, you know," she said in a soft, sweet voice.

Clay turned back toward her.

"You still can. Right here, right now. Just untie me."

Shaking his head, he turned for the door.

"There's more than half a million dollars to be had. We could go a long way on that. Just you and me," she called out.

Clay reached for the doorknob, his head still shaking.

"Are you just going to leave me here?" she cried as he turned off the light and left the room.

Clay was shaking badly as he went into the bathroom. The adrenalin was wearing off and he held onto the countertop to keep his knees from buckling.

He looked at his face in the mirror and saw a blood smear from where Carol had spit on him. He also noticed blood on both sleeves of his jacket. He took it off and rinsed the sleeves as best he could. Then he thoroughly washed his hands and face.

He had to sit down. He went into the dining room, pulled out a chair and sat, still shaking inside. It had been a scary encounter. But the scariest thing of all was that he wasn't absolutely sure he wouldn't have pulled the trigger. He was glad Carol had told him where Jo was—for all the good it did.

What good was it to know where Jo was if he didn't know how to get there? Carol had been so scared when she gave up Jo's location that he was sure she'd have told him the directions to it if she knew. That meant the she was probably telling him the truth when she said she didn't. Of course, Tom knew—

Where is Tom? Suddenly he was gripped with fear. *What if Tom is with Jo at this very moment?* He could feel rationality begin to give way to terror. His mind was becoming useless to him. He got up and paced, taking several deep breaths in an effort to force himself back to reality.

No time to be sitting down. Call Tom at work. See if he's there. No—better—call Jake Morgan and ask him if Tom is there. Jake is friends with Tom. Maybe he knows where Tom's cabin is located. Worth a try.

Clay searched until he found Carol's telephone book in a drawer near the phone in the kitchen. He looked up the number for Northern Fruit Wholesalers and dialed.

"I'd like to speak to Jake Morgan, in accounting."

"One moment please."

There was a short silence before Clay heard the phone on the other end begin to ring.

"Jake. Clay Ramsey. Please don't say my name."

"Okaaay," he said tentatively.

"I'm sorry to be cryptic, but I need to know if Tom Carlson is there, and I don't want him to know I'm calling. Is he there?"

Jake spoke softly. "He was. Hold on a second, I'll take a look."

Clay waited until Jake came back on the line. "He was here a few minutes ago, but he's left his cube. His computer's still on, so I'm sure he's here. He might be in the bathroom or something."

"Listen, Jake, this is serious. I am certain that Tom killed the auditor, and Amy—"

"What?" he interrupted.

"Please. Keep your voice down. I don't have time to explain it all to you now, so you're going to have to trust me on this. I guess I'm going to have to trust you too. Jo tells me you're a believer. That makes us brothers."

"What can I do for you?"

"I believe that Tom has grabbed Jo and taken her someplace. Has he been there all day?"

"No, he took a long lunch. I know he left the building, but I don't know where he went."

"I think I do. According to Carol, his girlfriend—"

"Yeah, I know her."

"According to her, he's taken Jo to his cabin—wherever that is."

"I know where it is. I've been there three or four times."

Clay breathed a huge sigh of relief. "Where is it?"

"North of here. North of Elk Rapids, on Wicks Lake."

"How do I get there?"

"Are you familiar with Elk Rapids?"

"Not really. I've been there once or twice, but that's about it."

"Well, as you go north on US-31, Elk Lake is on your right and the bay is on your left. Actually, as you near Elk Rapids, what you're seeing is not Elk Lake, but Elk River.

That's what connects the lake to the bay. US-31 crosses the Elk River. From that bridge, it's about 5 and a half miles. Look for a sign that says Wicks Lake and has an arrow pointing right. It's the next right. From there, it's about a mile and a half—you have to go across Carin Highway."

"Turn right past the sign, a mile and a half, cross Carin Highway."

"Right. It's a two-track on the left. There's four or five of them. I think it's the second, but I don't remember for sure."

"Second two-track."

"Anyway, the place looks like a garage without the big garage door. It's the only cabin that looks like a garage, so you'll know when you've got the right one."

"Okay, thanks. Now listen. I need you to leave there now and go to the police station on Boardman. Do you know where it is?"

"Yeah."

"Talk to a Lieutenant Burke, Rick Burke, and tell him that Tom Carlson killed the auditor and Amy Phillips, and that he has Jo, and I've gone after her."

"Rick Burke. Okay...just a minute, Clay. That's up in Antrim County. You're going to need the Antrim County sheriff."

"Okay. Go to Burke anyway and make him take you to Tom's cabin. Have him contact the sheriff if he wants to, but get him to go and take you with him. You're the only one who knows exactly how to get there, and I don't know how much time we have. If he dropped her off up there and went back to work, he's likely to head right back up there when he gets out."

"You want me to try and delay him?"

"No. I don't want to raise his suspicions. I'm in Kingsley, so I'm pressed for time as it is. I'd like to be gone before he shows up. I sure don't want him getting there before me."

"Okay, I'm out of here. Maybe I'll see you up there."

"Thanks, Jake. I hope I've got Jo out of there by the time you arrive. I owe you big time. Pray, will you?"

"I will. Via con dios, brother."

"Yeah, you too."

Clay looked for Carol's purse. When he found it, he took her keys. He put his jacket back on and ran out to his truck, checking his watch on the way. It seemed like he'd been there for hours, but his watch read 4:35. In reality it had been just half an hour.

His tires screeched as he backed up, and again as he set out. He figured he was at least 30 miles from Wicks Lake. Time was of the essence. Garfield is a curvy road and it was rush hour, he hoped he could make it to US-31 by 5 p.m. If he could, he probably had a chance of beating Tom to the cabin.

Chapter 30

CAROL ROLLED AROUND ON THE BED and tried to sit up. She made it on her fourth try. Scootching herself to the edge of the bed, she was able to get her feet on the floor. She stood.

Ramsey is weak, she thought. She didn't know what Jo saw in him. Of course, Jo was weak too. If Ramsey had hit her with the stun gun like she had hit Jo—in a vital spot and for a long enough time—she'd still be laying in bed, sick. But weak people always hesitate to go the distance. A major flaw—a flaw that was going to cost them.

She bent backwards and tried to get her tied hands below her buttocks. No luck. She couldn't bend backwards far enough. She sat down and strained against the pantyhose, trying to separate her hands. After several attempts she noticed that even though her hands were still bound, she could move them farther apart than before.

She stood again and opened her hands, laying them flat, the backs against her buttocks and as far apart as possible. She jumped backward, trying to get her hands to go under her buttocks as she fell back on the bed. It took 17 tries before she was able to get her arms in front of her.

She stood again, hopped to the door, turned on the light, and hopped back to sit on the edge of the bed. She tried to work at the knot with her teeth, but the way Clay had tied her put the knot underneath, and she couldn't turn her hands far enough to get a good bite on it.

She got up, hopped into the kitchen, and removed her sharpest butcher knife from the drawer. She held the knife point against the wood of the cabinet just below the counter top, and with the edge up. Then she pressed as hard as she could to seat the tip into the wood. Continuing to hold the knife with her abdomen against the handle, she sawed away at the pantyhose until she was able to free her hands.

She put the knife back in the drawer and removed the kitchen scissors. Bending down, she cut through the pantyhose binding her feet. As she stood, her eyes fell on the kitchen clock. 4:55 p.m.

Carol picked up the phone and immediately dialed, pacing the kitchen floor as she waited.

"Accounting, Tom Carlson."

"Tom. It's me. Ramsey's been here. He knows we have Jo, and I think he's gone after her."

"What? Did you tell him where she is?"

"I told him she's at your cabin."

"You stupid broad! What the blazes did you tell him that for?"

"He worked me over with the stun gun, *okay?* You have no idea how much that thing hurts. Look, I didn't tell him where it is. But I think he might have found out. I know he used the phone before he left—I could see the in-use light on in the bedroom. Then he tore out of here."

"What were you doing with him in the bedroom?"

"Judas priest, Tom! He tied me up, *okay?* Look, just get your butt up there! He's got a head start on you, but he's got a lot farther to go. I'll be up there as soon as I can."

Carol grabbed her coat out of the closet and headed for the door, grabbing her purse on the way. She locked the door from the inside, pulled it shut, and got in her car. Her purse was sitting on her lap as she looked for her keys.

IT WAS 4:55 P.M. when Clay turned right on US-31. He'd made good time up to this point, but traffic was much heavier here than it had been on Garfield. 45 MPH was the best he could do. Still, the farther away from Traverse City he got, the thinner the traffic became. His watch read 5:26 p.m. when he got to the Elk River Bridge. It had taken him 51 minutes to get this far.

Once he got north of Elk Rapids, traffic was light. He was able to go 70 MPH almost all the way to the Wicks Lake cutoff.

Clay turned onto Wicks Lake Road, slowing once he past Carin Highway. He passed a sign that read 'No Outlet,' and started looking out the driver's-side window for two-track roads. After he passed the first one, he slowed even more.

The area was overgrown with tall grass and trees lined both sides of the roadway; much of their now-spent verdure lying brown and scattered over the cracked asphalt. It was hard to see where the two-tracks were, and he drove past the second one before he realized it.

He backed up and turned onto the road, doubting it was the correct one. It looked like no one had traversed it in a long time. After about an eighth of a mile, he came to a clearing. Beyond it he could see Wicks Lake. There was no cabin; just a concrete pad with a utility pole next to it. Obviously where someone parked their motor home or trailer. He circled around and drove back out to the road, turning left.

The next two-track was about a quarter mile further down. He was sure this was the one as the grass had recently been flattened by tires. He turned in and again drove for about an eighth of a mile before spotting the garage-like cabin. He stopped before entering the clearing, surveying the site. Nobody appeared to be around.

Not content to trust luck, Clay slowly drove around to the back of the cabin. He spotted Jo's car, stopped next to it, and shut off his engine.

The sun was low in the sky and a chill had returned to the air as he quietly exited the truck. He looked into the Mazda. The keys were in it. Then he looked in the back window of the cabin. It was fairly dark inside. He could make out small rooms along the side walls, but couldn't see into them. He walked around to the metal front door and tried it but found it locked.

Clay tried wrenching the knob, turning it back-and-forth hard several times hoping that the lock would give. It didn't budge. He put his shoulder against the door and pushed, but it wouldn't give either in spite of repeated hits. Obviously the deadbolt was also locked.

He knew he wasn't going to get in this way, so he walked around to where his truck was parked to find something to break a window.

JO AWOKE TO SOUNDS AT THE FRONT DOOR. She had spent the afternoon alternating between terror, prayer, and sleeping from her emotional and physical exhaustion. Now Tom was back, doing something to the door. Her terror was also back, his last words playing so vividly in her mind that she could hear his voice saying them: *"You and me gonna have some fun...I'll be back later by myself and we'll have lots of fun."*

She was praying again when she heard the glass break. She fought against her bonds for the umpteenth time that afternoon, but still was unable to break free.

He was coming through the window now, she could hear him. Why wasn't he using the door? She heard footsteps, and wished she could get her hands free to cover her mouth and stifle the sobs that were trying to force their way out. He was in the doorway.

"Jo!"

She began to scream.

CLAY CAME TO HER, knelt, and embraced her. "Jo. Shhh, it's me."

She writhed against his arms, the volume and intensity of her screaming increasing. She was in hysterics. He backed away.

In the movies it's always a slap on the face to stop hysterics. He couldn't bring himself to hit her—at least not yet. It broke his heart to see that she was already bruised on her forehead and cheek.

He mustered up his most stern and fatherly voice. "Joanne Elaine Phillips, you *stop* that...*right now!"*

To his amazement, she stopped. Then she opened her eyes.

"Jo. It's me, Clay."

"Claaay." Her face softened. "Oh Clay, please, please get me out of here."

"I've got to find something to cut you loose," he said, looking around. "I've got some cutters in my truck; I'll be right back."

Clay went back out the window—why, he didn't know, and got wire cutters out of the small tool pouch in his briefcase. He went back in to Jo, clipping first the tie that

Justice for Amy

held her hands, and then the one that held her feet. Then he helped her sit up on the edge of the bed.

"I'm dizzy," she said, closing her eyes for a moment and slowly opening them. "That's a little better, but my feet are asleep. And I hurt. Oh, I hurt all over." She was shaking her hands, trying to get the circulation going in them again.

Clay bent down to pick her up, but she threw her arms around his neck, pulling him to herself. "Hold me."

He stood, scooping her up in his arms. "I love you, Jo, but there's no time. Come on, we've got to get out of here. I'll carry you out to the truck."

They heard a car drive into the clearing, and Clay, still holding Jo, stepped into the main room to look out of the window.

"It's Tom!" he said, carrying Jo back into the room and laying her back on the bed.

"Let's get out of here!" she said in a hoarse voice, just above a whisper.

"There's no time. He'll have us before we can get anywhere near the truck."

They heard the car door slam.

"Listen, Jo," he whispered. "You do exactly as I say—no argument."

She nodded her head.

"Lay here like you're still tied up, and I'll stand to the side of the door. When he comes in, I'll hit him—hard. Then *you* get out of here. Your car is out back and the keys are in it. When you get to the road, turn right."

They could hear Tom put the key in the locks.

"I can't see without my contacts," she whispered.

"Just go—no arguing. Do the best you can."

"I'm not going to leave you, Clay."

"Go!" he said in a loud whisper. "The police are on their way."

The outside door opened and Clay flattened himself against the wall next to the open bedroom doorway while Jo assumed her previous position.

Tom spoke to her as he walked from the main room to the bedroom. "Sorry, princess, our fun is going to have to wait. Your boyfriend's on his way, and I thought he might like to watch." He stopped in the doorway.

Clay was already reared back in anticipation of his entry, and he hit Tom as hard as he could in the face, sending him sprawling on his back into the main room.

Tom lay on the floor, momentarily dazed, his nose bleeding. Then, realizing the peril of his situation, he immediately went for a gun tucked in the waistband of his pants.

Clay dove at him, grabbing his wrist as he yelled at Jo: *"Go! Get out of here!"*

Jo hobbled, holding onto the wall, until she got to the door. She opened it and started to step out. She couldn't leave Clay.

Clay was sprawled on top of Tom, holding onto his wrist with his left hand, while he tried to pry away the gun with his right. Tom was repeatedly slugging Clay in the head with his left fist.

Clay's ear was bleeding and lights were flashing in his head every time Tom's fist connected with it. The pain was excruciating. He didn't know how much more of it he could take.

He stopped trying to pry the gun out of Tom's hand, concentrating his right hand on fending off the blows to his head. He was trying to get a grip on Tom's left wrist when the gun went off next to his ear. He flinched, his hand going up to his ear, and Tom broke out of his grip.

Tom managed to get out from underneath Clay. He was starting to stand as Clay also sprang to his feet, once again grabbing his wrist with both hands in an attempt to keep him from raising the gun.

Tom pulled the trigger again and Jo saw blood spray out of the back of Clay's right leg. Seconds later, she heard a car door slam behind her. She turned and saw Jake Morgan and an older man trotting toward her.

Jo ran to Jake. "Jake! *Please* help him! Tom *SHOT* him!"

The older man pulled a semi-automatic pistol out of a shoulder holster and started for the door as they heard another shot come from inside.

Jo turned and began to rush back into the cabin, but Jake grabbed her. She fought to get away, crying and screaming at Jake to let her go.

The second bullet had hit Clay in the side, but he instinctively knew that the leg shot had done more damage.

His leg was soaked with blood. He could feel himself fading, no longer able to hold onto Tom's wrist.

He fell to his knees, letting go as Tom staggered back. Clay saw him raise the pistol and aim it at his face. He heard, or perhaps perceived, two shots. Then he felt himself falling forward as everything went from gray to black.

Chapter 31

LIEUTENANT BURKE KEPT HIS WEAPON DRAWN as he walked past Clay to where Tom had fallen. Tom's gun was lying a few inches from his hand and Burke kicked it away. He kept his Glock pointed at Carlson while he felt his neck for a pulse. Tom was dead.

Jake heard a sound behind him and turned to see an Antrim County Sheriff's car pulling in. He relaxed his grip on Jo and she broke free.

She ran into the cabin in time to see Burke holster his weapon and hurry toward Clay. They reached him at the same time and she helped Burke turn him on his back. His right pant leg and his shirt were soaked through with blood.

Burke felt Clay's neck for a pulse and looked at Jo. "He's alive...barely. Is there a phone in here where you can call 9-1-1?"

Jo couldn't leave Clay's side. Tears were streaming down her face as Jake and the deputy came in the door.

Burke looked at the deputy. "Get Life Flight in here—fast."

The deputy keyed the microphone on his epaulet and spoke into it as Jo opened Clay's belt.

Jake, observing her, immediately came and pulled off Clay's shoes. Then he grasped the fabric of both pant legs and pulled as Burke and Jo facilitated the removal of his trousers.

"Chopper's on the way," the deputy spoke up. "I'm going out to move the cars to clear a spot for them to land."

Blood was pouring out of the wound in Clay's leg and Jo, now crying profusely, clamped her hands over the entry and exit points in an attempt to staunch the flow. "It won't stop bleeding," she choked out, her eyes filled with terror.

Burke had already pulled the belt out of Clay's pants. He wrapped it around Clay's leg above the wound. Then he pulled it tight and spoke to Jake. "Hold this."

Jake took the loose end of the belt from Burke and held tension on it as Burke ripped open Clay's shirt. The wound on his side was not serious. The blood flow had already begun to subside, but Burke pulled a handkerchief from his jacket pocket and applied pressure to it. Then he looked up at Jo. "Hold pressure on this."

Jo crawled over and relieved him.

Burke got up, walked to the sink, and washed his hands. Then he returned to the others. Clay's bleeding had pretty much stopped. The question was, had they stopped it in time?

Burke relieved Jake from holding the belt taut. Jake walked around, shaking his hands. He attempted to relieve Jo, but she wouldn't let him. He went back to Burke and the two traded off keeping the tourniquet tight, waiting for the helicopter to arrive.

Burke spoke to Jo. "Are you Joanne Coale?

"Yes."

"What happed here? Why was this man shot?"

Jo broke into tears again, unable to speak.

Jake took the end of the belt from him and Burke hunkered down next to Jo putting his hand on her back. He spoke gently to her. "I'm sorry. Can you tell me what happened here, Ms. Coale?"

Jo dried her eyes with the backs of her hands and struggled to explain everything from the time she arrived at Carol's house. Burke took notes. He put his spiral book back in his jacket pocket when the helicopter arrived.

As the emergency medical technicians were stabilizing Clay with an IV and attending to his wounds, Jo washed her hands and collected Clay's belongings from his ruined clothing.

She wanted to go with Clay in the helicopter, but they wouldn't let her. She was crying again as she watched it take off and fly away. She set out toward the back of the cabin.

"Where are you going, Ms. Coale?" Burke spoke up.

"My car's out back. I'm going to the hospital. He needs me."

"I'm sorry, but we'll need to process your car for fingerprints. I'll let you know where you can pick it up when we're finished with it. If you can hold on for a bit, I can take you to the hospital myself."

"Please Lieutenant Burke, I need to go to him now. His truck is around back. I'll take that."

Jake spoke up. "You're in no condition to drive, Jo. Come on, I'll take you." He looked at Burke and received a nod. "Give me his keys."

Burke had more questions for Jo, but he knew he could ask them later. Clay's injury was severe. He'd lost a lot of blood, and if he survived at all it might be at the expense of his leg. That was why he'd asked for the helicopter. Beason Memorial was the only facility in the region equipped to deal with such an injury and it was 25 miles away.

JAKE AND JO HAD BEEN ON THE ROAD for over 20 minutes and had just entered Traverse City. Jo was staring straight ahead. She'd been silent since she'd gotten into the truck.

Jake finally spoke. "Jo, please don't be angry with me."

"You should have let me go to him."

"I couldn't. There was nothing you could have done for him in there as long as Tom still had the gun. He might have killed you."

"If Clay dies, do you think that I want to *live?*" she shot back.

"He called me at work, you know. Asked me to get Lieutenant Burke and take him to the cabin. He knew he was, at best, just minutes ahead of Tom. But he didn't know if Burke was there, or if he'd even come with me. So, believe me, he understood the danger. But he went anyway, for you, because he loves you. He put his life on the line for you, Jo. I know you love him, but don't talk like that. Don't invalidate what he did for you...and for your daughter, who still needs you."

Jo began to cry again and took a tissue from the box in the console between the seats. "I'm sorry, Jake," she said, through her tears. "I'm so afraid that he'll die. He's lost so much blood. He was so pale—"

Justice for Amy

"You go on inside," Jake interrupted, pulling onto the hospital emergency entrance. "I'll be in as soon as I get the truck parked."

Jo exited the truck and hurried into the hospital.

When Jake entered the emergency area he found Jo in a heated discussion with a nurse at the triage desk. "...Please! I need to be with him."

"I'm sorry ma'am, it's against hospital policy. I could be fired for letting you in there."

"And he could die alone. Not that you care!" Jo crossed her arms and spun around, fuming.

At that moment another nurse approached from down the corridor. She saw Jo's tears and came to her. "What's wrong? Is there something I can do for you?" She looked at the other nurse behind the desk. "You can go, Theresa. Thanks for covering for me."

She put her arm around Jo. "My name is Lorraine Bulson. Now, how may I help you?"

"Lorraine, please. Let me in to see Clay."

"Clay?"

"Clay Ramsey. He's been shot, and I'm afraid he's going to die, and they won't let me go to him."

"Clay Ramsey, the medical equipment guy?"

"Do you know him?"

"Yes. He just installed a monitoring system for us." She turned and spoke over her shoulder. "You wait here for a minute; I'll be right back."

Lorraine hit a plate on the wall and the double doors slid open. Then she disappeared into one of the trauma rooms. Jake approached Jo and pointed to a row of chairs against the wall. "Why don't you sit down for a few minutes. I'm sure she'll be right back."

"I can't, Jake. I can't sit. I can't do anything until I know he's all right." She paced the floor.

The doors slid open again and Lorraine Bulson walked directly to Jo. "They're getting ready to transport him to surgery. Come with me."

They were wheeling Clay out of the trauma room when Jo and Jake arrived. A unit of blood was hanging on the IV pole attached to the gurney, and Clay's color had improved a little since she'd last seen him. However, he was still unconscious.

Jo trotted beside him as they wheeled rapidly toward the surgical suite, her hand on the railing of the gurney. When they reached the suite, the doors automatically slid open from pressure on a floor mat. They entered and Jake waited outside.

"I'm sorry, but you can't go any further," Lorraine said to Jo. "They need to take him into the operating room."

Jo took Clay's hand in hers and leaned over the railing, her tears falling on Clay's face as she kissed his lips. "I love you, Clay. Please come back to me, my darling."

Another set of automatic doors opened and she watched them wheel him down the corridor until the doors closed again. Then Lorraine put her arm around Jo. "They need you to get Clay registered, but let me first show you where the surgical waiting room is."

They exited the suite and Lorraine led Jo and Jake to the waiting room. Jake immediately went to the pay phone while Lorraine led Jo to registration. When they got there, Jo hugged her and thanked her for her kindness. "I'll be praying for him," Lorraine said as she turned to leave. Jo was comforted by that. She had been trying to pray for Clay since the cabin, but had been unable to get out much more than, "God, please let him live."

When Jo finally returned to the waiting room Kathy Weldon was there. She immediately came to Jo and hugged her. "Jake and I have just been praying for Clay...and for you. I called Pastor Giles and he's alerting the deacons. He'll be here as soon as he can."

"Thank you, Kathy," Jo said, finally sitting down. "Oh!" she stood again. "I've got to call Chrissie!" She dug around in her pockets for change, but came up empty handed. She sat again. "I guess I can call her lat—"

Kathy handed Jo the cell phone from her purse. "Here," she interrupted. "Use my phone."

Jo called Chrissie to be sure she was all right, and to assure her that she herself was all right. Chrissie cried when she told her about Clay and what had happened. But she agreed to stay at home for the night, then have Shelly's mother drive her to the hospital the next morning with a change of clothes for Jo, her glasses, and Clay's Bible. Chrissie could drive herself home in Clay's truck.

It was just past 8:30 p.m. when Jo hung up. Pastor Giles and his wife were arriving and Judy Giles hugged Jo before they all sat down.

Pastor Giles assured Jo that the church had an active prayer chain and that many people were praying for Clay. They, too, all prayed together while they waited for the doctor to come with news of Clay's condition.

Finally, at 10:45 p.m. the doctor walked into the waiting room. "Mrs. Ramsey?"

Jo stood as he extended his hand, choosing not to correct him. "Roy Cottrell. I just left Clay. He's in the PAC-U." Jo's look became curious. "The recovery room. I have to tell you that it was touch-and-go for a while. He has in his favor that he never stopped breathing, but he lost a lot of blood. Whoever got that tourniquet on him saved his life."

Tears were once again coming from Jo's eyes and the doctor put his hand on her shoulder. "I think he's going to be okay. The next few hours to few days will tell us for sure. As for his leg, I think we saved it. But it's too soon to tell. I'll be monitoring it closely for the next day or so to make sure everything pinks up like it should, and we'll want to do a vascular study on it. I'd guess he's a runner by the musculature in his legs. He probably won't be doing much running—maybe ever, but I'm fairly confident he'll walk again if we get good blood flow in there."

"Thank you, doctor. Can I see him now?"

"Let's let him finish up in the PAC-U. Then we're going to transfer him to the Surgical ICU." Jo's face reflected her renewed fear. "Just as a precaution. I'd have been much happier if he would have regained consciousness in the emergency room. I want to have him where they can keep a closer eye on him. We'll move him to a regular room as soon as we're sure he's out of the woods. I'll have someone come and get you when we move him."

"Thank you," she said as the doctor turned to leave.

Jake still had to pick up his car from the police station, so he and Kathy decided to leave at about 11 p.m. Pastor and Mrs. Giles stayed with Jo and they spent many hours talking and praying.

At about 1:15 a.m. a nurse came and took them to the ICU waiting room. Jo was allowed to see Clay for 15 minutes. She stayed the whole time—holding his hand, talking to him, crying. But he remained unconscious.

At 7 a.m. the Giles' bought Jo breakfast in the hospital cafeteria, then took their leave. They promised to continue praying for Clay and her, and to visit again later.

Jo returned to Clay's room. She was exhausted, but she couldn't make herself leave his side. If, no, when he woke up, she would be there for him. It didn't matter if it took hours or days, she would be there for him.

There was a soft knock on the door and a nurse entered carrying a Styrofoam cup filled with coffee. She handed it to Jo. "Hi. I thought you could use this right about now." She was in her mid to late 50s with auburn hair that was graying. Freckles were barely visible on either side of her nose.

"Thanks," she looked at her name tag, "Ms. Stuart."

"Why don't you call me Jean? Are you Mrs. Ramsey?"

Jo shook her head. "No." Her face was sad. "Everybody assumed that, and I let them believe it so I could sign the consent for surgery and stay with him. But I won't lie to you, I'm not his wife. My name is Joanne Coale." She sat her coffee on the bedside table.

"You love him very much, don't you?"

Jo began to cry. She couldn't speak so she just nodded her head.

Jean put her arms around her. "It's okay. I know what it's like to love someone. We'll just keep this our little secret." She let her go. "I'm his nurse today, and tomorrow too. You can stay as long as you want. If I still had my husband, I'd want to be with him every minute. I'll order you lunch and supper trays so you'll have something to eat."

"Thank you, Jean."

"Now, let's see how he's doing."

Jean listened to Clay's heart with her stethoscope. Then she pulled the covers back and thoroughly checked his leg.

"How's he doing?" Jo had stepped back to allow her room to work.

"Well, he's breathing on his own." She looked at the monitor and then back at Jo. "His heart rate is 62 and his blood pressure is 110 over 64. That's a little low, but he's in good physical condition so it might be normal for him. His leg is pink and warm all the way down to his toes. This is for the doctor to tell you, but just between you and me, they saved it. Why don't you come over here and watch while I change his dressing. You're probably going to have to do this for him in a while, so it won't hurt to know how."

Jo came around and stood next to Jean, watching as she cut away the dressing on Clay's leg. She cried when she saw the surgical wound, but continued to watch as Jean applied fresh bandaging.

"He'll be all right. There are no outward signs of infection and we're monitoring his white blood cell count. I've seen worse than this and seen them walk again. He'll need some physical therapy, but he'll be all right."

"Why doesn't he wake up?"

"Well, he's had a significant trauma and he lost a lot of blood. I wouldn't be overly anxious about it right now. Let's give him 24 hours or so. Then, if he's not awake, we can start to be concerned. Now I've got to go do my work, but I'll check on you both in a little while. In the mean time, drink your coffee while it's still warm. Then talk to him, hold his hand, sing to him. It's not going to hurt anything, and it might even help."

She turned and left, and Jo realized that the older woman had mothered her. But she also realized that was just what she had needed. She felt much better for her encounter with Jean Stuart.

Jo drank her coffee, then spent the next little while attending to Clay. His forehead was bruised and dirty, and there was dried blood around his nose and in and on his right ear. She found a washcloth and wet it with warm water. Then she gently cleaned away the dirt and dried blood.

She gently caressed the side of his face with her hand and kissed him before pulling the chair up next to the bed. She sat facing him and held his hand. If she could make him better by sheer force of will, he'd be up and walking around already.

At just after 9:30 a.m. Jean Stuart knocked lightly on the door again. "Your daughter is in the waiting room asking for you."

"Thanks," Jo said as she got up and put the chair back in its original spot.

As Jo entered the waiting room, Chrissie ran into her arms. "Oh *Mom*. What *happened* to you? Your face is bruised, and there's blood all over your jeans and sweater."

"It's Clay's blood," she said as they sat together on a sofa.

Jo explained, in detail, all that had happened between her and Carol, how Tom had kidnapped her, and Clay had rescued her. "Tom is dead, and as far as I know the police have picked up Carol. The doctors and nurses seem confident that Clay is going to pull through—I just wish he'd wake up."

Chrissie pulled her into a brief hug. "He will, Mom. I know he will."

"In my heart I believe that. I can't escape this feeling I've had that we have a future together. Right now though, my mind is not so sure. He's hurt really bad. But there are a lot of people praying for him, and the doctors have done everything they can. I guess he's in God's hands now."

"I think so, too...Oh, I hope you don't mind, but I called Clay's sister. I got her number out of your address book."

"Oh, good. I'm glad you did. I wanted to call her, but my phone and everything else is in my purse, and that's over at Carol's house. I've got Clay's wallet, but I don't even have change to make a phone call."

Chrissie gave her all of the change she had in her purse, along with her cell phone. "I gave Gwen directions to our house, and I think she's going to be here around noon. I'll be sure she gets something to eat, and then I'll bring her here. I'll bring you some make up, too; for those bruises."

Jo hugged her. "Thank you, sweetie. I love you."

"I love you too, Mom," she said, standing up. "Don't worry, he'll be all right—I just know it."

Jo pulled Clay's keys out of her pocket and gave them to Chrissie. "I think his truck is parked outside the emergency entrance." She extracted money from Clay's wallet. "Here's money for gas; I'm sure it will need some. I'll see you when you get back, and I'll call you if anything changes. I've got to go back to him now. Drive carefully, honey."

"I will, Mom. Don't worry," she said, hugging her mother again before she left.

Jo put her glasses on and took the department store bag that Chrissie had packed for her back into Clay's room. When she arrived, Jean was in the room checking Clay's leg. "How's he doing?"

"About the same. How are you doing?"

"I'm okay...I guess. Is there a somewhere around here where I can get cleaned up? My daughter brought me some fresh clothes."

Jean led her to the nurse's locker room where she could shower, stopping on the way to pick up a blow dryer from the utility room behind the nurse's station. "Be sure and bring this back when you come; it's the only one we have," she said as she turned to leave.

"I will. Thanks again, Jean."

Jo resisted the urge to take a long hot shower so she could hurry back to Clay's bedside. Nevertheless, she felt remarkably better for having had a short one. The towel felt rough and invigorating as she dried herself.

She examined her face in the mirror when she finished blow-drying her hair. The bruise on her forehead was oval-shaped, and she could still feel a small lump where her head had hit the coffee table. Turning her head to the right, she saw the clear marks of Carol's fingers in the bruise on her left cheek.

A wave of sadness passed through her as she touched her cheek. What had happened to Carol? Why hadn't someone seen it happening and intervened? Why hadn't she seen it? Had she been too wrapped up in her own life, or had Carol been too good at hiding it? Different people react differently to the same events. Maybe there was some underlying pathology in Carol's case. Whatever the reason, Carol had become the victim of her own bitterness and rancor. It had ruined her life, cost Jim his life, made it possible for Tom to take Amy's life, and made victims of those who loved her.

She thought of her own bitterness toward Mike and realized that she had to let it go. It suddenly came like a revelation to her that real love and bitterness cannot coexist, cannot live at peace with each other in the same human being. Either love will drive the bitterness out, or as is more often the case, bitterness will stunt any hope of love reaching its full potential.

She knew that she loved Clay, but she now also knew that she could never fully express that love to him, or give him the kind of affection he deserved, as long as she chose to harbor bitterness.

She had loved Chrissie from day one, but she realized that her own bitterness had taught Chrissie how to hate her father. It became clear to her that she could never be the mom Chrissie needed, could never be the example of how to love a husband that Chrissie needed to see, could never be truly happy herself, as long as she held on to bitterness.

She cried for Carol and for herself, and asked God to forgive her for her bitterness. Then she determined with all her heart that Clay would never have to guess that she loved him, would never want for the affection that would keep his heart warm and joyful. That she would confess her bitterness and its effects to Chrissie, and live before her as an example of love. With God's help she could do this—she could let her love drive the bitterness out of her heart.

Chapter 32

JO RETURNED TO CLAY'S ROOM, dropping off the blow dryer on the way. Her mood had improved with her shower and with her decision to leave her bitterness behind. She felt better on the inside as well as on the outside.

Clay remained unconscious, in the same position as when she left. Really, he looked like he was sleeping. His expression was peaceful, and it filled her heart with warm emotion as she bent over the rail and kissed him. "Hey," she said softly. "You going to wake up for me?" She let her hand caress the side of his face, holding it there for a moment—willing the love she felt in her heart to somehow flow out of her and into him. He didn't respond.

Remembering Jean's words, she took courage and put down her anxiety. No need to be concerned until tomorrow. He'll wake up. *Dear God, please let him wake up.*

She pulled the chair around to where she could sit facing Clay. She retrieved his Bible from the bedside table and sat down, opening to the ribbon marker Clay had placed at the beginning of the book of John. She began to read.

At 12:05 p.m. Jean came in the room with a lunch tray. She set it on the over-bed table, then pulled the table out and lowered it. "I hope you don't mind Salisbury steak. It was too late to get a menu in for you, so it's take what you can get."

"No, I don't mind at all. I'm just glad to have something to eat and to be able to stay with Clay." Jo put the Bible back on the bedside table and turned her chair around. She lifted the lid. "Smells good."

'Yeah, well, remember this is a hospital. We have a person here whose sole job it is to remove the taste from the food."

Jo laughed. "I'm sure it will be just fine."

"Are you a believer?" Jean asked. Jo gave her a curious look. "A Christian? I see you're reading the Bible."

Jo shook her head. "Clay is. We've been talking about it. That's his Bible. He suggested that I read the book of John, and that's what I've been doing. How about you?"

"Yes. Since I was a teenager."

"How do you do it, Jean? How do you keep your faith in the face of all the suffering and dying you must see?"

"I really don't. It's not my job to keep it. Jesus keeps me. I simply commit myself to him every day, to be his hands, to be his feet, to minister to others on his behalf. Don't get me wrong, he doesn't keep me as a reward for doing good; it's the result of believing. And the offer's open to anybody. He said in John, regarding those who believe in him, that he gives them eternal life, and they will never perish. That he holds them in his hand, and nothing or no one can touch them there. That's where I am—in his hand. And because the life he's given me is eternal, I'm completely secure there."

"I haven't got to that part yet."

"You'll get there. It's in chapter ten—near the end. Look, Jo, I'm not saying that I never have a bad day or that I never get discouraged, or that I never commit sin. The world we live in is not the perfect place that God created. Mankind's sin has had a devastating impact and we all are affected by it. What I am saying is that when I believed, the Lord Jesus gave me the Holy Spirit to be my comforter and guide. *He* keeps me in the faith. *He's* the faithful one. *He* is the earnest of the inheritance that God has reserved in heaven for me."

"Earnest? You mean like earnest money? Sorry, I work in a bank, and that's a term we use all the time."

"That's exactly what it is! The Holy Spirit in the believer, apart from being comforter and guide, is the evidence of God's pledge of the inheritance, and that all his promises are true. He is also how you know that you belong to Christ. It's like he whispers it in your heart.

"And you commit sin, and it's okay?"

"I do, and it's not okay. I don't set out trying to commit sin, and sin is not the practice of my life, but I'm human,

250   *Justice for Amy*

and like all humans, I've been impacted by the sinful world in which we live. God knows that. But if I confess my sins to him, he is faithful to forgive those sins and make my heart clean again."

"You talk like Clay...and like my sister, Amy, used to talk."

"Well, there's only one true faith, and it's based on God's Word. Believers know that because the Holy Spirit convinces their hearts that it's true."

"Sounds complicated."

"It really isn't complicated at all. Tell you what—you finish reading John, and we can talk more later if you want."

"Okay. Thanks, Jean."

Jean smiled at her. "Maybe, when I come back, you can help me turn Clay. Now, you should eat your lunch before it gets cold."

JO HAD NOT MUCH MORE THAN FINISHED her lunch when Chrissie arrived in the waiting room with Gwen and a man whom Jo had not met. Gwen's look was tentative and Jo could see that she had been crying. Jo opened her arms as she approached her. Gwen ran into her embrace and they both fought against their tears.

"How is he?" Gwen said.

"Well, he hasn't regained consciousness yet. But he seems to be doing okay. The doctor and nurses are not overly concerned. I'll tell you what, though, I'm going to feel a whole lot better once he wakes up."

"Jo, this is Bill Douglas, my fiance."

They exchanged pleasantries as she shook his hand. Then Jo turned her attention back to Gwen. "Come on in with me," she said, putting her arm around Gwen and leading her toward the ICU. "I don't know if they'll let us both be in there at the same time, but we can see."

"Have you been with him all morning?"

Jo led her into Clay's room and closed the door most of the way. "I haven't left his side for more than a few minutes since he got here."

"I'll bet you're exhausted."

"I don't know. I think I must be on my second wind. There's a very nice nurse here who let me take a shower in the nurse's locker room a couple of hours ago. I guess it woke me up. At least I've felt better since then."

"I'm glad he has you, Jo."

Suddenly Jo began to cry. "I'm afraid I'm the reason he-he's here."

Gwen embraced her. "Chrissie told me all about it. You had no way of knowing your sister was involved, so don't blame yourself."

"I love him so much," she said through her tears. "I feel so bad. I wish it were me laying there instead of him."

Gwen continued to hold her. "Shhh. I know you do. But he wouldn't want that. He loves you, Jo. Now you and I have to be strong and pray for him, that God will give him back to you."

The two women held hands as they stood there; Jo praying silently as Gwen prayed out loud for Clay.

Clay was facing the other direction since she had helped Jean turn him, so Jo walked around to the other side of the bed and kissed him. She looked over at Gwen. "I'm going out to the waiting room and let you spend some time with him. His nurse is an older woman with reddish-brown hair. Her name is Jean Stuart, and she's been an absolute angel to me, letting me stay with Clay and letting me help with his care. She keeps pretty close tabs on him, so she'll probably be in here in a little while. Just tell her you're his sister and I'm sure everything will be all right. If it's okay with you, though, I'd like to come back in a little while. I just need to be with him."

"Of course it's okay."

Jo went back to Chrissie in the waiting room. "Do you want to come in and see Clay, honey?"

"I'd love to. I've got some things I'd like to say to him, but he has to be awake to hear them. So I'll just wait till they move him to a regular room. Right now, it's more important that you and Gwen get to spend time with him. I think I'm just going to go home, do my homework, and clean the place up a little."

Bill then stood and spoke. "I think I'm going to take off too. Will you tell Gwen that I went to visit Jerry, and to call me on my cell phone when she's ready to go?"

"Sure, I'll tell her. What are your plans for later in the day?"

"I don't know. I guess we haven't thought that far ahead yet."

"Well, you and Gwen are staying at our house. You can sleep in the spare room and she can stay in Chrissie's room." She turned to Chrissie. "Honey, you can sleep in my bed tonight."

"What about you?"

"I'm going to stay here."

"You sure you're going to be all right?"

"I'll be fine. If he wakes up, I don't want him to be alone."

"Okay, Mom. I'll make sure there are clean linens on the beds. But I'm going to have to pick up some food."

"I can pick up something," Bill spoke. "Or we can order out. Don't worry about that. I'll cover it."

After Chrissie and Bill went their separate ways, Jo went back to Clay's room. She and Gwen spent the rest of the afternoon together there, talking quietly.

At 5:30 p.m., Jo opted to go to the hospital cafeteria for supper, leaving Gwen with Clay. When she returned, Gwen called Bill, and he picked her up at about 6:30.

Jean went off duty at 7 p.m., and was replaced by Connie Proctor. Jo helped her get Clay flat on his back. He groaned a little when they moved him, but otherwise remained unconscious.

Once again alone with Clay, Jo pulled her chair around so she could sit facing him and continued her reading. She had nearly finished the book of John when Pastor Giles came in at almost 8:30 p.m.

He read a passage from the Psalms, and they spent several minutes together in prayer for Clay. After that, they talked together for nearly an hour. Jo thanked him for coming and for everything he had done, and made him promise to thank his wife for her.

At 10 p.m. Jo helped Connie move Clay back to his left side. This was difficult for her because he was now facing the other way. After Connie left, Jo slid her chair around to the other side of the bed.

Connie had pulled the room door almost closed and turned the lights out, leaving only the dim illumination from the built-in night lights and the monitors. It was quiet and dark, and as Jo sat back down in the chair her exhaustion caught up with her. She leaned back and almost immediately dropped off to sleep.

She awoke to a noise. At first she didn't know where she was. Then it came to her that she was at Clay's bedside and he was moaning.

She stood, her neck hurting from her head having drooped to the side as she slept. Leaning over the bed rail, she put her hand on the side of Clay's face and spoke to him. "What is it, darling? Everything's okay. You're in the hospital. Can you wake up and talk to me?"

Suddenly the lights came on, blinding her. Connie entered the room and approached the bed. Jo stepped away to allow her room to work.

Connie put the railing down and listened to Clay's heart. Then she looked up at the monitor.

Jo's anxiety was building. "Is he okay?"

"I think so. His heart rate was up a little, but it seems to be going back down now. His ECG tracing is normal, and his vitals are all good. I think he may have had a bad dream, or maybe he's uncomfortable. Why don't you help me put him on his back."

Jo helped her move Clay onto his back, and Connie raised the head of his bed a little. Then, looking at Jo and perceiving her anxiety, she said, "Don't worry. If he's dreaming, that's a good thing. It means his brain is functioning. I wouldn't be surprised if he wakes up sometime today."

Jo looked at the clock. It was 2:15 a.m. as Connie turned the lights off and pulled the door back to its previous position. She went back to her chair and sat.

Even though she was still desperately tired, she had never been able to go immediately back to sleep after having been awakened in the night, and this night was no exception. It didn't help that her neck hurt and she'd just had an adrenaline rush.

Connie had left the bed rail down, so Jo pulled her chair as close to Clay's bed as she could get it. She spent the next couple of hours talking to him, sometimes holding his hand, sometimes stroking his hair. At length, she laid her head down in her arms on Clay's bed and fell asleep again.

Chapter 33

IT WAS ALMOST 6:45 A.M. when Clay's eyes fluttered open. He was severely disoriented and his right leg hurt. He stretched and looked around, noticing the monitor. He realized he was in the hospital.

Suddenly everything came flooding back to him. He'd gone to Tom Carlson's cabin to get Jo. He'd fought with Carlson. He'd been shot, but he was alive.

Horror began to seize him. Jo! Where was Jo? He had *not* rescued her! Carlson had her! He had to get out of this bed and find her—now.

Clay made a move to get out of bed, but about the time he realized there was an IV in his right forearm he felt Jo stir. Then he saw her. Then he relaxed and settled back, elation filling his heart. He laid his left hand on her head. Touching her was like an elixir to him.

She stirred again, lifted her head, and looked at him through sleepy eyes. "Claaay," she said softly.

"Hi, gorgeous," he said tenderly.

"Ummmm," she purred. "Hi, my handsome prince. I love youuu." Her voice was sleepy.

"I love you, too, sweetheart. I'm so glad you're okay. You are okay, right?"

Suddenly Jo was wide awake. *"Clay!* You're awake!" She stood, and then bent down and threw her arms around his neck, pulling him into an embrace. "Oh Clay, I missed you so much. I was so worried about you. I love you, I love you."

He held her close with his left arm and gave a contented sigh. "You are better than any medicine. I think a kiss might just cure whatever I've got."

She gave him a long and tender kiss.

Justice for Amy

"Uh-hmm," Jean Stuart cleared her throat. "Nice of you to wake up and join us, Mr. Ramsey." Once again, she held a Styrofoam coffee cup in her hand.

Jo stood and blushed. "Oh Jean! He's *awake!* He just woke up!"

"I can see that," she said. "And you're not happy or anything are you?" she laughed.

"*Yes!* Yes I am!" Jo blushed again, realizing that Jean had been joking with her.

Jean held out the cup to her. "Why don't you let me check him over?"

Jo took the cup and went around to the other side of the bed to allow Jean space to work. She took a sip and set the cup down on the bedside table. "Clay, this is my friend, Jean, Jean Stuart. She's been your nurse both yesterday and today, and she's an absolute angel."

"Nice to meet you," Clay responded.

"Nice to meet you, Mr. Ramsey," she said as she went about her work.

"If you're Jo's friend, you're my friend. Please call me Clay. What day is it, anyway? Why am I here? How am I doing?"

"One question at a time, Clay. It's Sunday morning, a little after 7 a.m. You were shot in the leg while rescuing this lady here." She tipped her head toward Jo. "You've had surgery to repair a serious tear in your femoral artery, and extensive muscle damage in your right leg. You're in the surgical ICU at Beason Medical Center. And you're doing just fine."

"Seems I'm a fortunate man."

"Yes you are. And not just to have pulled through. This woman has been at your side almost every minute since you've been here. She's cried for you, prayed for you, cared for you, changed your bandages, held your hand, and willed you to get better. You don't know how fortunate you are."

"I knew that God had it in his heart to bless me when he brought her across my path. But you're right, I didn't know how fortunate I am. Thank you for telling me." Jo blushed again as he picked up her hand.

Jean pulled the covers back up over Clay's legs. "Is there anything I can do for you before I go?"

"I could use some of that coffee."

"We'll see what the doctor says. I'll be back in a little while. We'll most likely be moving you out of here today. Need to make room for sick people."

Jean left the room, pulling the door mostly closed as she left.

Jo leaned over the railing and faced Clay, continuing to hold his hand, "Clay, I'm so glad you're—"

"Shhh," he interrupted. "She's right, you know. I am a fortunate man. Fortunate to have your love." Tears began to run from his eyes. "I wish I could tell you how much I love you, but I don't know any words."

She pulled a tissue out of the pocket of her jeans and dried his eyes. "I know, darling," she said softly. "You and I went past words a long time ago."

She put the bed rail down, and they held each other for a long time.

When at last they released, Jo put the bed rail back up, went around to the other side of the bed, sat back down in the chair, and picked up Clay's hand.

Clay looked into her eyes. "Tell me what happened. The last I knew, Tom had his pistol aimed at me and I heard two shots. I didn't know if he'd shot me or you."

"Actually, it was Lieutenant Burke who did the shooting. Tom was about to shoot you again when he shot him, twice. Tom is dead, and as far as I know Carol is in jail." She went on to tell him the whole story.

When she finished, Clay responded. "I'm so sorry about Carol, Jo. I didn't even have a clue she was involved until I had lunch with Mitch and he mentioned that she owned a Bronco. Then I got up here as fast as I could, but it was too late. They already had you. I had a bad feeling about you going over to her house. I should have insisted you not go. I'm so sorry for what you had to go through."

"It's not your fault, Clay. There was just no way to know. I feel bad for Carol. I have no idea what happened to her; if there was some trigger somewhere in her past that put her on a bad path—" She threw up her hands. "I don't know. And I don't know if I ever will know. I think, more than anything else right now, she needs our prayers."

"Yeah, you're right."

"I, uh...wouldn't want to go through that again. And I certainly wouldn't want you to have to go through what you went through again, Clay. But I learned a very valuable lesson about love. And you taught it to me."

"Me?"

"Yes. See...I guess I've always known about love as a feeling, and really, I suppose, even more than a feeling. But when you came for me, knowing that Tom was likely to be just minutes behind you. And then you practically forced me to leave while you faced Tom and his gun. I began to understand about a different kind of love. Thank you for loving me, Clay. Thank you for loving me so much that you were willing to give your life for me."

"Jo—"

"Let me finish," she interrupted, tears beginning to form in her eyes. "Last night, Pastor Giles came to visit you and we had a nice long talk." She wiped at her eyes with her hands. "I was so afraid that you would die, but he told me you were ready, if it came down to that, just like Amy had been.

"Clay, if you hadn't come for me I have no doubt that Tom would have killed me, and I knew, without anybody having to tell me, that I wasn't ready. So we talked, and he showed me in the Bible why the Lord Jesus came to earth, why he had to take on human flesh. That he loves *me* and that he gave himself for *me*—for *my* forgiveness." Tears were now also running from Clay's eyes. "And I understood perfectly. I understood, Clay. And I prayed and gave my heart to him. And I know, don't ask me *how* I know, but I know he heard me. It's like he was waiting for me with open arms, ready to take me in. It felt like a tremendous weight had been lifted from me, and I know that, down inside, I'm different now than I was before."

Clay held out his arms to her and she came into them. He held her close. "I love you, Jo. Thank you for telling me. This is, far and away, the best news I've ever heard."

When they released, Jo looked at the clock. "I've got to call Chrissie and Gwen and tell them you're awake. Did I tell you Gwen was here? She's staying at our house. Then I want to go to church. I promised Pastor Giles and his wife that I'd be there, and it's also a good opportunity for me to thank God for letting you live. But I have to go out in the waiting room because nobody's allowed to use a cell phone in the ICU. So, if you don't—"

"Go," he interrupted, laughing. "Just don't take too long. I'm already starting to miss you."

IT WAS 1:30 P.M. when Jo and Chrissie arrived back at the waiting room. Jo went into Clay's room, but found the bed empty. A wave of panic swept through her until she remembered that Jean had said they'd probably transfer him today.

She found Jean at the nurse's desk. "I'll bet you're wondering what we did with him," she smiled.

"Yeah. I thought I ought to stop in and see him at least once. I wouldn't want him to think I didn't care or anything." She smiled back.

Jean stood and handed Jo an index card with a room number written on it. "I'll walk you out and point you in the right direction."

"Thanks," Jo said as they walked to the door.

They stood in the open doorway and Jean explained how to get to Clay's new room. When she finished, Jo hugged her, "Thank you, my friend, for being so kind. I will never forget you."

When Jo and Chrissie arrived at Clay's new room, they found him dressed in pajamas and sitting on the edge of his bed drinking a cup of coffee. His hair was combed, and his IV and catheter had been removed.

When he saw them, he set his cup on the bedside table and opened his arms to Jo. She came into his embrace as he spoke. "I missed you."

"I missed you, too," she said before kissing him.

She stepped back and looked at him. "Should you be sitting up?"

"No. But they finally let me have a cup of coffee, and I was afraid I'd spill it if I tried to drink it lying down. Don't tell the nurses. They're horrible taskmasters up here. They've already had me up for a short walk, and I've been bathed, shaved, and had a shampoo. You wouldn't think I'd be so tired after having slept for so long, but I'm beat."

Chrissie stepped toward him. "I'm glad you're okay, Clay."

He opened his arms to her. "Thank you," he said as she stepped into his embrace.

She kissed him on the cheek and stepped back. "Thank you for saving my mom." She stood next to Jo and put her arm around her waist. "You knew Aunt Carol had her, didn't you?"

"I didn't know for sure, but I strongly suspected she was involved after finding out some information about her while I was in Grand Rapids. I'm sorry I didn't tell you, but I didn't want to worry you needlessly if I was wrong, and I certainly didn't want to put you in any danger. I hope you're not angry with me."

"I'm not angry, Clay. I'm just glad you're okay, and glad to have my mom back."

"I'm glad to have her back, too." He looked longingly at Jo.

Chrissie, ever perceptive, spoke again. "I should be going." She looked at her mother. "Call me when you'd like me to pick you up."

"You don't have to go, honey."

She looked knowingly at Jo. "Yes I do."

Jo gave Chrissie the keys to Clay's truck, they hugged, and Chrissie left the room.

Clay picked up his coffee cup and took another sip as Jo sat next to him on the bed and held his hand, interlacing her fingers with his. "I hope you don't mind, but we're driving your truck. The police have my car impounded while they get fingerprints off it. Worse, we've been using money out of your wallet. My purse is at Carol's, and it has my checkbook and credit cards and driver's license and everything in it. I'm not sure when I'll be able to get it back."

Clay set his coffee down and squeezed her hand as he leaned into her, bumping his head against hers. "Of course I don't mind. Sweetheart, everything that I have is yours. You must be running low on cash. I'll write down the PIN to the ATM card. I know there's a machine in the lobby because I've used it before. It's over by the reception desk. Get as much as you need."

Jo leaned in and kissed him. "I see Gwen was here. She said she was going to bring you your pajamas. They were gone when we got home from church. I guess Bill had to get back."

"Yeah, he's preaching tonight. Thank you for taking care of her." He leaned in and kissed her.

"Has the doctor been by to see you?" She leaned in and kissed him.

"Yep! He says I can get out of here, most likely on Thursday, maybe Wednesday if I do well." He leaned in and kissed her.

"I'll be here to take you home." She leaned in and kissed him.

"We need to talk about that." He leaned in and kissed her.

"About what?" She leaned in and kissed him.

"About what constitutes home. From now on, the only place that will ever be home for me is the place where you and Chrissie are." He leaned in and kissed her.

"What are you saying, Mr. Ramsey?" She leaned in and kissed him.

"I'm saying that you are so deep in my heart that I can no longer tell where I end and you begin. I love you, Jo. I love you with all my heart. So I'm asking you to marry me— if you'll have me. The most horrifying thought I could think is that I'd have to live my life without you."

She stood before him and took both of his hands in hers, tears escaping from her eyes. "Oh Clay...you silly," she spoke softly. "Of course I'll have you. You are my Clay, my very heart. In all my life, my one true love. And I am your Jo; made for you—just like you were made for me. So yes, I will marry you. And I will make you happy, every day of your life."

"Jo, you've already made me happy; the happiest man in the world." He tilted his head up and kissed her, putting his arms around her, and standing with her help so they could hold each other closer.

When at last they released their kiss, Clay had to sit back down. Jo helped him, and he continued to hold both of her hands as she straightened up. "I promise you," he said, looking into her eyes, "that for as long as I live, you will know every day that you are loved and cherished. I love you...*my* Jo."

"Ummmm," she purred, as she bent down and kissed him again, still holding his hands. "I love you...*my* Clay."

Epilogue

Hi Andy,

It was nice to meet you at Hopkins International in Cleveland. I never met a writer before. I hope you had a good trip to Denver (my trip home was a little bumpy). I'm not so sure I'd like a life where I had to travel a lot. I'm sure that must sound strange coming from somebody you met in an airport, but I guess, down deep inside, I'm really a homebody.

Sorry I wasn't able to get back to you sooner (I know you were eager to hear the rest of the story). But with traveling to Grand Rapids and then up to Houghton, getting my e-mail account set up, and with classes starting and all, I got bogged down. But when I remembered what day it was, I knew it was time to e-mail you.

It's hard to know where to begin, so I guess I'll just tell it as it comes to mind:

Jake Morgan is now the Accounting Manager at Northern Fruit Wholesalers. For a while he was the only one in the department. Now they've hired two new employees to fill both his and Tom Carlson's old slots.

He and Kathy Weldon did get married. I think it was last June, maybe July. My folks usually try to touch base with them when they're in Traverse City.

Aunt Carol was transferred to the Scott Women's Correctional Facility down in Plymouth (that's by Detroit) on the day after Labor Day. She was sentenced to life in prison for what she did to my Uncle Jim, and for her part in Aunt Amy's death. Mom and Clay have tried, but so far she won't see them.

Gwen and Bill got married on the Saturday after Thanksgiving, last year. Liz Ferguson was matron of honor. Clay gave her away. They live in Duluth (Clay calls it Freeze Butt), Minnesota. He's the pastor of a church there. Did I tell you that already? Oh well.

Clay has been off his cane for over six months now. He doesn't run anymore, in fact he walks with a slight limp. It doesn't seem to slow him down him much though.

Of course he and Mom got married. It was on Saturday, November 1st, last year. It was a simple ceremony at Northpointe Bible Church, out in Acme. Mom wanted Pastor Giles to be the one who married them. I was maid of honor and Mitch Ferguson was best man. I'm sure the timing must seem sudden to you, but they were both more than ready, and they wanted Gwen to be able to be there. They went to the Virgin Islands for two weeks on their honeymoon.

We stayed in Traverse City until school let out, and then moved to Clay's (our) big house north of Grand Rapids. But we kept the little house in TC, and use it when we're up there as a kind of a home base.

I honestly don't think I've ever seen my mom so happy. They work together, you know, Mom and Clay. He handles the engineering stuff and she handles the finances. She doesn't have to work, but she wants to. Between you and me, I think it gives them an excuse to spend more time together. What can I say? They love each other. No, it's more than that, they're in love with each other and their thing is being together. I hope, when I get married, it will be like that.

I may end up working there myself. I'm good at math and I'm taking electrical engineering at Michigan Tech. Unlike the rest of the women in my family, finance bores me. Clay says the business will be mine someday, if I want it.

Did I tell you they got me a car for graduation? It's an all-wheel drive Subaru Outback. I picked it out myself. It's dark metallic green. Clay wanted me to have something that was good in snow, seeing as I'm going to live in the U.P. for four years.

Anyway, back to Clay and mom. They bought a tandem bicycle last summer. They like to ride the local bike trails with Mitch and

Liz Ferguson. I join them sometimes—when I can get Steve to come along. (Steve Ferguson, Mitch and Liz's son). He's also starting his freshman year, but at Grand Valley State University. He's taking criminal justice. We dated a lot over the summer and have even talked about a future together, but we both want to get through college first. So, who knows?

As I mentioned, I was in Cleveland visiting my father. I know what I said, but I really don't hate him. My mom and I had a long talk about it, and we decided that bitterness is not what we're about. Mind you, I don't think I could ever think of him as 'daddy,' but I don't hate him. To be honest though, Clay has been more of a dad to me in one year than he ever was. Clay told me that he counts himself blessed that my mom and I have come into his life. Me, a blessing. Is that rad or what? I've got to tell you, I really love that guy. On the day we left to come up here, he took me in his arms and told me that he'd miss me, and that he couldn't love me more if I was his own flesh-and-blood daughter. That's when I started calling him dad. He cried—we both did.

Of course, as you already know, Aunt Amy is with the Lord. It's been one year today. I miss her. But by God's grace, I know I'll see her again someday.

I guess that pretty much ends it. Let me know if you ever do write the story. I'd like an autographed copy.

Best Wishes,
Chrissie 'Ramsey'

Acknowledgements

Writing is a solitary occupation, but not one that can be done in a vacuum. Most writers have a difficult time seeing their own small errors, and even fiction needs to present factual information factually. The bottom line is that writers need help to produce a credible work. The following people have contributed greatly to this book:

My wife, Lora. Thank you, sweetheart, for reading and rereading until your eyes practically fell out, and for your patience during the long process of writing.

My son, Andy, for his help in understanding and interpreting credit reports.

My editor, Ann Byle. All I can say is that you're the best.

Paula Brooks, for getting me a nicely detailed map of Traverse City, Michigan.

Dr. Norman L. Geisler. Some of the information in chapter 14 is based on his excellent work in the *Baker Encyclopedia of Christian Apologetics,* a book I highly recommend.

Dave Parmerlee, for his helpful description of aircraft/tower radio procedures.

Susy ten Haaf, RN, for her encouragement and sharp eye for manuscript errors.

Mary Carol Brouwer, RN, for her help and timely encouragement.

Adrienne Hentermann, RN, for her helpful information on hospital morgue viewing procedures.

All the many manuscript readers who offered suggestions and encouragement.

Thank you all! Any factual errors appearing in this book are mine and mine alone.

A preview of the
next book by

Andy Van Loenen

Please turn the page
to read an excerpt of

Missing and presumed Dead

Chapter 1

U.S. Coast Guard Station—Grand Haven, Michigan
Saturday, October 14th. 7:54 a.m.

SEAMAN APPRENTICE, ANGELA CRUZ knocked sharply once and stuck her head in the door of Lieutenant Commander Roger Estes' office. "Sir, they're asking for you over in radio. There's a mayday coming in."

Estes immediately dropped his pen, pushed his chair back from his desk, and stood. "Notify air operations to have a hee-lo standby," he said as he hurried past her, heading with purposeful speed to the Comm-Room.

Even before he entered, he could hear the edge of panic in the voice crackling over the radio speaker. "Mayday, mayday, mayday! This is the cabin cruiser, Marti Celeste. I think I'm somewhere near the south buoy. I have a strong smell of gas and my engine's acting up! Mayday, mayday! I'm in trouble! Please help me!"

Several of the enlisted personnel were huddled around the radio operator. "You people have jobs to do?" Estes snapped as he approached from behind them. "Yes sir," they said in near unison as they broke away and headed for their desks.

"What's going on here, Mason?" Estes put his right hand on the back of the radio operator's chair as he leaned over, placing his left hand on the desk.

Petty Officer Second Class, Ed Mason kept his intent focused on his work. "Sir, I'm getting a mayday. This is the fifth or sixth time it's come in, and I think the guy's in a panic 'cause he's holding his mic' keyed and I can't talk to him."

The panicked message came in again as Estes stood and turned. "Parsons, contact Milwaukee and Calumet Harbor. See if they're picking this up. Let's try to triangulate a fix on this guy."

"Mayday, mayday, mayday! This is the cabin cruiser, Marti Celeste. Please help me! The gasoline smell is getting—"

The *whump* sound of the beginning of an explosion ended the radio transmission.

"Cruz!" Estes yelled out into the main office area. "Get that hee-lo in the air! Head them toward the south buoy! See if you can get another one from Milwaukee while you're at it!" He turned back to the radio operator. "Mason, sound general quarters. I'm heading for the boat. We're going out."

Grand Rapids, Michigan
Sunday, October 15th

MARTI FORRESTER ROLLED OVER and looked at the clock in the headboard of the bed she'd shared with her husband, Greg for 5 years. It was 1:47 a.m.—7 minutes later than the last time she'd looked. It had been Sunday for almost 2 hours now. The horrible day had past, but the horrible feeling in the pit of her stomach remained.

Saturday had started out much like any other Saturday. No rush to get up and get going; the warm blankets wrapped around her felt good in the chilly house. It was her favorite time of the year: too cool for the air conditioning and too warm for the furnace. Greg had wanted to make love, but she'd put him off. Now he was gone, and the words of the newscaster played over and over in her mind:

Tonight's top story: The Coast Guard, this afternoon, is reporting the wreckage of the cabin cruiser, Marti Celeste in the chilly waters of Lake Michigan about 10 miles northeast of the south buoy. Missing and presumed dead, tonight, is prominent commercial real estate developer, Gregory Forrester.

The Coast Guard is reporting that the older,

wooden hulled vessel exploded and burned sometime during the early morning hours, today. This from a non-specific mayday call that ended abruptly and prompted an air and sea search. Wreckage spotted by a Coast Guard helicopter was later confirmed to be from the Marti Celeste when a search vessel picked up a piece of the wreckage that bore the boat's name. We go now to our lakeshore reporter, Keith Grimm, for more details:

"Thanks Rick. Standing with me is Coast Guard Lieutenant Commander, Roger Estes. Commander Estes, have you found anything else or any sign of Gregory Forrester?"

"No, not much, I'm afraid. We've picked up 5 life belts, and 2 life jackets floating in the vicinity. That number leads us to speculate that perhaps Mr. Forrester was not wearing a life preserver. Two Coast Guard hee-los, uh...helicopters, have grid searched the immediate area from the air, but so far have not spotted any sign of Mr. Forrester."

"What are the chances he might have survived the explosion?"

"I would say, slim. The boat was completely destroyed. However, assuming he was blown clear, the water temperature at the south buoy is about 57 degrees, Fahrenheit. The chances for survival beyond about 3 hours in that kind of cold, and without a life preserver are virtually nil."

"How long do you plan to continue searching?"

"We'll continue searching the surface until dark, and if we don't find anything, resume again tomorrow. That's all I can say for now. Unfortunately, the lake is about 540 feet deep in the search area; making it impossible to do much more that a surface search."

"Thank you Commander. That's all for now from the lakeshore, Rick. This is Keith Grimm, reporting live from the Grand Haven Coast Guard Station. Back to you."

Thanks, Keith. Gregory Forrester's wife, Martha, spoke briefly with reporters today and confirmed that her husband had taken the boat out. However, now she is said to be in seclusion and unavailable for comment. We'll have more on this developing story as more facts become known.

In other news tonight, the Vice President, on the campaign trail in Florida, announced today that, if elected...

She got up and went into the kitchen for a glass of water, stepping lightly so as not to awaken Jenny. Dear Jenny. She'd dropped what she was doing and immediately rushed to her side, bringing Liz with her, practically before the phone was cold. They'd spent the entire day with her on the lakeshore waiting for news that never came. Now she was asleep in the next room, and Liz, down the hall; while their husbands slept alone at home. They were true friends, true sisters—both of them.

Marti took her water and walked out onto the three-season porch. She set it down on the glass-topped table and pulled a blanket around herself before sitting on the white wicker sofa. She brought her feet up onto the flower print cushions and adjusted the blanket to cover them as she leaned against the wicker side and stared into the inky sky. She was dead tired, but would not be sleeping this night.

She closed her eyes to thoughts of Greg; sorry for what happened, sorry she had put off his advances yesterday, but unable to cry.

Chapter 2

Sunday, October 30—Five Years Later

GUNSHOTS! THERE GOES THE PERP! Mitch is down! I've got to get to him! Run!
"No! Harry, get down! There's somebody behind—"
Muzzle flash! Ohhhh! More gunshots! Falling...
"Harry!...Harry! Hang in there, man! Help is on the way!"
Where am I? Who is that laying on the ground?
"Mulvaney, help me get his jacket off!"
It's meee!
"Give me your handkerchief...I've got to stop this bleeding."
Linda? Linda, don't go!
"It's not time yet, Harry. You have to go back."

HARRY BRANNAN WOKE UP in a cold sweat; another nightmare, and his right shoulder hurt like a bad toothache. He looked at the clock on the nightstand next to his bed. 5:37 a.m. Close enough, he thought, as he got up to take more painkillers. He didn't know why they called them painkillers. They didn't really kill the pain and they made his stomach hurt if he didn't eat something with them.

He limped into the kitchen, got a glass of water, and ate four small soda cracker squares. Then he went into the bathroom and took the pills. They did help—some. And anything was better than nothing. If only they'd keep the nightmare away he'd buy stock in the company.

What to do? There was no sense in going back to bed. The adrenaline rush from the dream pretty much guaranteed he'd not be getting any more sleep for a while. He pulled open his top dresser drawer. He could get dressed and go see if the Sunday paper was in the press tube, out at the curb. He looked at his watch. *It would be a miracle,* he thought, *if that stupid girl who delivers it could get off her cell phone long enough to get it here much before eight.* He'd never seen anything like it. How could you drive a truck, talk on a cell phone, and deliver papers, all at the same time? Who was there to talk to at that time of the morning on a Sunday?

Old Mr. Humboldt had always had the paper there before 6 a.m. He was a good old guy. Had one of those old Post Office Jeeps, with right-hand drive, that he used to deliver newspapers. Actually, it was his only vehicle. The thing was rusty as all get out, but it always started, no matter how cold it got; and old Mister Humboldt had never failed to have that paper in the tube by 6 a.m. on Sunday mornings. Sometimes, if the pain or the nightmare had awakened him early, Harry would see him coming down the road from his window and go out in time to talk with him for a few minutes.

He worried about the old guy and went over to Radio Shack one day and bought him an amber strobe light for the roof of the Jeep. Best 25 bucks he'd ever spent. He could have sworn he'd seen tears in the old man's eyes when he gave it to him early one Sunday morning—and again when he'd helped him install it in the driveway of the little two-bedroom house where he lived alone, out in Plainfield Township.

Then one day the paper didn't come. It was a Monday, and the paper was always in the tube by 3:30 on weekdays. Finally, at 5 p.m. Harry had driven out and found the Jeep, still parked in the gravel driveway. He knocked on the back door. When nobody answered he tried the knob, and finding the door unlocked, walked in.

A heart attack had claimed the life of 74-year-old John Humboldt. Harry found him laying dead on the kitchen floor, a broken coffee mug lying next to him, its contents spilled out in a puddle that had collected in front of the refrigerator; the Sunday paper lying in a disheveled heap nearby. For the first time in his recent memory, Harry cried.

HIS FOREARMS WERE RESTING on the top edge of the open dresser drawer when his thoughts returned to the current day. His service pistol was in his hand. He didn't realize he'd picked it up. He pulled it out of its belt-clip holster and hefted it in his right hand. A Glock 27, one of the finest semi-automatics made. The so-called subcompact pistol fit his hand perfectly. At just under half an inch in diameter, the .40 caliber bore was big for a small gun. Unlike the .38 police special he'd carried in the early days, the 155-grain Ranger hollow-points in this thing had considerable stopping power—although he'd never fired it at another human being. He hadn't even fired it at a target in over a year.

He ejected the clip. Eleven shots—12 if you counted the one in the chamber, and he always kept one in the chamber. He turned the clip over in his hand a few times and then reinserted it into the handle of the gun. He could feel oil residue from the clip on his hand as he pulled back the hammer. *It would be so easy,* he thought. *Just press the thing up against my temple and pull the trigger—one big boom, and no more pain, no more nightmares.*

He lingered there for a moment. Old John lay dead in his kitchen for a day and a half before he'd found him. He may have been the old guy's only living friend—at least he was the only person aside from a brother and his wife who attended the funeral.

Harry wondered how long it would be until somebody found him. After all, if the paper hadn't been late he never would have driven over to old John's house. *And,* he thought, *nobody is depending on me for anything these days.* He was just a 51-year-old former cop with a shot-up shoulder and titanium alloy knee. *I haven't had a personal phone call in, what, a month? Who knows how long I'd lay there? On the other hand, why should he care? After all, when you're dead it just doesn't matter any more.*

But it did matter—at least to him. He'd walked into crime scenes before where the victim was in an advanced state of decomposition. He'd had to put the Vicks Vapo-

Rub under his nose—not that anything could mask that awful smell. He didn't want to be found in that condition. Besides, it's not like he had no friends at all.

Mitch is a friend—among all the people I know maybe my only real friend. He'd groomed that southern boy, preparing him to one day take over his job. It's just that he'd never thought the day would come so soon. Mitch would care. And so would his pretty wife Liz—the lady with the hugs. The thought of Mitch finding him in that condition made him shudder. The thought of disappointing him made him ease the hammer back down, holster the gun, and put it back in the top dresser drawer. *It's not that bad...yet.*

HARRY DRESSED, WALKED OUT TO THE KITCHEN, and washed the oil off his hands at the sink. Then he got a gel ice pack out of the freezer above the refrigerator. He held it against his shoulder as he walked out to the living room of his small apartment and lay down on his back on the sofa, the ice pack trapped between his shoulder and the seat back. He closed his eyes. The cold felt good. In concert with the pain killers it would relieve the inflammation in his shoulder.

He awoke to the phone ringing and quickly sat up, making his head swim a little. He picked up the cordless phone from the coffee table and pressed the talk button. "Hello," he said in a sleepy voice. He looked at the clock in the VCR. It was 8:27 a.m.

"Harry? It's Mitch—Mitch Ferguson. Did I wake you up?"

He rubbed his face with his left hand. "Umm, that's okay. It was time for me to get up anyway. What can I do for you?"

"Well, it's more what I can do for you. Remember we talked a few months ago about you maybe going out on your own. Well, I have something you might be interested in."

"Yeah, what's that?"

"It's a woman, a friend of Liz's—"

"You're not trying to set me up, are you," he interrupted.

"No, nothing like that. Her husband died 5 years ago—killed in a boat explosion out on Lake Michigan. They

Missing and Presumed Dead Excerpt

never found his body. Well, somebody thinks they saw him up north last week."

"Yeah, right! You know how common that is. And it never pans out."

"I know. And that's why the brass won't let me investigate it."

"I'm surprised you even asked."

"Yeah, well, ordinarily I wouldn't have, but she's a good friend of Liz's, and she's had a hard way to go these past 5 years. She pretty much lost everything after her husband died, and not having a body to bury, she's never had any closure."

"Look Mitch, I'm not even licensed. You know that. There's no way I could do it—at least I couldn't do it and charge for it."

"Well, she couldn't afford to pay you anyway—at least not much.

"You want me to go traipsing all over...wherever it is, for free?"

"Look, I just thought it would be a chance for you to see if you were interested in going out on your own. Clay, Clay Ramsey, you remember him. He and I have agreed that we'll cover all your expenses, whatever they might be."

"You must really like this woman."

"Yeah, she's a good friend. Look, I'd do it myself if I could, and I'll give you whatever help I can, unofficially of course."

"Yeah, well, I'll think about it."

"Why don't you come over for lunch today and talk to her? I didn't make any promises on your behalf. I only told her that I'd run it by you, that you're not a licensed investigator, and whether you did anything or not is strictly up to you. What harm will it do to talk with her? Besides, it's a free lunch."

"Yeah, what are we having?"

"It's just hamburgers on the grill, but it's going to be a nice day. We'll eat out on the deck. Who knows how many more opportunities we'll have to eat outside this year?"

Harry gave a heavy sigh. "Yeah, okay. What time do you want me?"

"Well, we'll eat between 1:30 and two, but why don't you come over at one so we can spend some time catching up. What's it been, a month or two?"

"Yeah, something like that. Okay, I'll be there. See you about one."

Harry rang off, put on his shoes, and dropped the ice pack back in the freezer, as he went out to get the Sunday paper. Then, throwing the paper in the car, he set out for André's Grill to enjoy their big sausage and cheese omelet; a cholesterol laden extravagance he allowed himself once a week while he sat and read the Sunday paper. It was also nice just to be around people, to hear the chatter—even if it meant putting up with Nancy-nice-waitress, who always called him, "honey."

IT WAS 12:55 P.M. when Liz opened the front door and greeted him with a hug. "Harry! It's so good to see you. We don't see near enough of you anymore." She put her hands on his shoulders and pushed him back a little while she scanned him with her eyes. "You're looking good. Looks like you've taken off a few pounds."

"Yeah, I guess," he said as she took his hand. "Once I healed from the surgeries I've been able to be more active."

She led him toward the back of the house. "Come on through. Mitch is out on the deck getting the charcoal going." She led him first into the kitchen, where two other women were busy preparing food. "Harry, this is Jo Ramsey and Marti Forrester. Ladies, this is Harry Brannan, Mitch's old boss."

Harry shook their hands and exchanged pleasantries with them. Both women, like Liz, were in their mid-40s. Dark haired, Jo was obviously Clay Ramsey's new, well, not so new wife. That meant the auburn-haired, Marti Forrester was the woman with whom he was to meet.

He took her in with his eyes. She was about 5-foot-4 with a good figure and a pretty face. Very feminine.

An uncomfortable silence was beginning to develop as he turned to Liz. "Where did you say Mitch is?"

"Out back on the deck. Clay's out there with him. They're waiting for you."

"Well, uh...I guess I'd better get out there, then," he said, as he turned and walked off. He thought he heard them giggling as he stepped out through the sliding glass door, and wondered if it had anything to do with him. He chastised himself for being paranoid.

At lunch he was given one of the "seats of honor" at the end of the rectangular table. Mitch was seated at the other end with Liz on his left and Marti next to her. Jo sat on Mitch's right with Clay next to her. That put Marti on Harry's right.

An outsider, looking on, might have imagined a scene of domestic bliss: three couples enjoying lunch together on a Sunday afternoon. But Harry was uncomfortable, feeling he'd been "paired" with Marti as they all held hands while Mitch prayed for the meal. He wondered if she felt the same. Maybe they arranged the seating this way so she and I can talk. On the other hand, Mitch, of all people, knew that you can't carry out an effective interview as part of the general conversation around a picnic table.

After lunch, they all took their plates and other items back into the kitchen. Marti stayed and helped Liz and Jo with the clean-up. When she eventually returned, she took a seat in a padded chaise lounge on the deck.

Harry pulled up a chair and turned it so he was sitting at her left hand, facing her at an angle. He bent down, putting his elbows on his knees and folding his hands. "So, Mitch tells me you think you might need the services of a detective. Can you tell me a little bit about why?"

Marti scootched around in her chair a little so she could face him better. "Yeah, I guess. My husband died, or at least I thought he did (they never found his body), in a boat explosion a little over 5 years ago. Well, one of the sales guys where I work thought he saw him up in the U.P. a couple of weeks ago."

"Ms. Forrester—"

"Please call me Marti," she interrupted.

"Marti," he continued. "I have to tell you that this kind of sighting is a fairly common occurrence. But in 30 years of police work, I don't know that I've ever heard of it panning out. Truth is, unless the person is wanted for a serious crime, police agencies won't touch something like this. The problem is, even if it turns out to be true, you can't force an adult to come back against his will. I'm telling you this up front because you need to know that, even if it turns out to be him, you'll most likely be wasting your money."

"Yeah, I know. That's what Mitch told me too. Thing is, Gary was so sure it was Greg. And I just haven't had a moment's peace since then."

"Gary? Gary who?"

"Gary Hammond, one of our sales guys. See, Greg was a partner in a commercial real estate company, and Gary sold them their health coverage, so he knew him."

"Greg was your husband?"

"Yes, Gregory Baines Forrester."

"Where do you work?"

"I'm an administrative assistant in the sales department at Choice Care HMO, here in Grand Rapids. We've recently been licensed to provide coverage in the Upper Peninsula. Anyway, Gary Hammond was up there, calling on the Waishkey Bay Casino, when he saw, or thought he saw Greg. He went over and talked to him, but the man denied he was Greg. Said his name was Alan something. I don't remember. I have it written down at home."

"Okay, Marti, the fact that Gary Hammond had more than a passing acquaintance with Greg adds some weight to the idea that it might indeed be him. If you're sure you want to go ahead with this, I'd be willing to check into it for you. But you need to understand up front that I'm not a licensed investigator. I guess Mitch told you that."

"Yes, he did. And I do want to go ahead with this— assuming I could afford whatever you'd charge me."

"Not being licensed, I couldn't charge you. But I would need to have my expenses covered. Maybe we can meet at a restaurant or something, and sit down and talk about this at length. I'm going to need as much background information as you can give me to help me get my head around what might be going on here. I'm also going to need to talk to this Gary Hammond fellow. Can you arrange that?"

"I think so, but it would have to be after working hours. I'd be uncomfortable about him taking off on company time for my personal business"

Ah, a woman with integrity. "Sure, that would be okay. Something early in the week?"

"I'll see what I can do. And if you don't mind, how about we have dinner at my house, seeing as I'm covering expenses; say...Monday or Tuesday? I have prayer meeting on Wednesday night, and I'd like to get going on this as soon as we can."

"Sure, either will be fine."

"Okay, how about Monday? I'll try to set up a time with Gary for you on Tuesday."

"Sounds like a plan. What time do you want me?"

"Would six be okay? We'll probably eat around 6:30."

"Six it is. Where do you live?"

Visit the author's web site, www.andyvl.com, to find out more about *Missing and Presumed Dead.*

About the author

Andy Van Loenen founded a hospital clinical engineering department and spent over 20 years in the field before moving to a second career in telecommunications. The author of technical articles for print media and articles on Biblical subjects for Internet publications, Andy caught the bug to write after being challenged by a high school English teacher. *Justice for Amy* is his first novel.

You can visit Andy's web site at www.andyvl.com. And if you'd like to find out what happened to Jo, go to www.andyvl.com/jo.

Time is a valuable commodity and a non-renewable resource. Thank you for taking some of your valuable time to read Justice for Amy. I hope you enjoyed it. If you'd like to contact me, I'd love to hear from you. You'll find my contact information on my web site. While you're there, please sign up to become a member of my mailing list. I'll keep you apprised of my book releases and maybe ask your opinion about book covers and things like that. I also give away free Sherlock Holmes adventures every month. It's a pretty good deal, and I'd love to have you "in the family."

Best wishes,

Andy